I0761521

THE GODS MUST BURN

THE GODS MUST BURN

T.R. MOORE

First published 2026 by Solaris
an imprint of Rebellion Publishing Ltd,
Riverside House, Osney Mead,
Oxford, OX2 0ES, UK

www.solarisbooks.com

ISBN: 978-1-83786-599-4

10 9 8 7 6 5 4 3 2 1

A CIP catalogue record for this book is available from the British Library.

Designed & typeset by Rebellion Publishing
Cover design and chapter art by Holly Macdonald

Printed in the United Kingdom

To the versions of you that have been forgotten—
for I will always keep them.

CHAPTER ONE

WAR STORIES ARE the best stories to tell, since any story is true when you're the only one left to tell it.

At least, it's what the rest of them must think as they sit around the glass-housed candles flickering against the moonlight, dented tin mugs full of ale, making merry with tales of battle and blood and brutality.

Basuin sits alone, away from the lanterns and the rest of the fleet, and listens to the thrash of the waves against the hull instead. The ocean is cold here, even many moons away from the glacier and ice he was last sent to occupy—and sent away from in defeat.

But for as cold as it is, the ocean burns mean. It sprays sea-salted water at him. Flicks her fingers at him and says, *Go away. Your ship does not belong here, soldier*. As if he doesn't already know that.

The ocean is much more unforgiving than war.

"Captain!" one of his men calls with a hiccup, raising his mug to Basuin. "Won't you join us, sir?"

Laughter rumbles through the crowd gathered on the deck, rough and drunk and melodic with cruelty. From here, Basuin can recognize a handful of shadowed bodies belonging to his fleet, adrift on liquor and treacherous seas. A squadron sergeant of Ariche's Fleet sits in the orange glow of a lantern, face all lax and loopy, gesturing wildly for Basuin to come and join their misshapen circle of cargo boxes and supply barrels.

Basuin's hand, pink scars illuminated by the moon hanging low in the sky, reaches for the collar of his cotton shirt. There, his fingers trace the outline of the stone he keeps hidden beneath his clothes.

The rest of the men, he's sure, do not wish him to come any closer than he already is.

"No," he answers, more gruffly than he intended. "Not tonight," he adds in an attempt to sound less bitter. Not that it matters anymore. These men know who he is. They fear his anger. In the dawn of day, they speak to him in respectful, quiet words; yes sirs and of course Captains. But in the dark, like tonight, they whisper unkindly, grinning with teeth pearly and warm in the candles' light.

Everyone on the *Ha'ria Drokha* knows his story. Basuin doesn't need to sit around and tell it again to ears that have heard it over and over, in all different genres—horror and tragedy and comedy and error.

Some stories, like war stories, are best left untold.

The hatch is kicked open with a squeaking hinge and Kensy steps out of his quarters and onto the deck. He's dressed for the cold still, or perhaps he has no other attire in his wardrobe but the long cloak of a black panther's coat and tall, hare-lined leather boots. Perhaps it's a status symbol. A reminder that, surrounded by his men huddled under cheap yak furs and wool-socked hands and feet, Kensy is the commander of this legion. His sharp eyes, a calculating blue caught in the light shared between men, survey the deck as if it were a battlefield.

An ocean breeze blows through, ruffling the loose hairs that have fallen from the worn tie at Basuin's neck. He reaches up to tuck the dark strands behind his ear, and the small movement has him pinned under Kensy's wandering gaze.

"Basuin," Kensy calls to him, voice not unkind but not kind, either. If it wasn't for how his smile stretches thin over his lips, Basuin wouldn't know if it was a call to share a pint or if it meant the ship was under attack.

"Commander," Basuin greets with a curt nod, not moving from where he stands leaning against the bulwark. The throng of men has grown quiet. Some shuffle to refill their tin mugs with more ale. Others, too drunk to keep their tact, look on at him and Kensy curiously.

"You must be bored, sitting there alone," Kensy says, showing a flash of his teeth. He takes five steps toward Basuin, slow and metered. "I'm sure Ariche's would welcome hearing the Black Wolf's tales of battle."

His heart stutters at the moniker, like his lungs might stop working. An ache shatters through his spine, breaking bones on its way through. He shivers under the cool night, the roar of the waves begging him to come back as he pushes off the wooden bulwark. *Black Wolf*, the waters whisper to him as he takes rigid, mechanical steps toward the lamp light. *Black Wolf, won't you come with us?*

Captain, the dead still whisper to him, choking on their own blood and spittle and fear. *Will you take my body back home, to my wife—in Ilham? My girl, she'll be waiting on her da, so will you take me home to her?*

Kensy's smile widens until the sharp line of his teeth peek out from the crack and curl of his lips. The men are still as quiet as they were before, staring Basuin down like predators hunting their prey. To them, it must feel opposite. For the same reason the men of Ariche's Fleet find that their only stories to tell are war stories, Basuin's sure these soldiers must feel like he is the only predator roaming this ship.

They are all soldiers, but only one of them is a murderer.

His boots come to a stop outside the scattered, uneven ring of drunken men, fingers curled into clenched fists at his sides. Basuin stands tall, taller than most, and looms over them with his broad figure. Behind his lips, his teeth cut into his tongue.

"You want to hear my stories?" he asks them, eyes cutting from the crowd to land back on Kensy.

And Commander Kensy, blue eyes hardened beneath the flickering light of flames that hide behind their glass walls, nods his head.

Basuin bears the brand of that name and becomes it—a hero of war, scars tattooed over his body by battle. Like a good soldier, he follows his orders and begins to spin a tale that only Captain Basuin of Ankor, the Black Wolf, can tell truthfully.

Because war stories are only best when you're the one left to tell them, and Basuin knows this best of all.

After the First Fleet have all stumbled off to bed, some drunk on tales of battle and some sobered on tales of blood, Basuin wakes wracked with pain, too breathless to even scream. One hand covers his left eye, a burning, searing flesh wound beneath his palm. Another clutches his chest, fingers scrabbling beneath his sweat-soaked cotton undershirt to find the stone he wears on a worn leather string around his neck.

He pants, barely audible under the creak and groan of the ship as it rocks back and forth on the water. Pathetic. Worse than a child, awoken from a nightmare and crying in fear for their mother. Basuin's fingers dig into his skin as he holds himself, choking on dry sobs alone, wrapped up in his damp bed sheets.

In the dark, when he wakes from the visions of Valkesta frozen in hues of black and white, it still feels fresh. Real. Flesh crawling, as if something's slipped under the sheep's skin he wears like a wolf in disguise.

Basuin kicks his sheets off from where they've tangled around his legs and falls out of bed, stumbling to the mirror hanging on his wall above his wash basin. There is no light, but his hands know where the matchbook sits near his oil lamp. With clumsy, panicked fingers and a seared thumb, the match strikes and his quarters illuminate in a faint glow, light enough for him to peer into the mirror.

When he removes his hand from his left eye, there's no wound. No blood or fester or rot. Just a jagged scar running from above his brow down past his cheekbone. He can still taste the pain in his mouth like someone ran their sword through his tongue. As though he were chewing the copper coins of beggars, tarnished from rain.

Hanging around his face in limp, tangled strands, his hair is a mat of sweat, dirt, and blood. But in the dim light of the lamp, he can see what seems to be the dark, dried flecks are simply shadows from the darkened room fading into the long locks of raven that tumble over his shoulders.

Every night, he sees them without fail. The broken bodies of dead men, hacked and slashed into pieces like a king might saw through a raw steak, their blood lit up on the snow. Basuin had never seen a color as brilliantly red until he saw the remnants of his squadron laid out and screaming for help, rubies spilled across the ice.

Captain, they called for him, hands still twitching. *Those gods you believe in… Will you ask 'em to take me to the Winter River? I'd like to meet my sister again.*

He plunges his face into the shallow wooden basin, the water as cold as the snowfall felt when he laid in the berm, waiting for death to come and send him away from this world. He stays there, not breathing, until his lungs burn. And then he pulls back up with a gasp, drinking down air, water running down his copper skin with a shiver.

On nights like these, Basuin wishes for things he knows can't come true. To scream, or to cry. To sink to his hands and knees in his private quarters and sob until his throat is raw and his voice is nothing. To go back and change it all. To go back and tell himself that Valkesta is a trap—before they march to their death.

His hand darts underneath his cotton sleep shirt, yanking at the leather tie around his neck and pulling it free. The stone, light and weighty all at once, sits in his palm as he closes his fingers around it. The uneven edges, smooth from something before his time, are familiar against his skin as he squeezes it tight.

If he could see his mother again, he would tell her that he loves her.

Staring at the ceiling, rolling the old jade stone between the ridges of his palm, Basuin lays in his bed and doesn't sleep. He moves and shifts with the waves rocking the ship and replaces the images of that snowy battlefield—that icy graveyard—with the last memories of his mother.

My Bass, she called him, her frail hand squeezing his. Strands of gray mingled with the inky black mess that was her hair. He would have to brush it again for her, braid it back loosely so she could sleep.

The gods say you're destined, she told him. *Destined for something awe-some.*

I'll be great, he said to her. *I'll be a war hero. I'll bring peace to our home, Ma.*

Awe-some, she amended for him. *But war, my son, does not bring peace.*

LIKE BASUIN, COMMANDER Kensy is up at dawn as well, leaned over the *Ha'ria Drokha*'s bulwark to watch the sun rise up from beneath the ocean. And it is a sight, no doubt—how the orange rays cast the waters in gold like an illuminated script only the nuns and their habits know mastery of. It shimmers, something magic, as the sky above their heads turns from a deep violet to an indescribable pink.

It smells of morning and sea salt, the air on the main deck. Crisp, but not fresh.

Though his hair is cropped short, Kensy's blond locks are

disturbed by the early breeze blowing off the ocean, which ruffles through the wavering sails dyed a menacing red. He no longer dons his cloak, but rather wears a pair of dark trousers with a white shirt tucked into the hem, not so unlike Basuin's own outfit.

"This land is beautiful," Kensy says, perhaps sensing his presence from behind.

"There's not much land to see," he answers, and Kensy looks back to catch Basuin's dark eyes in his blue gaze. Then, Kensy huffs a laugh and gestures for Basuin to join him at the bulwark.

"Bass," he says, almost melodically and not like Basuin's mother would. "Maybe you can't see it, but this will all be ours one day soon."

"You wish to own the ocean, too?" he asks.

"The queen wishes to own the ocean, and while she's at it, the rest of the land."

Basuin shakes his head, letting his chin drop to his chest so he can stare at the waves, glittering golden with dawn's light. "The ocean can't be owned."

With another laugh, Kensy pushes off the bulwark and turns to lean back against it, elbows hanging over the sides as he stares at Bass. He has that grin on his face, where his teeth flash dangerously, that makes Basuin not want to meet his eyes.

"Is this another one of your god-things, Bass?" Kensy licks his chops. "Is there an ocean god I should know about?"

It pricks at something deep inside him. Makes his hands feel hot as he curls them into fists and tucks them under his arms where they're crossed over his chest so his commander cannot see. Against his chest, warmed by his skin, his mother's jade stone grows heavier with Kensy's flippant words.

Ithika, he knows her name to be. If Ithika were to hear Kensy's words right now, the *Ha'ria Drokha* and all its men would not make it to shore. But Basuin can't say so, won't lay her name at the feet of a non-believer of a man. Basuin is a soldier—he's not a preacher, and they didn't build a church in the barracks either.

Gods don't belong here anymore. The queen made that clear when she outlawed them; when the legion began arresting priests and killing god speakers.

And almost as if Ithika hears him, stone flat to his skin and growing ever warmer, a wave roars up and reaches for the sun as it climbs higher into the sky and crashes against the hull of the ship, rocking them both where they stand. Basuin raises a thick eyebrow at Kensy, whose laugh doesn't reach his icy eyes.

"Did you pray for them to make proof for me?" Kensy asks, teeth straight and lips curled.

Basuin's nostrils flare. If they weren't on a ship sailing toward new land left to conquer—if they were still on the front lines of the war—he would say, *Perhaps you should try praying one day.* Instead, he kicks off the bulwark, still staring out into the ocean where they sail west.

The gods might even talk back to Kensy. How lucky he should be to not bear the silence Basuin does. But Basuin isn't supposed to believe in gods anyway. Kensy only allows it because of their history. Years at war together makes for twisted bonds.

Now, as the sky begins to lighten, more soldiers and sailors alike shuffle on deck to start their morning duties. It smells faintly of bitter coffee that wafts from their tin mugs. He begins to walk off, leaving Kensy behind to watch the sun continue its ascent, but the call of his rank makes him stop.

"Captain." Kensy stares at him, all pretenses dropped. He gestures with a nod of his head out into the distance, toward where the ship sails, an empty horizon. "When we arrive, I hope you and your gods will not cause too much trouble."

It's spoken with an edge, with more teeth than when Kensy flashes his own. As if he knows there are gods in this land—and Kensy wouldn't know that to be true. Even Basuin wouldn't know that to be true.

Basuin stares back at him, mouth set in a firm line. A soldier's smile. "The gods don't belong to me. I'm a soldier, Commander. But the gods—they are gods. And these are their lands. Their waters."

Kensy's eyes narrow into sharp slits, jaw tightening almost imperceptibly.

"Then maybe you should pray to them again," Kensy says. He smiles, lips thin, and looks off to the point on the horizon they've traveled toward for many nights now. "Warn them that we are coming."

CHAPTER TWO

THEY ARRIVE THREE days later, but Basuin has been watching the forest amass on the line where the sky and the water meet for two nights at least. The island makes him uneasy; the stone he wears around his neck creating indents in his skin from how tightly he holds it in his fist. It makes him nervous.

But it's better than going back to a country he can no longer call home.

Once they lower the boats and begin to row toward shore, the men all cheer at the sight of land and jeer that they were certain they would never make it here. After so long on water, solid ground seems precious.

"I could cry!" a soldier from the fifth squad shouts, wading through shallow water and onto the beach. He falls to his knees, running palms over the dip and crest of the rocky shoreline.

"And Cap'n Mitros would have you scrubbing latrines if you did. Quit with yer sniveling!" another yells back, laughing, tossing a handful of stones to pelt upon his comrade's back.

Basuin rows himself and his lieutenant toward the new land, grunting with every stroke of the oars as they drag through the water. Here, the foam is snow white as it glimmers under the sunlight. He could strip off his clothes and jump in, lay out in the pebbled sand and feel the earth against his back again. But it would look shameful.

Across from him, her tanned, golden skin radiant in the warm sunshine, Tehali grins.

"Lighten up!" Unlike him, she's already stripped out of her shirt, wearing nothing but a black band that runs tight around her chest and shows off the muscles rippling through her shoulders and arms. "You still look like you want to die, Captain."

He grunts again. They're close enough to jump out and wade further in. "I wonder why that is."

Tehali laughs, full and just, the golden rings lining each of her ears twinkling as she shakes. Seeing her look so free makes the corner of Basuin's lip quirk up in something that could maybe be a smile.

"Has anyone ever told you that you're dramatic?" Her fingers drag through the water, creating soft lines and ripples.

"Tehali," he warns, but she twists her wrist and flicks water toward him. Flecks meet the sun-warmed skin of his cheeks and he hates that it feels like such relief. He hates that she looks so pleased with herself, because when glee stretches across her mouth like that and boisterous, booming laughs escape her, it's always harder for Basuin to frown at her.

"I said it before, Captain. Lighten up!" Tehali throws her arms up in the air, gesturing to the land behind her, the land Basuin has been staring at for many nights now. "Aren't you happy to see land again? My feet ache for mud and dirt."

After forty nights spent on the *Ha'ria Drokha*, he should be. But he can't look at the rocky shore they approach by rowboat and feel anything but dread and shame. Basuin tried to pray, but the gods have yet to answer him the way they would've answered his mother.

"No," he says. Not if it's land that doesn't belong to them. A new island to conquer and colonize in the name of the queen, may she be well.

Tehali lets them fall into silence instead of pushing him. The gentle waves, lapping against their boat as Basuin rows through them with a grunt, don't help to carry them toward land. It almost feels like Ithika and her oceans are trying to keep him away from the island. Basuin would rather be anywhere but here, his mother's stone heavy around his neck.

Tehali jumps out of their boat first, her breeches turning heavy and dark with water. She gestures to Basuin to do the same, offering an outstretched hand for him to take. It's a simple, kind gesture, and one he should take. When he stands, the boat beneath him rocks unsteadily, threatening to tip him over.

He refuses her hand and misjudges the depth between the boat and the ocean as he hops out. It nearly lands him and his pack of supplies in the shallow water. Graceless. Frustration fills his chest like molten metal, tangy and searing hot.

Tehali is kind enough not to say anything.

They wade through the water, waves catching his legs and pulling him back. He's slower than Tehali, who forces her way through the shallow seas like a knife cuts through flesh.

Ithika, he prays to himself as they make their way onto the new island. *Thank you for your guidance and safekeeping.*

As the last rowboat meets the rocky shore, the men gather their things and start down the marked path. There, at the end of the trail outlined by piles of rocks the other fleets marked for them, the bastion awaits on the other side of the tall, thick oaks.

There's an undercurrent of something running through the island. It prickles the dark hairs on his arms, like how the air grows thick and charged right before lightning calls home and strikes. In the hollow of his throat, the stone he wears is humming.

Basuin doesn't know which god keeps this forest, because the gods don't speak to him the way they spoke to his mother. But he feels it—familiar, but inexplicable. From a memory.

The soldiers march into the forest together as if on their way to war, but behind Basuin, Kensy stops on one of the massive rocks lining the shore of the new land, scratching his beard as he stares into the unending trees stretching toward the sky. A breeze blows through, off the ocean and into their hair, ruffling the light collar of Basuin's shirt. In the light of the sun, his mother's jade stone glints softly, dully.

"Welcome to Yesua, Bass," Kensy says, his voice honey but his eyes steel. Then, he turns on his heel and starts down the rock-marked path. "May your gods bless it, or what have you."

Basuin's feet feel fused to the ground. He doesn't know why Kensy's brought him here; why Kensy sailed five fleets of men to an island that should be uninhabited. He cranes his neck back and stares up at the dark, verdant canopy that shelters the island Yesua from the smoldering sun above.

There is no going back from here. Basuin cannot go back home. The only home Basuin knows anymore is war—and the smell of it isn't just the burn of the hearth and food that cooks over a flame. It makes his eyes shut and his fingers tighten into fists at his side, ocean water easing down the length of his forearms until he shakes it from his knuckles.

And when he opens his eyes again, there's a flash of something white outside the left field of his vision. He turns his head in a snap, but when he looks through the gaps between the trees, there's nothing there at all. Just a trick of the light.

Underneath Basuin's cotton shirt, his mother's godstone burns hot.

It isn't a long walk before the forest becomes sparse, charred and burned and dry where Atun's Fleet cleared way for the bastion and began to build. The southernmost watchtower bursts through the treetops, made of basalt bricks and wood harvested and stripped from the new island. With its height, the tower clears the entirety of the beach they arrived on and a long stretch of the ocean they sailed. Basuin's sure it can be seen from the godrealm, wherever such a realm may be.

"Shaelstorm," Kensy calls from behind him, a hint of pride, or maybe something poisonous, in his voice. "Welcome home, soldiers."

Basuin almost laughs, but his teeth spear his tongue instead. He could be anywhere but here. Anywhere. Still in the freezing tundra of Grimmalia, fingers rotting black and toes raw as he marched his men into occupied territory and back out, carrying bodies that belonged to them on their backs. Where he saw the frost on his lashes in the reflection of his tin mug, warm from cider as they sat in wait on the border of enemy territory.

But here he is, at the Shaelstorm Bastion, five men dead and only scars to show for it.

Five men whom Basuin sent to the Winter River, to the afterlife of the blessed and holy and kind, to be received by their loved ones in the wake of gods. Those five men are the reason that Basuin's here at all.

Kensy said Shaelstorm was a second chance, but Basuin knows it's punishment. No one goes from being a war hero on the front lines to tagging along on an expeditionary crew, colonizing a new continent, if not in punishment for graves and grave decisions.

But it's still better than going home. Still better than looking for the little shack on the outskirts of Ankor that he built with his own hands and hoping to find his bed still warmed by the fire and his mother still sitting by the window, awaiting his return.

He squashes the image and swallows it back, tongue pressed to the back of his teeth.

As they get closer, the smoke he saw from the shore becomes thicker and hangs heavy in the air. It smells of roast meat, of industry and machines—and then it smells of gunpowder.

Basuin claps his hand over his mouth, index finger pressed against his nostrils to block out the stench. He can smell it anywhere, recognize it before it's left the barrel, before the striker has hit the flint and fired it. It wraps around him like a thick blanket, suffocating him. His lungs curse at him, begging for air, but Basuin can't breathe. He can't breathe that scent in, can't let it coat the back of his throat the way that blood might.

Blood. He can smell that too, from the edge of a memory.

No, no. He can't do this right now. He can't do it. He has to get out of here.

His head shoots up, looking from side to side, searching for a way out. In front of him, men still march down the path toward the bastion within sight. Behind him, Kensy and the captain of the *Ha'ria Drokha* linger at the back of the pack, discussing something he can barely make out with the blood pounding in his ears.

"The crops are all dead!" one of Shaelstorm's sergeants growls, throwing a clump of tiny, shriveled potatoes in front of Kensy. "We're running out of supplies."

The *Ha'ria Drokha's* captain argues, "My crew need more than a day to rest before we go back to the mainland."

"We'll starve before then!"

The ground is uneven beneath his feet. Roots running under the ground despite the lack of trees surrounding the bastion. Where do roots go when their mother is cut from their body? Isn't it the other way around, child cut from their mother's belly? There are green vines looped and growing up around the signage that was constructed crudely. Grass shooting up from the holes skewered and dug out for the lamp posts lighting the way.

Basuin stops in place before he trips, eyes darting back and forth between the sawed-clean trunks and the ribbons of vines climbing up the Shaelstorm Bastion as if to say, *give it back to us*.

His body is still fighting against his brain, the smell of gunpowder lingering in his nose. Burning, his lungs are screaming and pleading for air. He can feel his shoulders shake as he tries to regain command over his body, struggling for control.

It's just gunpowder. A military bastion will be covered in it. Just gunpowder.

Then, Tehali's hand falls upon his shoulder in a tight grip, and Basuin feels the ache shuddering through his spine as his muscles work to keep him from jumping in surprise. His fingers fall away from his face and he inhales sharply, chest expanding. Tehali doesn't let go of him, but her hand smooths over his back and she presses him forward.

"You're all right, Captain," she tells him, rather than asking. He's glad for that. "We're nearly to the bastion now." Then, she yanks something off her belt and shoves it into his trembling hands. His fingers recognize the yak fur of her waterskin, and gratefully, he pops the cork and tips it back against his mouth.

The clean water washes away the taste of blood he isn't sure is real—from his bitten tongue—or his imagination.

He wipes his mouth on his sleeve as Tehali takes her bladder back to hook at her waist again. Through it all, she hasn't let him stop moving, eyes glancing over her shoulder at their commander as though she worries he might see.

And she should be worried. Basuin should be worried. If Kensy were to see him having another attack—

That's what got him here. On the island Yesua. Brought him to the Shaelstorm Bastion.

If Kensy saw him having another attack, he would discharge Basuin for good. A captain who panics in the middle of battle is a dead man. And Basuin would rather be a dead man than be discharged. Pulling him from the front lines was shameful enough.

He doesn't thank Tehali, but he doesn't snap at her to stop coddling him either, which is as grateful as he can be right now. His chest still cries for reprieve, smoke stinging his eyes and the taste of blood coating his mouth. But in a blink,

Basuin stands before the iron-barred gates of the bastion, following the rest of his fleet inside.

Shaelstorm is lively. More so than the legion's headquarters back in Ha'riste, the capital city. The citizens of Ha'riste are all products of the war, trudging through the city of mud and stink and gambling on whether they will die from famine or from a shanking first. Shaelstorm is warmer than he thought it would be. He passes by soldiers who have shed their cloaks and outer layers, whose sweat glistens upon their backs in the golden sunlight.

One such man, bent over a forge that glows brightly and emits a heat unlike any other, stands to stretch and wipe away the waterfall of sweat from his brow. His eyes roam over the soldiers marching off the *Ha'ria Drokha* in an easy curiosity, until his gaze falls upon Basuin.

The man barks out a laugh. Basuin's first instinct is to clench his fists at the disrespect, the soles of his feet hot and itching to barrel down a soldier beneath his rank who would dare laugh at him. But then shame floods him, and his fingers unfurl.

"It's an honor, Black Wolf," the man shouts at him, a grin on his lips and a snicker cutting through his teeth.

"Watch it," Tehali snaps back, and Basuin can see how the soldier's legs straighten and his chin raises to greet her at attention, that simpering smile wiped from his dirty mouth. Once, Basuin had the power to make men cower that way.

Now, he's laughable.

Basuin shakes Tehali's hand from his shoulder gruffly, sick to his stomach at the thought of her protecting him yet again. He picks up speed, stomping through the trail and past the other men from his fleet to get away from her—from that lone soldier, from Kensy—and she reaches for his elbow in protest. He jerks away.

"Enough," he says, looking over his shoulder at her with eyes hot like embers, words as sharp as the sword on his hip. Basuin doesn't look long enough to see how her face might contort into fury, or maybe something worse. He pulls away and lets his long legs carry him past the gates of the Shaelstorm Bastion.

CHAPTER THREE

CHAPTER THREE

Shaelstorm looks out over the water they arrived by. Standing at the top of the southern watchtower and holding his mother's jade stone as he looks over the balcony, the view is the one good thing he's found since beginning the journey to Yesua. From up here, the ocean can't draw him back. The salt in the wind isn't enough to pull him into her depths.

After scaring off the soldier on watch duty, it's quiet. The sun sinks down, melting into the horizon, as his fingers fumble with the stone sitting atop his sternum.

Captain, Aless reached for him with hands stained red, *am I going to die?*

Sa-cha, he prays now, to the god of the Winter River, *please tell me that Aless has found peace at the mouth of your body.*

But there is no answer to his prayer. There never is.

Some people deserve to go to the Winter River—kids like Aless, who died honorable, horrific deaths—and rest undisturbed in sanctuary. The beautiful afterlife; the peaceful death, where Basuin's mother went. And then there are people who don't deserve to go to the Winter River, like Basuin.

When he was a child, his mother used to try and teach him. She explained her connection to the gods as a tree still growing its roots, reaching far down into the groundwater of the earth and searching for sustenance, unfurling and extending until it found its life source.

Your heart-bone is the tree, she told him, tracing a line up his sternum and tapping against the hollow of his throat. *You must reach and stretch and grow, my son.*

But no matter how tall Basuin grew, no matter how much he stretched himself thin between his duty to his mother, to his deities, and to his country—the gods eluded him. And still, even as he carries his mother's godstone and prays on every sun dawning and every moon waning, they do not call for him. He listens, but they do not speak.

He misses his mother.

The sound of footsteps, quick but steady up the stairs of the watchtower, makes him tuck the warmed jade back inside the collar of his shirt. Basuin stares out at the water as his visitor comes to stand beside him. All is quiet again for a moment, sans the crowing of birds in the trees that have yet to be cut down. Then, his visitor grabs onto the balcony bars, slipping their legs through the holes in the wooden banisters to sit dangerously on the edge.

The familiar sight of Tehali's many piercings, hair braided tight along the side of her head to show off her golden trinkets, makes him sigh, shoulders slumping.

"This island is grayer than mine, but still feels like home." She stretches out, breathing a noise of relief out through her pierced nose. "I miss it. Don't you miss home, Captain?"

A prickle of annoyance hits the back of his neck, but he brushes it off. The air between them is left unchanged, unending. He doesn't answer.

"Why didn't you go home?" she asks instead. Basuin chokes. "Why did you let Kensy bring you all the way out here?" Her words slither around his ankle like a snake, a warning hiss before the strike. This isn't a social visit.

He inhales through his nose. "I am a soldier."

Tehali laughs. Short, blunt. "And when you die?"

"I'll die a soldier."

The waves have picked up, crashing violently against the cliff's edge. The shore beneath them spells death.

"Then tell me," she says, looking up at him, coal-black eyes meeting his, and Basuin snaps back into the present. "What does it mean to be a soldier?"

Cryptic nonsense. He doesn't understand what Tehali is trying to pry at, though he knows her well enough to think she must be trying to pry at something. Tehali's favorite thing in the world is taking logic and twisting it into a weapon that could kill a man in his own argument.

"To fight for your country. Your people. To be strong and loyal. To be brave, and courageous," he tells her. "To follow orders." The way he was always taught to follow orders. Even his mother taught him that. To follow the trail the gods blaze for you without question. "That's what it means to be a soldier."

Tehali goes quiet again, rolling his words around in her head. Basuin wouldn't know what that's like—to take a thought and simmer on it like a stew. Basuin thinks and then he does, the way he was always taught. The golden rings adorning Tehali's ears glitter magnificently in the setting sun, and if magic still existed, she would've possessed it.

But magic no longer runs through this land; all that's left are the bodies of forgotten gods.

When Tehali finally looks at him, her face is a blank slate, but her eyes are narrowed like the eyes of an animal readying to hunt. Basuin is not afraid. He meets her gaze with steel, stubborn and unyielding.

"And what if you were no longer a soldier?" she asks.

He recoils like he's taken a blow to the chest. Crippling, because if he's honest—to Tehali, and to himself—he doesn't know the answer. His heart-bone, the trunk of his tree, is reinforced with militant commands and strengthened by break after break after break where his body had to regrow bone and heal again, organs reincarnating themselves after his blood painted every border that Grimmalia ever thought they had.

"Who would you be?" Tehali's eyes bore through him. "When you take off your armor, who are you, Bass?"

No one.

"The same," he answers instead, but his body feel heavy—like he's strapped in plate armor, readying to run to the front again.

He expects her eyebrow to raise, the corner of her lip to quirk into a knowing smile, her eyes to soften in the slightest. That's always how her countenance shifts when she's played her opponents like they're her own pieces from up her sleeve. A triumphant look.

But instead, Tehali looks away from him, eyes back on the sea beneath them. At the top of the world the sky is turning violet, the darkness bleeding into the light, edges blurred. She's quiet, chewing on his words and mashing them between her molars before digesting them.

"But who were you," she asks, voice low, "before you were the Black Wolf?"

The leather string around his neck tightens into a noose. If his mother weren't dead, she would say: *You were my son, strong and so brave, to go marching to a war you didn't want to fight.*

But she's dead, and Basuin doesn't know who he used to be. They must have beat it out of him when he enlisted. Only seventeen and primed to fight. Eighteen and promoted to a rank he should've never been given.

"Basuin of Ankor," he says, and he knows it to be the wrong answer because Tehali pulls herself up by the railing of the watchtower and climbs to her feet. She wipes her hands off on her breeches, shaking her head.

"Do you want to know what it means to be a soldier?" she asks, but Basuin doesn't answer. "It means you fought for your country." Tehali pushes her hair behind her tanned shoulder. "Nothing more. Nothing less."

"I know that, Tali," he says, a snap of his teeth, a growl in his throat that he swallows back. "I know."

"Bullshit. Because ever since Valkesta—"

Like glass breaking, something pops and shatters in his chest, puncturing the organs he's worked so hard to keep.

"—I've watched you struggle. The memories—"

He shakes his head. Please, no.

"—and the nightmares—"

"Stop," he pleads.

"—I still hear you screaming in the middle of night and it's been months."

He wants to lunge for her. To throw her over the goddamn watchtower and into the ocean. Fall to his knees and beg her not to say anything else. To pretend as though she'd never seen a thing. To act as though he's still the same, as if Valkesta never happened.

He wants to ask her if she is still his friend, after Valkesta, or if she blames him too.

Basuin's hand comes up to clutch at his chest, where beneath the skin and below his mother's godstone, his heart is racing faster than light. In front of him, Tehali's eyes have turned gentle again, alight with concern, but still the familiar dark irises he's always known.

"You aren't just a soldier," she murmurs, as if trying to soothe him. "You aren't Kensy's puppet to string along for another ten years. You are more than that, Basuin of Ankor."

Then who is he? If he isn't Captain Basuin of Ariche's Fleet, the Black Wolf, if the scars the war braided into his skin don't distinguish him, if he sails back to Xalkhir and drags himself back to that small hut in Ankor where his mother was laid to rest alone, then who is he?

If he leaves this war with nothing but a comrade casualty count and a bruised reputation, then what was it all for? Basuin couldn't save his mother, so what was it *for*?

Tehali's hand rests on the banister of the stairs. There's a look on her visage that he so rarely sees—guilt. "I just needed you to know that," she tells him, somber and quiet. Then, she descends the steps, and he watches until her head disappears and all he can hear is the tap of her boots on the granite.

There's nothing more that Basuin can learn, nothing that war hasn't taught him. It's been fifteen years and Basuin knows it all. How to march, how to kill, how to follow orders. The legion beat the boy out of him like a blacksmith beats the curve out of a sword. For fifteen years, he's learned. For fifteen years, he's been a soldier.

Tehali might think he's more than that, but she's wrong. What would she know of a failure so brutal it took human lives?

TEHALI WAITS FOR him outside the big tent pitched for the commander's meeting, arms crossed over her chest and dressed in the most clothes he's seen her wear since they left Ha'riste. She dons her lightest armor, a chest piece and her weapons belt, hair pulled up high on her head. Basuin dresses similarly, a hand on the hilt of his sword.

It's twilight now, the sun melted beneath the horizon—his favorite time of day. A shade of sky that can't be named, in swathes of blue and black and purple and brown.

Basuin nods, and Tehali nods back, and together they duck inside.

The rest of the captains are already there, their lieutenants standing beside them. A captain from the Third Fleet meets Basuin's gaze with sad eyes. Another, from the Fifth, glances at Basuin and then away, staring down at the floor. The tent is very, very quiet for a Commander's meeting.

Kensy stands behind a circular table covered in maps and military orders, his hands clasped at his back as he looks through Basuin. His smile widens into a grin, his blue eyes sharp and bright. Kensy raises his hand, gesturing to the pair of them.

"Everyone, meet Ariche's new captain."

Basuin looks at Tehali, but Tehali stares blankly ahead.

"Welcome," Kensy says warmly, "Captain Tehali of Jankri."

"YOU REPLACED ME," Basuin seethes, voice booming in the silence of the tent.

Leaning back in his chair, hands clasped together in front of his mouth, Kensy stares at him. The roar of the ocean outside the bastion walls isn't loud enough to cover Basuin's roar of fury.

"I gave the legion near fifteen years," he says, palms pressed against Kensy's oak desk. "I gave this war ten of them, and I gave you the better half of those. And this is what I get?"

There is begging in his voice. He hopes Kensy doesn't hear it.

"You brought me across the sea, leagues away from my home—" his words are heavy, breaths shuddering through his flaring nostrils, "—just to kick me out and leave me here for dead."

Fitting, he supposes, through the heavy fog of anger. That he should die on an island ripe with gods he doesn't know the name of, dishonorably, rather than on the godless, bloodied battlefield strewn with pieces of his men and his broken faith in honor and glory.

Kensy looks at Basuin through narrowed eyes. "Are you done?"

His nails claw at the wooden desk, fingers curling into fists alight like the fires they set upon the piles of dead enemies, bodies souring. No, he's not fucking done. But as he's rearing to go again, opening his mouth, Kensy holds up a hand with a snapped, "Enough."

And like the good, dishonorable soldier boy he is, Basuin's jaw clicks shut.

Kensy rises from his chair, shoulders rolled back and spine straight as he stands at full height. He is only a few inches shorter than Basuin, but twice as menacing. A spark of respect, an ember of fear, begins to burn in Basuin's chest as he meets Kensy's icy eyes.

"Don't you think," Kensy begins, and Bass feels his body slink back to stand at attention, "that if I was discharging you, I wouldn't have bothered bringing you here?"

No, he doesn't think that. He thinks Kensy is out to punish him in any way possible.

Kensy shakes his head. "No, Basuin. I brought you here for a purpose. A purpose much greater than what you serve as Ariche's captain. I need you here with me rather than running the fleet. Tehali is capable of that."

There's a stinging in his chest. "Tehali deserves to be captain," he says. He means it.

"I knew you'd agree." The corner of Kensy's mouth jumps in a weary smile, clasping his hands together and bridging his thumbs. "Let's face it, Bass. After Valkesta—"

For fuck's sake, he could scream. He'd tear down this whole bastion. Burn it to the ground and go with it. Just to make them stop mentioning Valkesta.

"—your men haven't seen you the same." Kensy looks solemn, but his eyes are still cold. "A captain needs the respect of his men if he's to succeed in the legion."

It never should've been Tehali who found him bleeding out in the snow at Valkesta. It should've been Kensy—Kensy would have finished the job.

Basuin says nothing. He barely breathes. Kensy walks around his desk and stands beside Basuin, not looking at him, but resting a hand on his shoulder. Basuin stares at the wall ahead.

"But I still need you," Kensy says. Needs him. Doesn't respect him. "There's only one person who can help me, and that person is you, Basuin."

Kensy's always said Basuin's strength was in doing. In following orders. It's why he chose Basuin to be his right-hand man—a rank that was Kensy's to give, and now Kensy's to take away.

So he swallows, and he asks, "What do you need, Commander?"

Kensy smiles at him. "A god speaker."

A prickle of fear, unlike any other he's felt, runs through his nervous system like fire struck from a match, racing to swallow everything in its path. The only thing that keeps him from visibly shuddering is the fact that Kensy is watching, and if Basuin shows any sort of weakness, it will only make it worse.

Why would Kensy need a god speaker? This is conquest. This is unholy.

And, worse than sacrilege, being blessed with the power to speak to the gods is murderous. A curse. God speakers never saw prisons. They were "kill-on-sight" targets after Queen Ye'suite outlawed the gods.

Basuin can't speak to them anyway. Only his mother, cradling her jade stone between her wrinkled and worn hands, was blessed enough.

Kensy walks away, out of Basuin's sight, to take a turn about the room. His footsteps echo off the wooden floors of his bunk house. It sounds like what Basuin imagines the death-bidden road to the Blacksalt Sea would, screams of emptiness echoing off the cavern walls as mortality is wrenched from the dead and their souls travel into the endless nothing of the afterlife for the damned.

Are we going there? a trembling hand clutching Basuin's shirt asked. *To the Blacksalt Sea? Captain, I don't wanna go—*

"Why?" he manages to ask through the bile rising in his throat. *Kensy doesn't believe in gods.* He repeats it to himself like a mantra.

"I'm looking for something," Kensy says. "Something sacred. Something only the gods know."

Basuin nearly recoils, blowing a breath out of his nose. "You don't believe in the gods."

"No," Kensy agrees, "I don't." He raps his knuckles on the wood grains of his desk. "But who built man?"

Who built man, Kensy says, as if man were a science. As if man were the technology that Ha'riste drives, the capital engineers soldering junk together to make weaponry. They did build man into weaponry. It's why he stands here now, in front of Kensy, unmoving.

Kensy, who doesn't believe the gods raised man.

Basuin doesn't answer and Kensy continues on. "I'm in search of a godly artifact for our queen. Something powerful." Kensy's hand tightens into a fist. "I know how much you care for your gods. Finding the artifact is the best way to protect them."

He bristles. "Protect them?"

Kensy grins. "Did you think I was so ruthless?" With slow, measured steps, Kensy approaches him, so close Bass can smell the lye of soap on Kensy's skin. "I'm not replacing you, old friend. I'm recruiting you." Kensy leans in closer, like he's sharing a secret. "Help me find it so I don't have to destroy the entire forest to get it."

Ruthless—no. Kensy is godless.

Basuin swallows. His throat is dry. "Where did you learn of it?"

"From a god speaker," Kensy says with a flash of teeth. "One like your mother."

The stone sitting in the hollow of his throat echoes the rhythm of his heart, making it feel alive. The heat of it stings his skin. A seed of dread buries itself in the gloom of Basuin's gut.

"That's why you've brought me, then?" he asks, knowing it's an overstep. "The queen wishes to own everything, but you—you've always known exactly what you want, Commander."

Kensy stares him down with an expression one would give a child, condescending but still warm despite the disappointment. It's a familiar look, one Basuin knows to mean that he's not clever enough to understand.

"It's your choice, Bass. You can stay in Shaelstorm and help me. Live out your duty honorably."

Basuin closes his eyes, chest tight.

"Or I'll send you home." Kensy's chair creaks as he sits back down, an ankle thrown over his knee. "Back to Ankor."

CHAPTER FOUR

Kensy doesn't leave any time. They pack their things and leave at first dawn. Basuin doesn't see Tehali before he leaves on his journey into the forest, and whether by design or not, he's grateful for it. He doesn't know what to say to her, not yet. *Congratulations* sounds rueful. *You deserve it* sounds biting. *You should be happy* sounds patronizing and mean, and hurt and sad, and angry, and all the things he won't dare to say aloud.

Soldiers don't have feelings—they aren't ordered to. And Basuin is still just a soldier.

"Do you smell that, Bass?" Kensy's hand falls heavy on his shoulder. "The greenery here is fresh. I wish we could bring it back to Ha'riste when we go."

Xalkhir is a dry, barren land. Browns and grays color it bleak, where the only green is in the capital, transplanted from the lush valleys of far off and conquered lands. Maybe every war they've fought was to steal the warmth and beauty from others to gift to the queen.

No, they went to war with Grimmalia because Grimmalia was the last country that worshipped the gods Xalkhir outlawed. Or, at least that's what his ma told him. That his father went to war and died over the gods she spoke to, on the nights when Bass could not sleep on the hard floors of their shack and sneaked an eye open to watch the glow of lavender light fill the room from his mother's prayer-eyes.

Mercel, the first continent Xalkhir colonized, believed in the gods. And they fell—just like Grimmalia will.

As if it might glean something from Kensy, Basuin says, "This is the gods' land."

Kensy moves past him, stepping over an overgrown root and ducking under the leaves branching out from the forest. Then, he pulls his machete from his hip and in a clean arc, swipes upward and slices through the thickets of the forest. It falls around him in green jewel-tones.

"Then they should start talking," Kensy says. "If this is their land, they should lead us to the artifact." Kensy presses his hand against a low-hanging branch and swings his blade again. It cuts. "I won't hesitate to make my own trail if they don't."

This forest is huge, taking up the entirety of the island and stretching far beyond what the watchtowers can see. And within it, Basuin knows there are gods. He can feel it, prickling the dark, dense hairs on his skin. Dead, perhaps, but there are gods.

Basuin still doesn't know what happened to all those gods, the ones who died. He's never known a god as a body. His mother said once, they had them. Bodies. But when they died, they ran through the land, like blood running through veins. They found hiding places, gravesites and burial grounds to mark themselves as real, but their magic waned under all that earth.

That's what his mother called them, at least. Hiding places, not shrines. They weren't homes—no god has a home, truly. And now, on this island, he still doesn't understand it.

Basuin isn't the most brilliant, but he isn't dumb. Kensy doesn't believe in the gods. He probably tricked some poor fool into spilling his guts, then killed the damned man for being a god speaker anyway. This island wasn't picked for conquest—whatever artifact Kensy is looking for, it must be powerful.

All Kensy believes in is war, and power, and weapons built by man.

But Basuin is a soldier, so he treks behind Kensy gripping his mother's godstone tight, begging in old prayers he hardly remembers the words to. He fears what Kensy will do if they can't find this artifact. Basuin might never leave Yesua. That, he doesn't mind so much. Death wouldn't taste so bitter in his mouth. But Kensy destroying a land the gods reign over—the idea quickens his heart, pounding in his ears.

He searches for signs and spirits. His mother taught him those, before he enlisted, when he was still a child and believed there was magic pooling in his mother's palms. Look for markings unable to be recreated by animal or man. Seek out shadows moving faster than eyes can blink. Find trails of light left behind by souls passing through the waters of life. Difficult in a forest such as this one, where the roots of tall oaks have branched out and grown intertwined with one another. Where fallen tree trunks close off paths, creating a maze.

When he looks up at the sky, he can no longer see the northernmost watchtower of Shaelstorm.

It's when he's resting against a tall, wide tree, panting as his hand palms the rough bark of the trunk he leans on, that Kensy becomes irritable. Basuin's strength is failing him, sweat dripping into his brow. He's lost stamina. Ever since Valkesta—

"Captain," Kensy calls, a few yards away and waiting. "You've lost your fight."

Basuin wipes the sweat from his brow and struggles to compose himself. "Not at all, Commander. We press forward."

But Kensy doesn't move, even as Basuin pushes off the tree, slides down a hilly mound of dirt, and strides toward Kensy. Instead, all he meets are those ice-cold eyes, stormy and narrowed by Kensy's blond brows.

"And what of the gods?" he asks. "Have they spoken to you yet?"

No. And no matter how tightly he presses his jade stone into the grooves of his palm, they won't. His ears are washed in the buzzing of the forest as he strains to listen for the gods. It's the dead leaves crunching beneath the leather soles of his boots as he strides across the forest. The birds chirping at one another and the flap of their wings as they take off into the sky, excited or maybe fearful. The swell of the wind like an inhale, ruffling the forest canopy in exhale.

Before he was dragged to this island, Basuin never would've thought things might be easier if Kensy was dead. Back when Kensy spoke to Basuin with camaraderie and respect, as if they both held the same rank. Two men, nothing but a war in common. Now, it might be easier if Basuin had never met Kensy at all. Never joined the military, never shipped off to Grimmalia, never became what the civilians of the capital city called a hero.

The sole reason he enlisted was because they swore his mother would get the medicine she needed so desperately. The medicine they couldn't afford, Basuin without work and his mother too weak. The villagers didn't trust them anyway. Not after the legion came and burned the church to the ground; not after they forced Basuin's ma out for speaking to outlawed gods.

If she was going to die anyway—if they were going to refuse her the medicine—Basuin would have stayed in that tiny shack with her until she passed, her hand wrapped in his.

A rustle through the brush. Basuin picks it up before Kensy does, who trudges forward with no care. The quick rustle of leaves against one another peaks in his left ear. But when he looks, there's nothing.

And when he looks again, Kensy has moved on without him.

With a curse, Basuin creeps forward, but he's never been good at keeping silent. His footfalls are too heavy. The clanking of his gear too loud. Out here, he carries only his sword and a dagger, but they still jingle with the shift of his body. The sound of whatever animal stalks them disappears under his movement forward, but it couldn't have gone far. It wouldn't have. Whatever it is, it's a predator.

He needs to regroup with Kensy. But he doesn't make it far before he hears it—a gunshot rippling through the forest. Basuin flinches, eyes shut tight. The moment will pass. It always does.

But then he smells it. First, the gunpowder. Then, the blood.

When his eyes flash open, it's Isaniel's face, stained with dark blood, that stares at him. His dear Isaniel, clay-colored eyes wild and wide open. The floor of dead leaves underfoot has morphed into cold snow. They aren't laying in Basuin's bed, naked bodies pressed together. They're still in Valkesta, and Isaniel's hand grips the heavy fabric of Basuin's undershirt, refusing to let him go this time.

You're coming with us, he says, eyes unblinking, lashes frozen with blood. *To the Blacksalt Sea, Captain. You're coming with me.*

Basuin clenches his eyes shut again—tighter, tight, aching—and then blinks awake. Isaniel is dead. Isaniel is dead, and so is he.

No, fuck. No, Basuin's not dead. Basuin could wish for death, but it would not come. He's alive, in this forest, and there's blood and gunpowder.

Basuin charges forward, following the smell perfuming from where the shot echoed. He runs after Isaniel. If he's fast enough this time, he can save Isaniel.

The sharp tang of a fresh wound flowers in his nostrils just as he arrives at the body. It runs a shudder through him. There is blood spilled among the snow. Red, splattered across white, oozing from a lead bullet.

A wolf, fur tinged pink, lays among the dead foliage of the forest floor. Dark blood pools around its body, leaking from the fat hole lodged in its neck. There's sulfur in the air. It chokes Basuin, watching the wolf's back legs twitch in death.

Why are there battlefields in the land of gods?

A bark of laughter bounces off the oaks as Kensy's boots approach, his rifle still gripped in his right gloved hand. Kensy shot this wolf dead. It lies at Basuin's feet, metal still bloodletting it even as the spirit leaves its body.

"See, Captain?" Kensy says. "This is why we have these." He taps the barrel of the flintlock rifle against his calf, but his finger still sits to the side of the trigger. "Would your sword have drawn quick enough?"

New guns—new technology. It bled his men in Valkesta. But it was still a blade that scarred his face.

Basuin crouches there, laying one palm on the wolf's snow-white fur, and grasps his mother's godstone. Even animals should go to the Winter River. Basuin presses the jade to his lips, infusing some of his own soul in the stone to act as a vessel. It's what his mother told him to do. It's what he did in Grimmalia, even when the bodies he culled were torn ragged and in scattered pieces.

Except Valkesta. In Valkesta, he wasn't given the chance to.

"What was it protecting?" he asks Kensy, wiping the wolf's blood on his boot as he stands.

Kensy raises a brow. "Perhaps it was hunting its dinner."

He shakes his head. "That's not what it felt like."

"Did your gods tell you that?"

Anger prickles under his skin. Simmering, Basuin strides forward, hand on the hilt of his sword hanging from the leather straps crossing his back. Kensy moves behind him, slower, the sound of brush beneath his boots much quieter than Bass' loud steps. There's something else in this forest.

An unfamiliar sound, one he can't recognize at first, cries over the crow of the forest. Pealing, bell-like, painful. An animal whimpering. Two, maybe three—he draws nearer. Young. He shoulders his way through the trees.

Sunlight shines through the canopy above his head, raining down on a thick, gnarled tree. Knobby and twisted, as if it grew wrong. He hears them, under the earth. Basuin leans his hand against the bark of the tree, a shimmer of light striking the worn, scarred skin of his fingers. No—he feels it. Something moving, squirming, beneath the tree. Basuin crouches at the base of the tree just as Kensy catches up.

"What is it?" Kensy calls.

The twisted tree, branches growing out of its trunk in all different angles, thick and old, sits upon a raised mound of dirt. There's a natural gap where the trunk meets the ground. Someone's dug underneath it, between the roots this tree has sent into the earth. There are animal tracks leading from it.

Basuin runs his fingers down the bark of the tree. "A wolf den. She was protecting her pups." And Kensy killed it. They got too close. Basuin should've stopped Kensy when he heard the mother circling them.

Behind him, Kensy approaches the tree with metered, swaggered steps. "A wolf den." He chews on a piece of stripped bark he cut earlier in the day, crouching down at the base of the tree. "Well, isn't that perfect?"

It takes him a moment too long, ears straining to hear the pups, for Basuin to recognize Kensy's words. He turns, the sound of something sharp rattling around, to see Kensy fiddling with a metal tin.

"What?" There's no reason for them to stir a den. These pups will die without their mother. A suffering death of starvation if a predator doesn't sniff them out first.

Kensy is silent as he pulls out a piece of flint and draws his dagger from his boot. There are paper slips in the tinderbox he holds. Every soldier carries one around; Basuin has one himself. He feels the pacing of paws from beneath the earth under his palm, the anxiety running like a creek through the dirt.

And it hits him too late. Too late.

"Those gods of yours refuse to talk," Kensy says, carving his blade against the flint. Shavings fall onto the paper. "So

I'll make them." He strikes his knife against the stone now and it sparks, catching flame on the edge of the paper.

"Commander—" Basuin reaches, but Kensy flicks it toward the tree. The pups cry, a grating sound that burrows deep in Basuin's eardrums. The flame races across the base of the tree, rounding the entrance of the den and catching on the dried grass circling the roots. It's not enough, at least. The tree won't catch.

But Kensy is smarter than that, and Basuin should know this by now.

"A perfect time to test out our new weapons," Kensy says, pulling what looks like a hand cannon from his belt. But it has a flintlock trigger attached, bigger than on a rifle, something Basuin has never seen before. The weaponry that Ha'riste engineers build, it all smells of steel and gunpowder. This, too.

"What are you doing?" Basuin shouts, widening his stance and growing large—nothing threatens Kensy, nothing at all, but Basuin palms the dagger at his hip. "Kensy, by the gods—"

"What gods?" Kensy growls, his blue eyes hardened into the same steel sitting in his hand. "What gods are there? If they won't reveal themselves to a godly boy like you," Kensy spits, "then I'll give them a show they can't refuse."

Basuin is too stunned to move. His mother—gods above, his mother. Kensy twists the barrel of the hand cannon, pulls it back with both hands aimed at the tree, and strikes the trigger back. In a flash, the forest is alight with fire, flames licking and curling white hot at the hanging branches and eating at the green leaves. The heat of it pushes Basuin back, his arms covering his face.

Fire races up the tree's trunk, and Basuin screams Kensy's name. Beneath the ground, the wolf pups scream in harmony with his own bellows, their claws scratching at the earth their mother dug them a home from.

In the wavering heat, Kensy stands unmoving, staring at the den. The cannon hangs from his hand, his fingertips singed black with gunpowder and burn blisters.

"Do your gods answer acts of cruelty?" Kensy asks, and he turns, a rueful grin on his face as he locks eyes with Basuin.

Basuin hears two choices—the crackle of bark as it splits under the sticky heat Kensy's created, and the animals still yelping as their home begins to burn. He doesn't think. He's never thought about anything on the battlefield. He moves.

Lunging, his hands grasp at the tree's roots as he dives into the fire. It's hot. The flames beckon sweat from the sides of his temples like a god beckons worship from those at their feet. Fire licks at the leather of his armor. The sound of it all is maddening. Crackle, pop, roar.

Smoke is coiling in his lungs and the hair on his right arm has been singed off as the fire continues to grow above him. Basuin reaches into the den but he's too broad to fit. Cursing, he rears back and strips his armor off, throwing it aside, his mother's godstone rocking against his chest. He'll kill Kensy for this. Fuck his duty, his oath.

Fuck whatever camaraderie they had. He'll kill Kensy after he saves these pups.

Again, he tries, and again, he fails. "Come here," he growls at the pups, fear beading across his forehead with the sheen of sweat. His heart thunders in his chest, lungs working too fast. "Please," he adds, as if they can understand him. But they are burrowed deep in their den, crying for their mother who lies in the forest already dead. They'll be next.

Basuin angles himself and shoves one arm down into the den hole, hand searching for the pups. His vision is blurry and black, ears straining to pinpoint their yelps. He reaches so far, stretches so far that it aches his muscles and he feels his joints lock up. He might dislocate his shoulder. The fire flicks at him.

Go away, Black Wolf, it warns him, blistering his skin.

"Please," he begs.

With quick, jerky motions, Basuin's fingers dig at the hole, scooping away dirt until it collapses. The earth here is not fragile—it's strong, but he's stronger. The fire is growing, tree completely ablaze, but he can't stop.

His hands worked Isaniel's breast over and over and over as the wind howled at him. If he shattered bone, he was unsure of it. But he kept going, and going, and going until Isaniel spit up blood and it dribbled from the corner of his lips.

The Blacksalt Sea, Isaniel said. *You're coming with me.*

So he digs and he digs and he digs, fingernails bloody and raw, coughing up smoke the way Isaniel coughed up blood. He digs until he can no longer dig, until the flames make him hiss where they kiss his skin, until the den entrance is big enough for him to fit through.

Basuin reaches again, into the hole, and there is nothing but darkness. Then, a sharp bite to his searching hands.

"I've got you." He grits his teeth, relief short-lived. "I've got you, c'mere—"

He wraps his long fingers around what he can, pinching the scruff of three bodies. He drags them toward the entrance even as they yelp and scream and scratch at his hands, the pain dampened by the fire that bites into him.

Their fur is soft against his chest as he gathers them there, pressing them to him as they squirm and struggle in his grasp. A paw gets tangled in the leather string around his neck, fighting for survival.

"I've got you," he repeats, finding a handhold at the roots of the tree to press himself out of the den.

And then the wood cracks above him.

It sounds like a rapture. Like lightning striking through the nothingness of the Blacksalt Sea, grounding itself in the sediment of tortured souls.

The den is collapsing, aflame. The tree above his head caves. Basuin pulls himself out of the den faster, hoping to beat the lightning home.

He doesn't, and the Blacksalt Sea is only its name—Black.

CHAPTER FIVE

When his eyes open, the forest looks unfamiliar. Thick smoke has blanketed the sky in white, unnatural and too calm. Behind him, the fire still rages—he can hear it, roaring and threatening and spitting at him. But he doesn't look back. That fire will swallow him up if he turns to face it.

In his blistered, scratched, bleeding arms, the wolf pups have stopped squirming. He can't feel their heartbeats, nor the work of their lungs, but he knows they still live. They must. When he glances down, he makes out three tiny, still bodies—two white, one black.

But he has to move. The fire, it's behind him. Crackle, pop, roar.

Ma, he prays, godstone beating against his chest as he runs. *I'm sorry.*

Basuin isn't sure where he's running, but he knows it's away from the fire. It's almost like the trees part for him, bending to make way for his journey as if they know he's trying to save these pups. He doesn't stumble, not once. He can't afford to.

He dodges another oak and then he sees it—fresh water. Glittering just on the horizon.

Pressing the pups to his body, cradling them like children, he sprints toward the river ahead. But there's a voice, calling over the shaking pants of his heavy breathing. He skids to a stop, a fork in the trees, ears alert. He hears her. From the right.

When Basuin turns to look, down a smoke-entrenched path as dark as the waters he arrived here on, a shadow dances through the fog. A body. She calls to him, speaks in a tongue he can't understand, but he knows. He knows she calls his name.

Basuin. He's sure of it. *The gods say you're destined.*

The jade stone on his neck sears his skin, enough that he hisses and tears his eyes away from the shadow. There's another path, tall grass and vines and gnarled tree roots, but the river is just past it. He has to get the wolves to the water, clear the debris from their eyes and make sure they can breathe again.

He flees toward the water, determined. So many lives have been lost. Not only in Valkesta, but in every Grimmalian city the legion stomped through in their crusade. There is so much death and not enough life, and so he must—he must—give these poor pups a chance. Animals like these, that walk on four paws instead of two feet, are innocent.

Humans shed blood for grace, not for survival.

He sprints forward, and then a woman steps out from the edge of the forest and walks toward him. Doesn't she see the fire behind him—does she not smell it? It warbles in hunger, looking to consume everything.

Her eyes, piercing and dark, meet his and widen. Now she must see it—the raging flames chasing him. Basuin picks up speed, racing against it. He has to reach the water before it's too late.

The woman thrusts her arms out on either side as if to stop him, shouting, "Go back!"

Go back to where?

"You must go back," she commands. "You're making a mistake."

"Fire!" he shouts back, lungs stinging and out of breath. "Get to safety, there's a forest fire! Run—"

But the woman never moves. She stands there, frozen, blocking his path with eyes that reflect the flames crawling through the forest behind him. The fire spits embers at him, flecks of soot burning his damaged skin. She won't move, even as he speeds toward her.

Basuin braces the wolf pups against him with one arm, reaching out to grab her and pull her to safety.

But she jerks away just as his fingers might gloss over her skin, eyes frightened, darting back into the woods and disappearing. As if lightning strikes the ground again, the smell of burned earth and ancient bones, a bright light flashes before him and he recoils, blind, again.

When he cracks his eyes open, all that's before him is crystal-clear waters, gently lapping against the bank. Two wolf pups slink out of his arms and onto the ground. As soon as their paws pad toward the river, their white fur blows away like the seedlings of an adolescent dandelion, and soon they're just shimmers of bright green light, fading into something that shines from the water. It's like he blinks and they're gone, without even a howl or a cry or anything at all.

In his arms, still and silent, the black pup turns to sand and trickles from his grasp.

He blinks again and a black wolf sits in front of him, looking up at him, tilting its head at him. The entire forest smells of blood and Basuin slaps a hand over his mouth and nose to fend off the stench. The wolf laughs—shakes its head at him—and then once more Basuin blinks and the wolf morphs into a man.

Standing before him, with human skin as black as ink, the wolf's head still laughs at him. This half wolf, half man, it reaches out to Basuin with long claws, arms tattooed with swirling red lines that glow, and if he wasn't unable to move, he would recoil in pure fear. But the wolf-man's sharp talon hooks around his leather string, bringing the jade godstone up to its red eyes to inspect.

Basuin almost falls to his knees and begs—*Please, no. Take anything but that.* It's all he has left of her.

But the wolf-man only huffs another laugh, dropping it back to Basuin's chest.

"You are lucky somebody loves you," the wolf-man says, if the sound oozing from between its canines could be called words. "So blessed to be Basuin of Ankor. Your choice was just."

And before Basuin of Ankor can even speak, the wolf-man's clawed hand collides with his chest, breaking his ribcage, shattering his tree-bone into splinters, puncturing his lungs and collapsing them inside of him. Something is forced out of him—his own spirit, his own soul—and something else so dreadfully cold and burning hot all at once replaces it like a light both black and white.

He's being burned alive from the inside out, the wound eating itself at the edges. And as the wound becomes ever bigger, the wolf-man climbs inside his ribcage, hollowing out his chest and taking up home where his heart used to be.

He is full. Of what, he isn't sure, but it aches like death and stinks like decay.

On the cusp of the Blacksalt Sea, Basuin floats once again.

I am your god, the voice of the wolf-man echoes inside of him. *You are my possession.*

CHAPTER SIX

"DON'T! DON'T TOUCH him," a young voice snarls. Just a boy, from the sound of it, as Basuin's eyes struggle to open.

"I'm not," another voice whispers—younger. "I think he's hurt."

The forest still looks unfamiliar when he blinks away the blur in his vision. The sky is blocked out by a canopy of leaves swaying overhead, the tall oaks' branches intertwining as if holding hands. They shelter him from the sun rising high in the sky. Basuin can't tell if it's risen or soon to set.

"It doesn't matter!" Angry and hissing. "He's one of *them*."

That stings worse than the smoke in his eyes. Basuin sits up—tries to, at least—with a groan of pain and a curse slipped from between his lips. His fingers clutch at his chest where the ache burns something fierce. Where his heart used to be. It feels empty now, and yet overflowing. Heavy, but with nothing.

Basuin rubs his eyes, gentle on his left where the scar is still fragile, aches radiating all throughout his body. He hunches over his lap, body curled inwardly, an arm braced against his stomach. There is soot, black as the earth, marring his palm, ash smeared on his skin. The fire was real, wasn't it?

His eyes search over his forearms. There are no blisters or burns, no scratches from claws, no bruises or blood. Just stretches of dark bronze skin fitted over twitching muscles marked by sunspots and dark moles from standing beneath the Xalkhan sun. Basuin's eyes trace over the white scars drawn on his body, flexing his fingers to encourage the blood back. When the needling fades and he regains feeling in his limbs, someone gasps.

Two young boys stand a few feet away from him—one with wheat-brown hair, holding tight to the elbow of another with gold-white hair messy and hanging in front of his eyes. Children.

"Shit!" the brown-haired one curses, yanking the other toward him. "Get back! Get away from us!"

The blond boy stares Basuin down, eyes big and childlike and filled with sincerity. "Hami," he cuts at the other boy, pulling his arm free. "He won't hurt us."

Hami's face shatters into betrayal, mouth trembling until he sets it in a line of anger. Then, he glares straight through the forest at Basuin, eyes the same dark shade as the leaves shaken from the trees above them.

"Who are you?" Basuin asks. Children, out in the forest. On an island, abandoned, and they're alone. No, this cannot be. With a grunt of pain, he pushes himself off the forest floor, struggling for air as he clutches his chest.

"Don't," Hami cries, but the other boy is faster. He advances quicker than Basuin can take a step back, until his sandal catches on a root running through the ground and he pitches forward. Reflexively, Basuin catches him by the shoulder.

"Yaelic!" the boy shouts, breathing hard. "My name is Yaelic and I—I'm going to serve you!" He pulls away from Basuin's grasp. Yaelic stands tall, forcing his shoulders back and his chin up, but still barely reaches Basuin's torso.

Basuin's jaw hangs. "What?"

"You saved us," the child Yaelic says. "My brother and I, you saved us from the fire." He glances over his shoulder at Hami, who stares on in fear.

"No," Hami seethes, but it's iced in dread.

Basuin's eyes flick between the brothers, slow realization

wriggling like worms in his head. The fire, the wolf pups. These aren't children. They're spirits.

Confusion, and a cold concoction of something else, sends a bitter wave rolling through his stomach. He doesn't know where he is anymore. Who—or what—he is. But it hurts. His hand sneaks its way to his collar, squeezing his mother's stone in his palm.

"I've done nothing of the sort," he answers the boy and hopes it's true. "Tell me which way to the bastion and I'll leave you alone."

It's like a cry for war, the way that Hami recoils and yells with rage. "I knew it! He's one of them, he's a soldier." Hami lunges forward, shackling a hand around his brother's. "C'mon, Yaelic!"

And yet again, Yaelic rips away from Hami. "No! I'm not going. He saved us. He's not a soldier—he's a god. And I'm going to serve him."

Basuin takes two steps back. No, he misheard.

The brothers stare one another down. One seething, breathing hard. The other calm, only glancing back once at Basuin. It's enough to make his hand twitch over where his heart used to be.

A god?

Basuin pulls at his hair, tangling the strands into a black mess tumbling over his shoulders. He's got to get out of here. Back to the bastion—yes. Kensy's waiting for him to return, Basuin has a job to do.

No, not anymore. Basuin defied direct orders. He can't go back to the bastion. Kensy will send him home. He doesn't know where he'll go, doesn't care. As long as it's not back to that fucking shack on the edge of the woods. But even in death, the heavy chains of guilt seem to follow him no matter where he goes. He takes another step backward, away from the brothers, only for the ache in his chest to hit him like a bullet. Basuin seizes.

Where do you think you're going? something asks from inside of him. *You belong to me now, little soldier boy.*

Staggered, Basuin's world spins and he lands on his hands and knees, gasping for air over the forest floor. He's going to throw up. Gods, he's going to hurl. And those kids—those fucking kids—are watching him. Basuin reaches for his chest with blackened fingers, but there is no wound. Just the remnants of the wolf-man, the empty chamber where his heart should reside.

Once, before he died, he had one, he swears.

Is he dead? It hurts too bad for him to be dead. He's been dead like this before, in Valkesta, where it hurt too goddamn much to be dead but he wished for it anyway.

That's right, the wolf-man says, curled up in the hole in Basuin's chest. *You've met me before. Your mother warned you about me.*

Basuin sits back on his haunches, hands covering his eyes. In the darkness, the wolf-man emerges. From the black fur of his wolf head and sinking into the black skin of his man chest, there is blood. It leaks, sticky and red, from his ruby eyes.

He flexes his fingers, covered in black soot. "What am I?" he asks, to the thing inside him.

Yaelic's eyes meet his, shining emerald in the light filtering through the canopy. "The Wolf God," the boy answers, and the forest lurches. His ears ring with the reverberations of bullets and war cries.

Your men have come and ravaged the forest, the wolf-man says.

He didn't ask to come here.

And yet, like a good soldier, you followed. So like a good soldier, you will pay your army's price.

A hand made of claws strikes something inside Basuin and he cries out as his flesh tears like tender, succulent meat roasted over an open flame. His blood, the same color as the wolf-man's, drips down his body, but when he opens his eyes and looks down at his chest, there's no wound.

With blood.

There's something desperate grasping at his limbs, climbing up his nerves. He was a son, once. And then a soldier. A war hero. A failure and a disgrace. But who is he now? What is this thing inside of him, not wolf and not man and not tangible? Basuin wants to stick his fingers into the nonexistent wound and peel that wolf-man out of him.

You were chosen. The wolf-man curls up inside of him now, black fur ruffled.

Chosen to what? His teeth bite into his tongue.

You are the Wolf God, it snaps its teeth. *Chosen to protect the forest*, it growls.

Basuin doesn't know whether to laugh or scream or run away. "I have to get out of here," he says to no one. No one who will listen, at least. "I won't be shackled to you."

The wolf-man huffs a laugh.

I own you, the wolf-man says from inside him. *What is a soldier without his duty? You wouldn't know, little soldier boy.*

"I'm leaving," Hami says among the echoing sounds flooding Basuin's mind, and then he's snapped back into the real world. "He's dangerous."

"He's our god," Yaelic pleads.

"He's our enemy!" Hami snaps back. "If you want to serve a soldier, you're stupider than I thought. Last chance, Yaelic."

"Please," Yaelic begs. His voice is scratchy and raw and aching. "Don't leave me."

"Last chance," Hami repeats.

Basuin's head swims. It happens too fast for him to catch ahold of. He's chasing something he doesn't know the shape of. Then, in a flash of bright green that blinds the forest, Hami morphs and changes. When the glow dies, in his place stands a small wolf pup, shoulders hunched and hackles raised. A pup he'd held—a pup he'd saved from Kensy's fire.

A spirit; a boy who lived in these woods until Kensy stormed them.

"No," Yaelic whispers, a shake in his voice. He outstretches a small hand. "Don't leave, Hami."

But his words are lost under the shuffle of paws on bark as Hami turns heel and leaps into the distant trees, leaving his brother behind. Something inside Basuin aches like rotting flesh, oozing acrid pitch and swallowing his insides with it.

All is quiet until Basuin calls his name. "Yaelic," he repeats, and the boy with golden hair nods. When he turns to look at Basuin, there are tears dampening his cheeks.

"You should go," Basuin says. "Before he leaves you behind."

Sharp and quick and unexpected, Yaelic's whole countenance shifts into something firmer. He mops up his tears with his sleeves, sniffling.

"I won't," Yaelic says. Instead, he bows his head. "I owe you my life." When he straightens, there's a fire in his green eyes. It smothers the pain of his brother abandoning him. "Please. I won't take no for an answer."

He reminds Basuin of the young boy, only nine or ten, who watched his father march off to war. Of the young boy, only twelve or thirteen, who buried his father's shield—or what was left of the dented metal. Of the young boy, only sixteen or seventeen, who had to join the legion so his mother would receive the medicine she needed to keep her heart beating.

Of the young boy he still sometimes sees in his dreams, floating away from his outstretched hand, hair shorn close to his ears. The one he still looks for in the mirror.

So he turns on his heel, facing away from the little spirit named Yaelic, and walks away.

"Go home," he calls over his shoulder, gruff and demanding. "Get out of here."

All he needs to do is get back to the bastion—he'll figure it out from there. Basuin isn't interested in picking up strays. He takes all of five steps before Yaelic is scrambling to catch up, his tiny boyish hands tugging on Basuin's belt and reaching for the edge of his shirt.

"Please! I'm begging," Yaelic cries out, the green of his eyes drowning in panic like sailors drown in the sea.

"You beg to serve me?" Basuin questions him, brows drawn. Something deeply painful settles in his stomach. Those who follow him, who serve under his command, always end up dead. Even his mother, whom he loved so fully, died at his hand.

"Yes," Yaelic says. "Please. I don't have anywhere else to go. There's no home I can go back to anymore." This poor little wolf pup, abandoned by his brother, dressed in a robe too long for his short, skinny legs. He needs to eat, put meat on his bones and grow muscle. And he needs warmer clothes, a good wash too. He needs to not be alone, Basuin realizes, as the boy's fingers tremble where he grasps at Bass' shirt.

I'll send you home, Kensy had told him. Basuin remembers thinking, what home? There's nowhere to send him back to.

Back to Ankor, Kensy said.

Home, where his mother's bones might be buried in the back of that little shack on the edge of the woods. Maybe the villagers burned it all to the ground instead, like the army burned their church. Maybe she was still inside.

His godstone, hanging around his neck where it hung around his mother's once, pulses and thumps in a rhythm that might match his heart if he still had one. He'd do anything just to have his mother here, to tell him what to do. But Yaelic, his head bowed to Basuin, shudders a sob and chokes it back. The sound makes him ache.

"All right," he murmurs, hoping it will not be heard among the ambience of the forest. But Yaelic's head shoots up, his eyes as wide as the moon when the month is grown and beginning to shed its skin for the next.

"Really?" Yaelic's emerald eyes almost glow. "Thank you!" he shouts up at Bass, too eager for his own good. "Thank you, Wolf God, thank you!"

Before Basuin has a chance to take it back, Yaelic's knees hit the damp, spongy earth beneath their feet. His hands sink into the forest floor as he bows his head to the ground, and Basuin takes a step backward, but it's too late. The green light of Yaelic's spirit bursts forth from the ground, spidering out like a crack opening the earth up, and breaks for Basuin.

It races up his limbs and hits him at the junction of his ribcage and his sternum, sending something warm through his entire system. It's nothing like when the wolf-man forced itself into Basuin's body; there's no pain and no struggling, no suffering and no endless noise. It's just warm, like the water his mother used to heat over the open flame of the fire for them to bathe in.

Basuin cries.

There's no sound, but tears burst forth from his lashes without permission and something thick creeps up his throat. His lips pull back from his teeth as if he might laugh, hit with this uncontrollable urge to wrap his arms around himself and fall to his knees the way that Yaelic kneels to him now.

Warm, wet tears run down his face as he clutches his chest, at the very point where Yaelic's spirit floods into his own—a braid of their threads, a connection—and Basuin cries.

I'm sorry, someone says. That little white wolf pup, who sits in the dark and looks up at him with sad green eyes. *I didn't mean to make you cry*.

"I'm not," Basuin struggles to say, choking on this foreign feeling. "I'm not crying."

He squeezes his eyes shut, wiping them with the heel of his palm, and when he looks down again Yaelic is crying as well. Yaelic sobs into the sleeve of his robe, wiping at his face that's gone wet and runny with snot. Basuin shudders a breath.

His hand descends on Yaelic's hair, brushing through it gently, ruffling it with his fingers. "It's okay," he says. "It's all right now."

But Yaelic cries and cries as a child does, without any shame at all. "My mother," the little wolf pup sobs, the sound echoing in the forest so empty and yet so full of life. "And Hami, too. Everyone's left me."

Without hesitation, Basuin pulls Yaelic to him, wrapping his strong arms around the boy. Yaelic clings to him, hands reaching for someone that no longer exists in this life—his mother is on the other side, at the Winter River, where he hopes Sa-cha received her. He hopes Sa-cha washed the blood from her fur, rinsed it out of her cotton dress when she walked through the river.

IN TIME, THE smoke and fog of the fire dissipates, leaving behind the smell of burned remains and decaying birth. He is sure he smells the same—char and ash from a graveyard and something made only to be destroyed. There's blood on his skin. He can't see it, but he feels it. Basuin needs to wash it away.

"The village isn't far," Yaelic tells him. "That's where Hami went."

Basuin doesn't mention the bastion again. He's felt the weighty shame of being called a soldier before, but it's never quite scratched the way Hami's clawed words did. That boy will never forgive Basuin for taking his brother. Even if it wasn't Basuin's choice.

He doesn't want to go to Yaelic's village, but damn, he's tired. He drags his feet as they walk, breathing hard and grunting in pain. His whole body aches, especially where the wolf-man has carved out Basuin's heart and made his ribcage into a home. A day of rest will be all he needs to get back to the bastion.

Anywhere would be better than here. He's told himself that before, when Kensy brought him to this continent. Anywhere would be better than home. Now, he'd rather die than stay here with a wolf or a man or a god in his chest.

Yaelic looks back when Basuin falls behind. "Are you all right, Wolf God?"

Gulping down a painful breath, Basuin looks up with a sharpness in his eyes. The poor boy doesn't cower one bit, too cheery to notice the storm that's overtaking Basuin's face. Wolf God. He is no such thing.

Black Wolf, Black Wolf, Black Wolf, the wolf-man snickers.

"Don't call me that," Basuin says, tone tempered.

"What should I call you?" Yaelic asks, blinking his jadeite eyes.

"My name is Basuin."

Yaelic chitters, his shoulders shaking and his gold-white hair swaying in the breeze that dances through the trees. Basuin frowns.

"I can't call you that," Yaelic says. "You're a god. The god I serve."

"Then I command you not to call me that."

Basuin pushes off the tree and strides past Yaelic. He's not a god. He's not even a man anymore—this thing inside him polluting him. Mocking him with every step. Shut up. Just shut up.

Yaelic trails behind him, trekking forward like a pup whose paws are too big for its body. It's not the most coordinated. A childish gait, but one with purpose and spirit.

"Weren't you a soldier?" Yaelic asks, kicking a stone out of his way and running ahead of Basuin. He turns to skip backward as they talk. "What did your soldiers call you?"

"Basuin," he answers.

"They must've called you something."

Black Wolf, Black Wolf, Black Wolf, the wolf-man jeers.

He stumbles, left boot catching on a thorned vine in dense brush he didn't see. Tangled, Basuin catches himself on the nearest oak tree, bark scraping his hands as he pants for breath. It feels like he's losing his mind. Basuin doesn't know who he is anymore.

There's movement to his left. He can hear it. But when he looks up, head turned toward the foliage, there's nothing but a flash of white. A trick of the light.

Something tugs on his sleeve and Basuin lashes out, ripping his arm away in a flash of fear. It broils in his stomach, a fire that the wolf-man breathes life into. The smoke is filling his lungs but when he turns, it's only Yaelic who looks up at him, eyes lost.

Aless had eyes like Yaelic's—as green and golden as gems, marbled with loss and a plea for guidance.

Captain, she looked at him with those same damned eyes, *I want to go home. I didn't want this, didn't think it'd be like this.*

We'll go home, he lied. *We're gonna go home, 'Less.*

But Aless never made it home, head still frozen stuck to the ground. None of them made it home, but only Basuin made it out of Valkesta. If he sheds his armor, if he tries to be anything but a soldier like Tehali said, what will happen to them? The pieces of them—the memories, the faces, the words—that he carried with him?

He's a soldier. Not a god.

"Captain," he tells Yaelic, not meeting his eyes, as green as Aless' were. "That's what they called me."

Yaelic takes a step back from where Basuin struggles for breath, bowing his white-gold head until those eyes of his disappear. "Captain," Yaelic calls him, voice boyish and flickering between a wolf pup's whine and Aless' cry for help before the sword swung down and beheaded her.

From muscle memory alone, Basuin's head tilts toward the boy. "What?"

But Yaelic just gives him a toothy grin, child cheeks grown round and chubby. "Nothing," he says, and then he continues to run forward. A pit of ache festers in Basuin's gut.

The wolf-man rumbles awake. *You're a god now*, it tells him. *Someone belongs to you.*

Basuin wishes he didn't. He wishes that Yaelic didn't belong to him, because the people that belong to him always die.

CHAPTER SEVEN

THE FIRST THING he sees when the trees part is a woman standing tall and straight in their path. Familiar, somehow, and not at all. The straight ends of her hair brush by her shoulders, blunt bangs ruffled by the breeze. But it's her eyes that he remembers.

A dark and oozing amber, a stricken look of horror marring her face. The woman from the forest, who told him, *Go back. You're making a mistake.*

Yaelic rushes toward her, dropping to his knees in a show of worship, same as he had to Basuin. His dirt-caked legs collapse into the brush, unbothered by any prickles.

But the woman's eyes don't leave Basuin, even as Yaelic bows. She stares straight at him, brows drawn derisively. He can't look away, locked in her stunned gaze. A line of ash angles over her jawline and down her neck. His godstone burns and buzzes against his chest.

"Am-sa," Yaelic calls her. "I've brought the Wolf God—he saved me and my brother from the fire."

The woman recoils, and her eyes drop to the boy at her feet. Her teeth grind, and then her lips part, but no words come out. Her swallow moves down the column of her throat and Basuin's fingers curl into a fist.

"Rise, Yaelic," she says. The command of it straightens her somehow, as if she's regained consciousness. Her face smooths out in a snap, everything angular about her becoming even sharper. Shoulders bent into spears, cheekbones set like a knife's edge. Even the slope of her nose seems dangerous.

As she reaches a hand toward Yaelic, he scrambles to his feet, patting dirt from his tattered robes. "Hami—Is he here? He left and—"

"Your brother is safe," she says, sweeping his white-gold hair from his eyes. "Go inside, now."

Basuin expects him to run off at her command, but Yaelic hesitates. He hides his hands behind his back where only Basuin can see, balling them up into fists.

"I've brought the Wolf God here," Yaelic repeats himself. His voice sounds small.

"I am no such thing," Basuin says. "I've seen to getting Yaelic back to his brother, which was all I set out to do."

Now, he'll go back to the bastion. Kensy might kill him.

And yet, it's the wolf-man that unhinges its maw and snaps its teeth around Basuin's lung, puncturing it with a squelch and a hiss of air. Basuin's teeth gnash into his lip to stop a groan of pain, choking on the taste of rancid meat.

Yaelic's look of pure betrayal knocks the rest of the air from Basuin's body. Those big, childish green eyes of his. Glistening with unshed tears now, mouth in a tremble. He's just a boy.

And Basuin is just a soldier. Not a god.

The woman returns with a curt nod. "Come, Yaelic."

His eyes widen even more as he looks between Basuin and the woman. "No," he protests, looking up at Basuin. Yaelic shuffles backward, toward Basuin, hand fisting in Basuin's sleeve. "You'll come too, won't you?"

Before Basuin can answer, she hisses, "No. He can go back to wherever he came from."

"Am-sa," Yaelic pleads. "He's a god, too. He needs rest."

"He's a soldier," she bites back, but all heat is directed toward Basuin. She raises her chin at him. "He belongs with his own kind—the dangerous kind."

"He saved us." Yaelic clings to him, even as Basuin tries to shake the wolf pup off. "He isn't dangerous, not like the others. He saved me and Hami."

"Yaelic," he interrupts, voice nicked into a thing with teeth. "I'm not staying."

"You're not welcome," the woman amends for him, and it takes strength for Basuin not to rise to her heckling. She's right—whoever she is. She's right that he's a soldier, and he's dangerous, and he's not welcome here. Wherever here is.

"Then neither am I," Yaelic says, a puff of his chest and a thrill of confidence in his voice. Determination and decision. "I won't go. Not without him." Yaelic's hand falls and the boy steadies himself alone. "I bound myself to him, Am-sa."

The cool, controlled look she wears vanishes, a flash of shock and horror flitting across her visage. "You what?" Incredulity floods her voice.

"He's my god now," Yaelic says. "If he isn't allowed in the village, then neither am I."

Children; how stubborn they are. Basuin's mouth moves around words, but none of them come out to tell Yaelic he'll do no such thing. This is where Yaelic belongs—his brother is here. The woman called Am-sa seems to care. Basuin doesn't need this kid stuck to his leg. He doesn't need another life to carry on his back.

But he's confused, too. He doesn't know where he is, who he is. Why Yaelic calls him a god, and why he bound himself to Basuin. Responsibility is red and hot in his chest. Kensy left Yaelic motherless, but Basuin was the one to pull him and his brother from the fire. Yaelic's life is a weight on his back.

This is for the best. To leave him here with this woman and his brother and march back to the bastion. Basuin can't be dead. If he were dead, it wouldn't hurt so bad. He can figure this out on his own.

Inside him, the wolf-man chuffs a laugh.

As he mulls on his words, something he isn't keen to do, the woman's shoulders droop enough to catch his eye. She takes a breath, chest rising and falling with a melodic sigh, and reaches to brush a hand through her hair.

"We'll talk more about this later," she finally says, voice hammered into a monotonous thing. "You can both stay—just for the night." Her eyes target his. "But you must leave in the morning."

It sends a measure of chill straight through him. If he wasn't trained into such a mean thing, he might have shuddered. But he stands strong and proud, despite wanting to shrink under her gaze. She sees him as an enemy; her dark eyes say as much. But Basuin's been an enemy for most of his life, so it doesn't matter.

Yaelic bows deeply. "Thank you, Am-sa!" But she's already turning her back to them and walking away.

Basuin lurches forward, unable to stop himself. "Who are you?" he asks after her. Desperation leaks between his teeth and spills onto his tongue.

The wolf-man howls in laughter.

"The Forest God," she answers, looking at him from over her shoulder. Then, a thread of blue light appears in a tangle around her wrist, and in one bright flash, the Forest God thrusts her hand forward. The air shimmers—like magic.

It's as if the wolf-man thunders in place of his heart, something deep within him thrumming from behind his ribcage. Beating at him, drumming in a march. *Her*, it says.

A dome appears out of the glowing lights that glitter from the Forest God's fingers, encasing the forest ahead of them. Then, her hand pierces the bubble and her arm sinks into the magic, creating a tear in the protective seal.

You'll protect her, the wolf-man barks.

It's feral. Wild and alive. His nonexistent heart hammers like it did on the battlefield—in Valkesta.

Fall back! someone called. *Push forward!* he shouted. The winds howled, *Kill, kill, kill! Protect, protect, protect!*

A command, he realizes. It's a command, one that's grown inside the house of his body from the once-god that now resides between his bones. The Wolf God, chosen to protect the forest. But not only the forest.

Protect, protect, protect.

The Forest God looks back at him again, face hardened and eyes cold. "Welcome to Gyeosi, Wolf God."

IT FEELS LIKE rain, the first time he takes a step through the magic barrier and into Gyeosi. Torrential rain beating down on him, sleeting across his shoulders and cutting through his skin, rolling down his back in chilling lines. It's heavy. He might drown in the downpour of the storm, thunder rumbling above the clouds he cannot see. The night is dark.

But then the Forest God walks through the trees and Gyeosi transforms entirely. It's as if the sun comes out—the shadowed trees of the forest blossom into a village that feels like home. Along the branches, strung up with twine, lanterns and glass balls housing fire and magic glow to life as if the Forest God commands them to, without even a word or a flick of her wrist.

The rain stops falling, the storm clouds race to clear the sky, and it's warm. Where his heart should be, the wolf-man laughs at him.

There is magic here, on this island. Running through the ground. What he felt before, when he first stepped upon the land, is nothing compared to the currents of energy sparking in the air of Gyeosi. Even breathing is easier.

"Isn't it great?" Yaelic, trotting along beside him, asks with a smile. "Hami's probably waiting for us."

For Yaelic, maybe. Not for him, an enemy. But Yaelic's grin glows in the village lights and Basuin can't bring himself to dim it. Not now, anyway.

As if summoned, there's a rustle in the brush to his right. His head turns, his eyes unfocused as his hearing takes precedence. Something takes shape and form as it moves through the foliage. Hami, maybe. Even the Forest God comes to a halt, steps ahead of them. As her footfalls pause, everything in their vicinity quiets as if bowing to her presence.

But it's not Hami at all. From the underbrush peeks out the snout of a small deer, its head following as it stretches out from the foliage and shakes leaves from its back. There are sticker burrs caught in its glossy chestnut fur.

A fawn, the puff of its tail twitching happily with a step toward them. Just a baby. It looks at him curiously, glassy black eyes staring at him. Basuin leans back, ready to put space between them.

"Qia," the Forest God calls out from behind him. "Come out, don't startle him."

With a snuff, the baby deer shakes out its fur again, and then a swarm of green light surrounds it, motes of dust like stars scattered across the sky. Before his eyes, like Hami had morphed into the wolf pup, the deer shifts and materializes into a human body. He tries not to blink—not this time—but the light is harsh and he flinches from it.

When he opens his eyes, a small girl stands in the place of the fawn. Roughly the same size, this girl seems to be a child as well, her features young. She wears a nervous smile on her lips, her eyes the same doe-like black as before. Her dark hair is pulled up into a long ponytail cascading down the back of the robe she wears, red fabric trimmed in gold, which moves fluidly as she bows her head to the Forest God.

"Sorry," she says, glancing up and meeting his gaze. "I wanted to receive you all properly."

"Don't play coy," the Forest God says, but her voice holds no anger. "You're too curious for your own good."

The girl bows her head again, deeper this time. "Sorry, Amsa. Forgive me?"

The Forest God steps forward, smoothing a few of the girl's

loose strands of hair back, and Basuin catches the faintest smile taking over her mouth as she does. It's a strange gesture, unlike the harsh front she's put on in front of him. Maybe the ice in her glare is reserved only for soldiers, like him.

"Go, then." The Forest God gestures toward Basuin. "Introduce yourself."

The little deer-girl steps in his direction, also bowing her head, but not as deeply. "I'm Qia. I serve the Forest God."

Basuin blinks down at her, grinding his molars, fumbling with his words. "Hello," he says, unsure of what to say. "I'm Basuin of Ankor."

"And I'm Yaelic!" He bounds toward Qia, bowing lower. "I serve the Wolf God."

Qia gasps, her hands flying to her mouth. Behind her, the Forest God looks away.

"The Wolf God?" Qia stutters, her brown eyes widening into the moons that mark the month's end. She bows her head again, hands wringing together in front of her. Basuin takes a step backward, grimacing. There's a sore on the inside of his bottom lip that his teeth want to worry.

"I'm not—That's not who I am," he says, waving it off, his eyes glancing back and forth between Qia and the Forest God, the trodden path beneath him and the canopy overhead. He doesn't know where to look. "I'm just Basuin, of Ankor."

Qia looks up, brows furrowing in confusion. She takes in his figure, worry swimming in the depths of her doe eyes.

"But—" she starts, and is silenced by a wave of the Forest God's hand which catches her gaze.

"Qia," she calls again. "You can show them the way."

In a fit of quick movements, Qia bows her head to Basuin first, then to the Forest God twice.

"Yes, of course, Am-sa," Qia says, grabbing the skirt of her robes. "Come this way, Wolf God, sir. Yaelic, too." She starts moving, her hands clasped together and hidden in the red sleeves of her robe. Every few steps she looks back to make sure they follow. Yaelic bounces right behind her, chattering about something, but Basuin stays a few feet behind.

The Forest God, as quickly as she came, disappears. She's done that before—in the forest, as he ran to save the wolves. He lunged to grab her and she spun right out of his grasp, dissolving into the trees.

The wound the wolf-man made inside of him rings with a searing pain. Though he doesn't bleed and there is no entry or exit made from his skin, Basuin aches. Not even a knife through his chest, not even a lead bullet, could hurt in the way this has.

There are other people in Gyeosi, he realizes, the further they move inside. Other spirits, maybe, but like Yaelic and Qia, they all look human. Small huts are carved out of the trunks of trees, tiny houses built from mud and fallen branches, quilted leaves and dried hay for roofs.

And more than that, sprawling roots from trees almost as thick as the watchtowers the Xalkhans build carry these homes as well. There are stairs made of thick slabs of bark linked by woven rope, ladders the same, that lead all the way up to the top of the forest until the canopy is so thick it blocks out the sky above.

Each spirit they pass greets Qia warmly, then shoots some version of a smile at Yaelic. But Basuin, they eye warily. Maybe he looks like a spirit, trailing after two children, still covered in ash. Or maybe, all they see is an enemy, like Hami did.

None of the spirits ask for his name, and for that, Basuin is thankful.

"Have you seen Hami?" Yaelic asks Qia, but she shakes her head.

"I was told he's here," she says. "We can look for him tomorrow. I'm sure you're both tired."

Once, he was. Now that he's stepped inside Gyeosi, it's like he's been recharged. As though drinking in the air here and filling his lungs with the fresh smell of leaves sticky with their life-sap and earth wet from the rains has given him a new reason to be awake.

Still, there's an air of unease running through the village, an undercurrent. Basuin can't tell what it is, but as they pass by the open clearing at the center of the village, a group of women are sitting on their knees and crying. They bow their heads low over a blanket spread with someone's belongings. Someone dead.

One of them looks up, toward the sky, but catches sight of Basuin. He looks away but their sobs continue.

"Elka," they cry for the sun god. "Stop the fires they brought here. Stop them from salting our home."

The image of Shaelstorm, cleared by fire and wood axes, burns his mind the way the legion has burned through the forest. The wolf-man nips at his sternum, his heart-bone. Basuin doubts even Elka, who bloomed the sun and throws it to rise and fall, could stop the legion. Ithika, god of the oceans, couldn't either.

He still doesn't know why Kensy brought them here in the first place. Kensy wouldn't have known of spirits like these, of gods on the island.

Then, quieter, from a girl who wouldn't be old enough to even join the legion, a scoff. "Pray to our god," she seethes. "Ask *our* god to do something about the godsdamned army."

Across the way, he spots her—the Forest God, again. She's standing among a group of two others—a tall, tall man draped in long and heavy robes, whose dark hair falls in straight lines down his back and shoulders to trail the ground, and a shorter, glaring creature with dozens of thin white scars standing out among their dark skin. They find Basuin first, beady eyes narrowed at him. Then, the taller spirit looks as well, much more at ease. Curious, if anything.

The Forest God doesn't look at all. But she bids them goodbye with a nod of her head, then turns to walk in Basuin's direction. They bow to her as she goes.

"Are you afraid of heights?" she asks, completely out of the blue. The first words she's spoken to him since he entered Gyeosi.

He snorts. "No." He wouldn't be a legion captain if he was. Soldiers, good soldiers, can't afford to be afraid of anything at all. Basuin doesn't fear even death. Not anymore.

When Yaelic answers similarly, she nods. "There's a hut for you two, beds to sleep in."

"And Hami?" Yaelic asks again, a thread of pleading mixing in his tone. The Forest God's whole demeanor shifts and softens to something gentler.

"He's safe," she tells him. "He's staying with Ko, the oak tree." She gestures toward the towering man and his unsociable companion. "You can visit him in the morning."

Yaelic shifts from foot to foot, fist balling in the dirtied fabric of his robe. "Okay, Am-sa."

The Forest God's eyes slide to Basuin, scanning over him yet again, and he prickles under her gaze. The hand he's clutched to his chest, on the left side, falls. Out of muscle memory, his spine straights and his shoulders roll back for routine inspection. Her eyes narrow, tracing the hard lines of his body. What is she looking for in him—proof that he's dangerous still?

Good. Basuin is dangerous. He hopes that everyone in his village knows it.

Then, she turns her back to him without saying another word. Qia scrambles to catch up, walking alongside the Forest God at double her pace to stay in tune. The Forest God is smaller than he thought. Qia's just a child, small and barely taller than the Forest God's waist. But the god herself, though fierce with her presence alone, is much shorter than Basuin.

He would tower over her if they stood toe to toe. He doesn't want to get close to her.

They're led to a larger house, one built on a platform that seems as if it were cut from a fallen oak; round and thick, like a saucer. When she pushes the maroon cloth aside to let him in, the interior of the hut is bigger. More room has been carved out of the tree it's built into, creating a large space in the front and an area for a few beds in the back.

It's not so different from the bunks in Ha'riste, the ones for squadrons, not much bigger than the length of a bed and enough space for a personal trunk and a washing basin. The captain's bunk, of course, was bigger. Not that Basuin ever spent much time there. He was a war hero, on the front lines. Not a political pawn.

"Qia." The Forest God gestures for the deer-girl. "Fetch them some water, please."

"I'll go with you!" Yaelic lunges for the chance, even as Qia's cheeks pinken at his enthusiasm.

"Sure," she stutters. "Of course." Then, with a whip of her long ponytail, Qia skitters out of the hut and Yaelic follows, skipping down the bark stairs.

"Don't worry, Forest God," he mocks before she has a chance to speak first. "I'll leave for Shaelstorm in the morning."

"Good luck." Whatever gentleness moved in at Yaelic's presence is gone, replaced by cold, hard eyes. "I'm sure you'll be accepted back easily, Wolf God."

"Don't call me that." He takes a step toward her out of necessity. The Forest God takes one step backward, out of his reach. "I'm not a god. I'm just a man."

She stares him down. "Do you truly believe that?"

The wolf-man inside him lunges. Its teeth tear into Basuin, shredding his flesh into nothing but dog chow. He covers his mouth with a trembling hand, so he won't puke up the entrails the wolf-man slices into paper-thin ribbons. There's so much blood.

Listen to me, it gnaws on one of Basuin's ribs. *You died, as all things do. But I gave you life again. I am the god that possesses your empty body. I've given you power so that you can serve your duty, little soldier boy.*

Duty, again. A soldier then, a soldier now. A soldier in life, and a soldier in death. Not until he lays in the Blacksalt Sea will he be free.

You are the Wolf God, it snaps again at him. *Chosen to protect this forest. Chosen to protect the Forest God.*

He looks at her, rage boiling him alive, eyes wide and searing. "I did my duty. I get to go home now." Home—when he thinks of it, he makes himself think of the Blacksalt Sea.

The Forest God cuts her eyes at him, onyx that could scar a man. "Do you get to go home, Black Wolf? When your people are killing mine?"

Basuin flinches at the name in shame, head swimming and hands hot. "I never wanted to come here."

"But you did," she says, and she's right. "You're getting in my way. I brought you here out of kindness, for Yaelic, since he's bound himself to you. How gracious a god you are."

A roar of protectiveness rises in him for no reason. "Don't speak of Yaelic," he spits out.

In a flash, the Forest God clears the space between them and is nearly slick to him—only a sliver of space between his chest and hers. Though she cranes her neck up to look at him, her glare is more fearsome. But Basuin doesn't cave. He stands straight and still, nostrils flaring as he looks down to meet her dark gaze. She's a bullet, quick as a gun goes off.

"My duty is to save the forest *your* army is destroying," she snarls. A wild animal. "You'd do well to remember that, god or not, you don't belong here. You've killed my people—be lucky that I've yet to remove you from the picture, Wolf God."

Her chest breaks with every heaving breath, eyes glittering with something silver and something deeper. Rage colors her glare into twilight. The dying light of day. He needs to look away—to anywhere but her. Anywhere else, because the way she wields her tongue she might as well hold a knife to his skin and bleed him now.

Fuck off, he wants to tell her. At that, the wolf-man digs its claws straight into him with a kind of pain that scratches at his brain and makes him want to vomit again.

Before he can say anything else meant to harm her, the Forest God falls back to her heels, the rift between them growing until he's left with nothing but the scent of soil and something floral. Then, she ducks out of his room.

Tomorrow, he'll go back to Shaelstorm. He'll do as Kensy says. He'll beg Tehali to undo her work in saving him and stitching him back up and make her kill him like he should have asked her to in Valkesta.

He'll ask to go home this time. Plead and beg and scream. *Take me back*, he'll ask at their feet and on his knees. *Back to Ankor*. Even if his mother isn't there anymore.

CHAPTER EIGHT

Sleep doesn't come, and neither does morning. Yaelic snoozes like a child, unaware of any danger that could fell him. His deep, quick breathing keeps Basuin alert, and he rolls around in his sleep so much that he falls from his mat leaving Basuin to roll him back. He never even wakes, just makes sleep-addled, nasal sounds.

So, instead, Basuin stares at the ceiling and replays his life's worst failure, as he does most nights. Names the people he lost over and over so his war-torn mind won't forget them. If he forgets them, then they were never real.

1st Sergeant Curk of Ferghit. The only man who ever matched Basuin head on, in height and strength.

2nd Sergeant Aless of Harker. She barely spoke a word to anyone when she first showed up. Basuin never expected her to become such a loyal ally in the end.

3rd Sergeant Isaniel of Medeia. Isaniel. *Isaniel.*

4th Sergeant Mekal of Altea. Basuin still doesn't know why Mekal agreed to go. They never should've gone—should've done their five years and left the legion as soon as they could.

5th Sergeant Tomaas of Olsten. Proof that the gods can be cruel.

Basuin lays awake and repeats them over, and over, and over, and over, until the numbers and names and cities bleed into the pulp of offal he saw strewn across the snowbanks. It's the one thing he can do for them, now.

Two days ago, he was the disgraced Captain Basuin, leading Ariche's Fleet to conquer a new land—something he never wanted to do. Yesterday, he was just Basuin. Disgraced, dishonored, and deserving of death.

Now, he's the Wolf God. A deity lives in his chest and has named him so. A boy belongs to him, has pledged his life to Basuin.

But in every iteration of his life, he's just a soldier tasked with a duty he didn't ask for. Basuin is tired. So, so tired.

Not tired enough to sleep. Basuin fixes the sheet over Yaelic's curled-up form, sighing. Then, he laces his boots on and heads out of their hut, into the village. The lights still glow, but dimmer in the darkness of night. It's so quiet now, no spirits to be seen. No Forest God, either. He's thankful for that.

But as he heads down the steps from the treehouse and toward the edge of the village, he catches sight of her. Just a flash—the back of her white, fluttering shirt and a dirt-stained calf as she disappears behind the foliage. Where is she going?

Without thinking, Basuin follows.

It's hard in the dark. She's too fast for him to catch sight of, and too quiet to hear—almost. Every faint rustle of brush that most people would miss, Basuin finds. And he holds on to that, letting it pull him through the darkened woods after the Forest God. The place where his heart used to be feels so empty, but if he were still alive, it would be hammering away as he chases after her.

He needs to know what she's doing to stop the legion. This duty she speaks of, what he's getting in the way of.

Then, he hears her voice. Quiet, and softer than it's ever been to him. "Wake, my friend."

He draws nearer, the Forest God's back illuminated by the moonlight streaming through the fronds that block out the sky. She stands before a tree, her hand placed upon its bark. At her words, it sways as though a harsh wind blows through, leaves raining over the crown of her head.

"Am-sa," a voice groans from the roots beneath her feet. Unlike Qia, the tree doesn't shift into something human in form. "Where do you go tonight?"

"That's not for you to worry about, friend." Her hand smooths over its bark. "But I would appreciate it if you would allow us passage."

"Of course, Am-sa. And then, I will sleep again."

The Forest God, slow and poised, turns around to face Basuin. "Well? Are you coming, or were you going to wait until I get back?"

He blanches. Shame is hot around his neck and crawling up his ears. Basuin rubs a hand over his mouth, wiry beard overgrown now, and takes a guilty step forward.

"To where?" he asks, spinning his shame into confidence.

But her lips twitch, flattened and mean. "To show you my god-given duty." Every word slipping from her teeth is sharp enough to cut into him.

It sounds like a challenge, and Basuin has never backed down from one before. So he closes the gap, eyes glancing between her and the tree. Its trunk is knobby, an uneven oval wrought into its bark, and the Forest God traces it with her delicate hand.

"This is Chiro," she says. A creak and groan of the oak meets her introduction. "He'll take us there."

"Hello," he says, awkward again. He doesn't know how to speak with the forest. But Chiro seems happy with his greeting, another gust of leaves spinning around them.

"Let's go," the Forest God says, and then that bright blue light pulses through her hand again. This time, it hits him with heat—hits him and drags him closer to her. The wolf-man teethes on Basuin's necrotic flesh, muzzle bloodied with his organs, and starts scratching at the rest of him. It feels the pull, too.

Then, within Chiro's trunk, a shimmering blue image fills the oval-like gnarled bark. It looks like water, but brighter. And when she puts her hand to it, her fingers go straight through it. Just like the dome that covered Gyeosi, she sinks into the magic. It's so quick, Basuin's afraid she'll disappear before his eyes.

"Wait," he calls out as blue magic swallows her wrist. She stops, turning to look back at him, confused. Flustered, Basuin can't think of anything to say. Nothing to protest with. He doesn't even know why he spoke aloud.

For the first time, she huffs a laugh at him. But it isn't kind. It's mocking.

"Are you scared?" she asks. "You're dead."

The wolf-man laughs and laughs and laughs at him, too.

Then, the Forest God outstretches a small hand with a toss of her head for him to follow. And despite her jeers, Basuin takes her hand, his large fingers wrapping around hers, and lets her pull him inside the blue portal of magic. It's warm, and it pops and sizzles on his skin, tickling him. He holds his breath as he dives in, but it doesn't last long.

And when he feels forest floor beneath his boots again, Basuin smells gunpowder. Like a sword taken to the gut, his legs give out beneath him and he stumbles, trying to breathe the scent of it away.

"We're here," she says, no fanfare.

Basuin looks up to the watchtower, to the lantern-lit walls of the Shaelstorm Bastion. The Forest God stands, staring it down like she's on a battlefield, outlined in the glow of the orange flames.

She takes off in a blink, rounding through the forest and toward the bastion. There's no guard in the tower—Shaelstorm has no defenses. That woman will be able to slip right through and slaughter everyone. He's seen little of her magic; he doesn't know what power she has. She could level the whole bastion. He has to stop her.

And wouldn't that be deserved? the wolf-man asks him, gnawing his insides raw.

Basuin sprints after her. But she doesn't head for the gates. She heads for the fields.

He's too slow, and before he can catch up, the Forest God drops into a crouch and knifes her palms into the upturned soil the legion tilled for farming. Blue magic pours, like water, through all the cracks and crevices in the earth and spreads in veins into the entire field. Instantly, the green growth breaking through the dirt withers, yellow and soured. The crops die.

Shaelstorm is meant to starve.

Her bare feet barely kick up dirt as she bounds across one field to the next. The mulch is wet with poison when he runs through it, and Basuin nearly can't catch himself as he slips to chase after her. The next plot of crops goes as quick as the last, god magic turning vegetal sprout into nothing more than rot.

The Forest God slips into a growing maze of corn, looking over her shoulder at him. Her eyes are near-black, even in the light of the torches lining the bastion walls. She disappears into the sea of green, her hand trailing over the ears of corn as she goes. Her touch leaves behind a blue trail, the smell of mold and ferment hitting his nose as he dives in after her.

"What are you doing?" he shouts, slowed by the stalks. She's small enough to slip through them with little resistance. He should've brought his sword, but it sleeps next to Yaelic in Gyeosi. How foolish of him, yet again.

"Not killing them," her voice, bell-toned and poised, finds him. "Not like your people are."

Basuin grits his teeth and speeds up. He hears her exit the field before he sees her leap away. She's fast, but his legs are much longer—and Basuin's had plenty of chase in his life. Not as kind then as he will be now. But the Forest God runs toward the food stores and this is his last chance to stop her.

When his hand closes around her arm, for the first time since he's seen her, she looks back with a flash of fear on her face. Eyes stricken and wide. Lips parted and gasping.

Basuin lets go.

And then he stumbles, shoulder hitting the ground with a wicked thud and a cough of dirt. Shit. Kensy was right. Disgraced Captain Basuin isn't much of a captain at all anymore. He's lost his fight. Basuin rolls onto his back, out of breath, staring up at the sky. There are no stars here, not with all the light and smoke from the bastion.

Where his heart should lie, the wolf-man snuffs a cruel laugh.

The Forest God's face appears before him and his breath hitches. He sits up on his elbows, tipping his head back to meet her gaze as she stands over him. Peering at him. Her eyes aren't angry so much as they are wary, but even still, he feels the ire radiating from her.

"Your world is so small and selfish," she hisses. "One woman against a militant base content to destroy a whole island, and yet you chase after her instead."

"You're killing a few soldiers who are following orders—"

"I'm not killing them," she snarls, and then she backs away from him. Basuin moves with her as if magnetic, pushing himself off the ground. "I would never kill them."

"And starving them is better?"

"Yes," she bites. "Your people won't starve as long as they leave this island."

"It's not their choice."

"Everything is a choice, Black Wolf." It's meant to cut, and it does. Basuin bleeds something awful. "You chose to come here, you chose to die, and your punishment fits your crime."

There is a war inside of him—there is always a war somewhere. The weight of it has bludgeoned him into nothing, shaped him into who he is now. She's as right as she is wrong. What choice did Basuin have when everything has been beaten out of him, until he's been made into the perfect soldier he was always meant to be?

"You know nothing of me," he says, voice quiet. "I wanted to die, not—"

"Perfect," she interrupts him coolly. "You're already dead."

"Good," he snarls back. "Great. I died, only for the gods to bring me back and command me to protect you."

"To protect this forest," she says.

"To protect *you*," he snaps again. He doesn't want godhood. Doesn't need another duty. Can't be a protector the way the wolf-man commands him to. Basuin couldn't protect his mother. Nor his soldiers, and certainly not Isaniel. So how, gods tell him, is he supposed to protect this woman and her forest?

He doesn't want to. He won't.

"I'll make them regret coming to this forest," she says. "And you'll regret it too, if you get in my way."

Then, as she always has, the Forest God turns and walks away from him. Back toward the forest, leaving Shaelstorm cropless. So Basuin starts walking, too. Following after her. But she flicks her hand out at her side and an arc of blue magic leaves her fingertips, and then Basuin runs straight into something solid—something midair that he can't see. A barrier.

She's leaving him. This time, for good. Rage and fury seeps into his skin until he's drenched in heat, anger dripping from his fingers until he has to make fists of them.

"Didn't you hear me before?" she asks, cutting a glare at him. "I said you weren't welcome."

It takes everything in him not to bang his fist upon the barrier, to try and break through. His nostrils flare. "You said I could stay until morning."

For the first time, the Forest God's lips curl into a smile as she looks to the horizon. "And you left to follow me. It's nearly dawn now. Let your people know that their fields won't grow anything."

He doesn't even want to go back to Gyeosi. Basuin could walk away, right now, and they'd both be happy. But spite narrows his brows and keeps his hands hot. She doesn't get to win—not when Basuin is forced to lose everything again.

The wolf-man stands up on his hind legs and howls. *You are weak!* it berates him. It sinks its canines straight into his flesh, tears chunks of it out until it can ravage his sternum, his heart-bone. *How far you have fallen from grace. I thought you to be a war hero.*

Once, maybe. But now he is nothing.

What a useless thing, the wolf-man growls, and then it breaks Basuin's heart-bone in one bite. He gasps for air, sagging against the magic wall the Forest God has barred him from moving past. *What a useless little soldier boy you turned out to be.*

It's better this way. For him to stay here at the bastion, to be rid of Yaelic, to offload the rest of his responsibilities so he can die—for good, this time. Basuin's tried to die twice already, and each time he's failed. Maybe this time, when Kensy kills him, it'll stick.

When Basuin finally takes a step back, away from the barrier, the Forest God turns her back on him. Then, the ground shakes. A chest-aching boom, loud enough to bleed ears, goes off with no warning. She recoils, shifting into a guarded stance as she looks to the sky. The barrier between them drops as the quietus of the forest is disturbed. The trees quiver violently.

"What—" she tries to speak.

And then another explosion goes off, louder and sharper, whistling into the air until it hits the ceiling of night and shatters into one thousand lights colored red like blood. The Forest God's face is awash in it, her eyes wide and fearful.

The place where Basuin's heart used to lie beats quick as a bird's fluttering wings. They're celebrating. It cinches something in his guts, twists his organs around each other. They're *celebrating*.

Another streak of fire arcs across the sky until it bursts into blue sparks, fizzling out with a whine.

Kensy, and all of Shaelstorm, are celebrating Basuin's death.

CHAPTER NINE

WITHOUT A SECOND to digest it, another cannon is fired and shakes the grass beneath Basuin's feet. She falls into a crouch, hands clasped over her ears. In a bloom of green lights, shrieking like something dying, he can see fear painted on her visage in a way he's never witnessed before.

Inside him, the wolf-man makes some half-growl, half-snarl sound and punctures Basuin's stomach with its claws.

He reaches, but she's quicker. She darts back into the forest and something yanks him forward. He chases after her—the wolf-man lunges at his organs and he's forced to move. She finds the nearest tree and begins to climb, fast, faster, and he lags behind. By the time his foot is braced against bark, she's already in the branches above his head. Basuin scrambles up the oak in pursuit. She's too quick for him.

Another firework explodes in the air. Red, again. And then another right after, bright white. The colors of the Xalkhan kingdom.

He wheezes as he pulls himself up over branch after branch, scaling the tree. His chest aches, muscles weak and weary. But finally, he reaches her. The Forest God stands rigid and upright on the topmost branch, extended out toward the south where the lights come from. Her head tipped up, mouth agape as she watches the fireworks gleam across the sky.

When Basuin catches his breath, he doesn't watch the show. He watches the Forest God, face alight with all different colors, and the horror spilling over her countenance.

"What fire is this?" she asks, her voice barely heard over the whistle of explosions and the boom of cannons. "I've never seen violence so colorful."

"They're fireworks," he says, throat dry as he swallows. "Haven't you seen any?"

In Ha'riste, they were popular. Common, even. Kingdom celebrations always held elaborate shows, new colors and new designs that would light up the dull skies of the city. Queen Ye'suite was a fan, someone once told him. But even street rats could buy tiny sparklers to light for a couple coins, kids running around trying to set fire to one another's hair or mark their skin with a burn.

But she answers, "No." Her voice choked and twisted. "No, I've never. What have you brought to my forest?"

Basuin cringes. He didn't bring them. But the legion did.

He remembers the vivid displays that sprang from their victories, the smell of blood at camp mingling with the sharp scent of gunpowder packed into paper hand cannons. The laughter of his men who lit the tail-end of the fuses and tossed them into the air.

Their greatest victory, in Ulenski, Grimmalia's last unoccupied trade city. When he couldn't wash the ash from his skin, blackened by death and sin and triumph. Kensy ordered a couple of soldiers to load the cannons, to shake whoever was left in Grimmalia and remind them of who held power—Xalkhir. Always Xalkhir.

Why the long face? Kensy had asked him, a burn in his sharp blue eyes. *You should be proud.*

But Basuin had flinched away from the cannons and held his head in his hands. Kensy clapped a firm hand on his shoulder.

You've freed them, Kensy said. *Unshackled them from gods who didn't bother to save them.*

And lights, the color of blood and fire, burst forth from their camps long into the night, punctuated by cannons that shook the earth and the oceans and Basuin's body as he lay on his cot, wracked with violent shivers. And Isaniel, who laid a blanket over him and left him to his demons.

"It's a celebration," Basuin says, voice as quiet as hers under the thundering of explosions. "The fireworks are harmless, mostly. They fizzle out, won't burn anything."

The fear that drenches her skin, the horror in her eyes, doesn't change. "What are they celebrating?"

My death, he thinks selfishly. But it's not true. He knows what they celebrate. He's watched it, city after city, the display of power and arrogance.

"Conquest," he says.

She whips around in an instant. The fear is replaced by an anger fueled by insolence. In two steps she's nearly toe to toe with him, head level with his chest, neck craned back to look at him with a glass-edged glare. Not evil. But a threat all the same.

But Basuin doesn't waver, doesn't lean back. She's too small for him to back away, pride licking at his nonexistent wounds. He won't back down, not to her.

It's not his fault. He didn't bring the army here—Kensy did.

"Do you think you've already won?" the Forest God seethes, low and steady. "How arrogant are you?"

His nostrils flare in anger. "I have won nothing. I'm not the one celebrating. *I've* lost everything. Again," he bites back, looking down at her. Another shower of sparks in the night sky, another display of impudence.

There's the slightest tremble in her mouth, lips silvered in the blue sparkle of another firework.

"I could never imagine someone so cruel," she says. "Cruel enough to celebrate the death of my people."

He can. And the cruelest of them all just set foot on this island. It's barely been two days and he's already slaughtered innocents—and killed Basuin, too.

His hesitation leaves time for her mouth to set in stone, for her brow to harden and for her eyes to narrow once more. A breeze wanders through her hair, blunt edges of her bangs shadowing her face until the next firework rolls overhead.

"Spare me your woes," she says, disgust coloring her tone. As if she's read his face and spun up whatever fortune she thinks. "Your self-pity can't stand against the destruction your army has brought here. I won't listen to it."

Basuin clenches his entire body to stop from leaning down to her and barking back. Even the thought has the wolf-man snarling inside of him, growling, snapping its teeth in warning. He breathes in, deep through his nose, and back out. The anger in him simmers despite it.

"You know nothing of me," he says quietly. Restrained.

The scream of another firework, like paint splattering across the canvas of night, makes her spin to look. He can't see her face, but he knows from the way her fingers curl into fists by her side—slowly, controlled, but raging all the same—that anger runs through her veins.

"I'll teach them," she says, voice low and tempered. "They won't celebrate a victory they haven't earned."

She raises a hand to the sky, pointed toward the bastion, and a blue glow encases her hand. Bright in her palm, between her fingers, then wrapping around her wrist and trailing down her forearm like growing vines. It pulses, alive.

Magic. Real and true and vivid and so close he feels it in his heart—no, he doesn't have a heart left. So what is this feeling?

Then, with a breath, the Forest God shoots a beam of blue into the night, the force of it blowing her hair back. But the force of it hits him too, tugs on his heart-bone and staggers him, nearly brings him to his knees. Basuin chokes on his tongue as a new pain grips him. He feels like his organs are being ripped out of his body. It hurts in the same way a flashbang hurts—sudden and bleeding without a drop of blood at all. Burning.

Her magic arcs toward the bastion, but fizzles out immediately. She inhales hard, glowing hand now clutching at her chest as if she feels the same thing Basuin does. The blue lights rain down into the forest below them in a sparkling of glitter, flitting away on the wind. A pitiful version of a firework.

She twists her fingers in her shirt, looking back at him. Her countenance speaks to confusion and surprise, knotted together by that look of horror.

"My magic," she whispers. "It's gone." Slowly, she unfurls her fingers, searching every line and divot as if for answers. There's a mark upon her palm, a series of white lines like scars. It makes his own palm pulse in tandem. Then, that same thread of blue magic twined around her wrist appears, glowing against her skin, and leads straight back to him.

The wolf-man scratches at the floor of Basuin's organs, making itself a nest inside him.

The Forest God turns to look at him, her eyes gone wide. "You're stealing my magic."

When he looks down, a thread of red is wrapped and knotted around his left wrist. Basuin, wheezing, upturns his hand. There, on his left palm, is a series of lines he's never seen before. They feel familiar, like they belong to him, but the edges are raised like a healing wound. It's black, like ink. Engraved into his skin. He stares at it, long enough that it almost flashes red like the color of the wolf-man's eyes.

"What?" He can barely breathe, barely cough out words.

"You didn't have magic," she says, but it sounds like a cry for help. Her chest unhinges with every breath she can't catch.

Magic existed. His mother spoke of it like a fairytale. Or perhaps a memory, he realizes now. *Magic existed, and it ate the world as you know it. Swallowed it up until there was no one left who believed in it.*

Then how are we still blessed to be alive? he asked with his teenaged snark.

The same way we always were, she told him, and he hated it. *If you kill a king, you take his castle.*

"They gave you mine," she says, a look of betrayal marring her face. "You're taking it."

If you kill a god—

THEY DON'T SPEAK after the fireworks end. Surprisingly, after she jumps from the branch she perched on, she waits for Basuin to climb down with her. Dawn is approaching, the sky colored in dark tones of lavender and periwinkle. She doesn't tell him not to follow, and Basuin doesn't ask if he can. Even when they reach the portal, they stay cocooned in silence until they are so far away from the bastion again that Basuin breathes without gunpowder stuffed in his nose.

She should have left him behind. Part of him would've preferred it. But it was he who followed—a searing need to know more, to understand what's become of him. Of them. Their magic, a frightening link. And it's he who speaks first, unable to keep himself from it.

"What's your name?" he asks, after all this time.

She doesn't glance at him. "The Forest God."

Basuin almost laughs, but he can only huff a breath of frustration. "That's not a name."

"I don't have a name," she says.

"Everyone has a name," he presses. If he can just prove that she isn't a god—if he can find something human in her—then maybe he can convince himself that it isn't real. Magic, and godhood, and duty. None of it is real.

Why did Kensy choose to conquer an island with magic running through its veins?

She pauses, one foot in front of the other. The Forest God looks at him from over her shoulder with dark eyes. There's something alive in them, slant and narrowed, as her gaze flicks over the length of his body. Perhaps it's the first echo of light, glittering through the canopy overhead, illuminating their color. Or maybe it's the way her cheekbones strike him like a weapon.

"Ren," she finally answers. "My name was Ren."

He thinks it to be sort of lovely—the way she speaks her name as if it does not belong to her. It silences him, and he chooses to taste the back of his teeth with his tongue.

"I know your name," she says before he speaks. "I know the name of every thing, living and dead, in this forest. The forest lives in me."

Just as the wolf-man lives in him, he understands. Not deification, not really. But possession.

I am your god, the wolf-man had told him first. *You are my possession.*

"We're all connected—Qia, Yaelic, Hami," she names. "And now you, too." She spits it like it's something souring in her mouth.

They linger outside of Gyeosi. She might not let him inside this time. But then she moves closer, reaching her hand out toward him. Her palm comes to hover over where his heart should be, and Basuin inhales sharply. But she doesn't touch him.

"You can't feel it?" Her brows furrow.

There's nervousness dripping down his throat and into his stomach. "No." The absence of it makes him believe they're not connected at all—that this is still just a dream he'll wake from.

And why him? Why him at all? Gods are never bound to one another, so why does it ache like a leash around his neck that leads back to her hand?

Gods don't belong to one another. The only ones he knows, the rare instance of a bond, are the sun and the moon. The push and pull of night and day. The rise and fall of sky.

But a forest god and a wolf god; they aren't bound. They never would be. So why him?

Whatever this connection is between them, the magic they now share, he doesn't know. His ma wouldn't even know what it is, he's sure.

For a moment, Ren stares at her hand just above his chest. Her visage doesn't change. Then, she nods and pulls away. All she leaves behind is that leash-tight ache he can't name, and then she releases the village's barrier and heads inside.

"You're letting me back in," he says, but his words are as weary as they are wary. It feels like a trick. He's too tired to discern whether it is or not.

She doesn't turn to meet his eyes. "You're taking my magic now." Only the fist she makes at her side gives away that she's capable of feeling anything at all. "I can't let you go back to the army. I need my magic—*here*, in Gyeosi."

His mouth is dry. "I don't want your magic." Silence, and then he wets his lips. "You can't keep me trapped."

"You're a danger here and you're a danger there." Her voice is rueful, withering. But her shoulders slump, and the way she relents makes him sick. "Fine, then. It's your choice—stay, or go."

Basuin is tired. He is so, so tired, and he has been for so long. So, without a word, he stumbles in behind her, choosing Gyeosi—for now, until morning, like he was promised.

CHAPTER TEN

Bass.

There's a whisper in the dark.

Bass!

A hand moves across his face. "What?" He sits up in his cot, rubbing sleep from his eyes. When he turns to his left side, there's no one there. Basuin fists his hand in the sheets.

What if they surrender to us?

He kneels in the snow, helping 'Less with her boots. She smacks at his hands, but he laces them tight. So tight she grunts when he pulls the knot. At the fire pit, Mekal covers the smoldering embers with snow. The smoke smells like roast meat, and when he looks over, Mekal's torch has been set aflame.

"Put that out!" he yells. The enemies will find them. It's too late. Mekal snuffs out the light in the snow and it all goes dark.

It's too late.

"I know," he sobs. In the cover of night, Basuin climbs the face of the mountain. His foot finds a hold, but it crumbles beneath his weight. His palm splits open as he slides down the sharp rocks.

Curk catches him by the strap of his bag.

Fuck's sake, you're soft.

He pulls himself over the edge of the mountain, lying half-dead in the snow.

Gods' sake, Cap'n.

Basuin scrambles forward, looking for Tomaas. Shit, shit, shit—Where is Tomaas? Fucking ginger head, it's brilliant in this white fucking hellscape, isn't it? But there's so much blood. Red, fucking red. He's drowning in it.

"Tomaas!" he screams. The wind is his answer.

Basuin charges forward, sprinting across the ice. Something grabs his ankle and he goes down, chin hitting the ground and blood bursting in his mouth. When he looks back, drooling red, Isaniel's hand is wrapped around his leg.

Will you defy your orders?

"Isaniel—" he chokes. "Isaniel!" he screams to the blizzard that swallows him whole. The white drowns everything else out. The snow floods his vision and Basuin holds his face in his hands.

Isaniel stands before him. Blood dribbles from his mouth.

Don't look at me like that, Isaniel says, his eyes black. *You fucking liar.*

Basuin sits straight up, clutching his heaving chest. Isaniel, Isaniel, Isaniel—his nails scratch his skin as he scrambles to hold his mother's godstone in his shaking hand.

Isaniel, again. Basuin clenches his eyes closed, trying to catch his breath. Gods, Isaniel will never leave him alone. He deserves it.

He's sweated through his sleep shirt, the cotton soaked all down his back. Basuin strips it from his skin, rubbing his eyes open. A sigh of relief leaves him as his vision returns. This isn't Valkesta and he isn't a captain anymore. He's in Gyeosi, the spirit village—and Yaelic is gone, blanket mussed where he laid. Slivers of light cut through the gaps in the cloth door. It's past morning.

Basuin lies back again, staring up at the oaken ceiling. He wipes the dampness from his eyes and rolls onto his side, but when he tries to sleep again, Isaniel flashes through his mind like a goddamn wraith.

He can feel the rage as it creeps up the back of his neck. It poisons his tongue and swells it until he can't swallow, steals his hands away from him. It's not often it shows up like this anymore, a slow crawl through his body that turns his flesh hot and his head hotter instead of a flash, like lightning that scorches the earth and cools as quickly as it came. His mother called him a stew pot, once. Put on to boil and even once the fire is put out, the cast iron bottom would burn skin at the touch.

Kensy always loved it when Basuin got heated like this. It made him the perfect warrior, a monster of rage. The perfect little soldier boy to do all of Kensy's dirty work—no questions asked.

Basuin doesn't plan on boiling over, but he feels it now. The urge sinking into his bones that scar them with char and soot. The palm of his left hand itches something rotten, like the unending itch of guilt under his skin when he feels sorriest for himself rather than the rest of his comrades he left lying in snow so red it no longer looked like snow.

When he unfurls his fingers, the black mark cut into his palm, bubbling with an angry red against the grain of his lifeline, stands out. It makes him want to vomit, looking at it. It makes him sick with a fury that starts in his stomach like the very stew his mother made out of him.

Isaniel is dead, Isaniel is already dead—

Captain? Isaniel says in that slick, slithering voice of his that Basuin would swear was poisoned like a snake's fangs, tongue rolling over his teeth, and Basuin whips his head around so quick that the vertebrae in his neck crack.

For a moment, for a flash, Isaniel is standing there. In the middle of the small village hut, the leather straps of his back scabbard crooked and hanging too loose—Basuin always laced it up tighter for him, tighter. So it wouldn't slip from his shoulders, less broad than the other men. If only he could tighten it now, grab the laces again and pull Isaniel to him, feel his breath ghost along his neck. To fumble with the belt of Isaniel's harness that was always more work to get off than it was to buckle around his trim waist.

He'd do anything for Isaniel to laugh that haunting, sultry laugh he always saved for when he snuck into Basuin's bunk during shift change, when the other soldiers wouldn't catch them.

He's desperate for it—and then blood pours from the holes in Isaniel's armor, drenching his tunic and running between the cracks of his mail. No, not this again. He can't touch Isaniel again. Basuin's hands are dangerous. He has to apologize before Isaniel dies again.

Then, Isaniel's hand grabs his shoulder. Touches him.

Basuin lashes out—all that anger, that hurt, that fear. He lashes out, fist curled. Swings, all air. Something hot and rotten bursts from him all at once. It smells of sulfur. Of blood and ash. Like fire ribboned between his fingers. A wave of red magic, pulsing and splashing, jumps from his fist and fills the hut in a bloom of panic.

Don't touch him. Don't touch him, Isaniel.

But it never was Isaniel who reached for Basuin first. And as the red glow of magic wanes, Basuin remembers Isaniel is dead. The body who stands a few feet away is too tall to belong to Isaniel. Nor to Yaelic, nor to Ren.

A man, hair long and trailing the floor, flinches away from the red god magic that's exploded from Basuin's heaving body. The sleeve of his robe has burned to smoldering cinders, revealing a stretch of pale skin beneath with a muddy-red burn. Basuin's mouth goes dry.

"My apologies for startling you, Wolf God," the man speaks, but Basuin's scrambling to his feet.

"You—" Panic laces his throat. He can hardly speak. "Are you all right?"

Basuin doesn't know what to do. He moves toward the man, reaching to tear the still-burning sleeve from its wearer, but the man jerks back. It sends another shot of icy panic through Basuin.

Shattered ceramic on the tent floor between them. Blood dripping from his fingertips. Isaniel flinching away from Basuin's red-stained hand. Eyes full of disgust.

He snaps his fingers into another fist—and another burst of uncontrolled magic floods the room awash in the same color as new blood. The man is quick. Prepared enough this time to dodge. But the sparks of magic catch on Basuin's sleeping mat. The black mark in his palm burns like the wound is fresh as he chokes.

"I'm sorry," he tries to say, but it's swallowed up by pure panic and rage coursing through him. His nonexistent heart beats and squelches in his ears. His hands are so hot now, like he just touched the still-cooling iron stew pot. He needs to beat the fire out of that pot. Drink the stew until it boils this feeling in his belly. Kick and scream until that pot cracks down its side, until the stew seeps out from it and sizzles on the fire, steam filling the house with something awful.

But the man in front of him is still burned, more red and angry than even Basuin is now, as he backs toward the wall.

"I haven't come to harm you," he says, voice somehow still calm as he pulls the tatters of his sleeve away.

"I didn't mean to—" Basuin can't even speak. "I don't know how to—"

Cap'n, we oughta stop! Curk shouted, so far away underneath the screaming of the wind. *It's not worth our lives, too!*

You'd leave your brother behind? he shouted back, digging his heels into the frozen earth. *You'd give up on Tomaas?*

He isn't there, Bass! Isaniel yelled again, again, and again. *He isn't fucking there! Stop!*

Basuin grabs his own shaking arm, digging his nails into his flesh in the real world, not in his glass-blown memory. Panic is still building within him, a sob bubbling up in him. Smoke fills the hut. It smells so much of death and he doesn't know what to do. He's trapped, halfway in a dream and halfway in a memory, and the man in front of him has paid for it.

Once more, Basuin reaches out toward his victim. And then a small hand catches his wrist, gripping it like a shackle, all bone and twist. In the blue light of god magic, Ren's eyes are narrowed into sharp obsidian. It could cut into him. Though he cannot see her mouth from behind her arm reaching out to clip his wrist in her hand, he knows her lips are set in a harsh line of fury.

Behind him, her magic stamps out the fire he's started. He isn't breathing—no one seems to be. All he can do is stare into Ren's dark eyes, which sear into him with judgment and distaste.

"You're just like them," Ren seethes. "You hurt the forest, you hurt my people—just like your people came here to do." She doesn't release his wrist.

Basuin flounders, biting his tongue. "It was an accident," he says in lieu of an apology. He thinks he should, but it doesn't slither out of his mouth. He can't make himself say the words.

"Do you always feign ignorance for your crimes?" she snarls at him. "You would hurt anyone if it meant fulfilling your needs, wouldn't you?" The spark of anger in her voice is so different than he's heard before. He nearly recoils in surprise, her words aimed for his throat and choking him. His mouth tastes of smoke.

Ren breaks her grasp around his wrist, unbinding him. Bass staggers back, free. When he can finally pull his eyes from hers, the man he burned is gone. Fled from the wrath of the Wolf God.

"I didn't mean to," he stutters out, but it changes nothing. Feigning ignorance for a crime. That's how soldiers operate. No—no, it was never ignorance. It was duty. Under oath and command. Soldiers had an excuse; they were given one. Kensy is the one who dragged him here. It's Kensy's fault.

But it doesn't keep the nightmares of his crimes away. It doesn't make Isaniel stop shouting and screaming and pleading for Basuin to let them turn back. It doesn't erase Isaniel shoving him across the tent, breaking the water pitcher, calling Bass a liar.

Men like us, Kensy once said, hand clapping Basuin's shoulder blades, *we can't help it. There's fight in our bones, in our blood. But we do it for good, even when it feels evil. That's the ugliness of being captain.*

He would hurt them, he decides. He would hurt anything if it meant he could go back in time and stop himself from marching to Valkesta.

Don't look at me like that, Isaniel had said, arms tight around himself. *You fucking liar.*

From the edge of his vision, Yaelic darts in front of him, putting himself between Ren and Bass.

"Am-sa," Yaelic cries out, bowing his head until it touches his knees. "We are so sorry, so sorry, so sorry..." The little wolf pup apologizes again and again, echoing in this little hut Basuin's almost burned down. Just like the legion. Yaelic apologizes the way Basuin should've.

I never lied, he told Isaniel. But he should have just apologized.

Ren's hand descends upon Yaelic's golden locks, her fingers combing back the strands. She reaches to tip his head upward, to guide him to look at her. Now, her face has gone gentle, softening as she frowns down at him.

"You mustn't apologize for him," she tells Yaelic, and her hands move to cup his cheeks. Ren's thumbs catch fat, hot tears that have started to stream down Yaelic's face, and Basuin looks away.

Yaelic hiccups with tears. "But I bound myself to him, to serve him as his charge."

"He is a god," she says. "You are but a spirit. Children do not apologize for their parents."

It feels like seventeen straps across Basuin's back in quick succession—a number he can't remember why he knows so well, but the lashes from his days in training are well kept in his mind. Punishment, to beat the gods out of him. How ironic.

Inside of him, finally, the wolf-man chuffs. It laughs at him. It scratches at his bones, wanting free. Basuin stands stiff and still, pulled into himself, gaze stuck on the floor. He doesn't care. He didn't ask for godhood, for magic. He doesn't know these people, these spirits. He's cared much less about many things. Soldiers can't care—they can't feel. It's why he never looked at any of their faces, the men and women who fought for Grimmalia and their gods.

Guilt twists his stomach. Basuin is a soldier, not a god.

When Ren finishes wiping Yaelic's tears away, she straightens and rolls her shoulders back, rising to her full height. Still small, but godly. Her eyes cut into him, icy and mean, but somehow burning hotter than the wild magic he's unleashed upon the room. Then, she presses her hand to Yaelic's back, leading him toward the doorway, and Basuin is alone again.

THE HUT WASHED in black soot stains doesn't smell of blood or even gunpowder—only the remnants of something burned. But his brain twists it, alchemizes it into smoke wafting from the barrel of a gun beside his head. The smell of death is poignant and fickle, but it coats the insides of his nostrils like tattoo ink, embedded into his skin. Tangible, rather than memorialized.

This isn't the first time Basuin's hurt someone, woken from dreams that are too vivid to just be dreams. And the first time was much bloodier.

When Tehali held her face between her hands, red blood spurting from a gap between her fingers, repeating over and over again: *It's okay, it's all right, you're okay, you're all right*. And he could not hear her chants over his own screams.

He cringes now, slapping a hand over his mouth and dragging his nails through his tangled beard. It smells of blood in here.

Squatting, he reaches for the still-smoldering sheet strewn across his sleeping mat, but his hands are shaking. Panic shoots through him, icy and biting. So different from the fire that shot from his fingers in fear.

He never thanked Tehali. His pride has always been quick to spit like a venomous snake at anyone who dared lend him a hand. Tehali let herself be poisoned most out of them all—because she was the only friend he ever had. If she were here, she'd sweep up the mess herself. Tehali always cleaned up after him, on the wintry nights when he'd ask her, until his throat ran raw, why she didn't leave him to die in Valkesta.

Movement from the doorway interrupts his thoughts, and Basuin turns. Ren stands among the wreckage of the hut, eyes scanning over the room all blasé. Her mouth is set in a hard, flat line.

He doesn't speak first. The stubborn streak in him won't allow his mouth to move.

"I'm not surprised," she says. "I knew you were a danger."

It makes his jaw tighten, but he doesn't reply.

"You need to learn to wield it." There's no room for argument.

Basuin turns to face her now, eyes meeting her ever-dark gaze. What makes this woman a god? She's so slight—nearly half his stature, thin-limbed and fragile and too pretty to be facing war with a legion like Kensy's. But it's the way she raises her chin and looks down the slope of her nose, the way her eyes steel over and spark with fire when anger makes her throat tighten, that makes him almost believe she would be a god.

The way she holds herself, standing in the treehouse, shoulders rolled back and one hand against her hip. All confidence, no room to be moved.

He can only bite back, it's all he has within him anymore. "Learn the magic you think I'm stealing from you? Is that what you want me to do?"

Ren's eyes narrow into knife-edged slits. For a split second, she makes like she might move. March over to him and rise to his height just to curse at him as she has before. But Ren stays planted.

"If you don't learn to control it," her voice seeps low, "you'll hurt Yaelic next."

That makes him freeze. All the fight wanes from his body in an instant, even as the bubbling broil of anger in his stomach heats molten. His whole body seizes, frozen in time, Ren's words engraving themselves into the hard-rucked iron of his brain.

Basuin can't stay. If he doesn't learn to control his magic, next time, it could be Yaelic he burns. But he can't leave, either. If he goes back, Kensy will kill him—and then he'll burn the forest down anyway, Yaelic still within it.

The wolf-man rolls onto its back, paws twitching in the air and making lazy, clawed swipes at his organs. It chuckles at him.

"All right," he says. Surrender. Basuin draws his shoulders up, hunching over himself.

"All right," Ren repeats, and turns to leave. There's blood speckling the left sleeve of her shirt, trickling down her arm in fine lines.

"You're bleeding," he calls out without a thought in his head, before he can consider the consequences. He hurt her, too. Somehow, he hurt her, too.

Ren stops in her tracks. "A scratch." She jerks her sleeve down, the collar of her robe flashing the slope of her shoulder to him, and lets the white cloth stain red as she mops up her own blood. "It will heal in time." Her collarbones are fierce, jagged, angry and sharp the way she is.

But the wolf-man snaps its teeth, and Basuin's god mark itches, and he can't find the words to apologize.

CHAPTER ELEVEN

THE MOMENT BASUIN exits his ruined hut, running from the sharp smell of smoke, someone yells above the noise of the village. A war cry.

Basuin turns, but not quick enough to dodge the body that barrels into him. They go rolling in the dirt. He gasps for air, wind knocked out of him as he hits the ground. His lungs are so empty they ache with a fever.

Black spots blur out the face hovering over him, but he can feel the press of ten fingers wrapped around his neck. He's choking. He is being choked by someone with skin ochre and dark, with eyes beady and black.

"I can kill a god," his assailant says, but it sounds far away. "I can. I can do it. I'll kill a god—I'll kill anyone!" They snarl like something predatory with teeth gnashed together.

The wolf-man inside him presses up on its four paws, stretching up on its hind legs and clawing into Basuin's flesh. Its hunched back grows into Basuin's spine and it balloons within his body until the black of its fur consumes him. Until wolf hair is spurting out of his mouth, coughed from his lungs like smoke and ash. Until he feels like he is trapped inside the wolf-man like the wolf-man stays trapped inside him, like they have taken each other's place within this prison cell of what used to be a heart.

The wolf-man howls, and then Basuin snaps like a broken neck and howls, too.

He shoves his knee straight into the stomach of whoever is on top of him. They wheeze, grip loosening long enough for Basuin to gulp down air. He kicks them off but they claw at his body and take him with them, rolling through the dirt. Basuin reaches for his sword but it's too far. He fights for his life, and his assailant fights back.

It's only once Basuin topples them and gets an arm pressed to their neck that Ren stops them.

"Enough," she says, voice loud but not yet a shout. It's cutting, firm as a command so that his attacker drops their hands and lies still against the ground. Basuin, heaving breaths above them, pulls back an inch to let them breathe.

Yaelic scrambles forward from the crowd of onlookers. His hands pull at Basuin's shirt, tugging him away until he is sitting in the dirt. Basuin touches the tender skin at his neck. It's skin, still. It's not fur. He's still himself.

Anxious, Yaelic's eyes glance back and forth between Basuin and the other. His assailant digs their nails into the dirt, crumbling it between their fingers. Their dark hair falls haphazardly over their shoulders, ends sticking out every which way.

They hiss at him, scrambling back on the forest floor. "What of a god who hurts those he's sworn to protect?" they spit out, beady eyes staring him down.

I swore nothing, Basuin thinks he says, but it comes out garbled. "You are nothing to a god, nothing to protect," he rasps out instead, but it sounds more like the scratching of the wolf-man's claws against his vocal cords. Nothing of him. None of him is left.

The assailant lunges again, eyes raging mad, but there's a burst of blue light that hits them both. Basuin flinches away from its brightness. There is no heat to it, no pain as he had anticipated, and he's left with his arm covering his eyes until the light fades from view.

There, between them and towering over them despite her stature, is Ren. She doesn't look angry, but the cool slate of her countenance isn't the same one Basuin's seen before. Her cheekbones are knives that could pearl with blood but she doesn't even sweat. Her eyes are darkened amber, fossilized magic threatening to burn out the sun in the sky.

"I said—" her hair whips on the wind, "—enough."

Basuin stares at his attacker still sitting across from him, steeped in the same shock. But then, just as quick, their eyes narrow back into sharp slits directed at him, and their nostrils flare.

"What kind of a god are you?" the assailant asks, wiping their arm over their face and smudging what looks to be ash painted in stripes down their cheeks. "A god who kills others? A protector who hurts those weaker than him?"

Again, the word clings to him. Wraps around his body and shoulders like it's trying to find his neck and strangle him. *Protector*. It makes the scar over his left eye ache with phantom pain. Basuin isn't a protector. He's a soldier.

A god, the wolf-man nips at him. It noses his insides, snuffing, pulling him toward Ren.

A man, he thinks.

Before he can say anything, Ren turns her gaze to the assailant.

"And what of a sparrow who flies toward the sun in hunt of its god?" she asks, voice breezy and nonchalant. "What of a bird who is pushed from its nest and builds a new one with blood as paste?"

They lunge at Ren, and before he can even breathe, the wolf-man howls something fierce and broken and Basuin is moving—he doesn't know who forced his feet on the ground. He plants himself, a rooted tree grown from his body, in front of Ren and blocks the incoming blow, arms held defensively in front of him and eyes raging mad.

But the blow never comes. A shadowed figure from the

forest wraps itself around the assailant—a flash of pale skin bared from a wide sleeve of black.

"Haaman," a deep, slow-crawling voice calls. "You traitorous thing."

Behind the assailant stands a tall, tall man—the man who Basuin lashed out at and burned. His eyes are closed as if he were asleep, long swathes of dark hair falling over his shoulder to hide his red-marked arm. Still, he looks at ease as he holds the assailant, Haaman, from attacking Ren.

Haaman slumps in the man's grasp, a look of shame crossing their face. Then, that shame turns to a boiling anger, head snapping up to look at Basuin.

"You tried to kill him," Haaman spits raggedly, voice shattered by rage. "Ko could've died at the hands of a careless god."

Basuin can't find the right words to counter. Though he hasn't drawn his sword against anyone since Valkesta, the wild magic that erupted in chaos had done the job for him. Magic he didn't even know he had.

"Little bird," the man murmurs, his head ducking toward Haaman's shoulder. "You tried to kill a god. Two, even. Are you any better?"

"Shut up," they bite back, bristling.

Ren holds her hand out to Haaman, halting him. "I understand your anger, Haaman. But it was an accident. The Wolf God did not intend to harm anyone, though he did."

"Intention is shit!" Haaman shouts back, anger foaming in their mouth. "The Wolf God was sworn to protect our forest, not hurt it!"

Ko snakes his hand around Haaman, covering their mouth. "Hush, little bird. I can speak for myself. Now, be quiet before Am-sa decides you've committed treason against her."

With that, he slinks forward, pushing Haaman behind him. Risen to full height, he is taller than Bass, but much less heavy and bulky. He sways when he moves, sleepy but somehow confident. Unlike Haaman's ripped-hem trousers and black shirt, he wears an elaborate set of robes that drape long and glide over the forest floor, his hair following it.

Of course, his left sleeve is torn at the seam, leaving bare and burned flesh. It's a dark wound, colored in bark-tones but already healing to a pink at the edges.

"My name is Ko," he says, bowing his head—first to Ren, deeply, and then to Basuin. "I am of the many oaks who make up this forest. I beg your pardon that I've yet to introduce myself to you, Wolf God. And for startling you this morning."

Yaelic kneels to the forest floor, bowing his head. "I am so sorry, Ko. My master—he's new to our way, our life."

Shame stabs through him like his own goddamn blade. He caused this, as he's always caused pain. Basuin curls his fingers into tight fists at his side. These hands are scarred from war. Soldier's hands. It's all they know anymore.

Haaman darts from behind Ko, snarling at Bass. "Bow to him," with a snap of their teeth. "You disgrace of a god."

The wolf-man cracks bones in Basuin's body, the force of it making him hunch over as his spine curves and his shoulders curl inward. Inside him, it snarls and snaps its maw like Haaman until there's foam on its snout and Basuin has a taste for blood. It brings a fever that makes him desperate to sink his teeth into a bloody steak and tear it into shreds.

Basuin sets his hand where his heart should be, shoving the wolf-man back. He straightens his spine, rolls his shoulders back, and draws to full height again. Not like this. He won't let the wolf-man puppet him like this.

"Haaman," Ren calls, her words with more bite than he imagines. "Your anger is heard." Basuin hates her words. He hates that she speaks for him, hates that she wears this constant countenance of calm as if nothing can touch her.

Under Ren's gaze, Haaman wilts. Their eyes fall to the ground as they shift from foot to foot.

"Would you have me bow, too?" Ren asks as the winds of the forest ruffle her shirt.

Haaman's eyes widen to black moons and they fall to their knees in the dirt. They bow their head, a display of submission and worship.

But Basuin doesn't stare at them. He stares at Ren, whose eyes aren't cold, but knowing. She waits, watching Haaman, the smallest movement of her throat as she swallows.

"Forgive me, Am-sa," Haaman pleads. "I meant no disrespect toward you."

"Disrespect to any god in this forest—to any spirit here—is disrespect toward me," Ren says, as easy as if it were but a conversation. "What would you have done?" she asks. "If you had killed me?"

A sound like a sob comes from Haaman, their nose pressed into the dirt. "I'm sorry, Am-sa. Truly, I'm sorry. Please, forgive me. I am loyal, I swear it."

"Stand up," she commands, and Haaman scrambles to their feet. "Wipe your face, sparrow. Look at me."

Though her voice is soft, light and airy and spoken with such a calm cadence, her words hold no room for argument. Basuin almost stands at attention under the spell of her voice.

Haaman does as she says, wiping their face on their arm. Then, they take a breath and look at her, eyes full of shame. Basuin knows the feeling. That look. He knows it well and he knows he would have done the same as Haaman.

He did, at one point. Fight an army for Isaniel, to protect him. But he still marched Isaniel to Valkesta in the end.

"You are free to leave, Haaman," Ren says. "You are not bound to this forest and you are not bound to me. I have never asked for your loyalty. The Wolf God has not either." Ren speaks so gently that Basuin isn't surprised when Haaman's eyes fill with fat tears.

She speaks like a mother would. Scolding with love. Disappointed.

I'm doing this for you! he once roared at the top of his lungs at his mother, until his shouts shook the very roof he built for her. *I have no choice but to go. Don't you understand that?*

And his mother, calm and gentle like Ren, but with sad eyes, looked at him from her bed and asked, *Do you truly have no choice? Is there no path but the one you see in front of you?*

Basuin takes his godstone into his hand and curls a fist around it. She was right. He had a choice, and he chose wrong.

Haaman cries into the crook of their elbow, hiding their face from the Forest God. Ko places his hand on their shaking shoulder.

"We are ever grateful to you, Am-sa," Ko says. "Even if you do not tie us to you, we are loyal."

Then, Ko turns to face Basuin, and he bows his head slowly and shallowly. Basuin doesn't mind it. In fact, he bows his head right back, quickly retracting to stand up straighter. There's the smallest quirk in Ko's mouth, as if he's amused.

"I apologize, Ko," Basuin speaks first. "God or not, I have much to learn."

"All is forgiven." Ko draws his hand from the sleeve of his robe to wave Basuin off. "I am glad that no one was seriously hurt. I hope you will forgive my little bird as well, Wolf God."

"Basuin," he corrects. "My name is Basuin."

Now, Ren turns her head. He can feel her stare on the side of his neck; she stands just outside the reach of his peripheral vision. What is she thinking? She's unreadable, has been since they met. But he'd burn to know what she thinks of him.

Haaman's dark skin has turned a shade warmer from their crying, but they wipe their face again and face Basuin. They hang their head, not quite a bow, but heavy with the same shame coloring Basuin's eyes.

"I'm sorry," they say, shifting from side to side restlessly.

Yaelic, hands dirty, clings to Basuin still. His golden hair is mussed, and Basuin resists the urge to fix it for him.

"Myself, as well," Basuin says, but it sounds awkward. In all his years given to the legion, Basuin's never surrendered. He's never had to—he's always been victorious. Until he wasn't. And even then, in failure, Basuin didn't surrender. And look where that brought him.

None of this belongs to him. Not the land, and not these people. Not the gods who speak to him now, after he's prayed for decades with no answer. Not the magic he never asked for.

Not even his own hands. He unfurls his fingers to reveal the scarred mark burned into his palm. Basuin couldn't even control his own hands—he hurt someone else, again. Shame is the tongue of the wolf-man that licks up the walls of his esophagus. And Basuin bends to its will, this thing, this wolf-man, that's possessed him. Like any soldier would.

He's just that—a soldier.

A bad one at that, the wolf-man laughs at him.

He agrees. A bad one at that.

CHAPTER TWELVE

REN LEADS HIM to a grassy field outside the village, far enough that he can't hear the murmuring of the spirits any longer. Close enough that the birds above the canopy sing down to them. It's bright here, the sea of trees parted wide enough for him and Ren to stand twenty feet away from one another. The shadow of Ren's hair darkens her face and obscures the color of her eyes, until she rolls her shoulders back and faces him with all the grace of a god.

"It comes from inside you," she says, holding her right hand out toward him, palm faced up. The curl of her fingers hides the white lines he knows decorate her skin the way the black scars do his. Basuin copies her, with his left hand, eyes tracing the lines he's studied before. He flexes his fingers.

He tries to picture it, the way Ren uses her magic so easily, effortlessly. He tries to remember the way that her blue magic coiled around her skin, dug into the earth of the Shaelstorm fields, burst from her fingertips like a firework shooting across the sky.

Imagining hers is easy—because remembering what his looked like washes him in shame. The way it felt, hot as molten metal, singeing his fingers as it exploded from him. The red of blood splashing against the walls of his hut, like fire, whipping and burning Ko.

Fitting magic for a soldier such as he.

"Do you feel it?" Ren asks him now.

No, but if he could, he thinks it would feel like a forest fire. Uncontrollable, and hot, and destructive. Basuin shakes his head, closing his open hand into a fist. The wolf-man huffs at him, and Bass doesn't know if it's laughing or frustrated with him this time.

Ren won't stop staring at him. "Not from your hand," she says. "From inside."

His eyes flick up to meet hers. The light of day passes over her as the clouds sail across the sky, illuminating the planes of her face. Her irises sparkle like amber in the sun. It makes him snap.

"No one taught me," he starts, defensive at the disappointment Ren's not even expressed yet. "I don't know what magic is or what's possessed me. So how should I know what's inside me?" He pulls his hand back to snatch the jade rock at his neck. He wouldn't have even known the gods were real if not for his mother. And he wasn't sure they were real after they let her die. After *he* let her die.

Ren says nothing in return, and he can't read her gaze. She pities him. Sees him as nothing but a monster with no brain. No insides. No heart left.

Does she have a heart still? Did her god let her keep hers?

"I don't know how to be a god," he snarls in admission. It feels like someone stuck a burning poker through his stomach and left him for the crows to pick over. He hurt Ko with his carelessness, and Haaman should have killed him. He would've killed someone if they hurt someone he loved, too.

If he were to hurt Yaelic because he can't control himself, Basuin doesn't know what he would do.

"Neither do I," Ren says, "but it's all I've ever known." She draws forward, closing in on him, the rustle of grass beneath every step as she shrinks their distance. "I learned, and you will too."

It feels like a truce. Ren floats closer and the breeze brings the soft scent of white lilies mixed with something bitter. Basuin inhales, hard, and his shoulders slump with his exhale. In this moment, Ren is kinder to him than she should be—more patient than anyone's been before. He yields.

"What's inside of me?" he asks, voice smaller than he means it to be.

Ren offers her hand to him, motioning toward him. "Here."

But he hesitates. She pities him.

The wolf-man scratches at his ribs like a sad pup wanting its master's attention. It makes something itch inside of him, so Basuin places his hand in hers. She clasps it, so large and scarred in her much smaller, much more delicate one, and overturns his palm so it faces upward. Basuin's palm is lined deep, not just with blackened marks, but with battle scars along his fingers and winding down his wrist and up his arm. Striking compared to her pale, unmarked skin. The only scars he's ever seen of hers are the familiar lines spread across her palm.

This is the closest they've ever been before, amicably, and the wolf-man's tail thumps in his chest.

"Right here," she whispers, tracing a line over the soot-stained mark engraved in his palm. "This is a god mark, like mine."

Ren sinks to her knees among the grassy field, and Basuin follows her down. Where Ren folds her legs beneath her, Basuin clumsily crosses his legs underneath his hulking frame. Each breath he takes is shallow as Ren holds his hand within hers.

"The vein here—it leads back to your heart." Her thumb soothes over his god mark like a mother soothes over a child's wound, and Basuin swallows at the softness of her touch. "A thread to your soul."

I don't have a heart anymore, he wants to say. *The wolf-man ate it. Do you still have yours? Or did the forest become it?*

A glow overtakes his hand, erupting from hers and drowning his. His god mark swims in the blue magic that bursts from her fingertips, and then it's shooting up his arm, following the same vein hidden beneath his skin. But the color shimmers, changes as it crawls up his limb. From Ren's bright aquamarine, it shifts into an array of colors until it runs bright red. The color of blood.

The threads seize him, trickling down to the place where the wolf-man resides, and the magic makes it howl from between his lungs.

Heat sinks into him, but it feels like it belongs to Ren at first. Like she's pouring lava straight into his god mark, injecting it straight into the vein she's made come to life on his skin. It surges up and through his arm until it fills the hole in his chest, and then like lightning, it races home back down to the soot mark scrawled and burned into his hand.

"Do you feel it now?" Ren asks, and she peers up at him from below thick, straight lashes dark in contrast to the moon-milk skin of her face.

"Yes," he says, because it feels like the pull and choke of an invisible leash when her magic fizzled out like the fireworks. He feels like the fire that erupted from him when Ko surprised him. "What is it?"

Ren's fingers press his own open, unfurling like a flower. Her fingertips aren't marred by callouses. They feel like silk against his work-hardened skin. She draws her fingers along his palm as if grasping for something he can only describe as light, pinching a fabric made of magic together and pulling it from his god mark. Dripping from her fingertips is the blue color that belongs to her, but as she extracts it like a puppeteer tugs the strings of its marionette, the light shimmers to the red color that sank into his veins. It pulses and wraps, like vines alive, around his bicep.

"Magic," she says, drawing her hand away from his—but the light stays. It rounds out in his palm, warm and wispy and somehow fragile.

Magic. His.

"Think of a light," she instructs. "Imagine it in your hand. Think of it as something inside of you and pull it out."

Bass takes a deep breath in. There it is. Deep in his chest, an ache. It burns, but it doesn't hurt. Like a fever growing inside of him. And the wavering light of magic in his hand starts to solidify, becoming an orb of light that pulses right from his palm. It's ruby red, spitting golden shimmer-embers. And it belongs to him.

It's so beautiful, so precious. It's a living thing, a collection of energy, like he bottled up lightning and laughter and the static on his skin when his mother's lavender light poured from her mouth late at night when she communed with gods in the godrealm. It's foreign, and yet so familiar. A kind touch, something he's known before, but hasn't felt in so long.

"I did it," he says. He flexes his palm and the ball of magic jumps. This magic, it belongs to him. He created something out of the darkness that festers inside of him.

From behind the glow of the ruby, artificial, magical light that bursts forth from his palm, Ren smiles. It eases her in a way that takes his eyes away from the brightly lit orb to focus on her. The curl of her mouth is so astonishing, so unfamiliar, but so perfect where it sits on her countenance. It softens her. Not so much a god now, but a woman.

"You did it," she says, and the way her lips mold words catches him a moment too long. "Well done, Wolf God."

There is so much inside of him. Too much—filling him up in the strangest of ways. The weight of that name hangs heavy on his heart-bone. There's something akin to pride, burning like a flush infecting his chest, that washes over him. The wolf-man is yipping, a soft pup keening to play with its master, rolling over onto its side and sneezing.

It makes him feel full, and that smile of hers—small and quiet but there—threatens something. He just doesn't know what yet. His magic is what he'll blame for the warmth in his face. But then, he curls his fingers over the red light he's created, snuffing it out. No heat races over his palm, only a sparkle of something once real.

Seeing her like this, more at ease here with him than ever before, makes words tumble from his mouth. "How did you learn magic?"

She hums, eyes flicking far off into the distance for but a moment before returning back to the space between them. "The spirits taught me," she says. "Ko was one of my first teachers—and one of my first friends." Admiration fills her voice. It's the first time he's heard it.

"He seems kind," Basuin says. Guilt shivers down his spine.

"He is," she agrees. "Very forgiving."

He hangs his head in shame, stretching his fingers out as if he could break them all. It might be easier that way.

"Long ago, I also had trouble wielding my magic." Ren doesn't look at him. "Before you came, I had much more. It was too much to control when I was young. Ko has seen many of my mistakes just as well."

The small admission—the fact that Ren's made mistakes before—makes something inside him seasick. Like he's back on that ship sailing to this island and he can't find the shore. Something claws its way out of his mouth and he can't stop.

"Who were you," he asks, "before you were a god?"

Ren's face falls, and Basuin feels the empty space he's forced between them. All warmth, all kindness that Ren once projected, is swiftly cut off. The loss of it is so sudden that the magic crackling alive between them dies—as all things do, anyway.

Ren yanks her hand away from his and stands quicker than he can press himself up off the ground to follow. She doesn't walk away, but she turns her back to him like she could close a door on the conversation. Desperation, for something he doesn't even understand, claws down his back.

"Did you want to be a god?" he tries, though he knows he should stop. His mouth has always caused trouble. "Or did you die—like me?"

Ren curls her fingers into a fist, drawing the magic that connects them back into her palm. It shimmers, disappearing into her glowing white mark, and the glitter of it dissipates into the air.

"That's none of your business," she answers coldly.

"But it is," he presses, a haze of hopelessness swallowing him. "I don't want to be a god." He takes a step toward her. "I didn't ask for this." It's shaking in his chest, this feeling. This desperation. But it isn't the wolf-man.

"And you think I did?" she hisses between clenched teeth. "I don't care what you want. Unwilling or not, they siphoned my magic into you so you could play god until your army kills us. You're leaching my magic and instead of doing anything to help, you're just feeling sorry for yourself."

"It's not my fault," he growls out. "As soon as I find a way out, you'll be free of me."

"You can't escape this," Ren says. "You can't escape duty."

"I don't want to escape duty," he snarls. "I want to escape *you*."

The wolf-man's teeth snap at his ribs, breaking one clean in two. Basuin hunches over, clutching his chest. All the air has been punched out of him. It aches, but when he looks up, the steel that's replaced Ren's visage in a way he's not seen before—it leaves him struggling for air.

He didn't mean to say that. He didn't. Not that he cares, but he didn't mean it.

Basuin's thumb finds the black mark on his palm, this scar the Wolf God's left on him. The runes of protection Basuin carved into the exterior walls of the shack he built for his mother and himself marked their house in the same way. Basuin has no heart left. The wolf-man, growling and chewing on the bone of his left rib, made its nest there. It makes a mockery of him even now, feeding off of Basuin's anger, and he presses harder against the mark burning his palm.

You can run, little soldier boy, the wolf-man huffs a laugh as it gnaws on his bones, *but she'll always catch you*.

Ren doesn't look at him anymore. "Then do so," she says, wicked of emotion. She waves him off with a flick of her wrist. "You know how to get back to your army." This time, staring straight ahead and refusing to meet his eyes, she walks right past him. The skin of her bare shoulder brushes by the sleeve of his cotton undershirt. That kindness, from before. Her patience. It's gone, and in its stead, walls of steel and ice and weaponry. How quickly she can change, like a chameleon adopting new colors. His fault, this time.

With no more preamble, and no more stopping, Ren walks toward Gyeosi.

I own you, it tells him, *but she owns us all.*

Something panicked and sharp drops in his stomach. She's leaving, and he doesn't know why he moves to stop her. As Ren presses forward, Basuin gives chase right behind her. With his long legs, Basuin catches up to her, and he rounds in front of her to halt her path. Ren's dark eyes flick up to meet his and there's an indescribable look painting her face.

"It's not that I want to escape you," he tries to stress. "I don't want godhood. I *can't* be a god." He doesn't know how. Basuin can't protect anyone; he's tried and he's failed and he's lost.

There's a long moment that stretches between them, Basuin breathing hard. He feels like he's outside his body, like he's still in those healing huts back in Ha'riste where all he could do was dream of a different life so that he did not dream of Valkesta.

And after a moment, Ren smiles, but it's unkind. Just like Kensy. But smaller, quieter. Softer.

"How lonely it must be," she says, "to be you, Basuin of Ankor. The only person in the entire world to suffer so greatly."

Ren storms past him. Basuin can't breathe, and it isn't the wolf-man pressing down on his lungs. It's something else.

* * *

Basuin tears through the forest alone now, content to get the fuck away from this place. Away from Ren, most of all. He hears water before he sees it, corrects his course, and then plunges into the river. The water is cold, soaking into his breeches and filling his boots. The only sound is the splash he makes as he thrusts his hands into the water, hissing. It's like he's shoving all his limbs in the snow again, freezing, burning, aching, awake, alive.

Violent and mad, Basuin scrubs his hands. The old dirt and blood covering his skin fizzles out in the water, but he continues to scrub until the river has washed away everything he is. Everything he's become.

Basuin yanks his hands from the river, water dripping down his forearms, and turns his palms over to look. But it's still there—his god mark, edges raised like a scar. This can't be permanent. This can't be real. He dunks his hands back into the cold water.

Someone laughs and Basuin freezes, head whipping up. This river cuts through the woods, surface glittering bright under the orange setting sun. It rushes over the rock bed beneath it with a babble that sounds like pure laughter. There's no one here. It's just him and the water.

Basuin pulls his arms from the river, but before he can stand, something darts out and grabs his wrist. A hand made of water, fingers like ice around his bones, tugs him forward. Panic floods him and he struggles, trying to wrench free, to no avail.

The laughter steadily becomes louder and louder, more realized. Out of the river, a stream of water rises into the air until it takes the shape of a woman, her curves deep and soft and highlighted by the burning sun behind her. Her hand, dainty and sharp with bones, releases him and he stumbles back.

"You wish to break your tie to Am-sa, don't you?" the woman asks. Her dark hair, wet and wavy, waterfalls down her back and into the river she stands in. Water droplets roll down her pale skin. But her eyes—they're a cloudy blue, the color of ice—but full of mirth when paired with the sly grin she wears.

"Who are you?" he asks, unable to look away from her.

"My sincere apologies, Wolf God," she says, and Basuin recoils at the name. The lilt in her voice and smile on her face makes him think she isn't so sincere at all. "I am the Hou-tou River."

Hou-tou doesn't bow her head, but another stream of water jets up so she can rest her elbows upon it, chin in hands as she stares at him.

"My name is Basuin," he replies, wary.

Before he can say anything else, Hou-tou laughs again. "I know of you, Wolf God. Tell me, have you come to save our Forest God?"

It sparks new fury in him, flint and steel catching paper fire. "I am not a god, and I cannot save anyone," he answers.

Hou-tou smiles. "Your mark says otherwise."

Basuin's teeth snap together, like a wolf about to growl. He closes his fingers into fists and jerks his head away, hides his god mark from this creature's sight.

"But you," she continues, "don't want that. You wish to rid yourself of this godhood that's been forced upon you. Isn't that right?"

He stops. Then, he turns back to look at Hou-tou, who grins with all her teeth. Even from here, he can see how sharp they are. Rows of tiny, shard-like teeth.

"I can help you." Hou-tou walks closer, her hips swaying. The wet fabric of her white dress clings to her skin. "I know something you don't know. Something even Am-sa doesn't know," she sings to him.

Hou-tou looks like a siren—he's seen the illustrations of them in books. She sounds like one, too. The sailors always said that a siren will get you before a man will, before a shark will, before the ocean will. Ithika willing.

"And what is that?" he asks her, drawing closer to the river again. If she wanted to, she could kill him like this. Take him and drown him. He's lured toward the water at the simple thought of leaving this world—this duty—behind.

"Have you heard of the elder tree?"

Basuin shakes his head. Hou-tou smiles, and Basuin feels like he's walking into a trap. He knows it, this time. But this isn't Valkesta. He's already dead.

"In the middle of this forest, there grows the elder tree. He is the biggest tree of them all, and the oldest. And it's said—" her voice dips down low, "—that if asked, his branches can sever godhood."

Basuin's eyes widen, but he looks away swiftly. He doesn't want Hou-tou to know how desperate he is, though he has a feeling Hou-tou already knows the depth of his wish to escape. Otherwise, she wouldn't be here.

The wolf-man lunges and sinks its teeth into Basuin's throat, puncturing his vocal cords. Basuin chokes, struggling for breath again, swallowing back the taste of blood. The wolf-man growls, but Basuin shakes it off and narrows his eyes at Hou-tou instead. Her lips are painted with the stain of crushed mulberries, and she runs her tongue over the top in wait.

"It's been done before?" he asks, words careful.

"There has never been a god who wished to try."

"Where is the elder tree, then?" he asks, and it makes Hou-tou's grin widen into something devious. Her whole face brightens.

"Oh, my good gods," Hou-tou hums. "I can show you the way." Another stream rises from the river, curling up her thigh and wrapping around her waist. She wades closer to shore, closer to him, and it takes everything in Basuin not to step away.

"I can go myself." He keeps himself tempered. River or not, Hou-tou sings like a siren. Basuin doesn't trust her.

Hou-tou stops with a giggle. "The elder tree is the biggest tree of all—his roots are what feed us, what made us. The grove at the center of our forest is where it makes its home. They call it the Crying Trees. How sad."

"If I go to the Crying Trees and seek out the elder tree to sever my godhood, what will happen?" Inside him, the wolf-man burrows somehow deeper into his chest. "Will it kill me?"

"No," Hou-tou laments. "But Sa-cha might, if that is what you wish."

The very mention of Sa-cha has Basuin leaning forward. "What do you mean?"

But Hou-tou draws back. With a twirl, she sinks back into the river. Her eyes lose their light as the playful act she's put on fades. Her dark tendrils of hair float atop the surface of the river. Only her eyes, blue and clouded, peek out of the water at him. Her sudden withdrawal feels strange.

"I thought Sa-cha lived in the godrealm," Basuin says, because it's what he's been told. Always what he's been told. Sa-cha, the god of all gods.

He didn't know gods could roam the land freely. All the stories his mother told him, they were just that—stories. Fairytales to pass the time, fables to put fear in him. Keep him out of that damned forest he was always coming home from bloodied.

Home to that little shack on the edge of the village, bordering the forest, hammering nails into the wooden boards he's built and rebuilt to house him and his mother, patching the leaking roof with big palms he's collected from the woods and woven tight together. He's there again, back there, with her.

"Son!" she calls for him, voice thin with weariness.

"Yes, Ma?" She's where she always is—in her bed, patchwork quilts pulled up her body, her frail hands working on something she shouldn't be. Darning a pair of breeches for him.

"Son," she says, eyes not meeting his, "don't go to the forest today."

"Why?" Basuin pulls up the little stool that sits beside her bed. "I've got traps to check. The other hunters will get to them first if I don't."

His mother lowers her sewing to her lap, hand reaching for the jade stone she wears, fingers closing over it. She bows her head, and outside the window next to her, the wind picks up, rushing through the trees and sending leaves spiraling downward.

"They've told me," his mother says, voice low. "You can't go to the forest, my son."

"Who?" he asks her, but he knows the answer lies inside her clenched fist.

"The gods." Her dark eyes are glassy from pain or from sickness or from something else. "They say you cannot go. Something is rotting inside the forest, and blood is the penance. You cannot go."

Basuin clasps his hands together over his mouth, elbows on his knees as he leans closer to her. His mother's fingers rub at the stone, wearing it with the warmth and oil of her skin.

"Okay," he says. "I won't go today, Ma."

From the Winter River, his mother told, *there arose a god, and that god was Sa-cha, and he was good.*

Hou-tou shrugs, her voice yanking him from the memory. "Perhaps you could go back to your bastion," she offers. No more mention of Sa-cha at all. "Turn yourself over to your godless soldiers. You're a big god now, aren't you?" She blows a whirlwind of bubbles his way.

Tongue between his teeth, Basuin barely breathes before Hou-tou bares her own sharp bite at him.

"They'll kill you," she hisses, "just like they'll kill my Forest God."

He tenses, stopping the shiver trying to race up his back. *Just like they'll kill Ren.* His cold fingers stretch out, and then he wipes his hands on his breeches and stands, knees creaking.

"You're keen for me to leave," he says, an acknowledgment.

Hou-tou rises from the river until her chin rests on the surface, teeth split into grinning splinters. "What shall it be—godhood, or death?"

Basuin tips his chin downward in a shallow bow that Hou-tou doesn't return. Instead, she watches him with her sharp, cloudy blue eyes as he backs away from the riverbank and climbs back up the hill toward Gyeosi.

Godhood or death. Is the artifact that Kensy searches for the elder tree? The ability to sever godhood from someone like him?

Or someone like Ren.

CHAPTER THIRTEEN

Basuin isn't ready to return to Gyeosi yet. Instead, he wanders the forest, lingering in the thought of Hou-tou's words. He asks himself the same thing she did: if it'll be godhood, or death. Does Ren know of the elder tree? If she did, she would've told him. All she wants is her magic back—the threads of it he's stolen.

But he isn't willing to face Ren, not after their last exchange of words. He winces at the thought. While it wasn't his finest of moments, it isn't regret weighing him down. No, he meant his words. He doesn't know what the heaviness is, but it isn't guilt.

There are bigger things to focus on. The elder tree, Kensy's artifact—the wolf-man and how to peel it out of his chest and where to find the remnants of his heart again. With the elder tree, Basuin has the chance to be a man again. It's a bright spot among the wreckage inside him.

He'll take that chance, to be human, again. Even if it means being a soldier once more.

The crunch of fallen leaves and other foliage beneath his boot is rhythmic as he marches through the forest. Side to side, his eyes scan through the trees. All of them, they must have names. That's what Ren said. Everything in this forest is a spirit, and she is connected to all of them.

He is, too. Everything—everyone—in this forest will be cut loose from him when the elder tree cuts him loose of the forest. It's a good thing. A blessing.

The best way Basuin knows to protect something is to remove it far, far from his reach.

Bass comes to rest before an old, gnarled oak tree, craning his neck back to look up at where it stretches tall into the sky. His left hand pulses, warmth heating the scarred mark on his palm. When he opens his fingers, the lines are red and puffy where he tried to scrub it away. He uses his thumb now to soothe over the god mark, but all it does is itch.

Above him, the sky is beginning to darken. The sun hangs low and ripe, waiting to fall beneath the horizon until tomorrow. The shadows in the forest begin to grow and lengthen, taking fuller shape. Turning back before nightfall would be smartest.

But Bass has magic, too. He made that light, the one Ren pulled from his palm. He flexes his hand again, watching the god mark pull and stretch. He could do it again and light his way through the forest. All the way to the elder tree, if he marches long enough.

The wolf-man snarls a laugh, and Bass thinks of anything but telling it to shut up.

"All right," he murmurs to no one—only the spirits that surely watch him from where they live. Bass takes a deep breath, materializing the image of Ren sitting with him, her small hand cradling his, to try to rouse the magic out of him from memory. She told him to feel it.

So Basuin burrows down, deep inside himself, past the wolf-man even. He burrows down and he pinpoints that place beyond his eaten heart, beyond the god-thing holed up in his chest and looks for the feeling of something warm. Something mirroring Ren's touch.

Another breath, and Bass opens his eyes. His god mark glows red, and it cracks a smile from his lips.

Then, a gunshot rings out—and the forest cowers beneath it.

Magic explodes from his hand in a shock of red. Light beams toward the sky, fire stretching toward the sun, its maker. His knees shake. He lands on the ground, somewhere, somehow. The only sense he has is to close his right hand over his god mark, smother out the flame. Quiet the red, angry, scared thing that's pouring out of him.

The light cuts off and Basuin falls, hands planted upon the ground as he pants.

And underneath him, the leaves turn to snow. White and so cold it burns. His vision blurs, wet with tears, and when he blinks them away the snow is splattered with blood. The same color as his magic.

Valkesta is howling: *Run.*

Basuin looks up. Above his head, a white crane flies over, darting through the sea of trees toward him. A crane shouldn't be here.

It opens its beak and caws at him. *Run, Wolf God! Run!*

He scrambles to his feet in an instant. The white crane sails over him, flapping its large wings, and then disappears into the woods. His eyes track its trail backward, into the distance from where it came, and he finds a body striding out from the trees.

Kensy barks a laugh. His blond locks have grown out just enough to hang over his forehead, dampened with sweat. In his hands, a cocked rifle waits. This is a different man. Not the same Kensy whom he fought with on the front lines. Basuin can't breathe. Whatever panic he tried to stave off starts to build again, swirling inside him on the brink of disaster and devastation.

"I'm not surprised," Kensy says, mirth and mistrust in his easy smile. "If anyone would escape death, it would be you."

Basuin can't hide the shock that widens his eyes, restricts his body. No, this isn't the same Kensy at all.

Kensy should be in Shaelstorm. Not with him, not in the forest. Not this close to Gyeosi. Basuin chokes on his own spit, all thick in his throat. If Kensy is this far into the forest, then he's still searching for the artifact. But alone? Kensy wouldn't think of sullying his own hands with god-things.

And if he is still searching for the artifact—what of it? Is the artifact he's been after at the Crying Trees, where the elder tree lives?

"What are you doing here?" he shouts across their distance, steadying his voice.

"Didn't you see the fireworks?" Kensy asks. "You should have stayed dead, old friend."

He coughs, a laugh caught in his chest. "That would've been easier for you, Commander? I thought we didn't leave soldiers behind."

Kensy grins. "Come on, Bass. You're useless now." It stings more than it should, coming from Kensy. "Face it—the gods abandoned you long ago. You were getting in my way."

Something in his chest aches. Ren would agree with Kensy, if she was here. That Basuin is getting in her way. He tries to hide the shake in his hands at his sides.

"They didn't." As soon as the words leave his lips, he knows he shouldn't have said it. "You might not be a believer, but I am the one who escaped death. Why bring me to this island just to leave me for dead?"

There's the slightest twitch in Kensy's eye. Something wicked. But Kensy doesn't advance; he slings his rifle over his shoulder and out of the way. A surrender, but a show of power. Of control. Kensy knows something; he has the upper hand. But Basuin doesn't know what. It feels like he's being eaten alive. As though Kensy can see everything inside of him—even the wolf-man.

And the wolf-man growls, muzzle pointed at Kensy, watching with beady red eyes.

"You think me cruel, but let me show you how kind I am," Kensy says, and he takes a step to the right, and right again, moving slow and circular to Bass. In turn, Bass moves to the left, keeping their distance. A careful, but unyielding dance. "Come back with me, to Shaelstorm."

Basuin stops. Kensy moves three steps closer. "What?" His mouth is dry, his throat tight.

"Forget and forgive," Kensy says, like it's easy. "We can still do this together, Bass. You can go down with honor."

Now, he understands. His mother's godstone feels so heavy around his neck, like cattle rattling their chains as they head toward slaughter. Kensy stills needs him. Kensy needs a god speaker—and Basuin is all he has.

It's familiar. Basuin's washed Kensy's dirty laundry for the last five years—broken necks and bled bodies and bludgeoned heads. Basuin was good at it. Of course Kensy wants him back.

"No." It comes out like a laugh. "I won't do that, Commander." It's the first time he's ever said no to Kensy. It'll be the last time, too.

Kensy nods, looking toward the trees. But a strange, tense silence closes in on them. "You remember what happened at Ulenski, don't you?"

Ulenski—his greatest victory. Right before his greatest failure in Valkesta. A whole city, razed to the ground, burned to nothing but black char beneath his boots.

A black wolf, a mother cried, praying to the moon and then praying to him. *Black Wolf*, she sobbed as she ran, as soot and ash stuck to his skin, *don't hurt us, please.*

This is a threat.

"I will do whatever is necessary to get what I want, Bass." Kensy bares his teeth in some perverse version of a smile. A sort of recklessness, so unlike Kensy, oozes from the corner of his lips. "And I won't be stopped. You're no stranger to that, Black Wolf."

The whole world is cold again. It isn't because he's in Valkesta. It isn't a memory, a flashback. Basuin's body floods with icy water, charging through his veins, as a pit of fear settles inside him. His teeth ache in his head. He knows.

Basuin knows Kensy will do whatever is necessary—because it was Basuin who always did the necessitating.

There's blood in his mouth.

"Now." Kensy holds his hands out in a shrug. "I'm not so cruel, am I?"

No, not at all. Kensy is the cruelest.

Basuin takes a step back, and then two, and then three. Toward Gyeosi. Kensy sighs, shaking his head.

"I always knew I'd have to kill you," Kensy muses. "But I really wish I didn't have to, old friend."

Kensy doesn't lie. Kensy never lies. He reaches for his rifle and Basuin runs. Flees into the forest, darts behind the trees. A shot goes off—too close, so close. It rings in his ears. Kensy didn't lie. The wolf-man howls until it shatters his eardrums, the same pitch as the bullet cutting through the woods. Something surges within him, more god than human, and the trees blur past him as he sprints faster than ever. Gone faster than Kensy can catch up.

Kensy meant it—and it lingers like the blood coating his tongue. He'll do whatever it takes. Burn down this whole forest to get what he wants, like Basuin burned Ulenski. A victory and a funeral march, all in one.

Basuin can't go back to Shaelstorm, but he can't stay here, either. Kensy's threat wasn't meant for Bass. It was meant for the gods. He should've known better; he should've known from the start.

But there's too much hanging in the balance now. Messy gods and duty and murder and death. His choice is just. He'll go to the elder tree and give up godhood. He'll give Ren's magic back so she can protect her people. And he'll be out of the picture.

When Basuin returns to Gyeosi, Yaelic runs to meet him. The boy clings first to his shirt, then gives a proper bow. He yaps on, like a pup would, about how he spent his day. How Ko taught him about Gyeosi, and how he and Hami are still fighting, but it won't last, it never does with them. And that there are newcomers. Refugees, from the south.

All he can think of, trembling hands tucked under his arms as Yaelic walks back to their hut alongside him, is that Kensy isn't going to stop. He won't stop until the forest is completely burned to the ground, until he finds that godly artifact for Queen Ye'suite.

And when he sees Ren, sitting among other spirit villagers, he nearly turns to meet her. To warn her. Kensy told him that first.

Warn them that we are coming.

Basuin pauses, staring straight across the village at her. She sits with the family of refugees, their heads bowed to her in thanks, but Ren holds his gaze instead. Her eyes are narrowed in that same glare, still soured from their earlier argument. Until something changes, and then her face softens into something else. Realization, and then confusion—a new weariness—moves in. It deepens the frown on her mouth, and Basuin hates that.

Then, behind her, a refugee raises his head. His eyes are full of hatred. Regret, and hatred, and blame, all pointed straight at Ren.

Refugees, from the south, where the army has razed clean.

Part of him wants to put himself in between them—shield Ren from those hateful eyes. But a better part of him knows she would first cut his throat.

So he swallows and continues onward, heading up the stairs with Yaelic pulling at him.

Ren can worry about the forest. Basuin is done being a god. She'll get her magic back, Basuin will die, and everyone will be happy.

These are her lands, and her people, and her problem. Basuin's presence is a pitfall. No more hurting spirits. No more learning tricks and playing games to try and make magic that doesn't even belong to him. None of it. This was a mistake.

Basuin coming here—Basuin being deified—was a mistake. And the sooner he leaves, the better the chance Ren has at saving her own forest. Right?

Something heavy presses into his spine, fissuring his bones. The weight of his supply pack when he carried it up the mountains and into Valkesta. The weight of the bodies they recovered, strapped to two soldiers each, and the pieces they found in the snow that they shoved in a bloody pack and carried back down to the encampment.

Can Ren really stop Kensy—alone?

CHAPTER FOURTEEN

THIS TIME, IT'S he who finds Ren—in hopes for a goodbye, maybe. Pitiful of him, to want something so simple from her, when their common ground is found in spite. But he can't deny himself. Not when this will be his last night.

The moon is shadowed by passing clouds threaded with silver light. She stands beneath it, still awake, leaning against the knot-rope railings and staring up at the sky. He climbs the steps to meet her, weight held by the rope-spun banister, and looks upward to gaze at the moon as she does. The moon god has a name, but he can't remember it. If his mother still lived, she would scold him, warmly, but all the same.

"Hwai-ga," Ren names her, just as he considers asking. "Do you think them enemies?"

"Who?"

"Elka and Hwai-ga," she says. "The sun and the moon."

Bass looks over, but Ren keeps her stare steady. The silver light pouring from the sky illuminates her face in a way that looks magical. Godly.

"No," he says, taken aback. "They're lovers. My mother told me their stories. How Elka would warm the sky because she knew that Hwai-ga gets cold without her. So Elka blanketed the world, hoping it would be enough to keep her love warm."

Ren's lips slowly, so slowly, curve into a smile. The smallest of smiles.

"How sad," she says. "To watch your lover from such a distance, not ever being able to touch them. All you can do is try and leave your warmth behind for them to remember you by."

Her words are a blade driven between his ribs, aimed for a heart he no longer has. It knocks the air out of him completely and Bass covers his mouth to keep from wheezing. How sad, indeed. He remembers so much of his time spent watching Isaniel from afar, curbing his glances so as to not arouse suspicion. The little things Isaniel would leave behind, proof that he existed and slept in the same cot as Bass, because by morning, he'd already slunk out of Bass' bunk and snuck back into his own.

Not only sad, but somehow unkind in its own way. Maybe he should see it as a kindness, as he always saw Elka's heat as a kindness to Hwai-ga.

"And you believed them to be enemies?" he asks Ren, eyes falling to the ground below them.

From the corner of his right eye, Ren shrugs. "In a way. Day and night are so different. They are the protectors of their own realm. I guess they don't have to be enemies, but..." She hums in thought, low and only for a moment. "But I never saw them close enough to be lovers."

"What about dawn?" Basuin's eyes are drawn to her yet again. "And dusk? What of twilight, if day and night are separate worlds?"

Ren turns her head now to look at him, still wearing that smile. She looks a little rueful, a little chagrined. But it makes him draw in a long breath.

"Well," she says quietly, "I guess you got me there."

It makes him crack his own smile, but he quickly wipes a hand over his jaw to hide it. Has Ren ever admitted to being wrong before? Never to him, at the very least.

He should correct her—say it's his mother, not him. But it feels too hard, like too much to say all at once. Wiping the smile off his lips, Bass wraps his hand around his godstone instead. But Ren moves, and her elbow brushes against his arm.

"I need your help with something," she says. Her gaze is stuck back to the sky. "With magic."

Basuin hesitates, only for a second. "All right," he agrees, but he doesn't know why. It's not like he's sticking around much longer. And Ren doesn't even like him—and he isn't very fond of her, either.

But she asked, earnestly, and Basuin is hemorrhaging her magic.

Once more, Ren leads him out of Gyeosi and into the trees, until they reach a familiar gnarled tree. "Chiro," Bass remembers, and Ren looks surprised.

The oak creaks awake, unbothered by them. "Am-sa, you leave again tonight?"

"We do," she says. "Would you be so kind as to help us?" She always seems to ask. Something he's come to learn about her, the very few days he's known her now. Ren cares most about these spirits. He knows how it feels—to care most about your comrades. To throw yourself on the cliff of a mountain trying to save them.

How Ren throws herself at the bastion over and over trying to save her people.

"Always," Chiro groans in response, and Ren lays her palm against its bark and the portal glows to life beneath her touch. She looks back at Basuin, face awash in blue magic. This time, Ren doesn't offer her hand. This time, she jumps into the portal without waiting, and Basuin leaps in after her.

The journey is the same, but where they land is different. It's dark here, and hard to see the ground at all. There's no light but the moon and even the moon can't illuminate their path. This isn't the bastion, he knows already. It smells of wet earth here, not of smoke. The smell of white lilies invades him next, and when Bass turns, Ren is waiting on him.

Without saying a word, Ren takes his hand and leads him through the darkened forest. Something stirs in him, half luminous and half pathetic at the way she always holds his hand with no hesitance. Guiding him the way she guides the other spirits in this forest. Ren isn't afraid to touch him.

There's no time to dwell on it. He follows behind her, sticking to her trail, trusting her. Ren moves with grace, but he moves with a reluctance. Her hand is the only thing that feels steady in the darkness of the forest. It isn't long before he hears it—the sound of soldiers on watch, their lightweight mail clinking against itself with every shift and move and march. It's a legion camp, far out from the bastion.

He jerks to a stop, clinging to her hand. Ren halts, looking back at him. Bass nods his head in the direction he hears the camp. From this distance, in the fog of night, they can't even see the glow of a lamp. Ren gives him a nod, a reassuring squeeze to his hand, and then she continues forward.

If he were a better man, he would pull ahead. Have her traveling behind his hulking form instead. Bass has always been on the front lines. But with her, in the here and now, Basuin doesn't feel much like a captain—not even a soldier. He's just Bass, and she's just Ren.

But as they close in on the encampment, the forest lightens with the familiar yellowing glow of oil lamps. "What is this camp?" he whispers.

"A hunt," she answers him. "They catch and kill the animals that keep your men fed."

He winces. Catch and kill spirits like Yaelic, like Qia. A horrible guilt settles in the very bottom of his gut.

Ren pulls him behind a large, thick oak. "This is what I need your help with. Can you do this?" She takes his arm and draws a finger down the line of his veins to his god mark like she did the first time she taught him magic. He presses his tongue to the roof of his mouth to suppress a shiver at her touch. "Paint a picture in your mind. Imagine their supplies."

Sabotage, again. Like she ruined the farms. It won't be enough to send these soldiers back to Shaelstorm, and it won't be enough to scare the legion off the island either. They'll just work on half rations until the next supply comes in. He's done it before—and he's asked his men to do it, too.

Basuin hesitates, torn between two worlds. Where do his loyalties lie? He is an enemy to both. That won't change.

But the wolf-man snaps its teeth at him, a warning. *Enemy or ally, you have a duty.*

He knows.

And what is a soldier without duty?

Nothing.

So Basuin closes his eyes and does as Ren says, imagining the bins and barrels of supplies he know the camp will have. Sabotage won't stop them, but for once, he isn't being asked to kill. Ren's told him before that she doesn't kill the legion soldiers, though Basuin doesn't understand it.

"Imagine it all turning to black. Dried up and spoiled." Ren's finger traces the lines of his god mark. This time, he can't stop the shiver as it crawls up the back of his neck.

All the food in their ration boxes they carry on wheeled carts, decaying. Oozing rot. Shriveled up and dried out. His mind burns their bandages into ash, turns their powders to soot and tinctures to dust. Everything he's ever carried in his packs on his marches through Grimmalia, he imagines destroying.

"Open your eyes, Basuin," Ren says, and he does.

His god mark is glowing, red light jumping from his hand. It snakes through the trees and toward the camp. Power and magic surges through his forearm, muscles jumping like he's been shot with electricity.

Ren shoots him this knowing grin he's never seen before. Something in his belly twists, seeing her eyes hold that glimmer. He can do it again. Make more magic. He doesn't care about it—but seeing her smile makes him feel much lighter than when she frowns. Less guilty. Less ashamed.

Less like a soldier, and more like Basuin.

"More," he says, leaning in closer to her. She smells of upturned earth and fresh-cut flowers. "Teach me more."

She nods. "Their weapons, now. Imagine taking them apart." Ren slips her hand under his, cradling him. "This should be easy for you. It was disastrous for me." There's that quirk in her lips again. Even as she looks down, he sees it.

"Really?" Bass has taken apart many guns and put them back together. Unstrung crossbows and bent metal. The only thing he can't shatter is steel—Kensy used to laugh at him for using swords long after the legion had rifles, but Bass knows how strong they truly are.

"I'd never seen weapons before," Ren admits, and everything that's risen in Basuin at seeing her smile drops, a weight sinking through him to the bottom of his gut. He doesn't know what to say. Nothing feels like enough to make up for what the legion has done.

Ren doesn't linger in it the way he does. She never does, and every time, he's awed by it. How she can turn from such a fierce beast into a gentle creature.

"Imagine it," she repeats herself. Once again, he closes his eyes. This time, he pictures the red thread of his magic zigzagging through the camp and invading every single weapon the soldiers carry. Taking them apart, breaking them, tossing away every screw and string.

He hears it—as if his mind is part of his magic—every bolt and spring it attacks. The click and snap of it assaults his head. Bass opens his eyes before Ren instructs him to.

"I did it," he tells her, and he can't help the grin that crawls over his face. More magic, yet again. Before, the only power he had was in his body as he struck down men and carved into their corpses. The only power he had was in death. It's a stark reminder that what he's doing won't stop the army at all. Whatever Kensy's plans are, sabotaging a single camp will only slow them. Kensy always gets what he wants.

"You did," Ren says, and then she draws her hand away from his. Blunt nails dig into his palm in a fist. She gazes off toward the camp, that smile long gone. "I'll teach you one more thing," she says. "It'll be more difficult."

Eyes stuck to the curve of her cheek, Bass nods.

Ren waves her god-marked hand over the camp, but no magic raises from her palm. "Thread yourself through their minds," she says. "The way you imagined yourself before, imagine yourself inside their heads."

Bass' brows furrow together, and he doesn't close his eyes. Being inside someone else's mind—it makes him uneasy. He wouldn't want someone else in his mind. He hates the wolf-man for it.

Still staring out at the camp, Ren doesn't even look at him. "You'll take their minds apart like you took the weapons apart. Creating nightmares isn't as easy—"

"No." He spits the word like it's a sickness. "I won't."

There isn't a world where Basuin will weave a nightmare into someone's mind. Not even his enemy.

Ren turns, her face unreadable. He looks at the floor instead. It's crawling all over him—her eyes, or the idea of barreling through someone else's mind. This was supposed to be easy; helping Ren by using the magic he's leached from her. It wasn't supposed to be like this.

No. He won't do this. Not to anyone. He'd take their miserable lives before he inflicts something like that. The power to kill is something he's come to terms with. The power to break someone's mind is something completely different.

"What?" Ren's voice is unsteady. Confusion and bite are laced in her words.

Bass brings his hands closer, turning his palms upward. The red glow of magic still lives under his skin, throbbing like blood vessels ready to burst and break. His god mark laughs at him the way the wolf-man does inside of him.

"I won't curse someone with nightmares," he says. "I wouldn't wish that on anyone. It would be better just to kill them."

For the past eight months—two of them taken to heal—he's woken in the middle of the night, punished by the blood that soaked his clothes. Forced to watch the macabre play of his career unfold on a stage illuminated by his sins. A theatrical rendition of his worst decisions.

He used to jump from sleep, still in Valkesta. Surrounded by snow and ice and all his misgivings. His body would be heavy with the weight of dead men, unable to do anything but thrash and yell and wait for Tehali to barge into his room and free him from the illusion—the memories. Bloody her nose, by accident, and keep his hands slick and stained with it. The same way he hurt Ko, in Gyeosi, too.

"I don't kill," Ren finally says, her voice controlled. "I will not kill."

"Then what will you do?" he asks, and the wolf-man snatches a rib from Basuin and splinters it. "Because this won't stop them. Do you truly believe you can starve out a whole militant bastion and send them home?"

Ren's eyes flash with something half malicious as she cuts her gaze to him. "Are you asking me to fight your legion?"

"No," he says first, because he doesn't think. "But you have to protect the forest. Isn't that your duty?"

And what of you? the wolf-man mocks him. *What will you do, Basuin of Ankor, to save the forest?*

He's giving up godhood. Giving his magic back to Ren. That's all he can do.

"I can't fight an army," Ren says, and while it should sound like an admission, a weakness, she makes it sound like something already decided and at peace. "I won't fight a war I cannot win."

Ren pushes off the tree as if she might walk away, but she only paces two steps before stopping. He doesn't understand it—that she won't fight a war. There's never been a time that Bass hasn't been in war.

Always a war you can win, the wolf-man reminds him with a painful nip.

That's true. Xalkhir has never had a bad hand in the war. They've always held high ground. Aggressive, always the one to start the fight and always the one to finish it, too. Even when Bass stood at the bottom of the Valkesi Mountains and stared up at their frozen peaks, even when he knew that it would be a lost mission, they were stronger.

But only because they made sacrifices.

What of the innocent? Basuin once asked Kensy as they stood across from one another, war plans on the table between them. *These bombs—we can't control the blasts, Commander.*

And Kensy looked up at him, eyes iced over. *What of them, Captain? This is war. We make the sacrifices that we make. Otherwise, we'll lose. Then what will we have left?*

Bass chose to climb those mountains. He chose to sacrifice himself and his men to the icy hellscape of bloody Valkesta.

"So that's it?" Bass feels the simmer of anger in his bones. "You won't fight them and the forest will die?"

"I am doing my best," she snaps at him. "Before you came, I had more power. Their crops withered and their weapons jammed and their men woke from nightmares that made them fear the woods. But you've taken that from me."

"Weak nightmares won't stop any man," he growls. He would know that best. "You're not protecting anything with your god magic, your games."

He expects her to respond with heat. But her shoulders only draw up, defensive, her eyes blank. Ren doesn't look at him.

"Then tell me, what would you do? What is your plan to fight them, Basuin of Ankor?"

Gods, stop saying his name like that. Say it like anything but that.

But he doesn't have an answer. Ren is right. The legion is massive compared to them, with weaponry and fire. They can't answer that. Basuin was supposed to find a way to protect them, but all he can do is give Ren back her magic. What she does with it, that's not on him.

But Ren will die. Yaelic, and Qia, and Hami, too. Once again, there are lives in his hands. Once again, he has nowhere to run but head on—toward the elder tree. He bites back the sting of selfishness he feels sitting on his shoulders.

Get it off of him. The magic, take it back. Drag it out of him with teeth and with claws, and take the wolf-man, too. He doesn't want this. He's never wanted any of this. If anyone would have listened, they would know that all Basuin ever wanted was to die up in those mountains, in Valkesta, honorably and unrecovered, with no war story left to bring home.

He doesn't want to care about people dying anymore. He shouldn't be here to care. This is Ren's forest, and these are Ren's spirits, and this is Ren's responsibility—and fuck the guilt that he tastes in the back of his mouth because it's *her* responsibility, not his.

Won't someone just let him die? For good, for once?

And when he looks at Ren, those dark eyes of hers and that flat nose and those high cheekbones, he doesn't see a woman right now. He sees a god with god magic trying to save her forest, her people, by weaving his biggest wound into her enemies' minds—and still failing, alone.

CHAPTER FIFTEEN

ON THE WAY back from the camp, Ren sucks in a hard breath and presses her hand to her chest. When he looks, there's a red mark crawling over her collarbone, peeking out from the neckline of her robe. Did he burn her?

He doesn't have a chance to ask. Ren picks up speed toward the portal, no words shared. But once her hands touch the gnarled bark around the portal, she looks up at him, lips parted in shock.

"What's wrong?" he asks. A fear shutters over him—he's drained all her magic. They can't get back.

Ren looks back down, where the blue, swirling magic pools in the tree's trunk. "One of my portals, I can't access it. It's gone. That's never happened before." Then, she turns her head, upward to the sky. "Something's wrong."

"Okay," he says, though it twists his gut with unease. Something bubbles between them, fizzling like magic. "Let's go."

They stand a few feet away from one another but Ren won't look at him. "This is a different kind of magic," she explains. "Not a portal." She demonstrates how he should hold his hands—fingers outstretched, curved like he holds a large ball. "We'll create a gust of wind, but you can't simply imagine it into existence."

Bass, staring hard at the space between his hands where he imagines the wind to be, grunts a noise of disapproval. Magic is hard enough already, without all of Ren's rules.

"We must ask the wind for help." Ren closes her eyes, and blue light begins to whip like ribbons between her fingers. "The forest works together. We won't have enough magic for both of us without its help."

Basuin hates asking for help, so he tries to think of it like teamwork. The forest and them, working together to create a gale that will take them to where Ren's portal has disappeared—back to the bastion. He doesn't know why Ren's burned, either, but Basuin knows that Kensy plays a part. Whatever's happened, it's because of Kensy, and that's enough for him.

He tries, but Bass doesn't know how to call upon the wind of the forest. Staring down at his hands, Bass asks, *Wind, will you help us?*

The wolf-man barks a laugh, wheezing. One of Ren's eyes opens, as if she heard the chuckle from inside him.

"It's like any other spirit," she says. "Their name is Ki-on. Treat them as you would anyone else—as a living being."

He huffs a sigh and closes his eyes again. *Ki-on, can you hear me?*

In answer, a breeze blows through the woods. Ki-on twirls through Ren's hair, tousling her bangs enough that the moonlight better illuminates her face.

We need your help, he asks it. *I still have much magic to learn, so please, help Ren instead of me.*

And, in answer again, a lighter gale circles them and makes Ren giggle. All bell tones and knotting shapes out of his belly. But the burn crawling across her skin rots that feeling into something gruesome. There's not enough time for him to look away before she opens her eyes again. But Ren reaches out, hand to the wind, letting it collect around her fingers.

"See?" she says. "Everything works in tandem here. Together."

Basuin copies her movement, letting the wind trickle through his fingers and curl up in his palm. It's gentle, and a little playful.

"Now gather it, and then channel it." Ren demonstrates, moving her hands in a circular wave, blue light mixing with the blowing breeze.

When the red of his magic hits hers, the gale turns to a bright purple—almost lavender in the moonlight. It reflects on Ren's face and illuminates all her high-boned features. Softening, rather than sharpening.

Together, they push the wind toward the south. As it rolls through the trees, it seems to pick up, and pick up, until he can hear nothing else but the whistle and rush of it.

"Ready?" Ren calls to him, holding out her hand. He hesitates, only for a moment, a touch of fear turning him cold. If he burned her before, he could hurt her again.

But he takes her hand anyway—they shouldn't be separated. Basuin gives her a curt nod. Then, Ren pulls them into the gale and he loses his footing. It's the strong, clutching grip of Ren's hand around his that keeps him from stumbling as they rush through the forest, riding on the spirit of the wind.

Ren looks back at him, a knowing smile sitting pretty on her countenance. He holds her stare, the way her eyes glow with this childlike glee in them, sparking something in his chest alive. It's magical. A head rush.

Until it's not.

Until they fly out from the trees into nothing. *Nothing*. A stretch of nothing at all.

Ren loses her balance first. Basuin's never been one to let go. His fingers are fettered around her and when she goes, he goes too. But he dives for her, wrapping his arms around her before they hit the ground. His feet land but the added weight of Ren against him topples him and they roll through the dirt.

Panting, Basuin surveys the area. But there is nothing—nothing here but cleared dirt and the light of the moon above them. It reeks of fire and ash.

Ren scrambles to her feet and Bass grunts as her elbow finds his stomach and her hand pushes off his shoulder. He jumps to his feet and trails after her, but he knows already. Acid crawls up his throat. His mouth tastes like cremation.

"What is this?" Ren asks, head tossing from side to side as she tries to take in the land. In the distance beyond the fog of the night, the bastion stands glorious and untouched. Only a few nights ago they were just here, watching the fireworks from atop a tree that's been logged now. Basuin says nothing, but Ren turns to look back at him.

Silver tears streak down her cheeks. Even Hwai-ga could call him a sinner for how the moonlight colors her crying.

"What have they done?" she asks him, and Basuin can't look away from her.

"They've burned it down," he answers. Just as he's burned cities down, too.

In the name of the queen, Kensy always said. For Queen Ye'suite, soldiers were always taught to say. Because the gods aren't allowed to be named anymore. Gods have no power in this world anymore. Just like the legion burned their church down, in Ankor, they'll burn this forest down too.

They already have.

A trail of tears drips off the edge of Ren's jaw in the same way a painter's brush makes a single stroke. Her eyes are two moons, bright and wide. Then, dark, in such a quick second Basuin would've missed it if he'd blinked.

Ren's eyes narrow, rage replacing her despair. Fury gathers around her so tangibly it stings his skin. Cerulean magic crackles as if crying for help—but who cries for help, and who is the help cried for?

With a scream yanked from her throat, Ren slams her palms down against the forest floor. Blue lightning surges across the clearing, cracking through the ashen earth. An acrid smell mixes in the air and Basuin slaps a hand over his mouth. Smoke. Gunpowder. Fire. Blood.

He's brought to his knees, the sound of shrapnel shrieking through the sky in his ears. The forest spins. The blackened, barren field floods with magic and out of it, light blooms. Painted in Ren-blue. Then, seedlings burst from the fissures in the forest floor—new, pushing through all the ash the army left behind.

It's incredible. New life, populating the clearing. All from Ren's magic.

Basuin chokes. Something is ripped from inside him; something is being torn out of his body. His skin is sucked to his bones. He can't hear anything—not even his own thoughts. There's no air out here. He can't breathe.

Strangled, Basuin is pulled to the ground on his hands and knees. Red bleeds from his hands and sinks into the field, drawn toward Ren. And on the other side, Ren is hunched over, too. Panting with pain, drawing ragged breaths. Behind her, the blue magic seedlings begin to recede back into the soil.

Magic. She needs his magic.

Basuin reaches for her. God mark outstretched. "Here," he pants. "Take it." Blood paints his palm.

Ren doesn't look at him. She slams her own palms down against the ground again, but a cry of pain leaves her. It shatters him. Enough to make him crawl on his hands and knees to her. It feels like something inside him is dying. Like everything that he is has been liquefied and now leaks from every orifice.

"Let me help," he begs. For the pain of watching her, and for the pain that she wrenches from his body as she tries stealing her magic back. "I can help!"

"No!" she screams, fingers digging into the earth. "I don't need your help. I can do this on my own. I've always done it on my own." Her body shakes. "I've always been alone."

From her fingers, blue magic bleeds into the dirt, but it isn't enough. The seedlings are dying. The ash is drowning them again. Ren sobs.

Reach her.

Basuin throws himself toward her despite the cost of it—the searing ache of all his meat and bones. When his hand falls to her back, Ren shrieks and tries to force him away, but Basuin stretches for her god-marked hand.

"You don't have to," he grits through clenched teeth. "I can help you—" *if you'll let me.*

His left hand finds her right. Beneath him, she's trembling. Every breath she takes is labored, sweat dripping from her skin. He takes her hand, trying to match their god marks.

"Let me help," he pleads.

A curtain of dark hair hides Ren's face from him, but another silver tear traces the line of her throat.

Then, Ren presses her scarred palm to his, and a violent purple magic colors them. Basuin curls the fingers of his right hand in the dirt, like Ren does, and their magic bruises across the clearing.

Please. Let it work. Let their magic regrow the forest his people cut down. End the pain.

Let this be his penance. Proof that he isn't just made to kill.

When he looks up, the seeds have begun to sprout again—violet, this time. Blue entangled with red. Ash peppering their homes as it does every living thing in this forest. This time, when their magic recedes, the sprouts look unbothered. They stand short and steady, planted in the earth, ready to grow again.

It isn't much, but it's a new start. A rebellion against the legion who tried so hard to ruin this place.

Basuin smiles. Until Ren forces herself to her feet and makes a sound like she's trying to choke back another sob. The loss of her hand in his feels so cold. Frozen, like snow beneath his hands biting through his heavy gloves to smart his skin.

"I don't need you," she cuts, breathing heavy. "I wouldn't even need your help if you hadn't come here and stolen all my magic."

Something inside him withers.

"I've always been alone." Ren wipes her tears away on her arm. "You being here won't change that. Ever."

Right. Basuin didn't help grow this forest—this magic never belonged to him. Proof that all he knows is how to kill.

But then, Ren wraps her arms around herself and cries, turning to hide her face. Basuin stretches his fingers out, unable to name if it's grief or guilt.

THE WALK TO Gyeosi is slow and metered, when Ren finally turns her back on the clearing. Time ticks away for an eternity and he lets it, unsure of what he can say. *I'm sorry the legion is destroying your forest. I'm sorry my people are killing your people. I'm sorry I didn't die the right way.*

In the end, neither of them say anything at all.

He can't even remember what the legion would tell the Grimmalian refugees when they came and conquered. It all blurs together, all of it the same. Comfort is a lie manufactured to make the winner feel better—and he's always been on the winning side.

By choice, he reminds himself. *By choice.*

Something tightens in his chest, and it's not the wolf-man's claws in his lungs anymore. Even now, he's making the same choice. Giving up godhood. Giving Ren's magic back so she has a fighting chance against the army. He's choosing to stay on the winning side.

Or, abandoning the losing side. What a haunting thought. What a cowardly decision.

"Why?" Ren's voice, quiet and flat, makes him jump. It's like she can read his mind.

He wets his lips. "I don't know," he answers, in truth because he doesn't know what she's asking.

"No." Ren slows to a stop and it sends a chill trembling through him. "Why are they leaving the bastion?"

Basuin turns to look at her. "What?" She said it so solemnly. Alarm bells, war cries, screams of help ring in his brain.

Ren meets his gaze. "The army is moving. Before you arrived, they stayed close to the bastion. Now, the camps keep changing. They're moving north. I don't understand why."

His stomach curls until he's out of breath. It aches, the realization born of Ren's words. Of Kensy's visitation, of the threat he laid between himself and Basuin. Ren thinks it was Basuin's arrival that changed things, but it wasn't. It's Kensy's.

She doesn't know—and he doesn't know what Kensy's looking for. Basuin opens his mouth, searching for the right words.

But then, a voice calls out, "Hello?" It comes from his left, deep in the woods, cutting through the darkness. "Is anyone out there?" a woman calls, but Basuin hears no footsteps on the ground. No movement, just the ghost of a voice. "I need help," she calls meekly, a needle of fear piercing her throat.

It must be a soldier. From one of the camps moving, pushed up from Shaelstorm. But they shouldn't be this far out in the forest alone. Ren is paces ahead of him now, looking back at him in wait. But Bass stands still, at attention, locked in place by the siren call for help that only he seems to hear.

The voice warbles with panic. "Captain?"

He knows that voice. He knows her. Basuin breaks into a sprint through the forest, racing toward her.

"Aless!" he shouts. The foliage is a blur around him. "'Less!" he yells again, until he bursts through a gap in the trees and sees her—back facing him, still armored, cloak missing. Her blonde hair is strewn from the braid pinned to her neck, mussed and frizzy. And when she turns around, she's exactly the same as she always was. Deep-green eyes and worried brow and smatterings of freckles along her nose.

Basuin skids to a stop in front of her, chest heaving. "'Less," he calls again, eyes searching her body for wounds. But her head—her head is still intact. No cut mars her neck. She looks exactly as she was before they climbed those mountains. He breathes hard, especially when Aless' face brightens with a streak of hope among the fear as soon as she sees him.

"Can you help me?" She rushes forward three steps in a familiar canter, hands pressed together at her chest. "I'm lost. I don't know how I got here. I need to get back," she says, her eyes widening as if she's realized something. "I have to go back—they need me." She raises a trembling hand to her mouth, panic coloring her eyes.

"It's okay, 'Less," he says, taking two steps forward to meet her. "It's over now. We can go back together." Basuin holds a hand out to her. They can go back to Shaelstorm, mourn over a pail of cold ale, get on a ship back to Ha'riste.

But Aless stares at his chest as if looking through him. "Do you know where we are?" she asks.

"Aless," he repeats, something ripping through the hole where his heart used to sit.

"I'm looking for the Winter River," she says. "That's where they told me to go—but I'm lost. Please," she begs. "Can you help me?"

Everything in him—every shred of hope and every star he could have wished on and every prayer he could have made—turns to rot in his organs.

"I can," Ren says from behind him, and his body goes shock-still, limbs rigid and shoulders back as he stands at attention. He stares down at Aless, her face flooding with relief.

"Thank you," Aless sighs out, and then her lips peel back to reveal that nervous smile she would always wear when she spoke with someone new. When the spotlight fell on her with her next promotion. And when he asked her to go to Valkesta with him. All thin lips with the press of her tongue behind her teeth.

Ren moves to stand next to him, her head at his chest, extending her hand. Aless takes it, but the skin of her fingers turns to a ghostly white where her palm meets Ren's.

"I don't know how I got here," Aless says, her voice growing watery and weak. "I really need to get back to them. I can't let them be alone." Tears begin to fall from her glassy green eyes, but she doesn't wipe them away. She lets them careen off her chin.

"'Less," he tries one more time, voice thin.

"I know it's scary," Ren tells her. "But we can walk there together."

"Where?"

"The Winter River."

"Will they be there?" Aless asks, and Basuin's fingers clench into a fist. "Did my friends wait for me?"

Ren inhales for a long time, then nods.

Aless' ghost-grip on her hand tightens. "Thank you," she says, breathless. "I'm so tired." She sags as Ren starts to walk them forward. Basuin takes another step, to follow after them. He should chase her down and apologize. Tell Aless that he truly cared for her, that he's sorry. But he can't move.

Sudden light blooms bright against the dark background of the forest. Ren walks Aless toward it; it's blinding. He almost shuts his eyes and flinches away but he doesn't. And before Ren lets go of Aless' hand, Aless turns back to look at him. He swears that she looks at him this time. But then, she fades into the nothing, a wisp of white that smokes from Ren's palm. Gone.

At least she made it to the Winter River.

Now, it's just him and Ren, ten feet apart from one another. Her eyes feel heavy on him, but not quite as sharp as they usually would. Yaelic's told him of this before, how Ren walks her dead spirits to the River. Basuin hasn't seen it until now. His mother used to tell him stories—of gods like this. Ones who shepherded their loyal devotees to the River so they wouldn't cross worlds alone.

She always said that when she passed, she hoped someone would walk with her. Not because she didn't know the way, but because it was a sign of love.

Would Ren have walked his mother to the River, like she walked with Aless?

Out of all spirits it could have been, of course it was Aless. She clung to him in life—clawed at him as they trekked up the Valkesi Mountains, begged him to let them go home. Of course it was Aless.

"Who was that?" Ren asks. He cracks under pressure and turns his head away.

"No one," he lies. Another moment of silence runs through the forest, long enough that he chances a look at her.

Ren's eyes have hardened into obsidian. "How did you know her?"

"I killed her," Basuin snaps, as hard as the wolf-man snaps its teeth at his ribcage. "Is that what you want to hear?"

Aless didn't have any last words. She never even made a sound. Not like Isaniel, who wrenched and spit at Basuin as he choked on the blood that sprouted from his stomach, damning Basuin for bringing them to Valkesta until the very end.

When her head was cut clean off, the only sound she made was when her skull hit the ground—the thud of it on the ice, rolling away.

Basuin did ask, though. He pleaded. Basuin begged on his hands and knees, prayed to every god he knew the name of, kissed his mother's godstone until his lips were raw as he tried to infuse every last piece of his shattered soul into it as an offering to Sa-cha, for them to go to the Winter River.

If 'Less made it, then the others did too. Or, he hopes so.

And Basuin—Basuin won't go there, so he'll never see them ever again. He'll never see 'Less, or Tomaas. Never see Isaniel ever again. But out of all of them—out of everyone Basuin has killed—he misses his mother the most.

He forgot, somehow. That he deserves whatever is waiting for him in the Blacksalt Sea.

The crunch of underbrush makes him look up, Ren beginning

to walk away. Something tugs on the raw edges inside his chest, the cavern where the wolf-man chews him ragged and septic.

"I knew her," he says, and Ren stops to look back at him. "She was my friend." He doesn't have anything else to say. Aless was his friend and he took her to Valkesta where he knew they would die, and she died.

Ren looks to where the light of the Winter River once shimmered. "She was very at peace," she tells him. "Most spirits who I walk to the River, they aren't like that. There was nothing lingering. No pain, no anger."

Something in his chest trembles. "She was lost?"

Ren's head tilts as she stares into the darkness. "No," she says, and for once, there's no barrier built into her voice. "She wasn't ready to go yet, so she simply followed you here. I think she wanted to say goodbye to you."

Basuin's hands feel heavy with grief, but something sinks into him that smooths away the twist in his gut. The god mark on his palm burns, and when he turns over his hand to look at it, the soot-black lines have turned to a scar-like red.

Like him, Ren upturns her palm and looks at her own god mark, the same hand she used to walk Aless' spirit to the Winter River. Her obsidian eyes trail upward, toward the sky above them, and her fingers curl back into her palm.

And though she doesn't look back at Basuin, Ren's hand finds his shoulder. A small, soft, barely there touch. Her fingers gloss down his bicep until she finds a wrinkle in his sleeve. Then, she gives it a tug, beckoning him to start moving again.

So, he follows. But for a moment, even as he moves, Ren's touch lingers. A second too long, like she's hesitant on letting go. But after that small, staying second, her touch fades, leaving only the echo of her fingers behind.

Basuin was wrong about Ren.

She isn't a woman who plays in the forest, who plays pretend as a deity getting lost in the woods. Ren is a god.

CHAPTER SIXTEEN

ONCE, WHEN HE was still a soldier and had yet to see a promotion, Bass was told his biggest strength was his mind and how he lacked it. The plain rank-cloth he tied around his upper arm every day spoke to that. His first stripe earned was for following orders. His second stripe was for swordsmanship. His third came from a bet—when he dueled a squad sergeant and won.

But Kensy was the first to name Basuin's real strength, the night before he promoted Basuin to lieutenant of Ariche's Fleet.

Decisive, Kensy called him. *No matter if your choice is right, you know what you want. You follow through. That's what it takes to be a winner, Bass.*

He still admired Kensy in those days. Captain Kensy, who chose Basuin to be his right-hand man. Captain Kensy, who understood sacrifice and how it would win a war.

Captain Kensy, other soldiers used to whisper, when he was still a mere sergeant. *Didn't you hear? He was part of that weird cult in Ha'riste, the one that steals orphan kids and puts 'em in the legion as soon as they can lift a sword.*

Commander Kensy, who never seemed to feel loss.

The decision to leave is easy. He makes it as he walks Ren back to Gyeosi. As Yaelic slumbers on, Basuin gathers his things. It's the worst part of leaving, that Yaelic won't understand why it's necessary. Poor pup has gotten so attached to a man he thought to be a god.

But Basuin knows he isn't a god. The wolf-man, who possesses as much as it pollutes him, is an infection.

Inside him, the wolf-man replies by sinking its canines into the meat of Basuin's chest and tearing a chunk away from the bone. It digs its snout into the mess it's made of his organs, bloody and stinking of rot.

Tonight, he's going to the elder tree. He'll pray on his hands and knees to be relieved of this duty—to be returned to the Blacksalt Sea. Yaelic does not need him. He's made a family out of the Gyeosi spirits. Hami will forgive him, once Basuin is gone. Ko and Haaman will help take care of him, too. They seem to have bonded, from where Basuin's watched from a distance. And Qia will be a good friend to him, maybe more someday. Yaelic doesn't need a caretaker.

Ren does not need Basuin either. He's getting in her way—she's made that clear.

There's another time of twilight that arrives right before dawn. When the sky turns to lavender and the first stirrings of the sun's coming warmth are felt. Bass slips out of Yaelic's grasp and fixes the sheet over the boy's curled, sleeping frame.

He doesn't understand how Ren could've thought them enemies—Elka and Hwai-ga, the sun and the moon. The sky is painted with proof of their love, their colors mixed on the palette and stroked over the world. This dawn before true dawn, this first twilight—it feels so much like Elka's hand stretching toward Hwai-ga, their fingers barely missing one another's.

But they'll pass each other by, as the cycle of day and night has ruled them so. Bound by duty, but suffering of love.

For once, the wolf-man is quiet, as if ignoring Bass now that he plans to leave. It tore him raw before, but now it lies on the floor of his chest cavity and stares at him through the darkness. Red pinpricks of light for eyes, always watching him.

But as he moves to leave Gyeosi for good, cool air fresh on his skin, the wolf-man presses its snout into his ribs and snuffs. It nudges him forward, and Bass descends the treehouse with no other thought. Something pulls him toward the center of the village and he follows. The wolf-man paws at him. His left palm itches where his mark is burned into his skin.

There's a small cottage on the eastern side of Gyeosi with a garden of wildflowers attached. He's seen it before, wondered how the flowers here grow so brightly under the canopy of the forest. But he's never seen anyone come and go. As he approaches, the wolf-man whines. Bass swallows and turns on his heel before he comes too close, but the wolf-man nudges at him again, more unkindly this time, and Bass walks an edge around the garden instead. It smells so soft and fragrant here, so familiar.

Then, a voice. "Maybe he's right." Hushed, and more delicate than he's heard it before. He can't help himself. His god mark pulses and burns.

Bass slows his steps, keeping silent as he draws closer to the voice. He sticks to the shadows of the cottage, but peeks around the corner.

And there she sits. She's perched atop a wickedly curved tree so nonchalantly—gracefully, as if the garden and the wildflowers and the entire forest has arranged itself around her. One knee pulled up to her chest, the other hanging down as her toes barely scrape the ground.

Ren stares up at the same lavender sky, her twilight eyes shining underneath the dimming moonlight.

"Maybe they aren't enemies," she continues as if she doesn't know he watches. "Maybe not everything is a fight."

He draws in a sharp inhale. She's speaking to the gods. Does she speak to the godrealm, or is there a god inside her too—like the wolf-man?

Even from here, he can see the smallest downward curve in her lips as she frowns up at the sky. "But this is a fight. It was always going to be. So, I ask you this." Ren's small hand parts the breeze in a slow ascent, one finger outstretched toward the moon. "Did you send him as an enemy, or was he meant to be an ally?"

He freezes, ducking back behind the wall of Ren's cottage and pressing himself flat to the darkness. She speaks of him. And though the wolf-man paws at him, claws at his ribcage as if it were a jail cell, Bass knows he should leave. He feels it in his boots, the driving need to bolt. But he stays.

"I think he could be," Ren says. "An ally, now. He's powerful, and he learns well enough. He could help save the forest. That magic—"

Basuin sneaks another look at her. Ren's eyes are locked on her right hand now, where a blue glow rises from the white lines written into her palm.

"His magic," she whispers. "I don't know what it is, but I've never felt so…"

Her fingers curl into a fist as she trails off, teeth biting into her bottom lip. Effervescent magic bleeds from the cracks in her fist, running down her wrist and dripping from bone.

Then, Ren slams her fist into her chest and snaps her head up toward the dawning sky. Her eyes are narrowed, fierce and angry and pained all at once out of nowhere.

"Tell me," she hisses, a sound he's learned well. "Tell me," she pleads, lips parted and empty. "Won't you tell me what to do this time? Or am I still unworthy?"

A heavy, rolling disgust floods him. Shame crawls up his spine, icy fingers like knife-points in his skin. It hurts. Hangs from him like a ghost trying to haunt him, like a bloated, rotting corpse he carries back to the graveyard. This moment was never meant for him to hear.

Basuin knows, best of all, the futility of praying to gods that never answered. Until the wolf-man made its home inside of him. A blessing, or perhaps a curse, that this dog of a god crawled inside him and speaks to him. Just like Ren, the gods never spoke to him—not until now. Basuin closes his eyes tight.

Does Ren have a heart? Does Ren still have her heart?

"Right," Ren tells herself. "Still not worthy enough to speak to the gods."

Something hammers in his chest where his heart should be, quick and unforgiving. The wolf-man's tail thumps against his ribcage, and then it throws its maw back and howls—a pained sound. Basuin scrambles back, panic racing up his throat. But he's frozen.

Then, Ren rounds the corner of her home, nearly crashing into him where he stands unmoving. He couldn't hear her over the pounding in his ears.

Fury colors her face, moonlight dripping like tears from her eyes and painting the blades of her cheekbones. Her lips part, poised in anger, but he opens his mouth first.

"I know of the elder tree," he says, words a swift slur pouring out of him.

Ren's eyes widen, but she culls her expression quickly. Her jaw tightens as she grinds her teeth together in anger. "What about it?"

"Hou-tou told me," he says, "that the elder tree can sever my tie to godhood, if asked." Basuin fists the godstone at his throat as if the edges could leave his palm raw. But for all he waits, Ren doesn't react. The rage in her dies, and she stares back at him, almost emptily.

"Do you know how gods are born?" Ren asks him.

Without hesitation, he answers, "Prayer and worship."

"Wrong," she says, and he grits his teeth.

From the Winter River, his mother told, *there arose a god, and that god was Sa-cha, and he was good.*

"From the Winter River," he tries again.

"Sa-cha did. But what of the rest of them?" He can't read her expression.

"It was said that Sa-cha bled into the Winter River, and from his blood, the water bred another god, and then another, and then when humans sprouted up from the earth that baked them like clay, they would pray to the gods and more gods would be born from their cries for salvation."

Ren laughs, but it doesn't sound light. There is a ruefulness, a darkness like the one he finds in her eyes, that taints her breath.

"If gods were born that way," she says with bite, "then godhood would be less painful."

"So, then how?" he asks, fist clenched so tightly it could bleed the god mark from his palm. How was he deified?

Ren looks away and the glittering light that falls from the cracks in the canopy overhead dances on her high cheekbones. "Living animals dismember ancient animals." Her voice carries on the wind.

New gods replace old gods, his mother said.

"People tear their gods apart," she says. "They feast on their gods, drink their blood, destroy their body, howl their name in jest for a chance to play gods themselves."

That's how they fall out of worship.

"And then—" her twilight eyes capture him once again, "—the god without a home finds a new one. The living eat the ancient. The dead come back to life."

To punctuate her words, the wolf-man's canines seize Basuin's lungs and squeeze the air out of him. Painful and sharp. A sword run through him, fire licking at his skin. Ren never stops watching him, even as he wheezes and clutches his chest.

The wolf-man built its new home there, where Basuin's heart used to lie. Maybe the wolf-man ate it, the way humans eat at their gods. Bone by bone by bone, slivers of sharp, cutting tools.

Like Ren's eyes. The edge of a blade.

"Ask me," she says, too lightly to be a demand but not hard enough to be a command. "Ask me how gods are born."

He sucks in a haggard breath and swallows his own blood. "How are gods born?"

From the Winter River, he thinks, there arose a god, and that god was Sa-cha. *Please Sa-cha, please let Isaniel make it to the Winter River*, and he was good.

"They possess the dead like humans possess houses," she tells him. "Like a child possesses its mother's stomach."

Something howls inside his head. The wolf-man blinks into his mind and takes up residence. Again, and again, and again.

But he *knew* this, that godhood is another leash tied around his neck, a knot he can't cut through. That he is owned once again, his fate another command in a long chain of orders he can't say no to.

And yet, to hear it out loud—to lose himself in Ren's eyes, as dark as the Blacksalt Sea itself—feels more damning than anything.

"Did they tell you? What happens if you fail the duty you've been given?" Her gaze is sharp. Shame, yet again, wraps around his throat.

"The gods," he says, voice wound tight. "I can't hear them. They don't talk to me." Just like her, he refuses to say. But her voice, the image of her fist to her chest as she begged for an answer, is burned into his memory.

Her brows draw together, eyes flicking down to his neck and back. "But you wear the stone," she says. "It's a—"

"It was my mother's," he cuts her off, an ache in his ruined chest. "It doesn't belong to me." Unlike Kensy, Basuin knows that not everything in this world belongs to him.

Ren walks two steps closer to him. A breath between them, umber eyes of hers locked on him. "If you fail to protect the forest," she says and draws nearer to him, "it won't mean death. The Wolf God will release your body and you'll disappear."

"To the Blacksalt Sea?" he demands, breaths quickening as his lungs grow heavy in his chest.

"No," Ren says. "You'll go nowhere."

Basuin pants, a tightness in his ribcage. Like the wolf-man inside of him is taking up too much space. Claustrophobic.

"What do you mean?" It hurts to speak.

In all his life, through all his mother's stories, Basuin's never heard of a nowhere. Humans go to the Winter River, or if they're like him, they go to the Blacksalt Sea.

And dead gods—gods who can no longer walk the mortal plane—they go to the godrealm.

But he is no human, and he is no god. So then, what is he? All he knows, for certain, is that he's dead.

The Blacksalt Sea is where he belongs. He has to go there. After everything, he's given up his chance to see his mother, his comrades, Isaniel—he gave it all up. Basuin deserves punishment. He deserves that penance.

Because if he doesn't repent, then what was it all for? Saying goodbye, leaving for war, watching everyone die around him. It's cruel, to make him struggle for atonement when it's all he's ever wanted.

Ren straightens her back, somehow more rigid than before. "It's as I've said. Your body will be left to rot as anything else. Your soul will die. You will go nowhere."

His hands shake. He can't breathe. The world spins away from him, his body attached to metal strings, and then he's looking down upon himself from above. Watching how mechanically he moves, how his lips crack open to speak.

"And what of you?" he asks. "You're the god of the forest."

"I'll die too," she says. "My life is irrevocably linked to the forest. If one dies, so will the other."

The hands he stares down at don't belong to him anymore. He's been made wrong. This whole thing is wrong. He's stuck in another nightmare, and he can't wake up.

"Then..." He gasps for air, wetting his lips. "Then, it's better this way." The words don't feel like they should belong to him, but his mouth tastes the same as it always does. He can't find the words to explain that he's doing this for her; to give her back what he stole. Basuin wants to claw his tongue out, feed it to the wolf-man in an offering. *Here, eat the rest of me, too.*

Ren falters, shifting her weight from foot to foot, but her eyes don't leave his.

Coward, the wolf-man laughs at him. It isn't even angry anymore. *Still a scared little boy left alone in the woods.*

"This is the last thing I will do for you, Basuin of Ankor." Her voice is steady, a harder edge than normal. She wields herself like a weapon once again, something he's no longer accustomed to. "We'll go to the elder tree—together."

As her back becomes smaller, and darker, and more distant, Basuin can't bring himself to move. This should be cause for celebration. Basuin finally gets the death he's wished for, the death he's deserved.

But if he doesn't go to the Blacksalt Sea, then it's all been for nothing.

CHAPTER SEVENTEEN

THE MORNING BREAKS sooner than he wished it would. He can't bring himself to tell Yaelic the truth of it, so he doesn't wake the boy. He's too young, too loyal. Bound himself to Bass without a second thought. If Basuin told him, the heartbreak alone would shatter the jade yolk of Yaelic's eyes, and that's too much for him to bear.

Ren's eyes, obsidian and sharp and resentful—almost sad—were heavy enough. Like a chain wrapped around his neck, stealing his last breath.

At the edge of the village, she's waiting for him, along with two spirits more than Basuin bargained for. Ko is draped along Haaman's back, still taller than Bass even with his back hunched. Haaman sees him first, blowing out a harsh breath through their nostrils and looking away. Ko turns at this, and Ren follows suit, and Basuin strides along toward them.

"Captain!"

He curses.

Yaelic barrels toward him, nearly losing his balance, eyes panicked. Behind him, Hami chases after his brother, a righteous anger scrunching his face.

"Captain," Yaelic pants, skidding to a stop before him. "Where—" He gulps down air, hands on his knees. "You're leaving me behind?"

Basuin frowns, but Hami latches onto Yaelic, tugging him away. "You're not taking him again. He doesn't belong to you."

It strikes him now how much older Hami seems than Yaelic. Not taller, but stockier somehow. When Yaelic balls his fists up, it looks petulant. The way Hami stands, one arm hooked around his brother, fingers curled by his side, it radiates a fury that Bass accepts. The sleeves of his robe stop well above his wrists. He's outgrown it already.

"Get off me." Yaelic struggles out from his brother's grasp. "You don't own me either, Hami. I'm going with him."

"You're my brother." Hami wilts, and it's enough that Yaelic finally pushes him off. Hami is bigger than Yaelic, yes, but he's still just a pup. A child who lost his mother and is scared to lose his brother.

"He'll be safe," Basuin says, before he has a chance to consider telling Yaelic to stay. "Yaelic will always have my protection. You have my vow."

But for how long? the wolf-man inside him huffs, rolling onto its back in laughter. Shame burns just below his skin.

"We'll be back," Yaelic tells Hami, shoving his shoulder. "Right?" Now, he looks to Bass, the green of his eyes sparkling with excitement and curiosity. Bass can't say no to that, so he just nods his head. Yaelic, at least, will be back.

As Yaelic skips off to greet Ren, Hami is left staring at Basuin with glassy eyes. "You're our enemy," he seethes. "Don't think I've forgotten."

"I know," Bass answers, biting his tongue.

Hami watches them with sharp eyes as they exit Gyeosi, lingering until the trees swallow them and Hami disappears from sight. Maybe he lingers well after, too. Basuin will never know, but he feels an emptiness settle into his body with every step they take.

"Where are we're going anyway, Captain?" Yaelic asks bright-eyed.

"Away from here," he says. *Away from you*, he hears, from a memory long ago that still tastes like the man he laid with. "To the Crying Trees."

Do you think I have anyone left to go back to?

You think I do? Basuin asked him, kicking at the broken porcelain under his boot that spilled over the tent floor. *Where will you go when we're done?*

Anywhere, Isaniel said. *Away from you.*

YAELIC IS AN unfortunate addition to their party of four. Soon, Basuin learns that Ko volunteered to escort them, dragging Haaman along too. Seeing Ren and Ko together—how she said he was her teacher, and her first friend more than that—creates a strange feeling inside him. It's like seeing a new side of Ren completely. Something not so harsh. Someone who has friends, not only followers. A woman, not just a god.

Basuin isn't sure if Ko and Haaman know why they journey to the Crying Trees. Part of him hopes they don't. A different, raging, tired part of him hopes they do. And that they hate him for it.

He hopes Yaelic will hate him for it, too.

They traverse the forest in near-silence, beyond Yaelic's chattering. Ko walks beside Ren, towering over her but keeping one step behind her, his robes trailing after him. They converse with one another, Ko's head dipping low to Ren's height, but it's so quiet Bass can't make out what they speak of. But sometimes, and only because he's staring, he'll catch the smallest laugh from Ren, the crinkle of her eyes—something Ko has said to make her smile so casually. It twists his gut.

Bass and Haaman, with distance between them, bring up the rear. They don't look at each other. They don't talk to each other. Yaelic runs back and forth between Bass and Ko, his growing legs carrying him with all the energy of a young pup.

"How tall is your tree?" Yaelic asks.

"I am one of the tallest," Ko answers. "My brethren all stand below me, except for the elder tree who connects us all." Ko smiles down at Yaelic, and Bass feels something crawl under his skin. It would warm his nonexistent heart if he wasn't colored by a stroke of envy. He should've been gentler with Yaelic. Now, it'll be Ko entertaining him like this. Good, then.

Basuin can't remember if he was ever soft. Once, though, he washed and combed and braided his mother's hair—he does remember that. When she became too sick to do it herself, too weak to stand for long periods. And then she became too weak to stand at all without Basuin to lean on.

He brings his hand up, studying the lines on his palm and the white scars drawn on the back. His knuckles have seen much violence. Bass remembers using the sharp point of a pocket knife to scrape the blood from beneath his fingernails.

These hands have seen much, and they carry that with him. Not for much longer.

He marches toward death quicker than he planned. At first, he thought it would taste sweet. But it's bitter, and sour, and acidic every time he thinks of it. He doesn't know what he'll do if Ren is right—if he doesn't end up in the Sea.

As the day sloughs on, Bass decides Ko isn't so bad. He's quiet, mostly, but polite. Haaman, he likes less so. They keep silent, but it's different than Ko's quietness. As if in spite. Like they're stonewalling the entire party—Ko, included.

Bass is intrigued by their relationship. An oak and a sparrow seem like a strange partnership. One nests in the crook of the other. One drinks from the ground and the other hunts seed.

Haaman though—he can feel their eyes on him as they walk. As hot as the boiling water the healers scrubbed his wounds in when he returned from Valkesta. When Yaelic runs back and forth to tell him something, to ask them how much further they have to walk, Haaman's eyes are always on Bass. It ignites irritation, like the endless itch of his god mark. The hottest days always made Bass mad, sun boiling him under its gaze. The heat from Haaman's beady eyes doesn't do them any favors.

"What are your nightmares about?" they ask, breaking the silence. Basuin stops in his tracks.

It's okay, you're home, you're all right, Tehali held him in her arms, on the ground of the healing hut, rocking back and forth.

Kill me. He clawed at her, drawing blood and still she wouldn't let go. *Kill me, please*.

When he closes his eyes, he can see them—the black, snowy, bloody scenes from his nightmares. But when he opens his eyes again, he can't remember them at all. Gone, like they never happened.

"Haaman," Ko chides. "You lack manners even around gods, now?"

Haaman stutters. "I didn't mean—"

No one ever means to. But this is the first time someone's asked him such a question. Even Tehali didn't ask him. She strayed from the topic, ran wide berths around it. He should've been more grateful for that.

When Bass looks up, it's not Haaman that's staring anymore. It's Ren, from across the forest. There's no emotion on her face, but her stare is burning. Like he's been set alight, the static of magic running in rivets down his skin. Her eyes are so different than anyone's eyes he's ever seen before.

Every time he looks at her, they're always a different color.

"I lost my squad in battle," he says, not to Haaman, or to anyone else. Just to Ren, whom he keeps gaze with. "We were too far lost in the mountains. I was the only survivor." He would kill to know what Ren thinks of him. Weak, perhaps. A nuisance. If they weren't chained to one another—if the gods hadn't forged this perverse binding between them—she wouldn't give a damn about him. He knows this. She's said it before, washed him in shame from how sharp her hatred was.

But her eyes—her eyes are ever changing. They shift and

shine with the light of the sun and the gleam of the moon. Unreadable, unyielding. But soft, right now, golden and warm like a sunset. Elka, grant him *something*. Anything, because he can't look away from her.

"I'm sorry," Haaman says, and Basuin finally breaks their stare to face Haaman. Even now, Ren's dark eyes don't leave him. The heat of her gaze is heavy and molten along the back of his neck.

"It's all right," Bass answers truthfully. It's all right, but he doesn't know why.

Maybe it's the way Ren is looking at him, because when she turns her back without a word, Bass grits his teeth. Haaman's face is streaked with shame, but they turn to follow Ren, and everyone moves on.

Fine, then. It's better this way. He doesn't want to speak of it. Of the snow he can feel on his back, the blood running rivers through the cracks in his fingers. The wolf-man doesn't have to laugh at him this time. Bass is already laughing at himself, chained, sunk, and drowned by the memories.

We have to go back, Isaniel screamed over the howling winds. *Won't you fucking listen? We have to go back—we're going to die.*

And, as if intended, the wolf-man inside him howls as loud as Isaniel did. Magic pulses hot and alert in his hands. He can feel it, for the first time. He can feel it strain against the rough and scarred skin of his palms, wanting to escape. Wanting to hurt something, to create something. To be wielded.

He makes his fists so tight his blunt nails dig into his flesh, caging that panicked magic away.

"We'll be at the Crying Trees before the sun sets," Ko says, ripping Bass out of his own head. "We've kept good pace."

It hasn't felt like good pace. It's felt like a fight at every step. Maybe that's the wolf-man's fucking claws in his fucking ribcage, or maybe it's the leash that keeps him dragging behind Ren.

He needs to focus on bigger things. On getting to this goddamn elder tree and cutting the wolf-man out of his breast. On dragging his dead, broken body back to Shaelstorm and begging Kensy to get out of the forest.

He needs to focus on anyone but Ren who walks, so confidently, through the forest. If he looks at her, she'll know. Somehow, she always does. But he can't stop himself from looking at her anyway.

She knows his greatest weakness now. His best failure. It's only fair for her to tell him why no one else calls her Ren. Why her name doesn't seem to belong to her. What her greatest failing was, or is, or will be.

But Basuin will never know.

It's Yaelic, in the end, who rips him away from Ren. Bouncing to him, tugging on his breeches, complaining that they left Qia in Gyeosi to help the refugees. It keeps him from the spiral of thoughts Bass gets locked in so easily. Yaelic's a child, just a child, really. Not so unlike Bass, before he grew big and tall and had to duck through the door of their little hut—the doorway he built when he was much smaller.

But Basuin wants Yaelic to grow up strong, like he did. Not because he's alone, but because he has Basuin and Ren and the forest to help him grow stronger. Only, Basuin won't be in that image much longer.

Funny, how fate works. But the wolf-man growls, chewing on his bones, and it isn't so funny then.

CHAPTER EIGHTEEN

THE CRYING TREES are somehow sadder than he imagined. Somehow grand, still. Like Gyeosi, it's made up of a huge network of trees. They branch out to their brethren as if holding hands, standing tall enough to block out the sky. But they weep. Every tree's head is bowed, back broken, leaves falling like tears all over Bass. The crowns all connect in some spiderweb of a way, as if a mother has braided all her daughters' hair together.

He can't stop looking upward. Who are they crying for? It makes something deep in his chest ache like his teeth did when he first bit into a peach pit.

"They are grand," Ko says, standing at his side. He raises a hand and gestures languidly toward the center of the Crying Trees. "From where we began."

And where he ends—a reminder of why he's here. Basuin shudders a breath. "They must be powerful. What magic do they hold?" Even here, where he is soon to die, Basuin tries to figure out Kensy's next steps. If the artifact he's searching for is here at the elder tree.

Ko hums. "Power only matters to humans. Here, we give life. The trees are full of it." When Basuin looks at him, Ko gives him a lazy smile. "There's no magic here for mortals. The elder tree only answers to gods."

Power only matters to humans. How true, and yet how ironic it is all the same. Did he ever care for power when he was human? When he was a soldier?

Basuin stares up at the Crying Trees and loses all sense of time, barely noticing when Ko begins his slow walk back. He wants to cry with them. He misses his mother, and there's nothing here for humans like him—like he used to be. No power, no magic. And nothing here for Kensy to find and break and steal.

Fear grows thick and fuzzy in his throat with each step further into the trees. Guilt, and shame, and—if Basuin was still just a soldier, knee bent to Kensy, would he have come here with hand cannons too? No Ren to stop them, no Ko to tell them there is no power here for mortals? It grows hotter in his chest until Ren approaches his side and everything stills in the radius of her presence.

"I love this forest," Ren says, out of nowhere. A declaration, but softer, said with her full chest. He's always known it. And more than that, this forest loves her back. She's lucky in that way, to love something so fully and to have it love her in the same way. More than loyalty. Less than self-sacrifice.

Her eyes shine with something right on that thin line of love and hatred when he meets her faraway gaze. Basuin didn't know eyes could be that dark and that bright all at once until Ren.

"Are you coming?" Ren asks, shaking him from solitude and forcing him to look. She's standing in that way he's come to know as familiar—her shoulder facing him, turned halfway, eyes locked on him. She's a waif of a god, thin from the side. As sharp as her mind seems to be.

He hates that she's so damn pretty.

"To where?" he asks instead of answering.

Ren stares at him, as if thinking for a hard minute. Then, her gaze falls and her chin drops as she turns her back to him. "I'm taking you to the elder tree."

He freezes. Right. That's what they came here for. All this way for him to see the elder tree, to ask for his godhood to be severed. This isn't a field trip; it's a funeral march. There's nothing left for him here.

If Basuin dies, where does Yaelic—motherless and scared and lonely—go? He'll have to get on his hands and knees and beg Ren to take Yaelic as her charge. If Yaelic doesn't run off into the forest and leave Hami without a brother again. The thought makes his hands sweat, his fingers curling into fists only to stretch out once again to feel something.

He begged for death before, same as he'll go to the elder tree. When Tehali sat by his cot in the healing huts, listening to Bass scream—in pain, in anger, in grief, in rot. She told him he would tear his stitches. He told her to fuck off.

Even now, he tastes blood in his mouth. This time, it's from his teeth biting into his tongue as he stares at Ren. She hasn't moved forward in his hesitance. Gods, he could take her by the shoulders and shake her. Ask her if she feels superior. Ask her if she knows everything, named and bloodied and dead.

Ask her—gods' sake—what will happen to her if the forest is burned to ash. If the legion leaves nothing but black fields in their wake, like the one she cried in for him to see; for him to bear.

"What will you do?" he asks instead. Her hair, cut blunt at her shoulders, wavers like the tears of the Crying Trees, shaken by a sweeping breeze.

And what will you do, Captain? he remembers Isaniel asking, sweat-slick and hot in his refusal to unlatch the tent window. It was a bruising summer night. Basuin doesn't even remember his own reply. Isaniel's words crawled over his naked skin on that night like mosquitos, like mean fingers searching to make new wounds in his flesh.

Here, in the present, Ren quietly asks, "What?"

Basuin takes a step forward. "Will you continue to sabotage

them? The legion. Killing the crops, rotting their food, destroying their weapons—Is that still your plan?"

When they sewed his eye up, they didn't tell him that tears would burn it. Salt in a wound. He hunched over his cot, Isaniel's long-sleeved undershirt strangled between his fingers—two broken, the others scarred.

And what if they surrender to us?

Now, Ren faces him. She raises her chin in defiance, dark eyes holding emotion he doesn't recognize. Her jaw tightens, and Basuin takes another step toward her.

"What will you do?" he repeats himself. "When I am no longer a god and I'm gone."

Will you defy your orders?

Basuin swallows, but he doesn't back down. He takes another step, and another, until she is just out of reach. She's always out of reach, it seems. Right outside the stretch of his fingers.

Ren's eyes narrow. "Things will stay the same, as they always have. We do not need you."

He hears it, her unspoken words: I *do not need you.*

But that's not true. It can't be true. If Ren doesn't need him—if the forest doesn't need him—then he wouldn't have been deified. It wasn't about being a chosen one. It wasn't about power or being god-full or being anything. Basuin is just that—Basuin.

He was deified for a purpose, not for himself.

They do need him. To protect Yaelic, who's entrusted his life to Basuin. To protect Ko, who he hurt, and Haaman, who loves someone as fully as Basuin loved someone before. To protect Hami, who hates him, but loves his brother enough to brave the enemy.

But most of all, to protect Ren. Ren, who loves this forest but doesn't know how to protect it. Ren, who would do anything for her people. Her dedication is strong, but her methods are soft. She truly believes her power can drive off the army, but she's wrong. Dead fucking wrong. Bass knows this because he's been a soldier. The legion was his home.

Starving them out, breaking weapons they can rebuild, sending them nightmares—soldiers have been through worse. He's been through worse. And he still followed his orders.

Not all will surrender, he told Isaniel that night. He remembers it now. He told Isaniel, *Never will they all surrender*.

Above Ren's head, the Crying Trees stretch tall. She looks so small, a figure painted against the backdrop of the forest, planted like a new sapling to grow among this ancient place. But this is her home—these are her people. When she walks through this forest, the trees sway in her stead and the birds in the trees sing to her, and even the breeze offers its worship through her hair.

The Crying Trees bow their heads to her even now, somehow further, leaves entangled and tears weeping, reaching for Ren as if to pull her into their embrace. They're all connected. The tangle of roots running along the ground aren't singular anymore. They don't belong to one tree, but to all.

This forest is all—and not all will surrender. Ren won't. This is her entire world, her family, that risks destruction. Ren loves this forest, and it loves her back.

Basuin can't go. He won't go to the elder tree. He couldn't protect Isaniel, nor the rest of the Valkesta unit, not even his godsdamned mother who he marched to war for. And yet, the gods still asked protection of him.

It's a second chance.

The wolf-man laughs lazily, rolling onto its side. *Humans and their chances. You all think so little of the world.*

Then what is it, if not a second chance?

A command, the wolf-man tells him. *A decree. We've given you a destiny—you should be thankful for it.*

Bass grabs at the front of his shirt, right where the wolf-man resides. It hurts, aches in a way it hasn't before. A destiny. This is what he was built for, where his choices brought him.

"I won't go," he says aloud.

The wolf-man snaps its teeth together, drool dripping from its jaws.

Ren recoils, her sharp eyes going wide at Bass' declaration. He'd give anything to know what she's thinking, what images he would find in her mind. What does she think of him? Behind that steel-forged gaze and those onyx eyes.

Isaniel wasn't like that. He wore every emotion on each facet and plane of his face. Basuin read him well—always.

"You won't go," she repeats his words, slowly, savoring each letter and rolling each word over her tongue.

"No," he says. And he means it this time. He's said no more than he has said yes, which is ironic. A soldier's only words are "Yes" and "Sir." There is no room for "No." And yet, Basuin has said it so many times.

The first time he killed someone. The first time he held someone dying. The day his dagger took the life of a child.

When Isaniel called him a liar. And when Aless asked if they could turn back.

No, no, no—no.

But when he says it now, to Ren, it feels different. They stand, on equal footing, together against the same tide threatening to roll in. With no one else has duty felt so much like a burden, and yet a relief all the same. He's drowning—but he's ducking down under the waves to grab her hand and drown with her.

Ren can't stop Kensy alone.

This is the closest they've been, he and Ren. She doesn't smell of the dirt coating her legs or the blood which once stained her shirt. It's sweat and it's white lilies and it's something else he can't name. Ren's face, once blank, shapes into something new. Confusion, laced with anger.

"I took you all the way here, and now you won't see the elder tree." Her voice is steady, but the cadence of it leaves him uneasy.

As if Ren did it out of the kindness of her own heart. He almost says it to her. Baits her response. But he locks a fist around it and hides it away.

"I've changed my mind," he says.

"And why is that?" Ren says, voice coated in venom.

Bass doesn't even know the answer. It's all jumbled up inside him, and if he could reach into his chest and force his hands into the wolf-man's cavity, maybe he could unravel it all and answer her.

He hangs his head, unable to hold Ren's intense gaze any longer. "I won't be the cause of someone else's death," he says. Not again.

It's so quiet, this moment between them, despite all the life that lives in the forest. Things that live are loud. Things that are dead speak in whispers, and he and Ren both speak low.

"You won't come back to life," she tells him.

"I know," he says.

"You will still be the Wolf God."

"I know."

"And you would accept such a sentence?" she asks, as though it were heavier than death. But Basuin is already dead, and he should've died many moons ago, and he still dreams of dying. But his death means Yaelic's. His death is the death of Ren.

"I'm a soldier," Bass answers. When his gaze finds Ren, her visage has fallen into something that makes him ache. Raw confusion, unmasked.

Softly, Ren says, "You're a god."

Bass' lip curls in a smile. "That, too."

Once again, Ren rears back, but this time it's completely different than before. Her twilight eyes hold something new—the smallest hint of fear. She shifts from foot to foot as if something has uprooted her.

Before she can say anything, or dance away as she so often does, Bass speaks. "I'll help you."

Ren bristles, her shoulders rising like the hackles of a caged dog.

He takes another step forward. "You told me that you can't fight an army. But I can—and I have. The sabotage—it won't keep them at bay forever, Ren."

The taste of her name is biting but sweet, almost as much as the shock that strikes her face. It's the first time he's thought to use it. To call her that. But by now it feels familiar, and it feels right.

She takes a long breath, staring down at the dirt beneath their feet. A long moment stretches out between them and Bass can almost see the link of their magic. Blue is tangled around her hand, wrist twined by her magic. And from his fingers, twisted and biting into his skin, red magic drips from his arm.

They meet in the middle, running taut and purpling as they reach one another. The color of bruises, he first thinks. Then, the color just before dawn.

Finally, Ren sighs. "I'm not too proud to admit that I can't do this alone. I may not like it, but you're right. The forest needs you."

Bass pretends not to hear her say *the forest* rather than herself.

"But," she says, "I do not want war."

He nearly bashes his head in. They had been making progress, finally, until that. They can't win without war. He can't protect the forest—the people he's grown soft for—without war. Ren doesn't understand that her pacifist tactics won't work.

Instead, he says, "We'll figure it out." Bass was never good with strategy, but he's always been good at killing. "I'll help you. I'll help protect the forest."

Ren looks at him, eyes wary. But she does take a step toward him, and if he wasn't so dutifully trained, his lips might've turned up into a smile. It's as if he's trying to befriend a skittish woodland animal. A doe. If he makes any sudden movements, she'll retreat as quickly as she came.

"I promise," he tells her, holding out his hand to her.

After a long pause, Ren reaches out and places her hand in his—not in a shake, but as a princess might give her hand to a knight. As if in a fairytale, he almost moves to kiss the smooth skin she's bared to him.

She has such a small hand. And yet she commands this entire forest, him included.

The wolf-man whines, nudging Basuin with its nose as if to press him closer to Ren.

It makes Bass smile, and he bows his head slightly to Ren. This is new to him, but everything in his body is screaming at him that this is right. No longer is he a soldier following orders, taking commands. He's a god, and so is Ren, and this is a partnership.

They'll protect the forest—together.

As he looks up, his eyes fall on her lips. Ren opens her mouth to speak, and then her eyes go wide and she spits blood. It dribbles down her chin as she chokes.

"Ren," he gasps.

Then, she collapses, and Bass goes down with her, cradling her body to his.

From the trees and in a flourish of green light, Qia bursts into the clearing. Tears are smeared across her cheeks, crystals in her eyes. She pants, her whole body shaking.

"Gyeosi is burning," she says. Qia falls to her knees, looking at Basuin like he's the last savior of the forest.

CHAPTER NINETEEN

SMOKE AND GUNPOWDER and everything he hates—it's choking him.

Gyeosi really is burning. Fire streams out of the hand cannons carried by legion soldiers, the same ones Kensy wielded. The pop-click-boom of rifles fills the air, screams and war cries the accompaniment. Orange and green should not mix. The flames swallow the forest until the canopy drips with hot black pitch.

Black Wolf, Black Wolf. He wants to vomit all his guts up and wash the floor with them.

Ren's blood soaks his hands, illuminated brilliantly in the face of the fire. He doesn't remember how he got here. An aching howl, a scream vibrating through his bones until his vision lost color and the forest became a blur. His joints breaking and reforming as he sprinted toward Gyeosi—riding on the winds of forest magic.

Beside him stands Yaelic, a steeled look on his face that speaks to the stubbornness of children. Bass kneels before him, hands swallowing Yaelic's shoulders as he gives the boy a shake.

"Listen to me." Bass holds Yaelic's green-eyed gaze. "You stay away from the fighting. Grab anyone you can, get them out of here, but stay away from the soldiers. You hear me?"

Yaelic nods, and Bass gives him another hard shake.

"Don't go near them. Grab who you can and go to the creek." Yaelic nods again, but it's not enough. "Do not go near those soldiers, Yaelic."

"I won't," Yaelic promises, eyes big and wide and terrified. That stubbornness is gone. "I promise, Captain, I won't. I'll grab the spirits and I'll go to the creek."

Bass gives him a hard nod. "That's right. Now go," he says, and he releases Yaelic from his grasp to stand. Yaelic hesitates, staring up at Bass, but then he turns and he runs toward the north side of the village.

Gods, protect him.

The wolf-man doesn't have to rip its teeth into Basuin for him to know he's too late. He swore to protect this forest too late.

He's never been too late before. Bass was never one to turn down a fight.

Haaman darts into his vision, something half human and half spirit, landing on their feet. Feathers cover the backs of their arms where their scars line their skin, silver and sharp and glinting with the light of the fire that burns Gyeosi. They look back at him as if waiting.

Bass unsheathes his sword, giving it a swing to remember its weight in his hand. His fingers adjust, his grip is strong. Wordlessly, he charges first, toward the growing flames, and Haaman follows. Their steps are so light they look like they're still flying. Bass feels like he's flying, too. This is a homecoming; this is where he belongs.

He strikes first dishonorably—a soldier whose back is turned—sword run through the gut. And next, another who turns at the scream of death and rushes Bass, with a sharp swing to the neck. Bass kicks the body away as the head rolls.

Haaman, not too far away, fights with their whole body. It's all fast lunges and quick dodges and swift, cutting movements that leave soldiers falling at Haaman's feet, dead. Those silver feathers are hard spines, now covered in a viscous red.

Other spirits fight alongside them, and he shouldn't be surprised but he is. They fight for their home, too. Basuin has seen so much rebellion before, but never on this side. Not until now.

The flames only grow as Basuin shoulders his way through the legion, his sword leaving bodies in his wake. It's hot here—sweat drips from his hairline. The smoke makes everything hard to see. Coughing, wheezing as he ducks a backhanded dagger. Hacking and spitting right after he disarms a man with a pistol.

It feels like too much. But a surge of something burning red and dark wraps him up in its clutches until it physically aches. God magic, filling him to the brim, fueling him. Basuin shatters through the ranks of Xalkhan soldiers, breaking each one that comes within reach. He cannot see. Blinded by smoke and rage and the image of the wolf-man as it moves within him. It doesn't matter—his body moves through the battlefield as if he's walked it a million times, because he has. Because he's trained to be a warrior.

Basuin is strong again, as strong as he once was when soldiers, allies and enemies alike, cowered beneath his shadow.

This is just like Valkesta, fucking Valkesta all over again. As strong as he is, and as he was, it never changes the outcome. He acted selfishly. His want for death, to ask the elder tree to sever his tie to godhood, resulted in this.

Gyeosi burns because his anger dragged the Forest God away. He was deified to protect them. He failed again.

Selfish bastard. He marched his own squad up the Valkesi Mountains to save one soldier—one they had lost due to his own fault. When the Grimmalians took Tomaas, Bass claimed there was no choice. No soldier left behind. He wasn't willing to lose someone else.

Basuin knew it was a trap and he still led his squad to death. Gods damn him.

He braces his foot against a legion soldier's shoulder blades for leverage as he yanks his blade from the soldier's spine. Blood blooms across the man's back, seeping out from underneath his armor. Ren's body looked just like his.

It invades his mind, the warmth of her blood on his hands. How pale her olive skin looked under the light of day. Red is not a color he thinks of when he conjures the image of Ren in his head. He thinks of blue, and forest greens, and white. Not the red that trickled down her nose and marred her chin.

Ko promised they would help her; take her to Hou-tou, who could heal even the worst of wounds. Basuin doesn't even know what happened to her, what injured her.

Whatever they did to her, they'll pay for it.

A howl builds in his chest. A compulsion to throw his head back and cry for blood. The veins in his neck pulse, a heart beating. A heart he doesn't own anymore. The wolf-man is loud enough for the both of them.

When he razed Ulenski to the ground, there was nothing left but soot and ash—no survivors. His bronze skin was painted in black, eyes wild and boots covered in offal. Far beyond, on an overlook jutting out from the Valkesi Mountains, a black wolf howled to its moon-mother.

Before he slaughtered them, the soldiers called it an omen. And when they died, they called him the Black Wolf.

You gave them a chance, Kensy lied to him. *But if you had given them two, you might have lost. Remember that, Black Wolf*, Kensy said with his unkind smile.

This time, he watches the men who were cut from the same cloth as he razes this village to the ground instead. His arms are covered in soot and ash and blood. But this time, there are survivors—only none belong to the legion.

Kensy was kind enough to warn Basuin—and Basuin wasn't smart enough to trust him. He knew, just like he knew about Valkesta. But he never learns.

Burning Gyeosi just like he burned Yaelic's den. Kensy will

set this whole forest aflame to find what he's searching for, whatever that may be. If the gods refuse to answer him, then the gods themselves must burn.

Somewhere behind them, to the north, a wolf howls. He turns, a cold shot of fear striking through him. Yaelic.

Without warning, Haaman muscles him out of the way and shields themself with their bloodied wings, blocking an attack meant for Basuin. He whirls around Haaman and dispatches the soldier with a clean, upward arc of his longsword.

"They won't fucking die," Haaman says through gritted teeth. "There's too many, and the fires—"

"We'll fight until they fall," he says, adjusting his grip on his sword's hilt. It's sticky with blood and sweat. "Go to the creek, with Yaelic."

He doesn't mean it as a slight, but Haaman thrusts their arms out and the spiny feathers covering their skin seem to flex and harden again.

"Not a chance," they say, and then they run back into the fray.

He follows, content to do the same—and then the howl of agony becomes the scream of a child.

"*Hami!*"

Basuin sprints toward Yaelic. That scream is a command, as powerful a guide as the magic linking him to Ren. He clears the battlefield, what used to be a village, charging through the army.

And there sits Yaelic, in the middle of the fighting, on his knees in front of an unmoving body. *No.*

But then there's a soldier, sword raised above his head, glinting like a guillotine about to drop upon Yaelic's neck.

No.

Inside him, the wolf-man breaks its own spine to contort into the shape of Basuin's ribs. Its bones drive into his bones, its blood becomes his own. And its fury, not so unlike the boiling in Basuin's gut, races up his throat until the veins in his neck thicken and pulse. His whole body burns with god magic.

The scar of his god mark burns. The wolf-man growls and rises onto both hind legs, sharp claws embedded into all Basuin's organs as it snaps its teeth, hungry for violence.

He feels it in his left palm, a pulsating heat that grows until his fingers are tight around the soldier's neck, god mark searing into the man's flesh as a brand. Bass takes the soldier's head and bashes it into his knee, and the force, backed by magic, ends the man's life and he crumples in Bass' hold. Bass tosses him away. He reaches for Yaelic.

At his touch, Yaelic screams. Jade eyes wide, tears streaming down his face, jaw unhinged. Boyish hands covered in familiar blood.

Fire rages around them, soldiers and spirits clashing. The air shifts and Basuin turns out of instinct alone to skewer a man on his sword. And another. And then another, before he can fire a bullet from his gun.

He walks circles around Yaelic and the limp, white body draped over the boy's legs, killing soldiers before they can kill first. Acting as a barrier between the battlefield and this bubble of grief Yaelic rests in. The boy is still screaming. Howling, staring empty-eyed at his brother.

Basuin kills them all. He takes, and he takes, and he takes—just as he was taught. *There is no god of death*, his mother once told him. *That belongs to us mortals.*

The spirits who are left alive bring water from the creek to stamp out the rest of the fire. Basuin fights the ache of his muscles as he yanks his sword from the last body, hand trembling from exhaustion. Beside him, Haaman's feathers are gone, replaced by blood that's still damp on their skin. There's a pain in their beady black eyes that speaks to the carnage and loss as they walk through the village, checking the bodies of soldiers to confirm they are all dead. There is so much blood. Too much of it.

But it floods Gyeosi—what's left, at least. Red is washed away by the creek water, but not enough of it. It stains the forest floor.

Yaelic doesn't move, nor speak, when Basuin crouches beside him. He sits kneeled amidst the sea of bodies, shaking, white fur laid across his lap. It looks like the white clothes of Ren, always clean and never stained somehow.

Hami's fur is soft, warm, and still. Basuin's god mark burns as he lifts Hami's head, black eyes open, and glazes over with a film of tears. Then, a red glow encases its body, magic pouring from his hand into Hami, and a spirit rises from it. Yaelic is washed in red, head tipped up to look, the splatter of blood across his face blending into his skin in the glow of magic.

Hami, small and scared, stands in front of them now. His hands, the hands of a child, are balled into fists. Basuin might hurl. Hami's eyes, shades darker than his brother's, are stricken with fear and pain. His mouth parts as he shakes.

"I'm dead," he whispers. "I think I'm dead."

A crushing pain fills his chest as he reaches, hands coated in red magic, for Hami. Tears spill down Hami's cheeks and catch on Basuin's thumbs.

"I'm scared."

"I know," he says, voice low. "It's all right."

Hami cries into his dirtied hands, eyes shut tight. Basuin doesn't hush him. He holds Hami through it, wiping away as many tears as he can, as the boy sobs through his own death.

"I'm sorry," he tells Hami. If he was any better with words, had any sort of brain in his head, he's sure he could come up with something better to say. But he can't. And truly, he's sorry.

And then Yaelic howls. His scream is so guttural it's inhuman—all animal and all newborn and all man and all pain. Excruciating.

Yaelic falls onto his hands in front of Hami's spirit, bawling. "No!" he cries, barely breathing. "Hyung! Please, Hyung, no—I can't, I can't, I can't." He reaches for Hami's ankle, for anything to hold onto, but his hand passes right through the spirit. Elbows in the dirt, Yaelic crawls toward his brother, begging over and over and over.

This was the duty Basuin ignored. The command he shrugged off. Soldiers do what they are told. Gods are given duties—things to protect, things to grow, things to harvest. Basuin should've been here, in Gyeosi with Ren, protecting the forest from his people.

Protecting Hami from his own comrades.

Hami was innocent in the way that only children can be. No weight of the world to carry on their shoulders, no blood wrung from their hands. But still, the dead body of Hami is laid at his feet, fur stained with blood and soot, and the spirit that's left of him wavers cool under Bass' burning hands.

"Will you take care of him?" Hami asks, eyes sheltered by fat tears. "I'll have Mama. But Yaelic's never been alone before."

"Yes," Basuin answers. "I swear it." There's a weakness in his voice. Something so quiet beneath Yaelic's grief.

Then, Basuin's hands begin to slip through Hami's image, just as Yaelic's had, and he yanks them away like he's caught fire. A shake in his bones, fingers growing cold to touch.

"Will Am-sa walk me?" Hami wipes his eyes with his fists. "To the Winter River?" His spirit fades more every second.

He feigns a grasp on Hami's narrow shoulders, fingers trembling just above the boy's waning form. If he still has a heart, he swears there's a weight tied to it trying to drown him. He's sinking, like his palms sink into the silhouette of Hami's arms if he isn't careful.

"She isn't here right now," he says. "I'm sorry."

Hami, so young and so strong yet, shakes his head. "I'm glad. Am-sa would've been hurt."

His chest aches. Ren is hurt. Her blood, and Hami's too, is on Basuin's hands.

"Would you…" Hami struggles. "Would you walk me, then? To find Mama?" Despite knowing him as an enemy,

Hami asks his last request with a shy innocence that any child would. Because what child wants to die alone? No human being, no spirit, wants to die alone.

But Basuin hangs his head. This hurts worse than if someone ran him through with his own sword. Worse than when the wolf-man shoved its claws inside of him and carved out a home as if he was a pig made for stuffing. To be eaten. If Basuin of Ankor ever cried, he would cry now.

He wets his dry lips and meets Hami's eyes. The boy is fading into the background, lost to the burned remains of Gyeosi surrounding them.

"I can't, Hami." He squeezes the boy's nonexistent shoulders. "I have to stay with Yaelic." All lies. He doesn't know where it is; doesn't know how to be a god. Lying to a dead boy, how cruel. "But your mama will find you, I promise."

At the sound of Yaelic's name, Hami smiles, his cheeks all round and full and pressing his eyes into thin, tearful things.

"Then I'm happy," Hami says. "I'm happy—I get to see Mama, and Yaelic won't be alone. Thank you, Wolf God." He bows his head, wheat-brown hair covering his eyes. "Tell him goodbye for me, please."

Basuin falls, sitting back on his heels and staring at the forest floor. His hands are outstretched before him, weak and empty. His god mark sits in his palm, black.

"I will," he says, but Hami has long been gone.

Yaelic falls atop his brother's body and screams into bloodied fur. But dead bones barely muffle his cries. He sobs upon Hami's body and Basuin lays a hand on his shoulder to pull Yaelic into an embrace.

He hopes they found each other, Hami and their mother.

Basuin reaches up to his neck, dirty fingers clutching his mother's godstone. He'd do anything to hear her voice. Just one more time would be enough. To hear her call Basuin her son again.

I'll miss you, my Basuin, she said when he stood before her in the uniform the legion provided him.

I'll be back as Officer Basuin, he told her, proud and also not so proud. His mother simply smiled at him, in that kind and consuming way she always did, patting his hand.

And yet, you'll always be my son, she said.

If he had never marched off to war, would someone like Ren have walked him to the Winter River, to see his mother again?

Ren sneaks up on him, her gentle hand falling to his shoulder. The quiet of it makes him jump, neck snapping to look up at her. Those eyes of hers, dark and knowing, could haunt him. It isn't hollow, that kind of sadness. It's so full and pure and it lives in him as much as it lives in her.

She leans her weight onto him, using his shoulder to hold herself up. Her head falls, as though she can no longer hold it up herself. Bass shoots to his feet, wrapping an arm around her, and she slumps into the shelter of him. She's sweating, the sickly coat of it making her blunt bangs stick to her forehead.

"I came too late," she says, eyes closed and head fallen to his shoulder.

"So did I," he murmurs. If only he could kiss her head, wipe the sweat from her brow, and banish her sorrows away. But he cannot, so he holds Ren in the aftermath of destruction, staring into the forest.

You see it now, the wolf-man says—not a question.

Basuin does. He sees it now.

CHAPTER TWENTY

THERE ARE NO homes left here for a funeral. Everything has been burned, and what hasn't is torn to the ground out of love. All who are left strip Gyeosi of everything it was as if they can cleanse it. But there is too much blood and too much ash. Still, the living take their loved ones down to the creek to wash their bodies. There is no rice to give them before they are buried, so they are buried with orchids and lilies and yarrow growing from their mouths.

There are still villagers out there now, crying. An older sister lying atop her younger sister's grave, clutching her chest, screaming. "Ya!" she sobs, clawing at the fresh dirt. "Answer me! Where are you going? Not without me—not without me, please," she begs.

Basuin never cried, but when he brought Isaniel back with him in pieces to bury, Kensy gripped his shoulder so hard it smarted and bruised. Soldiers don't cry. Soldiers move on, or they die in Valkesta, or they are sent across the sea to a new continent as punishment.

It wasn't just punishment. Kensy meant to use him—to manipulate the only man he knew to still worship the gods. Kensy's always used Basuin because Basuin's always let him. And now, he fears what Kensy looks for in this forest. He fears what Kensy will do if he finds any gods left here.

He fears for Ren. Because if she knows where that godly artifact hides, then Kensy won't hesitate to kill her, too. Kensy warned him the first time and Basuin didn't listen.

Ren is weak. Her clothes are stained red and her magic wanes—he can feel the loss of it. He's the one that took it, again. And again. And now—and again.

Among the remains of her village, Ren sits in the charred hollow of a tree that once held the homes of spirits, legs folded beneath her. Even when she couldn't find the strength to walk the lingering spirits of the dead to the Winter River, Ren didn't cry. She sits in her calm demeanor before those who are left, red mottled skin peppered with blisters and burns.

"You will leave," she tells them, "and you will never come back here."

There are gasps and tears among the villagers and Basuin swallows back bile.

"There is nothing left here for you," she continues. "The army has come, and they will come again. They will destroy this forest if they aren't stopped, so you must leave." For a moment, Ren's eyes drop, only to find the crowd once again. "There is still time. Go to the north—there are villages there where you will be safe. We will slow them down, push them back."

"But will you stop them?" a woman shouts from the crowd, her face screwed up and stricken. "Must we die for this?"

Someone yanks on the woman's arm, shaking her to stop. Bass feels his legs start to move, to shield Ren and to speak in her stead. It's automatic; he won't let another spirit hurt her for his crimes. But as if Ren senses it, her hand halts him.

"How are we supposed to believe going north will save us?" someone else, someone younger, yells. "You don't even know how to stop them!"

"I've not led you astray before. But I can't promise you anything, either," she says truthfully. "All we can do is try."

Behind the crowd, in the trees, Ko pulls Haaman into his embrace, folding them into his long swathes of sleeves. Bass should look away, but his eyes linger. From this distance, the image of them together is blurry. It makes something deep in his stomach ache.

There is silence, and no one moves until Ren speaks again.

"I am sorry," she says, though it's quieter than the rest of her words have been. A wave of crying ripples through the spirits, some bowing their heads and some hanging their heads and some leaned back and wailing for their dead.

One man stands, and he bows with his whole body to Ren. "Thank you, Am-sa."

Ren closes her eyes and bows her head back to him. She doesn't speak, but Bass reads her lips. The magic thread between them, linking their fingers from afar, pulses.

"Do not thank me."

She sits there, even as people begin to leave. Even as the dead are brought from the creek and buried in the shallow graves that have been cut to size. Even when Ko and Haaman disappear into the forest, saying they'll be back at dawn. Even when Yaelic stops crying after Hami's grave is covered, Qia hugging him and helping him back to the hut.

She sits there, and Basuin stands beside her, a stone guardian at her side. He'll be the last.

IT'S ONLY ONCE the moon has risen to the center of the sky, a sliver of it left, to signal that the darkest night is on its way, that Ren unfurls her limbs from the hollow of the tree. Bass reaches for her hands and catches her as she stumbles on weak knees. Her fingers dig into his arms and her weary body trembles in his grasp.

"I don't know what to do anymore," Ren whispers to him. It makes her seem so small, so vulnerable. Bass thought she would die at the Crying Trees when he left her. Even now, she's pained, skin fragile and chilled to the touch. Only the places where she's burned still hold a heat unlike any other.

"We'll figure it out," he says. "I told you that. We'll figure it out, once you've healed."

Ren laughs, cut and dry and sour and not at all sweet and church bells and starlight like he once heard before. "I may not heal this time," she says. "I may never heal from this." Her words are biting, coated in poison he could lick from her teeth.

"How were you hurt?" he asks, eyes drawn over the marks littering her body. He saw it before—the way she bled from her arm, the way blisters crawled across her skin.

"Gyeosi burned," she says, as if it makes sense. As if all the times he's seen her—cut and burned and bruised and hurt—should make sense. Wounds he could not place. Things she refused to say.

Gyeosi burned and Ren hurt for it.

The wolf-man snaps its teeth around his rib and Basuin feels all the force of it. The sharp pain throws him and he almost falters as he guides Ren toward the creek. He's stupid. He's so stupid—all fight and no strategy, Kensy said. *But my hand will guide you steady into the battle, and we will find victory together, Basuin.*

"The forest," he says, looking at her. "It hurts you."

Ren doesn't look back at him. "The forest and I are one."

It makes him ache. He's frozen, and Ren takes it upon herself to take a step forward without him. But she falls, catching herself on a tree before he can sweep her back under the stability of his arm. Now, she looks at him, and her eyes are silver in the light of the moon above them, something precious. Ren holds out her hand, and he takes it, and then she presses her right palm against the bark of a tree and a burst of blue magic fills the night.

Ren burns a hole through the tree, sap dripping like lava from its orifices. A burn, red and angry, crawls over the skin of Ren's forearm.

"I told you." Her face is grim. "When the forest dies, so will I."

KNEELING AT THE bank of the creek, Basuin washes Ren's burns with a fraying rag. He tries to be gentle—as gentle as his big, clumsy fingers can be—but anger simmers in his blood. Ren is quiet and still, watching as he cares for her wounds.

"Don't do that again," he scolds.

As he turns to dip the rag into the clean water again, Ren says, "I won't."

The wolf-man is restless inside him and Bass feels it. His fingers twitch under the pressure to be soft and caring, which he hasn't practiced for a very long time. Bass isn't soft, he isn't sweet. He is strong, and he is a soldier. But right now, he would rather be nothing at all.

When he fishes out a roll of bandages from his pack, fumbling with it as he unrolls it, he tries to remember who always wrapped his wounds. Sometimes, he ripped the gauze with his own teeth. Other times, it was the nurses in the healing huts.

But when Isaniel shared his tent, slept in the same cot, he always turned his back to Bass. He never watched when Bass rinsed blood from his hands in the water basin and wrapped his sprains out in the field. No matter what it was, Isaniel did not look at him.

His fingers shake from the work of being gentle as he wraps white bandages around the burn Ren suffered from her own hand.

"It doesn't hurt," she says.

"Liar," he says, jaw tight and aching. How stupid he was, stubborn. It's what burned Gyeosi down. It's what killed his squad, in Valkesta. His own boar-headedness. Regret tastes like whiskey and smoke and blood, and it makes his head swim.

Bass runs his thumb over the gauze, over the burn he hopes won't scar. Her body doesn't carry the white lines marking his bronze skin, the remains of war. She's fragile, but smooth like silk. Tough, then. Delicate but strong. He feels it in the muscle running under her skin, sinew and bone.

"We have to stop him," Bass says, turning to wash his hands in the creek. It's cold against his hot palms, against his burning god mark.

"Him?" Ren asks, falling back to sit on the rocky shore.

Bass curses at his thoughtless wording. He should've said the legion. "My commander." He does the same, sitting on the bank with a grunt. "The legion's. Commander Kensy." Bass can't help but say his name with something violent in his voice.

Ren draws her knees to her chest. "He brought the army here?"

"Yes."

"He brought you here, too."

Bass picks up a rock and skips it over the surface of the water. "Yes." But it'd be so much easier if he could say it was the ocean. That Ithika carried him here. It would feel better than to say that a godless man dragged him onto a godless boat which sailed to a god-full island in search of quest and conquest.

Ren is quiet, so he speaks instead, skipping another black flat rock. "Kensy is the one who wanted us to sail here. Colonize the land and turn it into another Xalkhan territory. As if we haven't taken enough land for the queen already."

Kensy's search for this godly artifact—it makes his mouth taste rotten. He should tell Ren, and his tongue runs over the back of his teeth trying to come up with the right words. But he fears for Ren. Basuin fears implicating her, more than he already has by being here.

If Ren were to know—if she were to try and stop Kensy—she'd end up dead.

Bass thought there would be no more bloodshed after Grimmalia. Naivety, or maybe exhaustion. Maybe he thought the world would stop when he died, and then he did not die, and then the world did not stop. Pity, that. Both the not dying and the not stopping.

The world felt like it stopped when he shook the godstone out of the letter wrapped in twine that wrote condolences. His mother was dead. But the world did not stop, for the legion nor for him.

Let me go home, to Ankor. Just to bury my ma, he pleaded with them.

And when they denied him, molten metal crawled through his veins, a slow drip driving him into insanity with every step he took, fleeing into the forest. Like plunging his whole hand into a bucket of liquid iron until it was so dead and numb that each pinprick of pain was drawn out, until he collapsed on his hands and knees as the rain came down on him, and he bowed his head against the ground, forehead to the tree's roots in prayer.

Ma's dead, he spoke to the gods who he had never spoken to before. *My ma's dead.*

Bass squeezes his mother's stone so tightly in his hand that he could crush it; to see if it'll cut into his hardened, calloused palm. The one not scarred with a god mark already. He tugs at it hard enough the leather tie will snap. But it never does, not through all his battles and not now.

"He's the one that will burn this forest to the ground," he says, without mention of Kensy's search. A choice, to protect her.

Ren stares off at the creek, glittering under the moon. When he blinks, he sees her covered in blood, and he blinks and blinks and blinks until she is clean of it. Until her skin is the same as it was before and the vision is gone.

"I don't know how to stop him," she says.

Bass laughs, shaking his head. "Me either."

"But we'll do it together?" Ren asks, looking at him with those twilight, silver, golden, everything eyes. He could look at her eyes until the end of time, in every color they wear.

"Together," he says. "I promised you."

Ren smiles, and it's shy but it's real. Her cheeks are round when she smiles, not so severe anymore. Not so godly. When she smiles like that, she looks like a woman. A woman not covered in blood and burns and god marks. It makes his chest fill with something incomparable to anything he's felt before.

The wolf-man's tail thumps quick inside of him, like the beat of his heart long gone.

It's what makes Basuin grab the jade around his neck and pull it over his head—the first time he's taken his mother's godstone off since he received it. The leather string is worn, by time and oil and blood and gunpowder. Worried until it's been frayed, and then worried more until soft.

That stone feels like it's a part of him, like it belongs to him now more than it does the ghost of his ma. She's in the River now, and this stone has never been a connection to the gods, but a reminder that his mother was real. She was real.

Basuin kneels before Ren, crowning her with his mother's godstone and slipping it over her head until it rests along her neck. It hangs lower on her, marking her collarbone, but it fits in the groove there perfectly. The hollow of Basuin's throat feels empty; weightless.

Ren's eyes are big, wide and as silver as the dishware served in the palace he's only been invited to as a hero. His fingers itch to feel the plane of Ren's cheek, to learn if it's soft like fresh snow or if it's as hard as tungsten. Would this war forge Ren into a weapon?

No, he won't allow it. And so his fingers ghost over her cheek. She closes her eyes at the touch, but doesn't flinch.

He was right—it's all silk.

"Your mother's," Ren remembers, and Basuin nods. "You

can't give this to me." Her voice holds an ache in it, unfamiliar and unripe.

He almost laughs at how concerned Ren grows, but he smiles instead. "Hold onto it for me, then."

"Why?" she asks. Basuin lets his fingers find the jade stone where it hangs from her neck, running his thumb on a facet that feels new, unexplored.

"Because I promised to protect you," he says, and he bows his head to her. Basuin brings the godstone to his lips, wishing he could imbue it with all the magic his mother could when she kissed it in prayer.

Basuin looks up at Ren, at her glassy eyes and her parted lips, and she meets his gaze with awe.

"It's only fair you protect something of mine, too," he tells her, and his lips curl into a grin. It almost falls when he realizes he hasn't worn such a smile in a long, forgotten time. "And now you'll know I won't be far."

If Ren calls for him, he'll be there. They'll go together—they'll figure this out together.

When Basuin pulls away, Ren's face wears a bruise the size of a fist and a smattering of freckles in the form of blood. He blinks, and he blinks, and he blinks until it's gone again. He won't let it happen again. Won't let her blood stain his hands again.

She's too good for that, too good to hurt for the sins of men who leave no fruit for gods. Too good to hurt for someone like him, who always brings war. Death rides on the hem of his shirt, on the heels of his boots.

Ren stays quiet, and that's all right. Basuin lets the godstone rest on her skin once again, fingers brushing against her collarbone by accident as he pulls away. Under the dark light of the moon, Ren's cheeks color like a peach and it makes something in his chest feel white hot.

They sit in that moment forever, staring at one another. Basuin listens to the sounds of the forest, so loud in his ears but as gentle as the lap of the creek's water across the stones in its bed. A dragonfly, buzzing in time with every breath he takes, flits over each silver lining that trails downstream.

But then the treetops shake and a flock of birds, black as the night, rush through the sky with a flap of their wings. They create a gust of wind that vibrates through the leaves of the forest's canopy, screeching and squawking as they fly away from the burned grounds of Gyeosi and toward the north.

He wonders if they're saying their goodbyes.

"We need to go," Ren finally says, eyes raised to the sky and trailing after the birds.

Basuin nods and reaches a hand down to her to help her off the ground. Instinctively, his arm winds around her waist to hold her steady, and their eyes meet once more. He opens his mouth to say something, but hears the rustle of feet on forest floor, of long robes brushing past foliage. He turns his head toward the sound, holding Ren closer to him.

But it's only Ko who appears from the thick wooded forest, long strands of black hair falling over his shoulders and robes askew as if he hurried here.

"We must leave Gyeosi now," Ko says. "More are coming."

CHAPTER TWENTY-ONE

As Ren commanded, they move north. Rain comes to wash away the horrors of Gyeosi, but when it falters, all it leaves behind is smoke coloring the skies in the same dreary gray. They've spent these last days gaining distance, but they need time to plan their next steps. Ren needs time to rest—her wounds from Gyeosi's attack still haven't healed.

"There is a village not much further we can rest at," Ko tells them as they travel. "I have an old friend there."

Basuin tries to keep count of the days. How many days has it been since he's been a god? More than he can count on all his calloused fingers, smeared with dirt and soot. He's been a man for ten thousand days, and now—now Basuin will be a god for much longer than that. Bound by duty, not fate.

It's been two days since Gyeosi burned, and when Basuin crawls into his bedroll on the eve of the third day, Yaelic is already asleep, breathing slow through his mouth. That gold-white hair of his reminds Bass so much of the slender soldier he first saw dressed in a forest-green tunic, laughing over a mug of ale with his buddies in the tavern, right before Isaniel was assigned to his fleet. Those clay-colored eyes, baked into hardened brick, challenging Bass to come over and join them for drinks.

He didn't, not that night. Regret grows in his gut as the

image of Isaniel's rage-stained eyes flashes in his mind. The smash of the porcelain carafe as Isaniel threw him into the table it sat upon, falling to the ground.

If you won't listen to me as a soldier, Isaniel shouted, *then listen to me as a man.*

Basuin shuts his eyes and tries to sleep.

But you won't listen to anyone, Isaniel hissed. *You didn't even listen to your own mother.*

Go to sleep, go to sleep, for the morning will come and the monsters will be gone. Go to sleep, my son.

And the morning of the third day does come, but unlike his ma told him, the monsters aren't gone. The rains slowed them, yes, but it will not stop them from marching forward. If the storms that the gods bring won't stop the legion, then it will have to be them—the Forest God and the Wolf God.

It's the spirits who have gone. They've outrun the monster. The village they traveled toward is empty, left behind in a hurry. Straw huts and tents are disheveled. Blankets and clothes and children's toys forgotten. No one roams here. Ko's friend can't be found. Everyone is gone.

"They left," Haaman says, even as they all stare at the same wreckage.

Qia picks up a colorful ball, dented and losing leaking air. Yaelic looks over the smudges of soot and dirt, frowning.

"It's for the best," Ko says. He looks to Ren, as if waiting for her approval.

But Ren says nothing. She squeezes the flesh of her bicep and turns away. Unable to look at the evidence of the danger that trails behind them. The army will come here, too. It really is for the best that they left.

"We'll make camp here, then," Bass decides for her. No one speaks, not at all.

"Of course, Am-ga." Ko bows his head before turning and motioning the children forward.

Bass frowns at the name, confusion making his brow twitch. Ren is Am-sa, a title he's come to know well.

As if she can read his mind, Ren comes to rest beside him and says, "Am-ga is what they have begun to call you. Though, Ko is old-fashioned, so he took to it first."

"And what is that?" he asks.

Ren glances at him. "A protector." Then, she follows behind their party into the abandoned village.

Ko graciously takes the children to walk around the woods, searching for any friendly spirits who may have stayed behind. Haaman volunteers to fly southward and scout out how close the legion is. With how damp the storm kept the island, no fire will survive for the next few days. But the flames will return.

Ren sits on an overgrown stump, legs crossed underneath her, as Bass paces a circle around what used to be a cook-pit. She's looking better today, skin less pallid and eyes more golden. The mottling has long been fading, few marks left behind.

"How did they find Gyeosi?" he asks out loud, though it's a question that doesn't have much of an answer. To it, Ren shrugs a little. "I thought only magic could bring down the barrier and open the gates."

She frowns. He doesn't like the look of it. "That's not quite how it works. I used god magic to create the barrier, but it only redirects people from the path—like an illusion." Her fingers tap on her knee. "In all fairness, I never expected people to come to the forest. When the soldiers arrived, I threw the barrier up as quick as I could. It wasn't…" She chews her lip. "It wasn't built to keep an army out."

Basuin blanches, the air stolen straight from his lungs. The barrier was made of magic. He knew that, of course he knew that. But Ren's magic weakened when he was deified. He stole it from her; their connection leached it from her.

"It was me," he says, not daring to look at her. "I took your magic—weakened the barrier. I left Gyeosi vulnerable."

It was his fault that Gyeosi burned, that Ren was hurt. It's his fault Hami died. He took her away from the village, made her journey to the Crying Trees so he could pawn off his duty. It's his fault.

Ren shifts just outside his vision, but he turns enough to see her right hand tighten into a fist. He hears her next words: *You're right, it was your fault. You are as selfish as I thought.*

"It could've been anything, Basuin." Ren's gentle voice brings him back into focus. "We don't know what magic they have."

"None," he snaps at her, and in turn, the wolf-man breaks one of his ribs off. He grunts and begins to pace again, not wanting to look at the way her face twists into something foul. "Xalkhir—the legion—has shunned the gods. The legion doesn't carry them, and no gods carry the legion. They have no magic."

"They truly don't care." It sounds like sorrow bottled up in Ren's glass throat. "They don't care if we live or die."

Hami's broken body, a white fur sack of bones loosened of blood, the wavering spirit of that little boy flashes across the blank plane of Basuin's mind. No, they don't. The legion doesn't believe in their existence, doesn't believe in the Winter River. If only Bass could have walked Hami there.

He stops in his tracks, a pause in his pacing.

"Basuin?" Ren's gaze lingers on him, but he's afraid to face her. She'll see the puzzle unfolding on his face as he slots pieces together as best he can with his big, fumbling hands. She'll see the guilt.

"Where do you walk dead spirits?" he asks.

"To the Winter River," she says, matter-of-factly. "But—" Her teeth pull at her bottom lip. "I haven't been able to take them all there. The army's distracted me. Gyeosi—there were too many." She turns her palms up, fingers trembling as if the spirits are slipping through her grasp.

Basuin wants to reach and pocket her hands in his, make them stop shaking. "Where is it? Can you go there?"

Ren bites her lip. "I don't actually walk them to the River itself. It's a vision, like a portal. My god magic links me to it."

Kensy is searching for a powerful artifact that only gods know of. Basuin thought it would be at the elder tree. But Ko told him the elder tree doesn't answer anyone but gods. No magic, no power, for mortals.

Help me, he almost asks the wolf-man, but he refuses to. He has the pieces in front of him, he just can't see how they fit together.

Basuin turns, eyes finding the jade stone Ren now wears around her thin neck. It catches the light shining through the cracks in the canopy, almost mocking him. He can see Kensy's clever smile so clearly in his mind, a snake flicking its tongue at Basuin, its prey.

Godstones are conduits, favors that gods bestow their speakers with. A blessing as much as it is a tool. If Kensy knew a god speaker, then he killed them—he could've taken their godstone for himself.

No. It's impossible. Godstones channel god magic through them, but only the blessed can use it. That's why Basuin could never speak to the gods—he wasn't blessed the way his mother was, with lavender light pouring from her eyes and mouth. And Kensy isn't blessed, either.

How do you know for certain? the wolf-man prods him.

Because he needed Bass. There's a reason Kensy asked him to come back to the bastion. He just doesn't know what. Bass shuts his eyes, tight as the fist he makes. He needs help.

"Kensy was looking for something," he says. He puts his hands behind his back and wrings them away from Ren's eyes. "A powerful artifact that belonged to the gods."

Ren's twilight eyes narrow in confusion. Then, they widen in realization. Fear colors her countenance and her hand darts up to touch the godstone resting upon her collarbone. And then, as quick as it came, that fear is replaced by a burning anger he's become so familiar with. Ren leaps to her feet to stand against him.

"How do you know that?" she asks, voice simmering. Quiet underneath the rustle of the forest. Accusing.

He swallows, hard. "Because that's why Kensy brought me to the island. He wanted me to help him speak to the gods."

Betrayal flares in her eyes. "You knew this whole time."

"I didn't." He holds up his hands, but it's futile. "I've never known what Kensy is after. All I did was follow orders."

Kensy's always been so eel-like. Slippery and in need of a kill. He feeds on his prey, uses their life to sustain him. Kensy isn't a liar, but he doesn't speak in truths. He's good at that, and Basuin learned that lesson hard.

"I should've told you," he admits. "I didn't think—" He cuts himself off, snapping his jaw shut. He did think, and to say anything less would be a lie. He did think, and he concluded that ignorance best served Ren's survival. Stupid and selfish of him.

It's the first time he's ever seen her pace. "I could have been tracking him rather than focusing on the bastion." She walks in circles, and a mean frustration bubbles up in him.

"Track him to do what?" His nostrils flare. "It's not like you would have killed him."

She whips around to face him. "Then why didn't *you*?" Ren leaps across the gap she's put between them. He looks anywhere but her eyes. "You've always said what I'm doing isn't enough—so why didn't you kill him instead?"

It shatters over his head like glass, his eyes wide, staring down at her. She's right. Why didn't he kill Kensy when he had the chance?

Ren's hand locks around the fabric of his collar, pulling him down to her height. He lets her. Until her nose is nearly touching his. Until her breath burns against his mouth. The smell of ash still lingers on her skin.

"I was wrong about you," she hisses. "You are everything I thought you were. I can't trust you."

But there's a moment, a breath—three breaths, even—of hesitance. She lingers, their eyes locked, and searches for something within him. He wishes he could help her find it. Every breath they share in tandem, a rhythm.

Then, she lets him go. Basuin flounders backward as Ren storms away.

"I am," he says. "I'm everything you thought I was—but it's different now." He catches up in three long strides, pulling ahead to block her way. Ren winds around him. "I didn't know, I swear it to you."

"How could you not?"

"I'm not very smart," he barks back. "I don't understand any of this. I've admitted that to you before. I've been honest."

Ren whirls on him. "Have you? Is hiding this not dishonest? You're a traitor. You are a danger to my people and I trusted you not to be."

"Must you always be a god?" It fizzles out, less angry and more desperate. "Are you not human, too?"

"No," Ren snaps. "I'm not. And neither are you anymore."

"But I was." He thumps a fist to his chest. "I was human, before I was a god. Weren't you?"

A shiver of rage runs up Ren's spine, her fists tightening at her sides. The nape of her neck peeks out at him when the breeze pushes her hair like a child's swing, revealing something of her to still be soft. She is soft, he knows. He's felt it before.

"No," she answers again, voice low and dark. "All I know is how to be a god, just like all you know is how to be a soldier. We're even, then."

His mouth feels dry and tastes rotten. "Help me understand."

The glare of her eyes is icy and mean when she looks at him over her shoulder. "Do you know what this island really is?"

Ren asks, a tremble of something not quite anger and not quite fear threaded in her voice.

"No." They were sent to colonize it, told it was an uninhabited island that needed to be claimed for the queen. But then Kensy pulled Basuin's rank and set him loose in the forest, commanding him to find something instead.

Basuin didn't have to follow that command—but he would've been sent home if he didn't. He doesn't know which one would be worse.

Ren turns, and the golden light of her eyes has cooled into the sharp obsidian he can no longer read. Her palms open, her god mark lighting up blue. In turn, Basuin's mark glows red and hot.

"This forest guards Sa-cha's shrine," Ren tells him. "The entrance to the Winter River."

CHAPTER TWENTY-TWO

THE STORY OF Sa-cha is a bloody one, like most stories he knows. It's a story of creation, but the way his mother told it, a story of peace. Stories of peace, he knows, are bloody in the same way that stories of war are. Because peace can only exist on the back of war.

How are gods born? Sa-cha bled them into existence. Out of his wounds, he created new life. The Winter River began as a place of birth, but once mortals were created and things could die, it became a place of rest.

Creation and extinction; life and death. What could something so sacred give to mortals?

Basuin has to find out. He made his choice, he stayed to protect the forest. Now, he needs to figure out why Kensy came to this island so he can get there first.

Otherwise, Kensy might do the unfathomable—the only option Basuin can assume from all these guessing games he's been playing since he arrived in Yesua.

If Sa-cha's shrine is what Kensy searches for, and Sa-cha's shrine guards the Winter River, then Kensy's out to destroy it. Without the Winter River—without Sa-cha himself—gods might cease to exist altogether.

Who built man? Kensy asked him in Shaelstorm.

* * *

THE ABANDONED VILLAGE, at the very least, is the perfect place to camp for a few nights. It's not as well built as Gyeosi is—was—but it's familiar. In the fire pit, huge flames made of magic roar across the small village. Bass doesn't know if the sweltering heat of the night is from that or from the anger and shame burning him up from the inside.

He sits alone, on the far side of camp, shoveling rice into his mouth. Across the fire, Ren sits between Ko and Qia, pointedly ignoring him. Yaelic is chattering Qia's ear off, while Haaman eats quietly next to Ko.

Once again, Basuin is the outcast among the people he fights alongside. He didn't miss it—when Ren called the army "them," rather than referring to the legion as his. Betraying her trust has lost him that privilege, surely. Bass never meant to betray her trust.

Ignorance is such bliss, until it crumbles.

Ren laughs aloud, all church bells and glee. It washes over him even from so far away, grip on his wooden cup crushing as Ren elbows Ko in jest. Something floods him, all bitter but filling him up until he's swollen with it. Envy, and desperation, flavored by something a little mean.

He wishes he could make Ren laugh like that. Like she's just a woman with no cross to bear, no duty weighing on her thin shoulders. Oh, what he wouldn't give to make her laugh like that. Not just a god, but someone once human. Like him.

Then, a blue-inked bruise blots the back of Ren's thigh. Out of nowhere. Edges purpling as it disperses through her skin. She doesn't even flinch, so he flinches for her. Bass is on his feet in an instant, storming over to her, his mission to fix it, fix it, fix it.

Ko turns his head as Bass approaches, but Ren doesn't even move. He lays a hand on her shoulder. "You're hurt," he says.

And Ren shrugs off his touch. Ignoring him. He draws his

hand back like she's slapped him. Ren doesn't say a word to him, doesn't look at him, doesn't do anything. She snubs him completely.

It makes him want to snort. How childish. This woman who claims that she is nothing more than a god is giving him the cold shoulder. How petty.

How human.

It almost wrangles a smile out of him, but then Ko leans over and says, "Allow me, Am-sa." With a yellow-green glow of magic, Ko passes his hand over the bruise that's formed. Not touching Ren, but glossing over her skin. As easily as Ko breathes, he heals the wound that the forest has dealt Ren, smiling all the way.

Basuin burns with a new jealousy. It's fierce and biting and he can't explain why it chokes him. He shouldn't feel so heated over this. He should be grateful that Ko eases Ren's pain.

He should apologize to her. It would make this rotten feeling in his stomach disappear. Eat the envy out of him.

The wolf-man rolls onto its back, paws in the air, sneezing with a laugh.

"Thank you, Ko." Ren's voice is almost startling. Basuin stares at the back of her head for far too long, willing her to look at him. If she would only look at him, he would apologize.

But then Ren does look at him. She whips her head back to him, glaring at him from over a stiff shoulder as if to say, *You're not welcome here anymore.*

Basuin takes a step back, and when Ren tosses her hair back and returns to her dinner, he turns and leaves.

Maybe there's no apology that will make Ren forgive him. But Basuin made a promise to her, and if she won't help him figure it out, then he'll figure it out himself.

He needs to learn to be a god before Kensy gets what he wants. And then he needs to learn what Kensy wants, so he can stop Kensy from getting it, from destroying the forest entirely.

It's no longer a duty. It's a necessity.

When the camp disperses for the night, Bass catches Ko alone for a moment. It isn't planned, but instinctual. Ko seems like the best option out of all the choices he has in camp—since Ren has decided to ignore him.

"Do you have a moment to talk?" he asks, feeling more diplomatic than ever before. Smart, for the first time.

A sleepy smile raises Ko's lips as he tucks his hands in the sleeves of his robe. "Of course. What is it that I can do, Wolf God?"

Basuin winces, and Ko notices. "Basuin," he amends. "How can I help?"

They walk to a circle of sitting stones, ground flattened in paths worn through years and now abandoned. A deep guilt boils in Basuin's gut as he follows the footholds to sit across from Ko.

"You've been a part of this forest for a long time," he says. "You must know much about the gods."

Ko laughs, a quiet chuckle. "Are you calling me old?" Before Basuin can jump to refute, Ko continues. "You would be right to." Ko leans back on his hands, long curtain of black hair falling in seams over his shoulder. "I am very old now. Much too old for war, though it is here anyway. How inconsiderate." Ko looks at him, but he wears a joking smile.

Basuin's mouth is dry. "I'm sorry."

Ko shakes his head. "No fault of your own." It's the first time anyone has said that to him. Ko, perhaps, is the only spirit in this forest that's never looked at Basuin like he was just a soldier, nor a god, and without hostility. "Yes, I know of the gods. I wouldn't say I know as much as you might think."

"More than I do."

"Yes." Ko chuckles again. "More than you would. So perhaps I can help."

Bass squeezes his fingers into fists, stretches them out, and then curls them again. "Where did the gods come from—and why do they possess us?"

Ko hums in thought. "Those are good questions to ask, though hard to answer, as many things are."

"I died," Basuin says, "and was brought back as a puppet."

At that, the wolf-man opens its jaws wide and snaps a chunk of his lung off to snack on. He coughs.

"Not quite a puppet," Ko says. "More akin to a shrine, of sorts."

He blinks. "What?"

Ko leans forward now, sleeves falling to reveal a pair of tightly clasped hands. "Gods cannot exist in our world without a body. Not anymore. There's so little magic in the land now. It's been whittled away by humans, bled from the ground and from the trees."

"There are no spirits left where I am from," Basuin says. "Nothing like the forest."

"If there were, gods could walk freely again. But without magic here to act as a conduit, their choices are limited."

"To shrines?"

"And bodies," Ko says. "You are a host."

"But the island has magic, doesn't it?" he asks. "There are spirits here. Sa-cha's shrine is here. So gods should walk freely here, too. Why am I a host for the Wolf God?" His chest is buzzing, burning. Lightning running through his blood, racing through him. "Doesn't the Wolf God have a body? A shrine?" Basuin asks, a hand on his heart—where it used to be.

But the wolf-man is silent.

"They used to," Ko says. "The Forest God and the Wolf God used to roam the forest together, even before they were bound by divine oath—before the Wolf God became the guardian of the Forest God. They were always together. But they..."

Basuin's jaw loosens. He leans forward. "They what?"

For the first time tonight, Ko looks away from Basuin and

into the forest beyond them. His Adam's apple bobs with a swallow.

"They were always together, until they weren't anymore." Ko takes in a breath, then shrugs, turning back to face Basuin. "I don't know what happened."

He lets out a sigh, head falling, thumbs twiddling, until he nods. "Of course. I wouldn't expect you to know everything. I appreciate what you've told me already. It's been helpful."

Yet no questions have been answered. It only solidifies what he already knows: he's a puppet being strung along by a god he knows nothing about. It's gotten him no closer to where he needs to be—the Winter River.

But Basuin can't help but wonder: Why did the Wolf God become the guardian of the Forest God? Was it duty bestowed upon the Wolf God, just like the Wolf God bestowed duty upon him? Bound by divine oath?

Ko smiles. "I'm glad. Is there anything else I can help with?"

"Actually... " Basuin draws a ball of light to his hand, red with magic. A part of him is excited at how fast he's gotten at the simple things. "I want to learn to heal, like you did tonight. Would you be able to teach me?"

But the look on Ko's face, the spot of pity where Ko's brows draw to and his forehead wrinkles, is answer enough before he shakes his head.

"My apologies. I'm not well-versed in god magic. It's very different from forest magic."

Basuin nods. "That's all right." The light in his hand quiets before dissolving completely, leaving behind red flecks of magic spattered across his god mark. "Thank you, Ko. I won't keep you up any longer tonight."

If Ko cannot teach him, he'll have to ask Ren's forgiveness after all. He'll have to pray that she'll receive him again.

Slowly and with a groan resembling the creak of wood, Ko presses to his feet and bows his head. Bass bows in response, drawing up the best small smile he can to bid Ko goodnight.

But as Ko begins his sluggish walk, Basuin calls after him. "Wait—"

Ko turns and Basuin freezes in response. He shouldn't ask this, he knows it. But it itches at him, in his palm where his god mark is burned into his skin. He has to know.

"Was Ren always a god?" he asks.

Ko stares across the distance at him for a long while, contemplating. The moon is a sliver of itself, no light to be cast upon the abandoned village.

"No," Ko finally says. "She wasn't."

CHAPTER TWENTY-THREE

IT TAKES HIM a long while to work up the courage to apologize. Far too long. Basuin spends a whole day contemplating what he might say to Ren, how he can gain her forgiveness again. How to convince her that it was not betrayal, but ignorance—and he doesn't wish to be ignorant any longer.

He doesn't have time to be wasting like this. The army is moving. Haaman returned, early in the morning, with news that the legion is marching toward them still. Whatever used to be his heart is steadily buzzing and his stomach keeps churning. He tried to speak with her then, but couldn't get his words together. Panic, whether at the army or at the apology, made him hesitate.

Then, after lunch, when Yaelic caught him to ask what their next plans were, since Ren said they'd be leaving soon. His last attempt was after dinner, but Ko swept her into a conversation before Bass had any chance at all.

Excuses, anyway. Basuin is scared shitless that Ren won't accept his apology.

How pathetic. A war hero, scared of a woman refusing to forgive him. Basuin considers, for far too long, whether he should go looking for some wildflowers to give her.

That's a memory he hasn't unearthed in so many years. Of his mother, before she was too sick to walk, who cut fresh flowers from the garden every week to set in the windows of their village home. Before they were cast out into that hellish shack Bass built, shoddy windows and his ma bedridden.

"What are you doing stalking around out here?"

Bass spins around, face to face with Ren, her arms crossed over her chest and annoyance sprawled across her countenance. He hadn't realized how far he'd paced away from their camp, on the outskirts of the abandoned village—almost as if he were walking to that little shack in Ankor.

And here Ren stands in the darkness with him. This is the first she's spoken to him.

Ren looks away, pursing her lips. "Are you leaving?" But she says it with a heaviness, a pit of sorrow in every vowel. The distance between them suddenly aches. No, it's always ached, but he feels it now.

The wolf-man whines, nosing at Basuin's flesh, pawing toward Ren.

"I'm sorry," he says like he's drowning.

Ren's eyes snap to his, burning golden in the moonless night.

"I'm sorry for hiding what I knew." Bass steps closer to her and she doesn't move away. "It wasn't malicious. I didn't mean to betray your trust, but I know I did. And I'm sorry."

His hands feel so empty at his sides, flexing and grabbing at his pants and then hiding behind his back so Ren won't see how he wrings his wrists.

Ren takes a moment before she responds, watching him. "You're sorry." Confusion lurks in her voice.

"I am." He sighs, glancing away from her. "I am ignorant, but I won't be anymore. I need to learn more magic. I want to," he says. Then, he looks up and meets her eyes. Holds their gaze steady. "Will you help me?"

Ren looks completely taken aback at his request, eyes gone wide. "You want to learn more magic?"

He swallows hard. "I want to save the forest."

She turns away, hiding her face from him. All he sees is a peek of her neck when the breeze blows her hair back and a still-healing series of cuts on the back of her arm. If only he could see her face, try and read her ever-unreadable emotions. If only he could save her the pain.

"I'm sorry, too." Ren's voice is quiet. "You said you would help, and I should trust that, after everything."

Relief floods him, washing away all the fear and guilt that once coated his insides. Ren's gentle hand finds his, her face shadowed by the night, and she tugs him toward the trees. Further into the forest.

She feared that Basuin was leaving. The thought sends a twisted thrill through him, the idea that Ren didn't want him to leave again. But her touch grounds him as they weave through the woods together.

Ren nestles into a bed of roots, back pressed to the trunk of an oak. It looks like she belongs there, right in the heart of the forest. As if this tree built its home to welcome her, to shelter her. The choppy ends of her hair blow across her face, hiding her lips as a cool night breeze coasts over them.

He sits across from her, lumbering a bit to get his legs in order. Too long, too big, too bumbling. If Ren is grace, then he is crude. She is balanced, he is clumsy.

But once he's situated himself, legs crossed beneath him, there's too much distance between them still. He feels the emptiness, the stretch of space separating them. Bass wants to recreate their closeness from before, somehow.

It feels so good to be close to her. The wolf-man's doing, he's sure.

Inside him, the wolf-man laughs and it echoes in the chamber of Basuin's chest where his heart is missing.

"I want to teach you something," Ren says, hand outstretched toward him. And as if she's the sun in the whole blessed sky, Basuin leans closer to her, seeking out her light and warmth. "Hold my hand."

He swallows hard. Then, he slides her hand into his from underneath, keeping her palm face up. No god mark ruins her left hand, and none wears his right. Like this, they're a mirror image of one another. As the wind rustles her hair again, it tangles with the long curls of his that have unraveled from the low bun he knots at the nape of his neck each morn.

Ren holds his gaze for a moment, but when her eyes drop away, his return to the stark white of her palm, milky in the dregs of light falling from the stars in the dark sky.

And then a knife slashes through her skin, drawing red blood to the surface, bubbling up hot.

Bass scrambles forward, fingers hovering over the gash in Ren's palm. Her eyes are unreadable, face smooth and even when he looks up. Her bone dagger gleams in her god-marked hand where she flips it in her grasp.

The cut is deep and it runs with the smell of rust.

"Heal it," she says, and Bass freezes.

"I can't," he says in one big burst. "I can't do that." His hands aren't for healing. They are for hell, and hell only.

"You can," she says instead, but when Bass presses his thumb to the cut to staunch the bleeding Ren winces. Her wrist twitches with pain and he can feel the icy grip of panic rise and curl in his throat. "Like I showed you, with the weapons. Imagine—"

"I can't," he snarls, louder, with an edge so harsh he could break a blade on it. Snap it, brittle and mean. These hands have never healed anything. Haven't saved a single soul, man or not-man. All they have done is killed.

The wolf-man sinks its teeth into him somewhere, but he can't even feel it. All he can feel is panic as dark blood oozes from the wound Ren's made in her own damned palm.

Like she can read his mind, Ren tells him, "It'll scar."

A curse falls from his lips. There's a shake in his fingers. Anything but that. She's too delicate to scar.

"Imagine threading your magic into the cut," she says,

softer this time. Lurid, somehow, in the darkness of the forest. "Imagine using it to stitch the wound. You've done that before, haven't you?"

Bass clenches his eyes shut. Pulling a tin needle through Tehali's calf with thick thread as she chewed on a leather bit. Fishing a bent needle out of his own shoulder with trembling fingers, hoping to god someone would come and save him from himself.

No one ever did, and the nightmares never fucking stopped. The nightmares only stopped when he came to this forest—this godsdamned forest where Ren sits in front of him and bleeds until he can dredge up some half-hero, half-killer courage that sprouted up inside him and withered to death in Valkesta.

"Basuin." She says his name quietly. Blood is crawling down her arm.

"Fuck," he curses again, culling his shallow breathing and shaking his head. "I don't know how to." It comes out more whine than words, like a kicked wolf pup. He sounds defeated, but he hasn't even tried. He thought he could do this; he needs to do this. But this is just a reminder that Basuin's hands cannot fix. They can only break.

"Listen to me," Ren says, and her voice draws his eyes to her face again. Unreadable, still, but softer. "Imagine your magic as needle and thread. Stitch it up. Use it as a balm. Mend it."

He swallows again. Her blood is smeared across her palm and sticking to his thumb.

"Mend me," she whispers, and Basuin shudders a breath.

Just as she's taught him—with the light and food and supplies and guns and weapons and the almost nightmares—Bass calls the red pinpricks of his magic into his mind. The pressure under his thumb lessens, but the weight of Ren's blood doesn't.

They can all heal her; Qia and Ko and Hou-tou. It's only him, the Wolf God, the guardian of the Forest God, who cannot.

But he has to. She's cut herself open for him, trusting that he'll save her. A second chance, to prove her wrong. She can trust him again.

Bass snaps the thread of his magic from where it's wound around his soul. Then he weaves it through the gash, the rift Ren has cut into her own palm. With his eyes closed, Bass moves his left hand over the wound, the heat of his magic sinking into her skin. He pictures it, stitching it closed. Using the string that's tied his spirit to hers to fix her hurt.

"Open your eyes," Ren asks of him, and he does. The gash is gone, leaving unmarked skin behind. The blood she wore has disappeared, like it never existed. All he can see anymore is the smile on her face.

It's so fucking gentle and so bright and graceful and fuck. He feels shattered by it. Like the light of her is bracing against the darkness caged inside of him, trying to slip through the cracks forming in the carefully crafted armor he bears on his back. She's trying to undo him. Break him.

Basuin would beg her to, if she'll keep looking like that. More a woman now than a god, with perfectly shaped lips and a soft sloped nose and kind slants for eyes, who was human enough to ignore him out of anger. Human enough to fear that he would leave her.

He could cry, she's so beautiful. Gods damn him.

"You're funny," she says, and it's so startling that he blinks. But she's wearing that soft, downy look still as she stares at him.

"What?"

"I thought, at first, that you were selfish."

That strikes him. Painfully. Then, honestly. "You would be right," he says.

But Ren shakes her head. "I was wrong. You worry so much for others, care for them so much, but you hide it. You fear it—being afraid."

Bass rears back. "Is that what you think?"

"I do." Slowly, Ren pulls her hand away from his and he watches her flee. He wants to snatch it back, to intertwine their fingers, even now. "You claim to not be a protector, that you don't want to be—but you do it anyway. Every person you try to protect is another fear to carry. Isn't it?"

His hand tightens into a quick fist, bones aching. "Very funny of me, then." Bass stopped trying to protect people a long time ago. The only reason he even cares to protect Ren is because of this godsdamned *thing* in his chest—

He beats his fist against his heart at the exact moment the wolf-man lunges, teeth bared, at Bass' ribs to crush them. That's not true. That's not true at all. He knows it.

And just like that, the light she's been projecting cuts off. He closes his eyes to pretend it's been dark this whole time.

"I just don't want you to fear me," Ren finally says, her voice low.

Fear for you, he almost says. He fears for her. But maybe that's the same as fearing her.

Instead, he presses his thumbnail into one of the lines of his god mark. "You're the same way." He can feel Ren's eyes on him. "You try to keep everything at a distance. Even the forest."

Eventually, his nail breaks skin and Basuin bleeds.

"But I don't fear you," he says. And he means it—even when he opens his eyes and sees the wrecked countenance Ren wears like a white flag.

CHAPTER TWENTY-FOUR

WITH REN'S FORGIVENESS, Bass feels renewed. Alive, again, and more determined than ever to understand Kensy's plans for the forest—and for Ren. It's a familiar feeling, out of breath and running straight ahead toward battle. But not as a soldier, this time. As a god.

So why does he still feel so powerless? His palm pressed gently against the back of the world, hand guiding the shoulders of the forest forward. The forest's body brushing against his side, her hip bumping his when their gaits match, crossing congruently every few steps.

Once, before, Ren would have stretched the distance between them into something easily measured. But now, he doesn't know what to call the small breadth of space separating them that she closes without even noticing.

How can he feel powerless when this power is one he's worked so tirelessly to gain?

It's so human, to trust someone. And Ren was human once. Just as he was.

"What was the forest like?" he asks when they stop by a creek to refill their waterskins. "Before the army came."

"Peaceful," Ren answers, eyes cast down to the water.

"Don't give me that," he shoots back. "What was it really like?"

She cuts a glare at him that isn't as intimidating as she must think it is. But then she hums, tilting her head and capping her waterskin. "Brighter. The sky wasn't filled with smoke. And louder. The spirits were so much livelier than they are now. It's so quiet now, so—"

The river splashes. Ren's hand cuts through the water as she catches herself on the bank, curled over in pain. Her gasp is swallowed by the run of the river. Bass darts forward, one hand on her back, the other searching for whatever wound has found her.

"Where?"

Ren coughs, wiping her mouth on her arm. "It's all right." But then she coughs again, holding her stomach. A spatter of blood covers her chin. She wipes it away again, quicker this time. "It's nothing."

But she sits at the river, still hunched over, even as he tries to help her. "Can you stand?"

She breathes heavily. "Give me a moment."

When he finally picks her up off the ground, carrying her weight until she can get her feet underneath her, Ren pulls the hem of her shirt up to reveal the bruising—purple and blue marring her stomach. The taste of sick rolls over his tongue and dries his mouth.

Ren pants, her eyes glassy with pain as she looks at him. "Can you heal me? We need to go—a spirit is calling for me. I have to save them."

His eyes go wide. Scar aching. "You're hurt."

"I have to save them," she snarls at him, and the agony in her voice can't crow over the fear that shakes her words. "Please, Basuin."

He can't deny her. He could never deny her anything anymore. So instead, he presses his hand to her body, coated in red magic, and concedes.

"Okay," he says. "We'll save them."

Together, they run through the forest—Ren is faster, but his strides are longer. She dances through the trees, twisting and turning, but he barrels through even as the branches whip and scratch his skin. Birds scatter overhead.

"We're close," Ren calls back to him.

"I can feel it," he answers. The sky darkens. The smell of smoke curls in his nostrils. He holds his breath because he's already sick enough at the sight of Ren's bruises. The army is close again. Too close, just as Haaman told them.

All too quickly, Ren skids to a stop, and Basuin nearly crashes into her. He pants, looking over the top of her head into a parting of trees. A sea of white and red. Valkesta.

And in the middle of it all, Kensy.

This is a nightmare. He's trapped again. He needs to wake up. Wake up. Wake—

Ren takes one step backward, into him, and his hands fall to her arms to pull her tight to his chest. This isn't a nightmare at all. He's wide awake. Ren needs to run. Please, run.

Kensy, standing among the wreckage of dying spirits like some king conqueror, upright and stoic, turns his head to look over his shoulder at them. The corner of his lip is pulled into a snarling grin.

A harbinger of destruction.

"So," Kensy takes a roundabout step to face them. "You've found yourself a god." His lopsided grin shouldn't be so menacing. Basuin growls, a deep-rooted fear in his nonexistent heart reaching up to escape his throat. He wants to blame the wolf-man for it.

Underneath his hands, Ren trembles. Terrified, or raging, he doesn't know. He doesn't want Kensy to look at her. He shouldn't be allowed to even know of her existence. He'll kill Kensy if he tries to touch her.

The dead, and dying, and bleeding, and twitching bodies of the rabbits laid at Kensy's feet make Basuin boil alive in his own skin. A black eyeball rolls to look at him, its owner's hindleg still thumping as if it can escape from its own death.

Help me, the spirit begs him. *I'm so afraid.*

Basuin's nostrils flare. "You did this." A statement; not even an accusation.

Kensy laughs. "Of course I did." He sets a hand on his belt, a holstered pistol at his side. "I forget you're as dumb as a dog, Bass."

It stings, but he barely feels it under the rolling waves of anger. "Dumb enough you thought you could manipulate me. Dumb enough you thought you could bring me here and make me do your dirty work."

Dumb enough to do it for nearly a decade. When did that start? When had their camaraderie transformed from friends, to favors, to force, to foe? For years, they've been on the same side of a fight. For years, Basuin thought Kensy only wanted the best for him. Kensy said he would help Basuin climb to success. But all he did was turn Bass into a war machine that killed when Kensy said kill.

They used to just be two men who had nothing—no family, no friends, and nothing to love. Nothing but war.

Maybe they're still that. So why did Kensy turn out to be so cruel?

And now, Kensy's lips press together in a knowing, snaking smile.

"Dumb enough that I did."

No, this isn't war. This is Kensy doing what he pleases. Being needlessly cruel for the fun of it. Killing for sport, hunting for game.

Basuin knows war best of all—and Kensy no longer wants war. He wants blood.

Resentment, mean and sticky, builds in his chest. But it's Ren who moves, who pulls from Bass' grip to throw herself toward Kensy. If his hands weren't so used to holding on to everything so tightly with dread, she might have slipped his grasp.

"How dare you," Ren seethes. He knows the look she wears even without seeing her face—she's looked at him like that before. "You are lesser than the rot of this forest. Even from rot, life can grow again. You are nothing," she spits at him, still lunging, a viper with all her viciousness.

His teeth are locked around her name, caging it in his mouth. Kensy won't hear it. He'll kill Kensy before he lets Kensy learn anything of Ren's.

Kensy quirks a brow at Basuin, a familiar look they've shared. "You've always liked them so feisty, old dog."

"Shut up," he barks back. The ring of broken bodies circling Kensy makes his hands tight. If he could shelter Ren behind his body, stow her away from Kensy's gaze, he would. But he can hear the quickness of her breath. The heat of her skin brought by anger. He lets her go, reluctantly, and stands beside her. Partners. "You don't get to speak anymore."

"Is that so?" Kensy chuckles.

"I told you this island was protected by gods." His eyes don't leave Kensy's. "Did you think you could get away with your cruelty? Do you think you'll be forgiven for your crimes?"

Kensy just laughs again. "Who will be left to crucify me when I burn this forest to the ground?"

It's not like you would have killed him, Basuin had said.

Then why didn't you? Ren had asked him. *Why didn't you kill him instead?*

The wolf-man lunges and snaps and breaks Basuin's skin with its teeth. It cracks his bones and rebuilds them with the foam from its jowls. The wolf-man howls.

Basuin growls low. "Me."

He darts forward. Reaches for the sword strapped to his back and runs for Kensy. Ignores the still-twitching rabbits that litter the forest floor. Hands enveloped in red. Hot. Magic. No human thoughts left. Only wolf. Only god. Only the Wolf God, who possesses his mind, his heart, his body.

And the soldier boy still lurking in the bones I pick your meat off, he thinks the wolf-man says. Or maybe it's him now. Maybe it's always been him.

The soldier boy who was betrayed by the very mentor who made him.

Basuin snarls, sword gripped in both hands, and aims for the canine grin Kensy's still wearing. Monstrous blue eyes still alight in glee.

"Basuin!"

A small, soft, strong hand wraps around his arm.

"Stop." Her voice is breathy in his ear. "Don't kill him." Not a command, but a request. Pleading.

He breathes hard. Panting, raging. Crimson magic drips off the edge of his blade. Kensy's eyes are wide, his body tense. He's afraid—not much, but a little. It's enough. Basuin can kill him.

Basuin will.

But Ren's other hand finds his shoulder and her arm twists around him. "Please, Basuin." The Forest God, begging him for something. It's rotten. Like Kensy. "I don't want you to kill him."

If she really wanted you to stop, she would've used magic.

No, no. She trusts him.

You are a protector. You are a killer. You will kill for her.

He will.

But in the brief moment of his hesitation, Ren pressed to his back and fingers curled in his sleeve, a hurried rustle of brush has his head snapping to where Kensy waits. But he's gone. Like he was never there at all. Kensy's sense of self-preservation is too keen. His close familiarity with what Basuin can do—what tragedies he's staged—bid him to run like a fucking coward.

A coward who Basuin could've slain dead, right here, to lay at Ren's feet. A dog bringing back a grouse to leave as an offering to the altar that she is. Proof of loyalty.

Basuin yanks away from her, and she lets him go with a gasp. That alone cracks him. Breaks him in half. She trusts him. She *trusts* him. He just got her to trust him.

But his mind is red with blood. With lust and rage. Hatred and betrayal. There's still time to catch Kensy. Basuin swallowed a god. He's faster than Kensy. But Ren's stare on his back is too heavy, and he can't move underneath it. He whirls on her, sword in clawed fist, looking down at her through eyes that don't belong to him.

"You don't want me to kill him?" he growls in question.

"No," she says, as if it were simple. "You can't kill him."

"This is what you wanted."

"I never wanted this!" Her hand comes up to grip the wide collar of her shirt, right over her heart. Does she even have one? "I said I don't kill. I won't kill. You told me you wouldn't."

"I never said that," he snarls at her. "I vowed to protect you—whatever that may cost."

"I said I didn't want war."

"But war is here." His teeth grind together. "If I kill him, it ends. It's done." Rage shocks through his spine. It aches, his want to kill. The need to slaughter. To end the war that Ren doesn't want. To taste the blood of the man who betrayed him. Manipulated him like the dumb dog he is.

He's a wolf now. He bites back.

"Don't kill him." Ren's twilight eyes are pained, as if it hurts her. "Please," she whispers.

Basuin lets his sword slip through his fingers and fall to the blood-wet ground.

He really can't deny her anything anymore.

Slowly, he reaches for her hand still twisted in her shirt. He unfurls her fingers from where they're tangled in the cotton. Ren takes her trembling hand and places it against his chest, right above where the wolf-man should reside. There's no flutter of his heart there anymore, only the hastened rise and fall of his chest. He closes his eyes, lets himself rest for just a moment.

"Thank you." Her voice is so soft. So soft. So soft, he can

barely hear her. It draws the wolf-man out of him, sings it sweetly back into its home among his ribcage. The boiling heat that frenzied him floods from his skin. The red of his magic recedes.

Once again, he's just Bass, and she's just Ren, and all that's left of Kensy are the dead rabbits, black eyes glassy and gone cold. He failed Ren—and their forest—again.

Basuin draws Ren into him, sheltering her from the grief. She lets her head rest against his shoulder, hand still drawn to where the wolf-man lives in him, and swallows in defeat. The wolf-man paws, claws retracted, toward Ren's fingertips.

If Ren won't let him kill, then she will let him die. Because Basuin will die for her. That's the duty he's been given. The duty that brought him back to life.

He waits for the wolf-man to agree, but nothing ever comes.

CHAPTER TWENTY-FIVE

PACIFISM IS SHIT-ALL for protecting Ren. Basuin is reminded of this—of how bad he is at the one duty he's been given—once the scorching starts again. The army doesn't just fill the sky with a glaze of smoke, a threat that smells of fire and brimstone and danger trailing behind them. Not just spirits who run from their homes and curse Ren's name as they look for safety. It isn't just Kensy, who knows Ren's face now, hunting them for the thrill of it.

It's Ren's skin, purpled with bruises and reddened with new burns.

It hurts Basuin more than it seems to hurt Ren, her head held high all the while. But when they stop to make camp in the forest for the night after hours of traveling north—trying to put as much space between them and Kensy as possible—Ren meets him alone, in the dark, and slumps against him.

Basuin folds her into a half-embrace and heals her wounds. It's all he can do. But he needs to be doing so much more. If only she would let him.

Once again, he lies awake under the night sky, staring up at the moon glittering above the forest canopy. The fire has died to a low spittle of embers, darkening their camp. Basuin, fist to his chest, breathes heavily.

He needs help. And he's never asked for the wolf-man's

help, but he needs it. Ren, Ko, and Hou-tou—they don't have answers for him. They don't know how to get to the Winter River, and much less, how to stop Kensy from getting there first.

Inside him, the wolf-man is curled up and ignoring him, chuffing a breath.

He beats his fist on his chest, the empty chamber the wolf-man lives in now, where his heart was eaten out of him.

Help. Gods, help him. If they want him to save the forest, why don't they fucking *help* him.

Basuin beats his fist against his chest so hard he can't breathe. And then, out of thin air, Basuin is yanked from his body and dropped into darkness.

He reaches, hands searching the black nothingness he's trapped in. Where is he? Where is Ren? His nonexistent heart hammers in his chest, panic building in his body and pumping through his veins. But he falls to his hands and knees, eyes open wide, the scar on the left side of his face twitching with pain.

When Basuin looks up, the wolf-man is standing before him. The body of a man and the head of a wolf, all black except for glowing red eyes and red lines drawn up and down its skin, tattooed like veins.

"Stand, Basuin of Ankor," the wolf-man commands, slamming its ruby-tipped staff upon the ground. Basuin scrambles to his feet, fisting his shirt right where his heart used to be. "You would ask me for help?"

Basuin swallows. "Yes."

"You are unworthy." The words are cutting as the wolf-man peers down at him. It tries to cow him into submission, but Basuin won't be rocked.

"Unworthy or not, I need help. If you want me to prove my worthiness, then help me do so," he spits back. "If you want me to save Ren, then help me." He labors a breath, chest rising and falling in quick succession.

"What is it you ask for?" The wolf-man's voice echoes in the endless darkness.

"To find the Winter River," he answers. "I need to find it before Kensy does."

He isn't smart, but he understands now. Kensy wants to find the Winter River. And Basuin knows him well enough—Kensy isn't here to worship. He's here to destroy it. The same way Kensy marched into Grimmalia to liberate its faithful from their godly fetters, Kensy marched to this forest to destroy what's left of the gods.

Queen Ye'suite wants to rule the whole world, but Kensy wants to eat it. If there's no way to get to the Winter River, then there will be no more prayer. No more worship.

But it's more than that. If Sa-cha's shrine is what guards the Winter River, then Kensy will destroy Sa-cha, too. Kensy destroys anything that's in his way. Ko said gods can't walk freely without bodies—without magic. If not a body, then a shrine. A host.

Kensy doesn't plan on outlawing gods. He plans to get rid of them.

The wolf-man looms over Basuin, golden eyes staring down at him. "What will you do, little soldier boy?"

Basuin closes his eyes. If Kensy kills Sa-cha, destroys the Winter River, his ma will go nowhere. The rest of the spirits, like Hami and Aless—they'll go nowhere, too. He is a god now. He has people who belong to him, who have sworn their lives to him in exchange for protection. The grief that's made holes and homes inside his bones is only a reminder that when people belong to him, they die.

The forest will die. Ren will die.

And Kensy wins.

"I'll stop him," Basuin answers, looking up at the wolf-man. He straightens out his back, leveling them head to head. Dead on. "I won't let Kensy get to the Winter River."

The wolf-man's maw opens, its long tongue licking its sharp canines while it laughs.

"How do I get there?" he asks, voice thick in his throat.

In a split second, the wolf-man swoops down, snout nearly pressed to Basuin's nose. Its fierce, angry eyes search his, looking for signs of fear, or hesitation maybe. But there is no hesitation inside of him. There is fear, yes. But it is fear for the forest, and fear for Ren.

When it's satisfied, the wolf-man pulls back only slightly. "I will lead you there, Basuin of Ankor. But it requires sacrifice, as all things do."

Hasn't he sacrificed enough already? Others, and his own. He's skipped death twice already and a third is on its way. And despite it, he's swallowed his protest and regrets and shouldered his duty, become the Wolf God. What else must he do?

The wolf-man reaches into Basuin's chest, painless this time, and pulls on the red string tied around his soul. It unravels, thread pulled from a spool, and the wolf-man wraps it around its wrist.

"What are you willing to give up?" the wolf-man asks him.

Basuin looks down at his hands. Ren's blood stains his skin, filling in all the lines and scars marking his palm. He squeezes his fingers into a fist.

"Everything," he says, and he means it. He would give up everything for Ren. That was his promise—to protect her. Even his mother's godstone he hung around her neck.

"Everything," he repeats.

And the wolf-man takes. It yanks on Basuin's thread so hard it sends Basuin sprawling on the floor of the darkness. He loses all senses except the feeling of a burning, searing pain in his heart. Razor-thin wires sink into his organ from where the wolf-man pulls him, trying to end Basuin's life again.

In the midst of the darkness, two black hands tie Basuin's red thread to a blue one, knotting them together. It's different than before somehow. When Ren showed him their connection, their magic, it was different.

This feels like death.

"You wish it was," the wolf-man says with a mean chuckle. "If you are so willing to die, then it means nothing that you are willing to die for her."

It aches. Oh, it hurts. Agonizing and bleeding. Basuin tries to catch his breath.

"It's different," he croaks out. "With her, it's different."

"You've wanted for death before, but hear me, boy," the wolf-man growls. "Your life belongs to her. It always has. But now, her life belongs to you, too."

"What?" Basuin gasps, looking for the wolf-man. He whips his head around in the darkness, but it's nowhere to be found.

In a blink, it appears before him, crouching to his level. "If you die again, little soldier boy, then she will die with you."

Basuin's eyes are wild, an ache overtaking his body. No, no, no—that can't happen.

"No longer will death solve your problems, Basuin of Ankor," it tells him, a laugh crushed between its canines. "You cannot squirm out of your duty any longer, even if you wanted to. Now, you have no choice."

He chokes on nothing but the taste of blood. No, this can't be true. Basuin doesn't want to die anymore—he doesn't. But what happens if he does?

You'll go nowhere, Ren told him once. Not even to the Blacksalt Sea. He'll go nowhere.

"And she'll go with you," the wolf-man says. "This is the sacrifice you've made. This is the sacrifice you'll keep."

It stands, leaving Basuin writhing on the ground. "But I'll lead you there," it says.

"Where?" he asks, gasping for the air that's been stolen from him. He can't die here; he needs to breathe. If he dies, she'll die too. He can't die.

"To Sa-cha," the wolf-man says, a harsh laugh filling the darkness. "From the Winter River, there arose a god, and that god was Sa-cha, and he was good," it recites in prayer. "Isn't that what you asked for, little soldier boy?"

He coughs, choking, and the wolf-man dissolves into nothingness.

Basuin, someone calls as he lies on the floor. *Basuin, wake up*.

He doesn't want to. Go away, go away, go away.

Basuin, wake up, they plead, voice so far from here. The darkness is sweeping him away, down the river, into the Blacksalt Sea.

Wake up, they say, hand on his face. And Basuin opens his eyes again.

Above him, Ren holds his jaw in her small hand, onyx eyes filled with concern. Her other hand is pressed to his chest, a blue glow tickling his skin. Bass captures it in his own, fingers swallowing hers, and she spooks.

Everything is murky, but this isn't the darkness and the wolf-man is happily inside of the cavity it carved out for itself. Bass surges upward, Ren sitting back on her heels beside him.

"Are you all right?" she asks, voice rife with anxiety. "Was it a nightmare? You—"

He doesn't listen. Bass takes the godstone where it hangs around Ren's neck, his hand coated in red magic. He squeezes; magic bleeds into the jade. Ren watches him, jaw slackened as the words she wanted to say tumble out of her mouth.

Ma, he prays, eyes open and hands desperate. *Ma, please, help us to the Winter River. Help me to find Sa-cha, before it's too late*.

Help him to save Ren. Because unlike Valkesta, where he ignored the prophetic visions laid before him, he's listening. He's seeing. Ren's fate is right in front of him, killed and cut and dressed and pickled and plated. He sees it—he won't let it happen.

Basuin is a god. It has to be different this time. Please, let it be different this time.

The wolf-man inside him stretches up and unhinges its maw, then howls so loud and so aching that Bass can taste blood in his mouth.

He looks up, his eyes finding Ren's. Gorgeous, her eyes, all obsidian and sharp. Right now, she looks at him like he's falling apart in her hands, and he's tortured by how easily he could slip his fingers through the spaces between hers.

A bright ruby-red trail appears right over Ren's shoulder, winding through the trees behind them. It stretches out until it's a wisp, disappearing into the forest, and he knows this is what his sacrifice paid for.

Go, the wolf-man pushes him. *Time will not be kind to you.*

Much of the world hasn't been kind to him. But his mother was, and Tehali was, and Isaniel had kind hands that made up for the unkind words he carried with every mug of ale.

Ren is kind, even when Bass hasn't been so kind to her. And she is kinder now, even after his transgressions allowed her village to burn. He killed her people, and still, she is kind.

"We're going," he says, squeezing Ren's hand delicately. "I know how to get there."

"Where?" she asks.

"To Sa-cha." Ren squeezes his hand back. "To the Winter River."

They'll move forward. He'll race Kensy to the end—of time, of life, of the River itself. Basuin has always been one of Kensy's pawns, strong and made for sacrifice. But Kensy can't sacrifice him if Basuin has already sacrificed himself.

CHAPTER TWENTY-SIX

Decisive. Basuin has always been decisive. One foot in front of the other, one goal to tackle at a time, one day of battle before the next. It lent him power, his simplicity a strength.

With a path in front of him, clearly marked by god magic the color of blood, Basuin wastes no time. He changes their course, closing the distance between them and Sa-cha. That's his only focus right now.

Getting to the Winter River before Kensy can.

Because if the legion catches up to them, Kensy won't let Basuin escape a second time. That act of kindness was a miracle. Ren won't make it out of that alive, because Kensy will kill Basuin. And Ren goes with him.

That's the sacrifice he made. The sacrifice he keeps.

They travel along the forest together in silence, but a comfortable one. The growing familiarity of it makes a warm feeling sway his stomach. In front of them, Qia clods through the forest with Yaelic chasing after her. Qia's ears are too big for her head in her spirit form, her little puff of a tail wagging as Yaelic bounces in a clumsy circle around her, showing off how fast he moves. He's growing into his paws, but his barks are still just little yaps.

It's endearing, watching the two of them play. Ko is somewhere behind them, the slowest of their party, while

Haaman flies over the forest scouting. They'll join Ko once they tire out and bring up the rear.

Ren leans close to him, a small smile on her lips. "How nice it must be, to have a friend your age."

He grunts in reply. "I wouldn't know."

"You didn't have friends?"

"Not until I joined the legion."

"How old were you?"

"Seventeen."

The smile she wears fades into a deep frown. "That's so young, to go to war."

But he sweeps right past it. "Did you have friends? As a child."

Ren's eyes fall, her brows narrowing. It takes her a moment before she speaks. "I don't remember."

It's sad—the kind of sad that he recalls tasting when she first told Basuin her name. How it didn't seem as if she knew it herself.

"Not at all?" he asks, ducking down closer to her height to see her face. But Ren blinks all emotion away, shrugging it off in the same manner he had.

"It doesn't matter." Ren looks back to where Qia and Yaelic play. "I am here to take care of this forest." She gestures with an open hand to the children, as if it can absolve the sorrow weighing down her voice and replace it with duty.

His lips part, ready to challenge her, but the light catches in her eyes and they sparkle golden. Yaelic's yapping, and Qia's bleating, and his blood rushing in his ears. Ren is happy. She's happy when her family is happy. Even as scrapes and burns bleed across her skin, marbling her like meat cut for roasting. Even as the forest hurts her—as the legion destroys her home.

"My mother," he blurts out. "She was all I had growing up."

Ren turns to him, and the admission is worth it when she smiles that kindly at him.

"Tell me about her."

Something blooms in Basuin's chest where his heart used to lie. "She was wonderful. Everyone was her friend, she was so kind. Until the fire, at least." He tries not to dwell on it—how their neighbors wouldn't even eat the fresh bread she would bake after god speakers were deemed witches.

"I was young, but when soldiers would come home—or when their shields would—my mother would wrap flowers from her garden into bouquets for graves. And she'd make big pots of stew, for the wives who were left behind."

Ren's eyes have gone all soft, a molten amber color he always gets lost in. Like sticky-sweet syrup. "She sounds very kind."

"She was," he says. "She would've liked you."

Ren tries to turn before he can see the warmth in her cheeks. It draws a grin to his face.

"You said Ko was your first friend," he recalls, prodding at her.

"Yes," she says, a smile growing now. "The first friend I remember, anyway. But that was once I was…"

Ren stops for a moment, the world around them closing in. Becoming small, and safeguarded by this closeness between them. He gives her a moment as her dark eyes glaze with the cool burn of something unsaid.

"Once you were what?" he asks.

She hums, pressing her lips together for a moment. "Once I was on this island. Ko was my first friend once I came to this island."

So Ren wasn't always here. She came to the island somehow. Ko told him Ren wasn't always a god—once, she had been human. Curiosity squeezes him. He wants to know more, more, more. It burns at his bones, he wants to know more about her. About what has hardened her, about what she can't remember. He wants to know everything that she's made of.

He gathers the strength to ask, then Ren speaks first.

"The fire," she says, and it grinds everything to a halt. "What happened?"

Everything slows. Basuin stares, but the colors blur into one entity. The smell of smoke lingers in his nostrils, better than blood—but then the tang is on his tongue, all rust and red. He keeps marching forward, like he was taught, but all he wants is to fall to his knees right now.

Fall at Ren's feet. Just for a moment.

"They burned the church," he answers. "When they outlawed the gods in Xalkhir."

Ren's voice is murky, on the edge of his mind like the shack on the edge of the forest. "I'm sorry."

Basuin tries to shrug, but his body doesn't listen. "She was a god speaker, Ma was. So, without the church, they told us we couldn't stay. We weren't welcome."

When his eyes regain focus, Ren's gaze is heavy on him. Her fingers are touching the godstone at her neck, all delicate as if it might shatter. "They made you leave?"

"They were afraid of her," he says. "Of what she could do." His hands feel tight. "Of what I would do."

"Afraid you would hurt them?"

There, in the middle of the woods, the march ends. Ren's eyes are heavy on his prickling skin. The whole world feels like it isn't real. Like this isn't his body. Like he wasn't the one who let his mother die.

"I could have," he says. "I could hurt you, too."

His throat is dry, lips wicked of moisture. He could if he wanted to. His whole hand could close around her neck and wring her dead. His boot could stomp her head into the ground like a stake. Basuin doesn't need a weapon. The sword strapped to his back has always been insurance.

His hands are enough.

All the pretty facets of Ren's face change in mere seconds. Her lips twitch, jaw tensing and slackening as she rolls something around between her teeth. She spends so much time thinking about what she says. Bass doesn't know what that's like. To think about what you'll say before you speak it aloud. To build a gate around your words, to only let dignitaries through.

He's crashed gates before. He's crushed locks and broken into homes. He wouldn't know how to swallow back any rotten words.

Ren takes a deep breath, lips finally parting to say something.

Then, her teeth gnash down on her lip in a clash of blood and her legs buckle beneath her. A sound ekes out of her as her eyes flash wide. Ren goes down, but Bass lunges to scoop her up in his arms, knees swept up in the crook of his arm. Blood drips down her arm, trickling off her fingers gone limp.

"I've got you," he whispers. He bars the panic from entering his voice as he kneels to the forest floor. "Hold on, Ren."

As soon as he lays her down, her head rolls to the side—she's fainted. A strike of fear pierces his heart, his palm holding her cheek. Her skin feels colder. His imagination. No, his worst nightmare. He doesn't know if he's awake or asleep.

But the spirits all convene, and now, it's real. Qia drops to Ren's other side. Her hands are already covered in the glow of green forest magic, ready to heal Ren's new wounds.

Then, a shot goes off, barreling through the woods from miles off. Birds crow and scatter. Basuin flinches, eyes shut tight. His body is so tense it aches, waiting for the smell of smoke and gunpowder and blood.

Blood. Tangy and rich. His eyes fly open. Ren is beneath the shelter of his body. Caged between his arms as she sleeps on, unconscious. Blood colors the foliage beneath her.

He's going to throw up. His stomach rolls. Fuck, he's going to heave. The green is turning white. The warmth is freezing around him. Ren is bleeding out on the ice; the winds are howling. Bowling through the plateau. Valley of death, they should have named it. Val-something. Val—

"Bass!" someone calls above the screams of Valkesta, and he turns his head. "Did you hear that?"

He stares up at Haaman, whose feathers stand sharp and at attention on the back of their arms. Ren isn't dead, he realizes. Her heart flutters beneath his hand. She's just asleep.

"Did you hear that?" Haaman repeats, and then another shot goes off. Bass flinches all the same.

Qia cries, "Am-sa! We have to—"

Bass looks down again. His palm is coated in blood. The wolf-man roars in his chest, a howl for war, and it reverberates through every single part of Bass. His sinew and his bone and his flesh and his blood. The crack of his spine sounds just like the gunshot as his body morphs into something not all human.

There's rotting meat between his teeth when he licks his lips. His eyes are wide, vision fielded by red.

"We need to move," Ko hisses, reaching for Ren. "I'll carry her on my back."

A growl leaves him before he can register it, body shielding Ren from Ko. *He'll* carry Ren on his back. That's his duty. He'll protect her. He'll keep her safe. He's her guardian. Her protector.

"Am-ga, please," Ko says, face twisting with grief. "The army is close."

He knows, but it makes blood fill his mouth. The wolf-man scratches at his ribs. Bass knows. They need to stop the legion, let Qia and Ko take Ren away from here. Painfully, he looks away from Ren. Haaman waits for him, still human, but ready to take flight. Yaelic shakes out his white fur, head down and staring at Bass.

He smells it now. The gunpowder. It makes him gag.

Beneath him, Ren grows paler. Sickly. She's losing blood and it's staining his trousers. She's dying.

Basuin takes her hand in his, clean of her blood, and presses his lips to the back of her knuckles. A blessing? A curse. A knight promising something to his lady. A servant vowing his life to his god.

"Take her," Basuin whispers. It aches to let go of Ren, but Qia wraps her in green healing magic and Ko labors her on his back. "To Hou-tou."

Haaman takes off before he does, headed straight into the forest toward the legion. But Basuin waits. He lingers. When he flexes his hand and red claws burst forth from his fingers, and when the wolf-man stands on its hind legs to take up all the space left in the chambers of Basuin's chest, he moves. He runs into the woods, spine hooked and picking up speed. Basuin runs into the woods until the trees are a blur of angry red passing him by.

Always too late, the wolf-man snarls.

Last to arrive, but first to leave. The only one who leaves.

It isn't a loaded promise, either. When he finally arrives at the blood-spattered site of marching soldiers and dead animals, Basuin tells them to run. He gives them that chance. And none of them take it.

He doesn't spoil their supplies nor break their weapons. Basuin burns them to the ground the way that Gyeosi burned. The way that Ulenski burned. Basuin recreates the same scenes over and over again, just like the nightmares do.

Have mercy, the women cried as they fled their homes with their babies bundled in their arms. A little girl clinging to her mother's skirt as they raced toward the Valkesi Mountains—the only side of Grimmalia that was still left unoccupied by the Xalkhans.

Black Wolf, one of them cried as she bumped into him, hands covered in soot so black he could not tell where the darkness ended and he began. *Black Wolf, Black Wolf, please spare us*.

And now, in the present, Basuin's hands pulse with red magic as he brings his sword down upon a Xalkhan soldier and slashes through the flesh and bone of his arm. Lumped bodies—more humans than heavy slumps of bears—burn with smoke and smell of fresh meat roasting over an open flame. He swears he hears the dinner bell ring, the one from Ilkana where he trained. Where he gave up his life to be as cruel as these soldiers are. Where he pledged to give up his gods, beaten until sick by iron bars, shoulders lashed bloody.

His hands are hot and they are violent. There is black fur sprouting from his tongue and he runs it over his teeth. Grown into sharp points, canines. Basuin growls from somewhere deep inside him.

More, more, more. With every man he fells he can taste their body. He'll slink on all four paws and rip the throats from these soldiers, show them how cruel this forest can be. Show them how the blood they spill grows claws that draw blood, too.

His fingers twist and click, curving into talons. He breathes, hard, heavy, quick—flexes his hand out to stretch away the claws trying to break free from underneath his nail beds.

Let it, the wolf-man snarls. *Let me.*

Basuin swallows, shaking out his hand. He hears a man lunging from behind. In a practiced swing, he draws his sword and slashes in an arc until the soldier falls at his feet, cut plainly and dead.

No.

Basuin's throat is parched. He craves blood. The wolf-man is panting for it, foam dripping from its jaws. He won't let it. He won't.

The magic that clings to his hands and winds up his arms in trails of red retract and dissipate. Then, he plunges his sword into another body. The smell of blood consumes him, but all it does is make him gag. He doesn't remember where he is anymore. If he's in the forest or in Grimmalia. If this is home, or if this is Valkesta.

If he's a boy again, or if he's still just a god.

* * *

For what it's worth, the blood washes off easily. He rubs his hands together under the slow-moving stream of Hou-tou's creek, a little ways from camp. There's a stubborn streak left on his cheek, blood threaded and dried in his wiry beard that he struggles with. It takes a few rubs with the damp hem of his shirt to budge. He doesn't want Ren to see any of this. If she sees the blood, she'll know what he did.

There wasn't any sabotage on this day. There was only carnage that turned to ash on the ground. Basuin is a bad, bad liar. But he washes the blood away before he checks on Ren despite it.

Of course, he isn't lucky enough to go unbothered. Before he can shake the water from his hands and dry off, he feels the watchful gaze of a spirit from upstream. Her blue-white eyes, sharp and narrowed at him. Hou-tou pokes her head up from the water in a cloud of bubbles, hands clasped together and cheek perched atop them.

"What a deceitful deity the Wolf God is." She hums. "Lying to our Forest God."

"Yes, Hou-tou." He plunges his arms back into the cold water and doesn't let her see him twitch. "I know you don't care for me. You made that clear when you told me to go die, before."

But Hou-tou doesn't giggle. "You're a useless god, are you not?"

"Yes, Hou-tou." He scrubs the blood off one, two, three more times. His skin is red and raw.

With a loud splash, Hou-tou jumps from the water, shrieking. "You're going to get her killed." Rage colors her cloudy eyes.

Basuin looks up at her, exhausted. Yes, Hou-tou. "You're trying to protect her, I know. But I am, too."

For a long moment, she stays there, glaring him down. But

the fight in her dies eventually, and Hou-tou sinks back down until just her eyes peek out at him, nose blowing bubbles on the river's surface.

"Do better," she demands. And then she disappears in a ripple.

Basuin is doing all he can do, but Hou-tou is right. It isn't good enough. He can do better.

Only the crackle of flames Haaman has started to keep everyone company breaks the quiet of their camp. As Bass passes by on his roundabout through camp, he stops to shake his hand through Yaelic's golden hair. Yaelic bats his hand away playfully, looking very bashful. Especially since Qia, who sits next to him, giggles.

Ren isn't in her tent when he ducks his head in, but when he looks up, her leg dangles from one of the branches atop the tall oak tree she sits in. He doesn't know whether to smile or scold her.

"Why aren't you resting?" he asks. "There's a perfectly pitched tent down here for you, Forest God."

Ren huffs and waves her hand at him. "Does this not look like resting to you? City folk should learn to go outside more often, breathe in the magic of the forest."

"There isn't much magic left on the mainland." Basuin leans his back against the tree's trunk. "None at all."

"The fault of your own kind, then." She doesn't say it meanly, but he still feels the heat of anger creep up his neck. He knows whose fault it is. He knows who burns down this forest. "It's peaceful here. Even the sunlight can heal you if you let it."

He tips his head and looks up at her. She stares off into the sky. "Is it healing you?"

Ren presses a hand against her stomach. "Little can anymore."

But Basuin can. He looks down at his hand, bloodied before but now clean of sin. He's a god; this hand of his can mend. He's done it before. The god mark swirling across his palm feels tight and leathery as he stretches his fingers out.

"Come down," he calls to Ren. "It's warmer in your tent."

Instead, Ren says, "I remembered something, from before. You made me think of it."

Though she says it lightly, it sits heavy on his shoulders. "What is it?"

Ren labors a breath. "When I was a child, we were celebrating something. I was given this sweet thing, in a bowl shaped like a flower. It was red, and I liked it." Her eyes are faraway. "I can remember how it tasted. Like cherries. But what was the name of it?"

"Do you remember anything else?" he asks. Basuin cannot give her much, so he needs to give her this. She'd been waiting for him, all this time. While he was off slaughtering men and planned how best to lie to her, Ren was waiting to share this memory with him.

She hums. "It bounced, when my spoon hit it."

Basuin could cry. "Gwapyeon."

Ren's eyes go wide, bright and beautiful as she looks down at him in shock. "Yes," she whispers. "Gwapyeon. It was my favorite." Once again, her eyes become distant, but a fond smile curls her lips. "I begged for my mother to make it for me every year. We picked the fruits fresh. How could I forget that? Gwapyeon."

She looks at ease now, leaned against the tree smiling, eyes cast toward the sky. Radiant, she's radiant. He reaches for her again, out of want. Then, he remembers where they are again. Who they are.

A woman posed in godhood. A soldier dressed in the fur of a deity.

"Won't you come down now?" he asks. Ren nods.

Bass moves to climb up the tree, to carry her down somehow. But then the tree's branches begin to unfurl, moving like a sway in the breeze. The spirit bends, bark and spines cracking as it lowers Ren to the ground, letting her slide off the branch she was sitting on and into Bass' grasp. He winds an arm beneath her, around the backs of her thighs, almost seating her on his bicep for a moment before helping her feet touch the ground.

She's still pale, and he suffers a breath at the sight of blood smeared on her skin.

Ren's fingers curl in the material of his shirt. "Would you take me to the lake? It's not far from here."

Bass, of course, nods. He turns his back to her, crouching low to the ground and gesturing for her.

"C'mon." He looks over his shoulder at her, grinning. "Hop on."

The press of Ren's thighs around his hips is almost as damning as her thin arms wrapped around his neck. Perhaps worse is the silk of her bare skin where he holds her legs, carrying her through the woods and toward the lake. Gods damn him, really.

The wolf-man aches for Ren's touch, where her fingers brush over his throat every now and again. On purpose or by accident, he's not sure. But what he's more sure of is that it isn't just the wolf-man preening at the feeling of Ren, smooth and plush on his back. It's him who aches for it, too. Aches more than death.

Bass squeezes his eyes shut, then opens them wide. He doesn't need to think about this. He doesn't need to consider it. She's wounded, for fuck's sake. She's vulnerable and hurt.

"You drove them away?" Ren asks him. "They hurt something, I know."

That kills the flare of light that was rising in him. He swallows. "Yes. They shot a pack of bears. Only two."

"Neither made it."

"No."

His hands feel tacky with blood. No matter how furiously he washed his skin, it sticks to him. Red the color of cherries—of Ren's gwapyeon. Bass adjusts her in his grip, careful not to jostle her too much. It makes her tighten her arms looped around his neck.

Then, a soft puff of her breath ghosts over his cheek as she lays her head against his. Softly, she says, "But you drove them off."

Drove them, scared them, killed them. Destroyed them in a war he promised not to bring. It doesn't matter. All that matters is the softness of her skin against his right now. He likes Ren like this—pliant and tender, as if all the weight has sloughed off her shoulders. When her fingers feel petal-soft as they glance over the muscles of his arms.

He likes her when she's sharp too. When she tries too hard to stay composed, poised. Limbs stiff and stubborn, but not her face. Not her eyes, graced with the futility of hiding the emotions she always tries to bite back.

Basuin likes Ren in every facet of the light. The feeling is so light he could laugh. Instead, he hangs his head and swallows hard as he trudges through the forest, onward to the lake.

CHAPTER TWENTY-SEVEN

BEHIND THE THICK woods, a break in the gnarled trunks and stretching branches of the trees, the lake glitters bright under the dying light of day, waters still. Nothing disturbs it, but ghosts of a gale break the mirror-glazed surface into ripples. Mossy rocks form a barrier between the lake and the forest. A glowing blue oasis. A pool of healing.

Ren inhales hard when her feet touch the ground, and Bass snakes an arm around her waist to help her find her balance. When she's steady, she pushes a small hand against his chest and evades his grasp. She moves toward the water like it calls her—like there's magic tugging her forward.

But then, at the edge of it, she pauses. Ren's foot is raised, but she's frozen in time. The smallest hesitation. He approaches in two steps, a hand outstretched to catch her if she falls. Ren looks back at him, a wrinkle in her brow, until it softens and her lips bloom in a smile. It shatters whatever held her captive.

As soon as her toes dip into the lake, she unties her robe's sash from her waist. The rest of the white fabric falls from her shoulders in a flutter, which she tosses away to the shore. Her back is a flaxen field of bone and beauty. Ridges of spine and sprouted shoulder blades and blood. Dried blood is smeared across her perfect skin.

There's a curve to her waist that Bass has only felt in touch, but deep bruises are creased in her skin following the line of the ribcage he can't see from this angle. His stomach rolls. His nonexistent heart is beating so fast. He's losing air. He can smell the blood from here—no, no, he can't. He's imagining it.

"Will you help me?" Ren asks, and he chokes. The delicate slope of her shoulders makes him tighten his fists.

"With what?" he struggles to speak. Even as Ren takes another step into the lake, Bass doesn't move. His feet are stuck to the ground.

"Bathing," she says. His mouth is dry. "Why else would I ask you to come here?"

If he squeezes his fists any more, his nails will tear holes into his palm.

"I want the blood off."

He does, too. But not—not like this. Bass can't touch her like this. It'll—

Ren unties the knot of her cotton shorts. Then, she bends and pulls the fabric down her legs, stepping out of them as the hem drags in the water only to be tossed aside with her top.

This is the end of him. This is where the gods will banish him to the Blacksalt Sea—how he looks at her like this. He squeezes his eyes shut and glances away because he can't trust himself to look at her. Bass doesn't trust himself to look at Ren without the thick heat rising in his body.

But even with his eyes shut, the image of her smooth, olive skin is burned into his brain. Not the flash of her shoulder he glances beneath her sleeve or the tendon on the back of her thigh running under the hem of her shorts—but barren flesh, the scales of her spine and the curve of her glutes.

"Haven't you seen a naked woman before?" Ren calls to him, but he doesn't dare open his eyes.

"Of course," he grits between his teeth, huffing. None like her. What would it feel like to let his fingers wander over the bones of her?

"And men?" she asks.

He exhales shakily. "Yes."

"Then why won't you look at me?"

Because when he opens his eyes, Ren's shoulder turned to reveal the dewdrop curve of her breast, his lips part and his mouth dries and a want courses through him in a way that it shouldn't. Shameful. And even more shameful, the fact that he can't turn away anymore.

Even as naked as she is, the leather tie of his godstone is knotted around her neck, the jade sitting in the rest of her collarbone and dragging his eyes to the valley of flesh he shouldn't be looking at. A thrill of desperation runs through him.

Bass' eyes flick up to meet hers, pools of obsidian hiding her thoughts from him. He doesn't want to read her now anyway. Fear of her judgment makes him stutter. Fear that she knows he looks at her so unabashedly.

"I am," he croaks out, throat stuffed with cotton.

Ren holds out her hand to him, the beautiful line of her arm stretched out as her fingers beckon him.

"Then help me into the water," she says.

How could he ever say no? Basuin toes his boots off at the same time he strips off his shirt, tossing both aside in a movement that feels too long. In three big strides, Bass meets her, slipping his hand under hers until their palms meet.

He wades into the cool water with her, breeches drenched and heavy. But a huff of relief leaves him without permission as Ren sinks further into the water, her olive skin disappearing into the lake and out of his hellish sight.

The sigh that Ren lets out as the water wraps her in its embrace is devastating in and of itself. It makes him think—for the first time since they've met—what other noises she could make and what they might sound like. Bass is careful not to squeeze Ren's hand out of the thought, but his jaw tightens into something painful.

Ren dips under the water, hair slicked back and bangs sticking to her forehead when she turns to him. Her lips split into a smile, almost in pride of something, and then she disappears beneath the surface again.

This time, the waters surrounding her illuminate into a glowing blue that matches the color of her forest magic, and when Ren rises, her skin is flecked with it. A feral thought tears through him—her skin freckled in god red, instead. Not of blood, but of his magic.

It makes him move closer; closer for the first time. As he wades into the ring of blue waters surrounding Ren, he feels the soothe of magic upon his skin. She's healing herself. Trying to. It's weaker than he's ever felt, and it wrecks the haze of want in his mind long enough for Bass to recognize the dip in their connection. Ren has nothing left to give, and his own magic races through their god-thread trying to offer his own energy up.

Bass takes Ren's soft arms in his hands, gentle but drawing her near. Careful to keep space between them. He would die if he felt her body right now. He would drop straight into the Blacksalt Sea and drown.

"Quit it," he scolds her, watching as her head tips back to meet his gaze. "Let me."

Ren opens her mouth, but before she can speak, Bass pours his magic into her. It feeds her through his palms, streams into the water around them. And all he can do is look into her twilight eyes, unmoving. He doesn't have to conjure any images in his mind because she is right in front of him.

He wants the blood off. He'll replace it with his own, color her with all he has.

Slowly, the water around them turns to a deep red, as if they bathe in wine. Ren's eyes flutter closed, fragile lashes pressed to her cheeks. She relaxes in his grip and he nearly bites his tongue in half to keep from pulling her into his embrace. But then she sinks, as if the weight of this forest comes down across the wings of her shoulders, and Basuin winds an arm around her waist.

The movement presses her into him, her breasts against his chest, and he swallows hard. Then, Ren brings her hands up, tracing the line of his shoulders, to wind around his neck. An ache pulses through him like the heaviness of guilt pitting in the bottom of his stomach. It's been so long—so gods forsaken long—since he's felt this, the heat is almost welcome in the way of a reminder that this is real. His touch, and her touch, and their closeness, is real.

"Thank you," Ren says, her voice quiet despite their privacy. "Thank you, Bass."

He doesn't trust himself to say anything. Not when her eyes open and reveal such beautiful colors. The rarest onyx, faceted with gold in the glint of the light. Warmth from the red of his magic a glaze over her irises.

Basuin's gaze traces down the length of her flat nose to the curve of her perfect lips—parted and wet by her tongue.

He doesn't trust himself, so he hangs his head until his forehead presses against hers, her skin damp but warm. Basuin closes his eyes, and still, all he can think about is how it might feel to kiss her.

Ren's hand curls around his neck. The other draws to his jaw, cupping his cheek as her thumb paints over a scar embedded in his beard. He shudders a breath he can no longer hold in.

"Can I try something?" He keeps his voice low, quieter than ever.

"Yes," Ren answers, no hesitation. Basuin's heart thunders in his chest like it might stop at any moment.

Then, Basuin dips his head and presses his mouth to Ren's. Soft—softly, taking her lip between his, plush and beautiful. And Ren tips her chin up, meeting his movement, clinging to him in a way that angles them somehow closer than they were before. It feels like sin, her lips against his, but it tastes like magic. Electricity on his tongue when he swipes it across her mouth but doesn't dare seek entry. Just to feel her.

In the haze of Ren, his hand has slipped into her wet hair to cradle her head. The other grasps at the flesh of her hip as gently as possible. When he finally pulls away, forces himself away, he's left panting in want for more.

Ren, gorgeous Ren, is staring up at him in the most dangerous way he's seen. Forget her sharp eyes and her stinging words. Her drawn shoulders and defensive stance. Here, eyes half-lidded and hazy, mouth pink and open as if asking for more, she's more insidious than anything.

Temptation beckons for him and Basuin is caught by it, leaning down until his nose bumps against hers.

And this time, Ren tightens her grip around his neck and pulls him down until her lips cover his. In shock, he folds, grasping at her waist for purchase, ridding them of any space between their bodies. He wants to feel everything of her.

It makes his breeches tighter and tighter, enough that he shifts his hips away so Ren won't feel it. Bass holds his tongue between his teeth painfully, but not as painful as the ache running through him.

His hands itch for more. To feel more. And when Ren sighs against his mouth, catching her breath, he needs to hear more of it. He needs to make her sound like that again—it's such a pretty sound. It drives him insane. Gods, fuck.

"Can I touch you?" he asks, voice ragged. He needs to.

Ren inhales, breath shuttering. "You're already touching me," she whispers.

In defeat, Basuin's head falls to the crook of her neck, spine bent to reach. His mouth is so close to her neck that his breath ghosts over her skin where water beads along her olive pulse point.

"But can I *touch* you, Ren," he says, not a question, voice a hum vibrating from his chest.

He can't see her face, but he hears the sharp inhale whistling through her nose. The way her body stiffens, locks up, enough that Basuin would pull away if she didn't have such a clutch on him. The fire quiets at her hesitance and a shame sets in that should've stopped him sooner than now.

But Ren doesn't let go, and her voice is a tremble of leaves in the wind when she says, "Yes." Then, "Please," in a watery beg he can't say no to.

Basuin's hands slide down Ren's body, following the deadly curve of her, thumb brushing over the soft skin of her breast, until both palms swallow her hips. He walks her backward, the shift of the lake around his legs heavy, mouth leaving kisses where he can. Her neck, where her jaw connects below her ear, her temple—anywhere. Ren's hand finds the leather tie in his hair and pulls it until it unravels, letting his locks free for her fingers to tangle in.

At the edge of the lake, Basuin finds a rock with the flattest incline and wades Ren toward it. He steadies his hold on her hips and lifts her out of the water to sit on the precipice. Ren's legs part for him to slot between, and it takes everything for Basuin to focus on her eyes as his breeches start to suffocate him.

His hands fall first to her thighs—he hopes they aren't too rough. Her skin is silk and spun sugar under his calloused palms and he's careful to keep his touch light. But Ren makes no protest, her chest rising and falling as she watches him. Her nipples, dusky pink contrasted against her flaxen skin, are peaked from the cold air or the hot arousal he hopes is coursing through her the way it sears him.

Slowly, Bass trails his fingers down to Ren's knees, then to caress her calves, then all the way until he brushes his touch over her delicate ankles. And when he drags back up her legs, Ren shivers. He can make her do that again. Again.

So he moves to lay a kiss on her knee, and then to her thigh, eyes catching her dark twilight gaze. Her stomach is taut and scarless. Then, a dark patch of curly hair above the apex of her pelvis. And when Basuin finally lets himself look—because gods help him, he's going straight to the Blacksalt Sea after he brings Ren to her peak—Ren's core glistens with evidence of the same need making him hard and heavy.

She's so beautiful. She's divinity in true form. And he'll pray. Sa-cha help him, Basuin will pray at her feet like this and worship her.

One more kiss to her inner thigh, close enough to feel her heat. "Can I?" he asks one more time.

Ren nods, her hand running through his hair. "Please, Bass."

His thumb swipes over the seam of her, a dribble of her honey collecting on his skin. Ren rolls her hips, the smallest, faintest gasp leaving her at his simple touch. It heats him, makes him crazy, makes his eyes flick up to hers as he tastes her.

And it isn't enough, this hint of her. It isn't enough. Without another thought, Basuin shoulders between her legs until her thighs surround him, locking his arms around her hips. His breath ghosts along her core, a last prayer for salvation after this is over, and then his mouth is upon Ren—enveloping her, tongue parting the valley of her lips and delving into her slick center, hot with need.

Ren makes a keening sound that calls for him, breathless as she falls back upon the rock. Strands of her wet hair make a halo around the crown of her skull and Basuin tightens his grip on her thighs to bring her closer. His tongue flattens on her point of pleasure, licking a path through her until it's well-traveled. Ren's fingers tighten in his hair, twisting, only driving him forward for more as he groans into her skin.

"Bass!" Ren chants his name in gasps and moans that make him want to grind his hips into something just to relieve the pressure. He aches, and he'll do anything to rid Ren of her ache and make her say his name like that again and again. Ren grinds her core against his mouth. She trembles under his hold. She clenches around nothing as her hand seizes his hair because he doesn't stop. His mouth does not stop and will not stop—the taste of her is addicting, and Ren makes such pretty sounds.

He is wicked. He's a sinner. There is no wolf-man here. It's just Basuin, worshipping his god until she will pray his name instead. And she does.

"Bass—Bass, please—" she pants, so pretty. So beautiful.

He wants to keep her here, riding this line, so she'll keep saying his name like this. But he wants to push her off that edge, to catch her as she falls, to hear how else she'll say his name. He wants to say, *Please what? Please what?* until she unravels beneath him.

Her thighs squeeze around him, nails turning to talons in his skin as she winds her hips over his mouth and on his tongue. He doesn't want it to end, the taste of her. He'll lick his fingers of her essence every single moment from now. But he wants to break her. See what Ren looks like as she shatters.

And so he does.

Basuin curls his fingers in the soft flesh of her hips as his lips envelop her pleasure point. A noise so stricken, so wanton, so lovely, tears itself from Ren's mouth like a howl that makes his blood run hot and his pulse quicken.

He pulls every bit from her that he can. Drinks her like the wine of the gods. Molten lava, eternal youth, blood of Sa-cha. He licks the magic from her skin, paints the apex of her thighs with her own makings. As quickly as she begins, she ends.

When Basuin pulls away from her core, Ren is slick to the rock, chest heaving from exertion. He loves it. He loves the sheen of sweat covering her skin, the glow of his red magic left behind. The way her eyes are soft amber, clouded by pleasure. He loves the brokenness of her, the beauty in her undoing.

He loves it—Ren, like this.

CHAPTER TWENTY-EIGHT

For the first time in his life, it wasn't a decision—kissing Ren was a compulsion, something he was meant to do. But his next decisions are easy. Familiar and what he's best at.

After watching Ren bleed again at the hands of the army, Basuin takes no risks. His anger is unbridled. The wolf-man hungers for death and Basuin hunts for it. At the next legion camp he and Haaman find in the night, men die. And at the camp they track after that, more men die. He trails their blood from one end of the forest to the other in hopes it will be an omen. This forest isn't for taking—they'll all die before he lets them take it. He'll kill anyone who tries.

More men fall, but Ren carries less wounds. And that's all Bass cares about. He promised Ren he wouldn't bring a war, that he wouldn't kill, but this war is already on their doorstep. This isn't the Xalkhan military marching into Grimmalia, bringing heavy guns and new technology and trained soldiers—trained Basuins. This is the forest, standing tall under the Xalkhan Legion's boot. He's doing what Grimmalia did. Fighting back.

It isn't even war. They don't have much to fight with. But every soldier he kills under the cover of night, a rank tied around their bicep the way he used to knot his, means one less bruise marring Ren's arm. He'll do anything if it means leaving her skin unblemished.

When he faces forward, he sees the red magic thread pulling him through the forest and toward the Winter River. But when he looks back, he sees the legion camps he's destroyed—and the ones he hasn't gotten to, yet. He needs to beat Kensy, to secure a future for this forest. But he needs to protect Ren, too. And killing is so much easier.

Killing comes naturally to him. Those soldiers, they're easy prey, and he's a predator with a violent magic he can't rid himself of.

Bass buckles his harness across his back and around his waist, tightening the straps in the dark of the night. The moon hides behind the clouds, blending into the velvet of the black sky that owns it. He moves by memory alone. Yaelic is at the small creek a few paces over, filling their waterskins as they ready for battle. Bass turns to follow after him when he hears hushed whispers bleeding from Haaman's tent.

"I wish you wouldn't." Ko, he recognizes. Then, a long pause.

"This is my home, too." Haaman—voice less cutting now. Soft in a way Bass has never heard.

"I am scared for you. They'll kill you."

"But my life, or yours?" A rustle of clothing. "They'll destroy us. I'd rather go down fighting than let them win."

"I cannot fault you for that." Ko sighs, loud enough for him to hear outside. "Then, be safe, little bird."

Bass leaves them to their silence, trailing after Yaelic. When the boy runs to him, arms full of water bladders, Bass ruffles a hand through his golden hair. Where once Yaelic would have laughed aloud, tonight the boy is eerily silent. He doesn't meet Bass' eyes, and a pang of hurt rattles through him. Guilt. Yaelic's bound himself to a god who doesn't know how to be a god. Basuin is still just a soldier.

Yaelic's caught in a war that never belonged to him, that he has no blame for. An inherited fault.

The pup doesn't speak even as Bass belts his waterskin to his hip, and it makes Bass linger. Then, Yaelic finally asks,

"Can I come, too?"

His answer is swift and immediate. "No." His voice cuts through the night. "You'll stay here and protect the camp."

It pains him that Yaelic would even ask that. He's a child. Children do not fight in wars. Basuin will not allow that. He walks away, content to not think of this anymore, but Yaelic runs after him.

"The army is far! Our camp isn't in danger. I want to come with you."

"I said no."

Yaelic runs around him, trying to cut him off, and Basuin stops. "Why not? I can fight—I want to." His eyes are steeled with determination, small fists curled up at his sides. But Yaelic is so small still. A child, not reaching past Basuin's hip. And so skinny; collarbones severe where they peek out of his robe and chicken legs all thin out the hem of it.

Basuin bends, crouching to Yaelic's height, eyes narrowed in a glare. "What do you know of fighting?"

It doesn't shake him at all. "I'll learn. You can teach me."

"Absolutely not." Basuin reaches out and shoves Yaelic's shoulder—not hard, but enough to make the boy go reeling back. "You'd get hurt. Worse, dead."

A flash of Hami's broken body slams into him, knocks the air out of him. The image of Yaelic's hair—white-golden and soaked with blood—crawls across his mind and he can't force it out.

Yaelic wears a look of hurt. Upset and betrayed. "I want to fight." He looks away, emerald eyes beginning to well up with tears.

"Why?" Basuin asks, though he's never been able to answer that himself. Never once did he wish for someone to save him from the devastation and death when he signed his name away to the legion. He always wanted to fight. He wanted to keep his mother alive, and if fighting promised that, then Basuin would fight.

"I want to protect them," Yaelic whispers, a hitch in his voice. "All the people I love."

And now, Basuin fights to keep Ren alive, too. What a cycle life is.

Basuin's knees creak as he rises again. "No," he answers still. "You won't be made a soldier." Not like he was forced to.

When he looks back—and he shouldn't have looked back—Yaelic is crying into the sleeve of his robe. Grief is so hard. Children shouldn't have to bear it.

In the woods, dagger in hand, Haaman sheathes the blade to loop their skein over their hip. Traces of sorrow crease folds at the corner of their eyes, and Bass pretends not to notice. Haaman looks to where Yaelic sits, still crying, and then glances back at Bass. But Bass refuses an answer.

"Ready?" he asks, giving Haaman a chance to back out. A door to leave through.

But Haaman gives him a curt nod. "Let's go, before day breaks."

And before day breaks, Bass runs his blade through the last soldier, blood from the wound trickling down his hand and dripping from his wrist as his boot shoves the body to the ground. He gulps down air. He feels like he's back in the past. Years ago, older than Yaelic is, when his hair was shorn on the sides and he wore his locks pulled back in a wolf's tail.

When he loved his sergeant, a man with bony hands and a slender form—a man he shouldn't have loved, but he did anyway.

Gods, Bass always loves people he shouldn't.

Haaman brings a dirty rag they found amidst the legion's supplies to the river near camp, wiping the blood from their arms before it begins to dry. They offer it to Bass, who does the same. He'll need a good wash in the river still, to rinse the smoke and blood from his hair, before—

"You have to stop." Yaelic finds them at the bank, eyes glazed over as he looks at all the blood Bass and Haaman wear. Bass wants to cover his emerald eyes with his bloodied hands. "Before Am-sa finds out."

—Ren finds out. Basuin needs to wash up in the river before Ren finds the blood trickling from his brow.

He runs the ratty cloth over his blade carefully before sheathing it on his back. Then, he crouches down, looking up to Yaelic.

"If you won't stop," Yaelic says, "then you have to bring me with you."

"This will be the last," he promises. And he means it. The blood has stained all the scars and creases of his hands. "We've bought ourselves some time." What an excuse for his bloodshed. Basuin acts as if he's done this to keep the army off their trail, rather than in return for how they've hurt Ren.

"And Am-sa will heal?" Yaelic asks, his eyes full of sadness. More than anything, there's trust in him when he looks at Bass. That much trust could kill him. That much trust could make Bass forget who he is. A god, this time. But a soldier, once.

But Bass nods. "She will," he answers, though he doesn't know if it's true.

Yaelic's sinks his teeth into his bottom lip. "What about the army?"

Something in him feels like death. Bass swallows, apple of his throat jumping, because no fucking boy should wonder that. Not even him, when he was a boy too, wondering if his father would come home. Wondering how he would take care of his mother after his father's shield was returned, body left on a battlefield.

No boy should ask to fight. To want to be a soldier.

"I'll take care of the army," he tells Yaelic, placing a hand on his small shoulder. "Don't worry."

Yaelic's eyes close, and then he nods. "Yes, Captain."

* * *

In the daylight, when his skin is clear of blood and no smoke lingers in his clothes, Basuin finds Ren sitting with Qia, young girl giggles mixing with the faint hum of a song under Ren's breath. Qia's weaving a mix of fronds and flowers together into a crown, which she places atop Ren's head as she bows for Qia to reach.

"Perfect!" Qia claps her hands. "A crown for the Forest God."

Ren touches it with gentle fingers. "It's beautiful, Qia. Thank you."

"Not as beautiful as you!" Qia chirps back, and Ren's smile widens into something blinding. And she is. So beautiful, flowers in yellow and white circling her head like a halo, eyes golden and radiant in the light filtering through the canopy. But he doesn't have the strength to tell her so.

Qia sees him first, bowing her head to him and to Ren, then running off. Ren turns to look at him, still wearing that smile on her perfect lips. She looks so easy right now—no pain, no responsibility. Just a woman.

Before she has a chance to greet him, he says, "I brought you something."

Her head falls to the side in question. "What is it?"

Basuin sits across from her, hands cupped together to hide the trinket from view. Then, he opens his palms to her. A maroon-painted ocarina, clay shaped by someone's careful hands. Ren's lips part, fingers gently running over the holes.

"A hun," she gasps. "Where did you find it?"

"We call it an ocarina in Xalkhir." He glances past her other question, not willing to lie to her right now. "You called it a hun?"

Her brows draw together. "It's the first word that came to mind. They would play these at…" Ren trails off, biting her lip. "I can't remember."

Instead of pressing, Basuin pushes the instrument toward her. "Did you know how to play?"

She shakes her head. "Do you?"

"No."

Ren laughs first—bright and clear and beautiful. And he barks a laugh in response, unable to help himself.

"Thank you," Ren says, taking the ocarina in her hands and turning it over and over, like she's searching for the memory in the rounded surface of it. "Maybe I could learn to play it, one day." There's a hesitance in her voice. The unease of it all. That there might not be another day for her to learn.

Guilt hits him in waves. He feels torn from side to side. Drawn and quartered. If Ren knew how he'd pulled this trinket off a legion soldier laid face down and slain, she would hate him.

But if he doesn't stop the army—if he doesn't win this war in any way he can—then Ren will die.

Basuin crosses his legs beneath him. "What else do you remember?" he asks instead of letting his mind linger on that. He can't.

Ren's head tilts again. She chews her lip in thought. "I don't know. But I remember that they played the huns. There were these… colorful things in the sky." Ren puts the little wooden instrument in her lap to free up both hands. She paints her palms along their own sky now. "It rode on the wind. I remember running, but I can't remember what it was. It was all different colors—red and yellow and black and blue."

"A kite?" he asks.

Ren lights up yet again. "A kite. Yes."

Bass' lips curl into a smile. "So, you flew kites as a child, and they played the huns, and you ate gwapyeon."

Ren's eyes get faraway again, lashes dark and blinking away the wet sheen that makes her irises sparkle golden. "Yes, I did."

He leans forward. "Was it fun?"

Now, she meets his gaze, and her smile turns into a grin with a hint of her teeth. "Yes, it was."

If Basuin could, he'd capture this moment forever. Lock it in a bubble of red magic, create a barrier around them that no one could enter. He reaches for her, fingertips brushing by the delicate skin of her cheeks to tuck fallen strands of her hair behind her ear. She turns pink beneath his touch and his lips curl at the sight of her. He wants this forever, this kind of Ren. He's terrified to lose it.

Basuin draws his hand back and clenches a fist he hides from view. He shouldn't touch her. The fear is heavy in his gut, a lead bullet leaking all his happiness he's found. He's trying to hang on too tightly. Everything he's ever tried to hold on to has crumbled beneath the crush of his grip. Ren might, too.

But he swallows that back, because she's sitting here in front of him, the most beautiful thing he'll ever see.

"I'll bring you one," he says instead. "When I go to the mainland again, I'll bring you back a kite. One in each color."

And Ren, gods damn him, laughs. So preciously, she laughs, her crown of flowers slipping off her head until he catches it for her and readjusts it among the nest of her hair, laughing along with her.

"*CAPTAIN!*" SOMEONE SHOUTS over the blizzard.

"I'm here!" he calls back. His hand is set to his brow, trying to keep the snow out of his eyes. Hail pelts his shoulders, plinking off his armor, the sound rhythmic and fading into the whipping winds that scrape by his ears. His boot catches on a rock hidden beneath the blinding white and he plummets toward the ice.

"Captain!" Someone's hands scramble to catch him. When he rolls onto his back, Qia is atop him, eyes alight with fear and the red of her robes drifting like a raised flag in the wind.

The flurry thickens and she's gone. Basuin heaves to his feet.

"If we keep going, we'll die." Ko's voice echoes behind him. "I am scared for you."

He whips around, but there's only an oak sprouted in the middle of the mountain. Valkesta screams.

"I won't leave him behind!" he screams back.

He loses his grip on the rocks and slides down the face of the mountain, hands splitting apart. There's nothing beneath him, no one to catch him. He doesn't make a sound as he falls, just shuts his eyes and hopes he doesn't feel it.

And when he opens them, the sky is gray above him. The battlefield is rife with gunshots. He flinches as one blooms close, shattering through glacier.

"Get up!" Haaman screams at him. Their hair whips across their eyes. "You marched us here—get the fuck up!" Then, a shot ruptures their gut. Haaman falls to their knees, choking, bleeding into the snow.

But he can hear it. In the dingy cells beneath the outpost, he can hear the screams of the captured. Tomaas is down there. He can still make it.

"*Captain!*" another voice wails. Bass turns, looking for the source. Who's out there?

"*Captain*," a pup cries. Bass whips around. Yaelic's gone. He shoves his arms into the snow, digging for it. Yaelic's underground. The tree above him is dead, all rotten wood. He can't find the den. He can't reach.

"*Help me*," Yaelic sobs.

"I'm trying." Bass gasps for air. His hands turn black with frostbite as he digs and digs and digs until his nails have peeled from his fingers and the snow has turned red. "Where are you?"

"*They trapped me*," Yaelic answers. "*I'm in a cage—I can't get out!*"

"I'm coming!" Bass stumbles to his feet, the winds of Valkesta pushing and shoving him back and forth as he teeters on the edge of the cliff. "Where—"

He looks to his left and there Ren stands. Blood leaks from her chest, saturating her shirt. Where her eyes should be, there are stitches closing the sockets.

"It's your fault," she tells him.

I know, I know, I know.

Her head tilts to the side. "He's already dead."

He knows. He knows that.

Ren's body breaks, collapsing into the snow. He dives over the ice for her. Her skin is already so cold. So cold. He cups her face in both his hands, blood-stained and aching.

"I'm already dead, too," she says, mouth unmoving.

Bass shoots to his feet, blankets tangling around his ankles until he falls to his knees with a curse. Forest ground is beneath him—not snow. Not ice. Not Valkesta. It's cold here, but not freezing. The fire has burned out but the smoke still permeates their camp. It makes him gag.

He beats his fist on the ground. Wake up.

Captain! Yaelic's shout reverberates in his mind. Wake up. Come back to the present. Get out of Valkesta, there's nothing left for him there.

But Yaelic's voice is so loud in his mind, so real, so vivid. It thickens in his throat, their connection. It burns in his gut. Basuin tears out of his tent, chest heaving. His stomach is twisted, his lungs empty. Wake up. He ducks into the tent nearest to him, rubbing remnant tears from his eyes. Wake up!

It's empty. Yaelic is missing. He's not dreaming anymore.

"Yaelic!" he shouts into the woods. A shake rattles through his bones as he pulls back the flap of Ren's tent. She's there, Qia wrapped in her frail arms, sleeping on. Basuin pauses, waiting to see if she breathes. And she does—chest rising and falling slowly.

"Yaelic!" he calls out, standing in the middle of their camp. Then, he rushes to the edge of the forest. "Yaelic," he warbles into the darkness.

A shadow moves through the trees and Basuin prays it's his little wolf. But the figure is too tall, and when the light from the waxing moon hits his face, it's only Ko.

"Am-ga?" he asks, nose wrinkled from being woken. "What is wrong?"

Bass' eyes are wide and wild. "Have you seen Yaelic?"

Ko shakes his head and Bass paces. He has to find Yaelic. That dream—*I'm in a cage, I can't get out*. It thrums through his head and he clutches his hair in his hands. He hears it, the same soft echoes he's heard before. Before, when Yaelic bound himself as Basuin's charge. How clearly he spoke to Bass without words at all.

Yaelic, he thinks. *Yaelic!* he shouts into the blackness of his mind, trying to reach the little wolf pup. *Yaelic, where are you?*

I'm here! Yaelic's voice stretches across the blank space of Bass' head. *Captain, they have me—please, help me!*

Where? Bass rushes to his tent, fumbling with his shirt and leather armor.

I don't know. I snuck out and—and they found me and—I'm sorry, I'm sorry. His voice is a whine of fear. He can't stand the sound of it. Yaelic whimpers again and it brings red magic to gather in Bass' hands. Into the hole of his chest.

And in that hole, the wolf-man howls until there's nothing but red left in Bass' world. Nothing but red. There's a thread of it, through the forest. The wolf-man paws at the ground and snarls against his ribcage.

Don't worry, he tells Yaelic. *I'll find you.*

Yaelic cries, *I'm caged. Please, Captain.*

Wait for me. I'm on my way.

He's knotting his boots when Ko pushes his tent flap out of the way, revealing a half-woken Haaman still rubbing sleep from their eyes.

"What's happened?" Ko asks, dark eyes weary and brows drawn in worry.

"Yaelic's been captured."

Haaman's beady, gold-ringed eyes widen into pucks. "Where?"

Bass jerks his chin in the direction that the wolf-man pulls him toward. There's no time for words. Then, he slings his harness on and buckles his sword to his back. There's no time to waste. There's no time when someone's been captured, made a prisoner of war. Tomaas didn't last. This could be a trap, just like Valkesta was.

But it didn't matter then; it doesn't matter now. Not for Yaelic's life.

It will be different this time. Basuin is a god. He was deified to protect. It will be different.

Haaman shoves their feet into a pair of boots and ties their hair back, dagger already strapped to their ankle. As they head for the woods, Ko catches Haaman by the arm to pull them into his embrace. As quick as he can, Ko presses his lips to Haaman's temple, then lets them go.

No words are shared. There is only silence. Bass walks, spine straight and marching the way he was taught to, trained to, toward Yaelic.

He flexes his hand. His nails have curved into claws.

CHAPTER TWENTY-NINE

THE CAMP WHERE Yaelic was taken to is miles away. Basuin finds the tracks of horses leading through the forest, his hand lit with red magic. But wolves are faster than horses. And Basuin is faster, yet. He won't let them have Yaelic.

Basuin runs like he ran in Valkesta. Like he's running out of time. He sprints through the trees, breaks through the forest. Like Tomaas is already dead, Sa-cha help him. Aless' head is seven feet away from her body, her blonde hair dyed red with her own blood. And Isaniel is—

Fuck, Isaniel is—

The wolf-man roars inside of him, lunging to tear his lung out of place. It feasts on his organs, muzzle bloody and rank.

No. Basuin leaps from a gnarled root and off an escarpment, boots landing heavy on the forest floor. But he keeps running. No. This won't be Valkesta again. Basuin won't let it be Valkesta again.

If he dies, Ren dies, too.

He hears Yaelic before he sees him, the soft whine filtering through his canines and whistling through his snout. The legion encampment is bigger than the others, and Haaman flies up to the canopy, circling the perimeter and scouting. But there is no dramatic entry. No stealth, no magic. This isn't a game—it's a reckoning. Basuin comes up behind the watchguard and slices his throat open with the dagger he wears on his hip.

Basuin presses his boot into the soldier's stomach and rips the legion rifle from his holster. He feeds bullets into the chamber and reloads, gun in one hand and dagger in the other. There will be no mercy here. None.

Haaman drops from the trees once they've found Yaelic's cage. In a flurry of quick movement, they dispatch the soldier who guards Yaelic, splattering blood across the kennel door and leaving entrails slick on the ground. Basuin hears the rattle and the piercing clink of Haaman breaking the lock. The squeak of metal as Yaelic rushes out, white fur dirtied. He runs straight for Basuin, but Basuin holds steady.

"Haaman," he barks. "Get Yaelic out of here."

Yaelic whimpers, rearing back on his haunches. The sight of him hurts, makes Basuin want to tear out his own throat, so he looks away before Yaelic's emerald eyes can soften him too much for the war he brings to this encampment.

Haaman hesitates. "You're staying," they say.

Already, the tents of this camp are rustling with movement, soldiers awake and alert. They yell orders at one another, screaming across the clearing they've cut out of the woods. Basuin sheathes his dagger to grab the lit torch they've set by the watchguard.

"Go," he commands them. Then, arm aglow and veins pulsing with god magic, he hurtles the torch upon one of the legion tents. The flames swallow the fabric, crackling with red wisps of his magic, and shouts of soldiers begin to swarm the camp. Weapons click, armor rattles, blades swathe along the air. As smoke disperses through the forest, Basuin doesn't look back, but listens as Haaman's footfalls disappear under the cacophony of the legion.

Basuin stands at the cusp of the legion's camp, blood boiling, red magic rising from his skin, body hot as sweat from the burning flames curling over his forehead. Once,

Basuin was a warrior feared across the legion. Praised as a war hero. Idolized by soldiers who coveted his strength and his devotion to the military. A perverted sort of worship.

But now, he's stronger. Basuin opens his clenched fist, spreading his fingers to free his god mark. Now, he is a god.

"There!" someone yells, and bodies begin to run at him. Basuin can't tell them apart from the shadows. His vision is dark. Everything is red. He moves by instinct alone, blind. But his ears catch everything.

And when he snarls at them—the legion which captured his wolf pup and threw him in a cage—his tongue swipes over sharp canines in a mouth that tastes like spoiled meat. Then, he lunges.

Basuin bleeds them and he burns them. If these soldiers had any gods left, they wouldn't have a breath left to beg for mercy. They don't deserve mercy. This is justice for what they've done. To Yaelic, to Ren. Clawed fingers strew vocal cords and innards across the forest. Black fur rises along his arms and legs, hackles tense on the back of his neck.

His teeth rip into limbs, canines creating sharp incisions that bloody his maw. Basuin runs through the fires he's set even as it singes the fur that's grown into armor over his skin, tackling soldiers to stab a dagger through their eye only to turn and shoot hot bullets through another man's torso.

Gunpowder fills his nose but he doesn't gag. He stretches his neck back and howls, bashing the butt of his borrowed gun on someone's temple until blood sprays across his face. He doesn't care. This is a frenzy. They locked Yaelic up. Tried to kill him. Not another prisoner of war. Not another Tomaas. This isn't Valkesta. Gods's sake, this isn't Valkesta.

Basuin tears a tent down with his claws that the flames haven't yet breached, barreling inside. A scream rings out from the corner where a man and a woman sit, cowering away from him. The man's arms are spread wide as if he can stop Basuin.

"Please!" the man begs, sheltering the woman with his body. "We're medics! We—We'll leave! We'll go back, please. I told them not to take the wolf. I told them it wasn't—"

"Shut up," Basuin barks, making them flinch. "You suffer the consequences of your brethren like everyone else. Like I did, like my men did."

But his claws retract. He curls his hands into fists around his weapons, hesitating. They're just medics. They're afraid. Just like little Tomaas, the medic who could barely fire a gun without his hands shaking, making the shot go wide. They had to train it out of him, beat it from his back the way they beat Basuin into form too.

When he blinks and the red recedes from his vision, just an inch, the man's face morphs into Tomaas', hair turning to ginger. But it's not him. Tomaas is gone like the rest of them.

His grip tightens. Medics know how to shoot, too. They're forced to kill like all the rest. They're not *just* medics, they're soldiers.

Behind him, heavy boots skid to a stop and Basuin whirls around, gun pointed at the medics and dagger braced against the enemy. Their faces all are blank to him, bodies black amalgam beneath the red filling his head.

"Bass?" a familiar voice calls, incredulous. "Captain, is that you?"

His head snaps up, eyes blinking away the bloodlust. There, a few feet away with a rifle in both hands, is Tehali. Her hair is pulled back in red-coated braids. Piercings have been ripped out, ears gored. Blood is smeared down her neck.

"Tali," he says, voice rumbling into a murmur.

"It is," she says, dark eyes widening in disbelief. "Captain, what are you doing out here? What are you—" Her eyes sweep over him. "What's happened to you?"

He tries to laugh but it comes out as a growl. The fire burns brightly still, heat licking at the tent now. Ash rains down across his boots.

"Why are you here?" he asks her, because there is so much death here. And his hands still beg for more destruction. For devastation.

"Who are you?" Her gun is loaded.

"The Wolf God," he answers. It burns from the hole in his chest and outward.

Tehali takes a step back. Basuin takes one forward, holstering his gun. And then another, and another until he snatches Tehali's armor and forces her backward, out of the tent and into the burning grounds, snarling down at her until her shoulders are shoved against a tin supply shed.

"Where is Kensy?" he demands.

Tehali stutters. She's afraid of him. "He hasn't been seen in days. He came back without you—said you were dead."

"I was."

She searches his eyes, fire reflected in her black irises. "What happened?"

"Where did he go?" he asks instead, shaking her by her armor.

"What have you become?" Tehali whispers. His eyes go wide, then narrow with a heavy anger hanging on his brow.

"A god." Dead, twice over. Saved first by Tehali. Saved again by the gods and made into this—this thing. He must look like a horror to her. Is his skin pitch black, has he grown fur, are his eyes bleeding red yet?

Is he monstrous yet, his outsides finally matching his insides?

"I'm sorry," Tehali says, barely heard under the crackle of fire as tents and tarps collapse around them, eaten away.

Basuin shoves Tehali away from him with a guttural sound. He would kill the whole legion if it meant keeping Ren safe, but why must it be Tehali who stands here before him? Tehali—his only friend left. Captain Tehali, of Ariche's Fleet, of the soldiers Basuin once led.

Please, not Tehali. Make Tehali go home so he doesn't have to kill her, too. Basuin closes his eyes, feels the fury ripen and sour within him.

Then, an explosion bursts through the camp, incinerating the vicinity. Basuin is thrown forward by the impact, heat sizzling on his skin with a hiss. He topples over Tehali, shielding her from debris as the blast shudders through the camp.

When he turns to look back, the tent where the medics hid is completely destroyed.

"Fuck!" he screams. He checks Tehali, fingers pressed to her neck until she coughs and sputters alive, and then he breaks into a sprint for the medics. But it's too late. Even as he sifts through the wreckage, hot and sharp, there's nothing but bodies. No pulse. Just blood and bits.

Nothing solid to drag away, like the Grimmalian soldiers dragged Tomaas away.

Basuin stands, flicking blood from his hands. His claws have gone; his mouth is dry. He runs his tongue along his teeth and find all of them flat again. But it doesn't stop the magic coursing through him. The need to howl. To track Kensy down and tear his throat from his body in hunger.

"Bass," Tehali pants from behind him, struggling to stand. He doesn't look at her. If she shoots him in the back, so be it.

"Get out of here, Tali," he says. "Get off this island."

"Will you come?"

A huff of a laugh leaves him in shock. After all the carnage she's witnessed, he can't believe she's asking that.

"No."

"It doesn't have to end like this," she pleads. "You can still go home."

He shuts his eyes. There is no home anymore, no shack still left on the edge of the village. No Ma waiting for him to come back from the forest, trappings for stew and fallen branches to sturdy the roof.

There's only Ren and the softness of her hand in his, the way her lips curve in a smile and the color of her bruises with every mark the legion leaves on the forest.

"Go, Tali. I won't give you another chance," he lies.

Tehali grunts in pain, almost quieted by the fire still ravaging the camp. "He went north," she says. "That's all I know." With a hard inhale, Tehali starts to walk away, footfalls still familiar, then stops. "Captain?"

Basuin cracks his scarred knuckles, but he turns to her in response.

Tehali pauses before she speaks. "Be well, Basuin of Ankor." Then, she trudges off.

The fire blazes around him, collects in a tornado which swallows the encampment. He waits until he can't hear Tehali anymore to murmur, "Congratulations." She's gone, but he still says, "Congratulations, Captain Tehali."

Basuin stands until his knees start to give out, and then he stomps out the flames. Culls them with the last of the magic sunk into his bones. He waits until there is nothing left but blackened bodies to leave the legion camp behind. It's quiet, the aftermath. No cicadas and no animal cries and nothing at all. Only the sound of charred grass beneath his boots, the crunch of twigs and ash.

Basuin walks all the way back to his own camp, the sky turning to a dusky lavender overhead. He turns before he comes too close, heading down to the stream that runs through the woods. Yaelic is fine—he can feel it through their bond. Ren, too. He doesn't need to check on them. He needs, first, to wash the blood and ash from his skin. It crawls all over him like fat centipedes wanting to burrow inside him.

He kneels at the bank, shoving his arms into the cold water. With quick, rough hands, he scrubs his limbs of what he can until his skin feels raw. Then, he splashes his face and rubs it clean, washing soot from his eyes and blood from his jaw.

Basuin sits back on his heels, wiping water from his vision. But when he looks down at his reflection in the creek, it isn't him.

Instead, he stares at the Wolf God—black skin, red lines, a black wolf's head. Basuin raises his hands to his face as the

Wolf God raises his clawed ones. No, it is him. Basuin is the Wolf God, just like he told Tehali.

What's happened to you? Who are you? he asks himself just as Tehali asked him. *What have you become?*

He plunges his hands back into the water, gritting his teeth to bite back the scream in his throat. His lungs feel empty. Choking. He's losing himself. He doesn't know who he is. He doesn't know who he was before. A man, a god, a soldier—who was he?

Basuin bows his head and grits his teeth to swallow the sob bubbling up in his chest as fear sinks lower into his stomach. He's dead. He really is dead.

When he looks again, reflection only seen by a sliver of moonlight, he's staring at himself again. Bronze skin, dark eyes, scar threaded white through his brow. And behind him, Ren is staring at him, too. Her skin is mottled with red burns. New burns. The ones he's given to her as easily as he could give her a fistful of wildflowers. The ones he's caused by setting a fire that burned black rings into the forest floor.

He hurt her again. He always hurts her. Basuin doesn't know any better than this. Horrified, ashamed, he hangs his head, hand covering his mouth to hide the tremble, eyes squeezed shut and burning with unshed tears. These hands—they only bring war.

But Ren, despite it all, sits beside him. And her hands—her hands made of peace—fall to his arms, gentle and soft and forgiving.

Despite it all, Ren lays her head on his shoulder as Basuin cries into the creek. The gods, they damned him. But not before he damned himself.

CHAPTER THIRTY

"KENSY'S NOT WITH the army," Bass says, thumb soothing red magic over a burn on Ren's forearm. He can't look at her right now. He can't hide the fear lurking in his eyes. "He's moving north, alone."

If Ren's face changes, he doesn't see. He busies himself with healing every new wound that crawls across her skin—the wounds he brought to her. This is the one thing he can control right now, as laughable as it is. Trying to find forgiveness in his own guilt and shame.

Godhood, it seems, is as despicable as being a soldier.

"For how long?" Ren's voice is a tremble.

"I don't know." He inhales, running his fingers down the rivulets of her knuckles, only pulling away when the urge to slip his hand into hers grows too heavy. "But I do know him, and this isn't anything new. Kensy's always been crafty. We used to move ahead of the legion in the middle of the night together, just me and him, and bargain with whoever was heading the opposition in whatever city we wanted to take. We wouldn't sleep, sometimes for days."

His vision dims. Ren must think him a monster for such horrific things. But it's true. All of it.

"And once we bargained," he continues, "we'd kill whoever we'd just conned, and when the fighting started, the legion had already caught up with us."

A chill crawls up his spine. Ren says nothing, nothing at all, and he chooses not to look at her.

"He's outpaced us. He could be there right now," he stresses.

Ren's free hand draws up to touch the godstone she still wears. She closes her fist around it, much like he used to do, and it makes his heart quicken. He wets his lips, the ghost of her kiss setting a blaze of want through his mind again. If only he could reach up now and cover her mouth with his. Banish that worried look she tries so hard to hide from him, the one that creases her brows.

He has to get to the Winter River first. He has to go—now.

"Don't worry," he says instead, and brings her hand up to lay a kiss upon her knuckles. It's the closest thing he can get. "We'll figure it out." He's said that too many times now, but every single time, he's meant it. He hopes Ren believes it, too.

"Let's go, then." Ren's eyes meet his, but she blinks and they wander down to his lips. Then, her gaze falls completely. "The army has slowed down. The spirits are safe, for now."

Right. Because he's slaughtered every camp they had.

He squeezes her hand. "I'll go, and you can stay and protect them."

"No." Her answer is quick and snipped, her nails biting into his skin. "You said we do this together." Those eyes of hers are so dark and so sharp, so cutting, and so beautiful. So sad.

His heart is so full and so heavy in his chest.

"We're partners," she says harshly. Then, softer, she asks, "Right?"

"Of course," he answers with no hesitation. "We're partners." Basuin clasps her hand in both of his, pocketing her away. He doesn't want to let go of her. Ever.

Ren's whole body eases, and she blinks what he thinks might be the blossoming of tears away. "So we go together."

It makes his chest ache something foul. Basuin keeps hurting her, but she still believes him a partner. Once, he thought he wouldn't find another human as kind and gentle and patient as his mother was—she didn't seem human to him in the first place, touched and blessed by gods. But Ren was a human once, and she is more kind and more gentle and more patient than even his mother was.

Ren lets him heal the rest of her wounds with magic that feels like it belongs to him now. The Wolf God. The acceptance tastes like rot and fester in his mouth. But he tries to believe it's worth something. He's a protector, and this magic allows him that. An extension of this feeling he harbors for Ren—this affection, the need to protect her and steal away her pain.

"You are going to the Winter River." Ko startles them both, a hitch in Ren's breath that he only hears because she's so close to him. Ko stands a few feet away, draped in his dark robes and looking as tired as ever. More, somehow. Bruised undereyes and mussed hair.

Basuin looks to Ren, who meets his eyes. What will they say?

But Ko doesn't wait for them, tipping his chin up to look toward the sky with a heavy sigh. "I wonder if Ithika watches this unfold, and if she is saddened by it all."

Basuin, too, wondered that. As he sat on the boat that brought him to this island, he wondered if Ithika might rise and swallow them whole in her seas.

"But she has long since been dead," Ko says. "She cannot protect the Winter River, as she did before, from up in the godrealm."

His eyes widen. "Ithika is dead?" Across from him, Ren closes her eyes and turns away.

Ko gives him a sad smile. "I told you before that gods cannot roam without a body or a host."

"Yes," Ren says before he can ask anything else. "We're going to the Winter River."

A sad silence covers them, then Ko nods. "Of course you are." Then, he kneels beside them, letting his eyes fall closed and his shoulders droop as he hides his hands in his lap. "You make her proud," he says.

"Who?" Ren asks. But her hand clasps the godstone at her neck. Can she feel the grooves that he's worried into the jade stone—the imprints of his mother's wishes and worries? Of his own fears?

"The Forest God," Ko answers. "The one who lives in you."

Ren's eyes flash wide and bright, a mirror of the moon above them. "You spoke with her?"

Ko's smile only gets kinder, but more somber all at once. "I knew her, before I knew you. The determination in you is the same that she bore. I know she feels pride in you, Am-sa."

Ren bows her head, touching her forehead to her clasped hands—a prayer that goes unheard. Then, she buries her face in Basuin's chest. His mother's stone is a heat between them, the only thing that keeps the place where their hearts might be from pressing together.

Ren has a heart, he knows. The gods don't speak to her because they let Ren keep hers.

BASUIN STARTLES AWAKE. He can't remember what he dreamed about, or what woke him at all. His eyes scan their camp, trying to listen for any other sound—but there's nothing but the whistle of the forest. Everyone is asleep in their tents. He checks on each one, counts heads and bodies, lingers until he can breathe.

It isn't enough. He pushes to walk the perimeter of the forest, too. Then, he'll be able to sleep again.

He traipses into the darkness, thinking better of making light out of magic. If there's something out here, he'll hear it before he sees it.

But there's nothing out here. Only the dawning light of day, rays of light beginning to color the sky as he makes one final round through the trees. He's tired—his eyes are starting to ache and his joints are stiff in the cold morning air.

Bass slows to a stop, ready to turn back and go check on Ren again. Then, he sees it.

Movement, in the forest. A flash of color. A glimpse of someone. Bass is pulled underwater in an instant, drowning, the rush of waves too loud in his ears for him to hear anything at all.

He drops to a crouch, creeping forward. Whoever is in the forest doesn't make a sound, disappearing behind a thick-trunked oak into another throng of trees.

Bass rushes them, leaping out—but there's no one there. No one at all.

He breathes, hard. A trick of the light. He turns to head back to camp.

There, a flash of golden hair. Isaniel.

No, fuck. It can't be. It wouldn't. Paranoia trickles in like ice water in his veins. Bass whips his head around, looking at all angles of the forest. *Isaniel.*

But when he looks back, Isaniel is gone. There was nothing ever there.

He's been fooled by his own mind. Again. Nothing at all.

Basuin sinks to his knees in the middle of the woods, breathing heavy and quick. That space in his chest is buzzing, like it's been set aflame. He's been through this before—seen it before in the darkness of his quarters, from his bed in the healing bay. Isaniel's ghost come back to haunt him.

It will never end.

There's an ache filling him as he trudges back toward camp. The feeling of Ren's hands on his face, calling to him, waking him from what she believed was a nightmare. If only he could feel that again. The softness of her. How is her skin so honeyed, still? After all the fires in her forest?

He falls to his bedroll, lying beneath the stars, catching his breath. It's over now. It's just a memory. Isaniel is buried beneath the snow on the Valkesi Mountains, never to return. He's at the Winter River. Basuin must get to the Winter River, before Kensy can.

Basuin has to get there first.

He's the last to fall asleep, still wracked with worry, and the first to wake, mouth dry and back aching. He sits up with a quiet grunt, rubbing his scar until the itch is gone, wiping the crust of sleep from the squinting crack that blurs his vision.

When he stands to stretch his legs, turning to head into the woods, he's stopped with a pit sinking into his stomach. An oak tree stands shrunken before him, no leaves on its withered branches. A large, uneven square has been cut into its trunk and stripped of bark. And in that trunk, words have been burned into the flesh.

YOUR GODS CHOSE WRONG.

Basuin chokes. He steps forward, placing his palm to the marred trunk—but it collapses, the tree shattering into dead wood to reveal a broken heap of a man dressed in long robes. Ko's long hair is stringy along the forest, matted to his face with blood.

He drops to his knees, hands hovering over Ko's body. "Ren!" One hand to Ko's face, the other searching for a heartbeat. "*Ren!*" he calls again, voice ragged.

Movement starts, quick and chaotic, as Bass' shouts make it across the camp. And then, a scream. Agonizing. Pure unfettered pain. It rings out so terribly that even Basuin flinches with the ache.

Haaman wails—an animal that's lost its mate—tumbling to the ground on their hands and knees before they can even reach Ko's body. They howl, head pressed to the dirt, and he can't bear to look. The sound of Haaman's screams vibrate through Bass' bones.

Ren slides across the ground on her knees, clutching Ko's face. She searches for something, then arranges Bass' hands on Ko's cold body. One on his chest, one on his stomach. She doesn't say a word, one hand on Ko's forehead, the other on his throat.

Clenching his eyes shut, Bass floods Ko's body with all

the magic he can, following Ren's lead. Her magic is more graceful and confident—much like she is—and his magic intertwines with hers to power it.

And then he's tackled, hands pulled from Ko's body, rolling across the forest. Haaman is bawling, making inhuman sounds like the screech and squawk of a bird.

"Haaman!" Ren yells, but her hands don't stop pumping healing magic into Ko.

Bass struggles beneath Haaman. He needs to help revive Ko. But Haaman takes his head and slams it upon the ground—once, twice. Bass' vision shutters.

"You killed him!" Haaman's fist strikes Bass' jaw. Then, his nose. Pain explodes as it cracks over his skin but Bass doesn't try to stop them. He doesn't raise a single hand to them.

Haaman strikes again, tears and spit dripping from their face onto Bass, and misses. Their hand hits the ground and Bass hears the snap of bone. Another scream is torn from between Haaman's teeth. They just switch hands, punching Bass again. And again. Until he tastes blood in his mouth.

There is no Ko to calm them. And Ren, when he has a split second to look, is slumped over Ko. Haaman's fist whiffs by, but their fingers catch in his hair and whip his head back into the ground a third time. Stars burst in the back of his mind.

"Haaman," Ren calls again, her voice exhausted. "You have to stop. You need to come to him."

Then, Haaman's weight is off him and they're shrieking again, kicking at the ground as they're pulled away. When Bass opens his eyes, vision fuzzy, Yaelic has risked violence to wrench Haaman away.

Still crying and heaving, Haaman crawls on all fours toward Ko's body, collapsing atop him. Basuin's stomach twists. It's sickening to watch. Horrific. If he squints enough, this forest turns into a battlefield, strewn with dead men and women and all their body parts.

Why are there battlefields in the land that he's been

entrusted? The land of broken gods and bitter soldiers.

No one touches them; neither Haaman, nor Ko. Ren moves to Basuin's side, reaching out to touch the bruised, broken skin Haaman's left on his cheek. He doesn't even flinch—doesn't look away from the scene before him.

"Don't go!" Haaman screams to no one. Ko isn't there anymore. "Please! Don't fucking—don't leave me!"

When Ren's blue magic lances over his skin, Basuin brushes her touch away. Instead, he takes her hand in his, holding tight. All he can do is watch as his heart aches in his chest worse than the wounds do. He doesn't deserve the healing. She's exhausted anyway.

She couldn't save Ko, but that's not her fault. It's Basuin's fault—because it wasn't Isaniel he saw in the forest last night, golden hair haunting it. He knows the man who would be this cruel. Only he knows how Kensy would curl his lips and bare his teeth in the most vicious of grins.

Kensy hadn't outpaced them. Kensy had *followed* them.

"Bastard," Haaman curses, choked by their tears. They struggle for breath. "You fucking bastard, don't fucking do this to me."

Haaman's screams echo through the forest, loud and shrill enough to scare off a flock of birds who take off into the sky in search of shelter.

They let Haaman cry and sob and curse and wail for so long that Bass loses track of time and stops counting each throb of his head. Yaelic's silent tears run down his face. Qia hides her face in the sleeves of her robe. Ren sits holding Bass upright, fingers pressed to his temple to sink what magic she has left into him.

Haaman wipes their face on their arm, struggling to breathe. They hiccup, catching their breath, and dissolve into bawls again. The cycle repeats on and on.

"Haaman," Ren finally calls to them. "We can let Ko rest now. I can—"

They whip their head around, beady eyes cutting. "Shut the hell up," they seethe. "This is *your* fault. This is all your fault. Ko died because of you."

Ren's face is still, but her hand tightens in the cotton of Bass' shirt. She doesn't say a word, doesn't move a muscle besides the twitch of her fingers. Qia, sitting further away from all of them, opens a trembling mouth just to shut it again without a word.

"You—" Haaman heaves a breath, "—didn't do shit to stop them. Your pathetic pacifist ideals killed him. You aren't a fucking god. You're just a naive little girl," they snarl.

Ren doesn't answer, but Haaman crawls to their feet, sluggish and yet burning with anger. Their face is red and streaked with tears, as if they've boiled alive in their grief.

"If you'd fucking fight, then Ko would be alive." Haaman staggers closer to them and Ren stands. She steps over Bass, toward Haaman, shouldering their words. Responsibility—guilt, maybe—squares her shoulders but keeps her small.

"But here's the truth," they spit, thrusting a hand toward Ko. "The truth is that you don't give a shit about this forest. Don't care if we live or die. All you care about is upholding your perfect version of peace."

Haaman sobs, clutching their chest. They fold, as if the weight of everything is too much. It's all compounded on them, too heavy to keep them upright anymore.

"Well, Am-sa? Is it fucking pretty?" they scream, throat raw. "Looking down from your godrealm—have we died just for your fucking entertainment?"

The trees shake. Haaman pants, shivering.

"I'm sorry," Ren says. Basuin closes his eyes, for it sounds just like Tehali's apology.

Haaman jerks back, eyes wide as a choked sound leaves them. For a moment they stand stock still, frozen in fear. Then, they turn on their heel and take off into the forest, running for the woods. Everything is silent. Too silent. So silent that Basuin doesn't think mourning could break it.

He hangs his head between his legs, skull still pounding. Blood drips from his nose into the dirt.

Ma, what can I do? he asks no one. She's never responded before—she won't respond now. The dead don't talk back. Ko's body, stricken and cold, is so starkly outlined in his mind even in his refusal to look. *Ma, I don't know what to do anymore.*

You do what you can, the wolf-man answers. It's curled in a ball inside his chest. *You must protect her—at any cost, man or spirit alike.*

But when will it end? When will I stop having to watch people die?

The wolf-man huffs.

Blood begets blood begets blood, the wolf-man answers. *War begets war. Debt begets debt that is never repaid.*

CHAPTER THIRTY-ONE

QIA HEALS THE rest of Bass' wounds, chasing away the ache and the dizziness that remained. Yaelic stays close by, but sticks to Qia when Bass heads into the forest for some air that isn't thick with death.

Ren disappeared, taking Ko's body with her. He hasn't seen her since.

The forest isn't quiet and that's what he likes. There's life here still. The fluttering of birds' wings and the croak of frogs. Buzzing insects and breezy canopy. Even the light, shimmering through the leaves, makes a sound that reminds him of a bright, melodic hum.

He should look for Haaman, even if he's the last person Haaman wants to see. Him, or Ren. But Bass doesn't want them to be alone out there, grieving their lover. He knows what that grief feels like. It wrapped Bass in its tight cocoon, suffocated him slowly, bit into him like glass.

Haaman shouldn't have to fight that by themselves.

Bass climbs the nearest oak tree he can find, smoothing a hand over its bark and murmuring a short apology. The trees will grieve, too. Every spirit will feel Ko's death in some way. He finds footholds in each branch until they thin out and the leaves begin to sprout densely, then he sits to rest his back along the trunk and survey the forest.

Kensy's cruelty knows no hesitance. Even if Ren doesn't wish it, this is war. And Bass—well, Bass is best at war.

He's torn in half by indecision, perhaps for the first time in his life. Part of him is screaming to run at Kensy now, to take off by himself and hunt his commander down. End this, here and now, before anyone else gets hurts. But the other half of him can't bring himself to leave without Ren.

Ren said she wanted to go together. But Ren doesn't want war, either.

Haaman wasn't wrong. He would've soaked up all the bullets for Ren if he could, but as sharp and killing as their words were, they weren't wrong. Bass should have worked harder to protect them. He should've gone against Ren sooner, met the legion head on and tried to save more spirits. Should've killed Kensy when he had the chance—should've bore Ren's anger, or hatred, or disappointment. He should go now. Track Kensy down, meet him at the Winter River, and kill him like he was meant to. Made a god to.

He has to kill Kensy.

Hami and Ko are yet another weight of guilt sticking to his back, something to carry in the grooves of his armor. Inaction—his fear every time a wound breaks Ren's skin—has made him weak. Protecting Ren should've meant protecting the forest, too. But he forgot. He won't let himself forget again.

He's going to kill Kensy.

Bass leans his head against the oak he sits upon, staring up at the sky. There's so much distance between him and the godrealm. He reaches for the godstone around his neck, but there's only skin and bone there. Maybe his mother could comfort Ren now. He would like that.

And, like the thought called for her, Basuin looks down and spots Ren wandering through the forest. If he didn't know her so well by now, he'd call it aimless. But Ren's never done anything without a goal in mind.

Without a second thought, Bass drops from the tree and lands on his feet right in front of her. The only thing that hurts is the creak in his knees as he stands, thirty years of war still in his bones.

Ren doesn't startle, but she does take a step back as if preparing herself to twist away from his touch. He doesn't move toward her, though, and she doesn't jerk away from him. He should say something, but his mouth doesn't move. He can't say a word; doesn't know how to comfort her. So they stand there, staring at each other, waiting for the other to break the silence.

It's him, first. Because Ren's nose is blushed and her eyes glassy. The last time he saw her cry, it was as beautiful as it was painful. Now, it cuts through him like a knife carving meat away from bone.

"Sit with me," he says, because he can't think of anything else but pulling her close and kissing the crown of her hair.

Ren's eyes fall. "I was searching for Haaman."

If he had a heart, it would ache. The blinding hole in his chest is too empty—the wolf-man has stolen into the shadows of his organs. He aches despite it.

Bass stretches his hand out toward her, fingers unfurling. His god mark runs red, magic pressing beneath the surface of his palm. And when she takes his hand, her god mark slotted to his, Bass' whole body jolts. Like lightning's struck, birthed him into a new man.

He doesn't tell her not to worry, and he doesn't say that Haaman will come back. He doesn't say anything at all, but he leads Ren toward the tree he climbed earlier and shelters her beneath it. Ren tucks her knees beneath her, leaned toward him, and Bass spreads his knees and leans back against the oak's trunk. It's quiet—a bird chitters above their heads, singing a song that no one returns.

Ren hasn't let go of his hand, and Basuin hasn't let go either.

"I've never left this island," Ren says, gaze turned upward

to the sky. "I've been here since I became the Forest God. It's all I've known."

It's the first time she's admitted it out loud—that she was once a human, before.

"You're bound here?" he asks.

"No." Ren turns her head away from him. "I've always feared the ocean. I can't remember it well, but I was just a child when I came here. The water—" Ren swallows, "—scares me."

Her voice is an echo-chamber of fear, full and unending. She won't let him see her face, but she sheds the spikes she wears on her skin for this one moment. He's looking. He hopes Ren knows he's looking at her.

"How did you come to the island?"

"She saved me," Ren says, her hand falling to his knee. "The gods gave me life and let me grow. Then, when it was time to repay my debt, I became the Forest God."

Debt begets debt that is never repaid. Basuin hooks his pinky around hers.

Ren was human, just as he was. But Basuin died old, with a life lived, even if he was nothing but a soldier. Ren was a child; a little girl, who died and became a shrine. How lonely she must have been. How gracious the gods were—how cruel they are.

Ren plays with his mother's godstone, all worried jade and desperate prayers. "I was jealous of you," she admits. "I've never spoken to the gods before. Not in my whole life."

The light streaming through the forest canopy creates a halo circling Ren's hair. There's a shimmer of red amidst her umber strands, a color he hadn't noticed before. A single bright tear rolls down the plane of her cheek, catching on her moon-curved jaw.

"Despite it all—despite how I treated you—you were kind." Her voice is so small. "Kind to Yaelic, and Qia, and Ko and Haaman. Kind to every spirit. Kind to *me*."

His mouth is too dry to speak, his tongue heavy.

"You always admit when you're wrong. I can't do that." She hangs her head, tears falling from the soft slope of her nose. "I had no one to guide me. No parents and no gods," she whispers. "There was only Ko, who taught me how to wield my magic. But he's gone now, and I don't know—I don't know what to do with this vacant space beside me."

Ren stares down at her trembling, empty hands. "What if I did it wrong, Bass? What if I've been wrong all this time?"

Basuin reaches, harbors Ren's cheek in the shelter of his large palm, and turns her gently to look at him. Please, look at him. See that he sees her, that he won't look away from her.

He's never seen Ren as Am-sa, nor as his god. She isn't the forest to him, a thing to protect.

She's always just been Ren. Who hated him. Whose tongue cut into his bones, whose eyes daggered into his own. A threat. A curse. A treasure. Something mean. Something benevolent.

Someone who bleeds. But bleeds for the ones they love.

Basuin doesn't give a shit if Ren doesn't love him—he doesn't give a shit. He would do anything for her, even if she did nothing else for him. He'll bleed for her. Cut him open, tear him apart. Fuck it, let the wolf-man hollow out his chest again. Take his heart, and his organs, and his bones, and all he is.

Anything that's left, he'll lay at Ren's feet. Even if she doesn't love him.

Because Ren is afraid of water. And she was human once. And even she questions if she's made mistakes. Ren sits here, now, and tells him that she fears water and that she was once human like him and that she might've been wrong.

Her tears are hot against his palm as she presses into his touch, and Basuin doesn't care if Ren may never love him. As long as she trusts him, he'll happily bleed out among these trees for her.

"And what if you were?" he asks, gently, as gentle as he can be after a lifetime of brutality.

Ren clenches her eyes shut and turns into his hand, trying to hide. But Basuin frames her face with both hands now, baring all of her to him. His calloused thumb wipes at the tears she cries.

"What if you were wrong?" he asks again.

"Then I've failed," Ren sobs. "Then everyone who has died has died because of me." When she looks up at him, her dark eyes glitter behind pools of tears in distress. "My first friend—my only friend—is gone, and I am all who's left to blame. If I'd let you kill Kensy, Ko wouldn't have died. You know that, don't you?"

A laugh, mean and guilty, is wrenched from her mouth. Her fingers are so tight in the cotton of his shirt it might tear.

"What sort of peace is that?" Her voice is broken. "This isn't the peace I promised. This peace brought death. I chose this."

Another aching sob blossoms in her chest and it takes everything in him not to kiss her forehead, kiss that wrinkle of anguish in her brow and soothe it all away.

"I chose wrong," she cries.

"You're human," he murmurs.

"I'm a god."

"You were human, first." Basuin gathers her in his arms and Ren crumbles. Fuck this distance he keeps trying to put between them, to hide how he covets her touch. He doesn't care anymore. Because Ren collapses, and Basuin pulls her against his chest and cages her safely in his embrace.

The whole forest—the whole world—is cradled right here between his two legs and two arms.

"You did your best," he murmurs into her hair. "You didn't bring the army here. Even if you killed, you couldn't have stopped them. You did what you knew how to do, and you did it well."

She was a child when she died, stuck frozen in time. They made her a god and didn't tell her what to do.

At least the wolf-man told him what he was made for. To protect her.

"But you're not alone anymore, Ren." Her grip in his shirt tightens. "I won't let you be alone ever again." He cannot fill the vacancy Ko's left behind, but he can help Ren plant rice and rain lilies in the shape of him.

The one thing he's always promised her is that they would figure this out together. From the beginning, that was his pledge. Together.

"I know," she says, curled up against his chest. It's heavy, this feeling. "But I wanted to. I wanted to kill."

The admission sears into him. His inhale is sharp.

"I think of killing all the time," she whispers. "I have wanted to kill, but I won't do it. I won't. It isn't right. I'm not made to kill." Then, she tucks her head beneath his chin, slotting herself perfectly in his embrace. Her tears run rivulets between his collarbones. "You're the only one I could ever tell that to, Basuin. You're the only one who could ever know that."

"I'll do it," he says. It burns so brightly inside him, the space he's carved out of his ribs for her. "I'll kill for you."

Ren stiffens in his grasp, and he almost regrets it. Almost.

After a long moment, she asks, "Is that what you want?"

"Yes," he answers. "I would kill anyone if it meant protecting you."

He would've killed even Isaniel for her.

It's inside of him—so much anger and so much guilt, and it's ruptured into pain like bones breaking to shred through muscle and flesh. It's cutting. Heavier than the armor he dresses in, and heavier still than the burden of the gods. Fuck what the wolf-man says—fuck whatever duty was bestowed upon him in return for a third chance at life.

Basuin will give up everything. Gladly put his warring hands to use. All for Ren. Just for Ren.

"Do you fear it?" Ren's voice is quiet. "What will happen if you can't protect me?"

Yes, the hole where his heart used to be begs him to say. That he fears her death.

"It infuriates me," he says instead. Ruins him. "I'm angry that they would come here. Angry that they've destroyed the forest. Hurt you," he stresses, and his hand turns to a fist so quickly that the shock of it makes him release it. "I won't let it happen."

Fuck whatever debt he owes. Everything he owns, everything he is, belongs to Ren now. Even his fury. Even his rot.

"But all anger stems from fear," Ren says, her hand right over the space where his heart should be. Her fingers press to it, itch for it. Like she wants to see if it's there the way he's always searched for hers.

Yes. He knows this because he fears for Ren the way he feared existing in a world without his mother. Because he feared Kensy, and what Kensy would do to the forest. He feared what he might be if he was no longer a soldier. He feared godhood.

And Basuin still fears exactly what she's asked—what happens if he can't protect her?

Ren will die, and it scares him.

"War and peace coexist." Ren tips his head upward until their eyes meet. Twilight, she's twilight. Her eyes could be the night sky or they could be stars of silver or they could be where the horizon and the ocean meet, tear-filled and still beautiful. "There cannot be one without the other. You can find peace even at war with them. But if you want peace, then you must forgive yourself."

Ren reaches for him now, pulling him down until their foreheads press together. "Forgive yourself," she repeats.

Basuin breathes, heavily, and rests his hand along the back of her neck.

"Have you?" he asks.

She's silent, and then her fingers curl into a fist resting against his chest. Basuin takes her cheek into his palm, a thumb on her jaw, and brings her mouth to his. He would die to taste peace from her lips. To know what it's like. To swallow her whole and feel what it means to embody peace.

The way she answers his silent request is with a soft kiss to the corner of his mouth, before she returns to take his bottom lip between hers.

"I swear," he says, breath against her gossamer lips. "I swear I will protect you, no matter what. Only death will stop me."

And without hesitation, Ren laughs. But it's laughter filled to the brim with fear. "But whose death will it be?"

In the darkness of his mind, his howl is a harmony to the wolf-man's own.

CHAPTER THIRTY-TWO

Basuin sits in front of the campfire, looking at the faces across from him through the wavering flames. The crackle and spit of the eaten embers blares through the campsite, blocking out any other sounds from the trees. He's thought about standing, pacing around everyone in a large circle. But Bass is no captain here. No god, either. Right now, he's just a man at war.

A man on the hunt for another. Basuin's last murder will be Kensy's. How bitter.

"I would ask one thing from you," he says, voice bent of steel. Two sets of eyes stare at him, but those obsidian ones that always haunt him are kept to the ground. Ren's knees are pulled to her chest, arms wrapped around them. "You will journey toward the forest that the legion has yet to reach." He isn't asking. "You'll be safe there, until this is over."

He's lying. Bass doesn't know if anyone will make it out of here alive. This forest may very well burn to the ground. But if he can give them the illusion of safety, in any way, he will. It simmers beneath his skin—an amalgam of guilt and anger.

There is no peace to be had here. No matter what Ren says.

Qia's black ponytail whips around with her head in an instant. "What? Am-sa—"

"You're going." Ren's words are sharp and cutting. "To the northwest."

"No," Qia begs. "I want to fight!"

Ren's eyes close, a movement in her jaw that gives away the hurt she feels. "Hush," she bites, and Qia's mouth shuts.

"Yaelic will go with you," Bass speaks up. And despite the wild look Yaelic gives him, desperate and crushed, he's grown up too much in these last weeks. He can pitch a tent. Start a fire.

Yaelic looks between Bass and Qia, and then again, biting his lip like he can't decide to agree or to fight. But ultimately, it's Qia who shoots to her feet.

"I won't!" she says, her eyes blazing with a heated anger. "I want to fight. For Hami and for Ko." Her voice doesn't sound so much like a child's anymore, no matter how much it wavers with newfound confidence.

"I won't go either," Yaelic says, a firm nod to his head. He looks over the fire at Bass. "I bound myself to you. That won't change. I'm not afraid."

Bass' hands tighten into fists. Yaelic sounds so grown already, though he is younger than Bass was when he went to war. "I can't watch over you in the midst of battle," he snaps, a growl on his lips. "You may not be afraid, but—"

But he is.

"Let them fight," comes a voice from the edge of the woods. Haaman steps out from the darkness of the woods, face and arms covered with dirt. There are red, angry scratches lining their cheeks and forearms; weariness glosses over their eyes. "This is their home, too."

These are the exact same words he overhead from Haaman's tent long nights ago, where they swore their life for Ko's. Gods can be so cruel.

But Kensy is not a god. He is simply a man.

Perhaps it's time for Basuin to be cruel now, for he's a god. This is his forest. Maybe it's time to answer the legion's cruelty—Kensy's cruelty—with his own.

If there are to be battlefields in the land of gods, then let Basuin be the god to level them.

"Blood will be spilled," Haaman says. "The forest has seen enough of it. But if we don't fight back, then what are we?" They stare into the fire, eyes glazed by heat and grief. "I'm not a coward."

They have nothing left, the wolf-man says from somewhere deep and dark inside of him, the cavity of his body. *They fight for someone already dead. We go to battle for someone still living.*

"Then we fight," Bass says. He stands, wiping dirt from his hands on his trousers. "Are you afraid to die?"

Haaman stares at him. "Are you?"

THE NIGHT DOESN'T sleep. Every cicada is out in the dark singing a song of futility and loss. The anticipation is lead in his stomach, anxiety bleeding from him. His mind is rife with nightmares cemented in reality. Nightmares that chase him even while his eyes are open and sleep eludes him. He goes through his list once again.

First Sergeant Curk of Ferghit. Rough-hewn and merciless for anyone but his allies. Run through with a serrated blade and stuck under a snow bank. Recovered.

Second Sergeant Aless of Harker. Always diplomatic, always soft-spoken, but packed a punch no one would see coming. Beheaded. Body not recovered.

Third Sergeant Isaniel of Medeia. Bled out on the snow from a stab wound. Fuck, Isaniel. Gods, fuck. Partially recovered.

Fourth Sergeant Mekal of Altea. A silent body that could move through the thinnest of shadows. They had a daughter at home, left waiting. Shot through the stomach. Recovered.

Fifth Sergeant Tomaas of Olsten. Just a kid. A prisoner of war. Body not recovered—didn't even have a family to return him to if he was.

He immortalized them—the Valkesta Squad. Made them carve out graves for the ones who didn't return. Asked if they'd dig him a grave, too, beside the rest.

You're fine, Tehali would say in the nights she steeped his wounds with hot water and an herb mix the healers gave to him. *You're all right.*

Leave me alone! he screamed—at her, at the ghosts of his squad sergeants. At the vision of Isaniel that stood in the corner of his bunk night after night after night saying: *Liar. Cheat. Traitor.*

He was. He still might be. Bass squeezes his eyes shut until they hurt, until someone moves his tent flap to the side to enter. Haaman, of course. Their footsteps are easy to tell apart from the rest, a little jumpy and not as heavy. Bass sits up on his elbow, rubbing his eyes.

"Can't sleep?" Haaman crosses their legs beneath them to sit.

"Never could before a battle." And never could after, either. He hasn't slept well since he decided he would kill Kensy—for all of his cruelty, Kensy's been with Bass for a long time.

What happened to the man he once knew? Have they changed so irrevocably, so unrecognizably? They warred at the front lines together. They killed together, bled together. When Basuin thinks of Kensy, he thinks of the man who sat beside him and drank ale from the same tin cups as Basuin until they laughed the horror of their crimes away. Ground their sins into the ash beneath their boots together.

When Basuin imagines killing Kensy, it's still that version of him. The version that Bass considered a friend. Not whatever gnarled, twisted, cruel thing Kensy became as he shed the man he was in Grimmalia.

Maybe Kensy was always that, and maybe it was easier to believe he was good. Because if Kensy was good, then Bass could be, too.

Haaman wrings their hands together, staring at the floor. "You should go without us," they finally say. "I didn't mean what I said earlier, but they're children. They don't understand." It sounds weary, like their words are too hard to even say. Terribly pained. "I'll take them to the northwest in the morning. Hou-tou said she'll help. I'll protect them," Haaman says quietly, "with my life."

If he could do it over again, Basuin would've dismantled the Valkesta squad before they even left. He knows this. He would've spared them, his comrades, from the death he knew awaited them at the top of that mountain.

He would've gone, alone. And he would've died there, at peace, alone.

"I trust you," he tells Haaman. But he doesn't apologize. There was never any moment that he wanted an apology after Valkesta, after Isaniel, and he's certain Haaman doesn't want one now.

"Then leave now," they say. Haaman digs into the crease of their knuckle as if to draw blood, nails bitten to nothing. "You can move with the night."

"Will you be all right?" he asks. "With the two of them?"

"I have friends." Haaman looks upward as if they can see them now. "There are still some who haven't left. Who don't want to leave their home."

He doesn't either—want to leave. Before this, he didn't even know if he had a home anymore. And that's why they must fight. Now, more than ever. Because they don't have much else to lose—so they have to fight for what's left.

Bass claps Haaman on the shoulder, squeezing them. "Thank you." He hopes Haaman knows how much he means it. Words are shit, don't mean a thing. But he'll kill Kensy, and he'll fight for the forest, and maybe that'll be enough.

Haaman's beady eyes have narrowed. "Don't thank me. There's nothing but death ahead of us."

A muscle in Bass' jaw twitches. "No one can read the future," he says, something he's spent the night staring up at the ceiling in thought of—if he could have changed anything with clandestine knowledge of the future. "Not even the gods."

He tucks the blanket tightly around Yaelic's shoulders and under his chin, resting a heavy hand on the boy's sleeping frame in a lingering touch. Then, he takes the dagger from his hip and places it with Yaelic's things. Boys and their sharp things—too young and too bloody. The sheath is worn, from his father, to himself, and now to Yaelic.

When he peeks into Ren's tent, she's asleep too. Her arms are locked around a slumbering Qia as if someone might try and take the fawn away. Everything about her is sharp and defensive, even as she rests. Basuin doesn't dare touch her for fear she might jump awake. So he watches her, the soft rise and fall of her chest, the way a sliver of moonlight graces her cheek the way he wishes he could.

He takes nothing with him. As he walks away from their camp, for the last time, he pulls his harness over his shoulders and buckles it around his waist, sword hanging from his back. He's ten paces into the trees before Ren's voice slices through the silence.

"You're leaving me?" Her voice is shrill, filled with betrayal. But something more than that.

When he turns to look at her, cold fear seeps behind a crooked mask of anger she tries to wear. He can see right through her.

"I'm not leaving you," he tries to stress. "If I leave right now, I can make it to the River before Kensy." He swallows. "I spoke with Haaman—they said they would take Qia and Yaelic westward."

"And where would I go?" she hisses. Ren's eyes, beautiful and glassy with the wash of the moonlight, are poisonous. "You were going to leave me behind."

"Ren—"

"Liar." The way she wraps her arms around herself, protecting herself, makes him wither. "You said I'd never be alone again. You lied. Liar."

There's always been something lurking behind that cool expression she likes to wear. Soft, and a little afraid. A woman wearing the clothes of a god.

But here, with him, she's a feral animal. Wild and scared. A deer caught in the scope of its hunter, gun aimed to kill.

And here, with her glaring at him like that, he's still just a wolf who bites at hands that come too close.

"I do fear it," he snaps at her, all teeth. "You, dying." He marches toward her now, and she doesn't cower away. Not even when he snatches her arm away from her chest and clasps her fist between his own, swallowing her small hand in a cage made from his fingers. "Do you even know who I am?"

Does she even know what he did?

Ren's eyes search his, and it breaks something deep inside him.

"I've trained since I was seventeen," he tells her. "Went to war under an oath and command. Let them beat the gods out of me, lash me until my faith bled from my skin. They didn't promote me because I was smart. They made me a captain because I fight good. Because I know war."

Ren reaches for him, trying to pull him closer. But he won't move. He locks his knees and grits his teeth.

"And what did I do?" Basuin huffs a laugh and looks away. "I marched all those people who were forced to follow my command into a trap that I knew was a trap. Valkesta was a mistake. I killed everyone in that squad. I let them die."

The anger burns out of him. Snuffed out. He intertwines their fingers, slotting their palms together—a perfect fit. God mark against god mark.

"It should've killed *me*," he says. "I couldn't protect them. Don't you understand that?"

Basuin's grasp tightens, but his hand is still entwined with

Ren's. He studies it, how their fingers connect, how fragile each bone braces under her skin. Someone's hand is shaking, but he can't tell whose. Maybe it's both of them.

"I couldn't protect them," he bites like a snake, afraid of contact. "So yes, Ren. I'm leaving you."

Just like he should've left them behind. Like he should've left Tomaas behind, because he knew that Tomaas was dead the minute he was dragged off. Prisoners of war aren't prisoners. They're dead.

"I wanted to die," he rasps. How pathetic. "I deserved to—in Valkesta. A captain goes down with his squad and I should've, too."

Ren reaches up and brushes her hand along his cheek, fingers finding the line of his jaw under the thick hair of his beard.

"Please." And it sounds so pretty from her lips. "Don't ever say that again."

Basuin bites back a sob he didn't taste before. "But I can't protect you." Teeth in tongue, Basuin forces back a sound only a wolf could make. "It's what I was made to do," he stresses. "I'm a *god*. The wolf-man changed me to protect you—but I don't know how. I don't know how to protect you, Ren."

Here, he isn't a soldier. Because a soldier would know what to do. A soldier follows orders. Here, he's a god. His hands aren't sure what to do with the power between them. He doesn't know how to carry out the duty he's been given.

If he was a bad soldier, then he is a worse god. But Basuin was a good soldier—so he was never meant to be a god at all.

Before the tears come, before he breaks in half, Ren gathers him into her arms and pulls him into an embrace that smells of fresh soil and something so Ren he can't even name it. Her hand paints patterns across his back as she holds him against her, so much smaller and still somehow enveloping him in all that she is. If the world was to end, if the forest was to die right now, he wouldn't be able to stop it. Not here, right now, in this glass bubble he's afraid might shatter.

"Basuin." She says his name so softly, so gracefully—it reminds him of his mother, the way it's said with love. "You must let go if you are to ever find peace."

"There is no peace for me," he says, canine teeth and all. "I always bring war."

"Do you bring war," Ren asks him, "or do you chase after it because you fear peace?"

He cries. Basuin has cried in this forest, cried before Ren, more than he has since his ma died. Soldiers don't cry. He knows that; he's known that since he was seventeen—and now, moons away from thirty, he cries not as a soldier, but as a god.

"I've become it." Basuin bows his head to her shoulder. His tears mar her skin and it's akin to the way his mistakes have marred her in the form of burns and bruises. It's not enough. He'll never be enough.

"And I'll wage war again," he hisses into her skin. "I'll bring war to them the way they brought war here—but I'll finish it. I will."

"You're scared."

"And I'm angry." His body trembles. "I'm an angry man, Ren. I am."

"They both exist inside you because they are both the same." Ren's hand presses to his chest, harder this time. Less gentle. Heavy in a way that makes him feel like she's real. "And like anger and fear, war and peace both exist inside you, too."

He knows what she asks of him, and he refuses to answer.

"Let me make up for what I've done," he pleads. "Let me learn from my mistakes."

Let him change who he is.

But Ren moves closer in his refusal to do so. "You promised we would always be together," she says, voice tight. "So we're going together." Then, with the heel of her palm gentle against him, she wipes his tears from his cheeks.

Off in the distance, weaving through the trees, Bass can see it—the bruise-purple trail of magic leading them toward the Winter River. The same color tied around their hands, a shade made from both their colors.

Ren starts to move, but Basuin doesn't let go of his grip on her. He doesn't want her to go. Doesn't want to risk her life. But how can he deny her?

Basuin can't break another promise. Not to Ren. And even if he could, Ren won't let him leave without her. She's too stubborn, too spiteful. She'd follow after him just to prove her point. And gods damn him, it would make him laugh.

So Basuin steels himself. Swallows back all that fear and anger.

"I will protect you," he swears. He has to. "No matter what."

This won't be a failure. This won't result in death and decay, not again. This is his last chance to get it right, before he loses everything.

"I've never protected anything," Ren says. "I don't know how to."

It forces a smile from him, a warmth in his chest that feels like he's held his hands too close to the fire and he's singed the top layers of his skin. Something inside him feels broken, pieces rattling like glass shards in his chest.

"We'll be okay," he tells her. "Together." But Basuin isn't sure that's true at all. Because he's said it before, and the last time he said it, he was a liar.

We'll be okay, he told Isaniel that last night, whose breath stunk of ale and venomous words. *Together*.

They never should've called you a hero, Isaniel said. *Killing people just because you can doesn't make you a hero. It makes you selfish. Makes you a monster.*

And he laughed, because it was honest, and because it was true. Because it didn't hurt him.

I would burn the world to save you, he said. *To save anyone I love.*

Well don't save me, Isaniel said. *I don't want to be saved by you.*

* * *

THEY RACE THROUGH the forest together. It's dense and dark until they exit to the river's bank and the moon above illuminates them. The water, slow laps of it against one another, sparkles like a collection of heavy gems.

Ren stares up at the sky, lips parted, her thin slant of eyes open wide, all silver and worshipping. She's beautiful, pale in the light that shows all the small sun-made moles and freckles dotting her skin like stars. All goddess. And not as the Forest God—not like that. Not the god he's meant to protect. She's something to worship. Something so bewitching you want to capture it, but she can't be possessed. Deadly and illusive. An enchantress, a witch.

Ren's cursed him. Of that, he's sure.

She takes the few steps to the river's bank, crouching on one knee to place her hand in the water. "Hou-tou," she calls, and her voice carries over the river.

A rush of water and a burst of bubbles finds them, swifter than the current. Dripping in silk and webbed in moonlight, Hou-tou rises from her domain with half a body. Her legs are still part of the stream.

"Am-sa," Hou-tou sings like a siren would. "You've called on me?" She smiles, and Bass knows of the teeth that hide behind those deceptive lips. "Even after all that happened to Gyeosi, you would ask something of me?"

It's subtle, but there's a jump in Ren's cheek that mimics something dark. Her fingers curl, scooping silt from the river's bank to crumble away.

"I would," Ren says coolly. "A favor."

Hou-tou tilts her head with a toothless grin. "Oh?"

Standing, Ren rises to her full height, shoulders rolled back and chin held high. Every move she makes is so dedicated. Purposeful. Each flick of her hand and toss of her hair is decided and full of a grace and balance Bass has never seen.

"Take us northward," Ren says, no waver in her voice.

"And why should I?" Hou-tou asks, words all melodic, a hum in her throat.

"Because I am too weak." Her voice is strong, even as she admits her faults. "The army will come if we don't stop them."

"You didn't stop them before they destroyed our village." Now, Hou-tou bares her teeth, slides her eyes over to Basuin. A mouth full of calcium weapons, all serrated edges and sharp points to rip into something.

"When this forest falls," Ren says, eyes narrowing, "you'll lose your home, same as we will. You won't remain unscathed. They will burn everything, like they burned Gyeosi—and they won't spare you."

Basuin feels like he's choking on thick, cloying air. This isn't a conversation. It's a negotiation, and Ren is winning.

Hou-tou's grin falls and her blue-clouded eyes turn sharp and cold. Like a lake iced over, brittle and deadly. She's lost, and she knows it. In an instant, she sinks back into the water, backing down.

"Yes, Am-sa," she cedes. The river bubbles and babbles and Hou-tou drops like dead weight into the water. Then, she races back up to the surface, body made of luster current and quick-moving streams. Her shape is outlined only by the moon, eyes clouded and blue, glowing pinpricks of light stemming from her body of water.

Hou-tou holds out a hand, but water pours from it. "Come, then," she says, voice all river babble. "I hope you can swim, Wolf God." Her eyes flicker to Ren.

Bass takes one step into the water, current flowing around his boot, hand outstretched toward Ren. But Ren hesitates, body rigid for a moment too long, before she places her hand in his. Her grip is shackling. Terrified. She takes two steps, wading into the cold stream with nothing but bare legs. As she moves to take her third, her fingers close over the jade godstone linked around her neck. It sends something in his chest wild.

Especially when she turns and looks at him, gaze holding a childlike fear. Ren has always been afraid of water, and this seems no different. Though her eyes are dusted silver with the moon's light, there's an innocence in them that reminds him of snow. Fresh, powdered, and something he, too, fears.

It makes him squeeze her hand and steady his arm and say, "I've got you." Ren's eyes widen, and he repeats it like a promise. "I've got you."

And she moves toward him, each step dragging through the river and cutting through the current as they approach Hou-tou. As they get closer, hand in hand, foamy water builds around their legs until they can no longer move. Beneath them, a surface that looks like ice constructs itself around them, a glowing platform the water anchors them to.

"Go with grace, my gods," Hou-tou says, and then she blows a kiss made of bubbles and they rush forward as if the river has burst through a dam, the trees blending and bleeding into nothing but blackness around them, wind blowing their hair back as they ride toward the north.

Basuin doesn't know what's more magical—the speed at which the river carries them with, or the way Ren clings to him in an embrace as they brave the gale that crows, *Go back, go back, go back.*

CHAPTER THIRTY-THREE

THE FOREST SOUNDS like bells—like the ringing of the bells in Ankor. They rang when his mother fell ill. They rang when his father returned from war as nothing but ash. They rang when the villagers burned the church down and drove Basuin and his mother to the outskirts of the forest. Gods, they tolled, don't exist.

They never did rebuild upon the ashes of the church. Sometimes he wonders what might replace it now, if Ankor still stands. If they built more little village houses, or if they built a casern.

He can feel it again—the press of the wolf-man against his body. The smell of singed fur as it grows along his skin. The blood of his nails as they sharpen to claws. They're merging into one, he and the wolf-man. The hole in his chest is filling up with red magic and burgeoning anger.

The moon, silver soldered to the sky as they run through the woods, begins to blur into the wisping lavender of dawn. The sun hangs just below the earth and the first streaks of light—not even knowing that it's light yet—begin to creep up on the shadows of the forest.

He hears them, the bells. They ring loud in his ears. His grasp on Ren's hand tightens.

"What will you want to do?" Ren asks, breath steady even

after all the land they've crossed. "When the army leaves."

Bass, struggling to catch his breath, asks, "What do you mean?"

"Will you want to leave?"

It almost makes him stop in his tracks, halt their movement. He hasn't thought of it. Ren can't leave the forest—she's a god. And not just any god, but the god of this forest.

"No," he answers. "There's no place for me in Xalkhir anymore." If Ren isn't with him, it doesn't matter. Basuin can't imagine a world where she isn't beside him anymore. He doesn't care that he's bound to her. He would still go wherever she goes.

Ren nods, but doesn't say anything else.

"We could rebuild Gyeosi," he says then. The image of it is familiar. His hands, scarred, working to thatch a roof. Carving large oaks who no longer have a spirit into a home. Something on the outskirts of the village. He's done it before.

"We could," Ren says, a twinge of wonder in her voice. "Would you live there?"

"With you?" he asks.

"With me." Her twilight eyes meet his and something warm runs through him, like a heat that belongs to him. Giving life to his veins. Damn him, he should kiss her. If he took two steps he could.

"Then, yes," he says. "I would build a home." A home for the two of them.

A smile curls Ren's perfect lips. "Would the Wolf God provide for his people?"

"As much as the Forest God provides for them."

He wants it. More than anything. For them to rebuild Gyeosi together, build a home together, build a life together. To wake up with Ren in his arms and kiss her forehead and—and to tell her how beautiful she is. Because he hasn't yet.

Basuin can't lose her. He can't.

There's a grim, heavy feeling in the air. Like something isn't quite right. He's felt it before, the hair-pin grenade waiting in the pit of his stomach, on the cusp of exploding. It's leaking out of him in streaks of red magic. If he closes his eyes, he'd feel the wintry blizzard of Valkesta upon his cheeks.

When he marched the five of them up the mountain, he felt just like this.

The way Ren shifts through the trees has changed and he knows she can feel it too. There's something static on his skin. Buzzing and lightning and insect stings. Inside him, the wolf-man howls, but it isn't a war cry. It's a cry for help.

Ren stops, and out of instinct, Bass moves to stand in front of her. But she holds out an arm, blocking him.

"Wait," she says. Then, she reaches out. Her hand meets something, palm glowing blue. There are indentations on the air in the shape of her fingers—an invisible wall. Beyond it, the forest looks as it always has. But under the shimmer of blue magic, there's something else. He can't see it, but he knows it's there.

Ren turns her head, twilight eyes gone big. "This is Sa-cha's domain," she says, voice dropped to a lull. She takes a long breath. "This is where everything ends. Isn't it?"

Kensy is on the other side of this wall. Basuin has never been good at guessing games. He is decisive and stubborn and he knows, without a doubt, that Kensy is just beyond this wall of magic, waiting for Basuin in Sa-cha's domain. His bones, weary and war-worn, know it.

This is what Kensy always wanted.

With a breath, Bass takes Ren's hand in his, their god marks pressed together. He's terrified—can already smell the blood of her and it hasn't yet spilled. He can't protect her. He's never been able to save anyone.

This really is his last chance.

"I'm with you," he tells her, gazes locked and hands entwined. Forever. Until death. Until he is nothing because he is nothing without Ren. Everything he knows and everything he desires is so easily her now.

Ren gives a curt nod, inhaling hard. Then, she presses her hand further into the wall. It gives, welcoming her inside, and every limb that travels through the shield is illuminated with blue. Ren tugs him after her, and he moves through it in the same incandescent blue light as she did.

And on the other side, the day has dawned. A field of green grass and wildflowers stretches out before them, lush and plentiful. Birds chirp and sing from where they sit in the trees, wings fluttering among the leaves. The rush of water carries through the clearing. Off in the distance, a waterfall careens down a steep cliff of rocks and feeds a creek running through the clearing. In the middle, a fat, round statue sits decaying, bottom worn and stained by the constant stream of water.

And beside it, Kensy. Standing there, leaned against the idol with his cruel smile, blonde hair ruffled on a breeze. Waiting for Basuin.

He knew that Basuin would chase him all the way here. Kensy told the legion that he was dead. Kensy *killed* him. And still, here he stands, waiting for Basuin to show up.

"You've slowed down, old dog," Kensy chastises. "The Black Wolf would have beaten me here."

Basuin locks his jaw and curls his lips into a grim smile. "The Black Wolf would have killed you by now."

The grin Kensy wears splits even wider. Like this is what he's been waiting for since the day Basuin was assigned to Kensy's fleet. Like this is what he's planned since he promoted Bass to his old position—Captain of Ariche's Fleet.

Calculating blue eyes stare across the field at him, then flick over to Ren with something sly in them. Bass' fist tightens, heavy at his side. He won't let Kensy anywhere near Ren. That's a mistake he's not willing to allow.

"You've become so bold, Captain." Kensy kicks at the creek running over his boots. "So, this is what happens to dishonorable men when they are given the gift of godhood."

Basuin blinks to keep his eyes from widening. He's known—he knew from the moment that he saw Basuin with Ren.

Kensy notices his hesitance. He always does. "That's right," Kensy says. "I know who you've become, Wolf God."

"Why are you here?" he fires back, hand itching toward his dagger. "What is it that you want?"

"Nothing so terrible," Kensy answers. "I want what you have." He leans his elbow on the statue to prop his chin up, eyes meandering between Basuin and Ren. "To be a god."

If you kill a king, you take his kingdom. If you kill a god, you take its home.

Something thunders in his chest. The wolf-man growls inside of him and it reverberates through Basuin's mouth. He swallows it back, the anger. The venom that courses through him. He was wrong again. Kensy doesn't want to destroy the Winter River.

He's going to kill Sa-cha.

Kensy hungers for power and feasts on those below him to get it. This has always been true, and Basuin hates that he ignored it for so long. His own need, to still be something good, allowed this. But Kensy was never evil—not until he dragged Basuin to this island to colonize in the name of the queen. Not until he killed a wolf and made to sacrifice her pups so he could lure the gods out. Because if Kensy was evil, it would make Basuin evil, too.

It was never in the name of the queen. It was all a ruse. It was in Kensy's want for power; his want to win. Kensy doesn't want to outlaw the gods. He wants to kill them. Become one.

"It was *wrong*," Kensy growls. "They chose wrong. They should've deified me."

"I was dead," he tries. "I didn't ask for this."

Kensy *killed* him. That's why he's a god now. It's Kensy's

fault—it's all Kensy's doing. And here Kensy is, wanting the very thing he forced upon Basuin.

There's a moment, a dead, long moment, between them. Ren is still beside him, unmoving and without even the sound of her lungs. Ren died, too. She drowned in the ocean surrounding this island, saved by a god without a body, primed to be deified in the same way Kensy primed Basuin to be his dog.

"The gods spoke to me, too," Kensy says, a countenance filled with pride. From under his armor, he rips a stone from around his neck and holds the leather string out for Bass to see. A black stone—a godstone—hangs from it like a dead man hangs from a noose.

"You never believed in the gods," Bass says, biting back the shake in his voice.

Kensy wraps his godstone around his wrist. "I always believed in the gods. But unlike you, I don't worship them. The gods spoke to me, and do you know what they said?"

From the Winter River, there arose a god.

Basuin's heart thunders in his chest. The gods never spoke to him—they never spoke even a lie to him—until he was possessed. Until his god took his body and made a home of it.

And that god was Sa-cha, and he was good.

"They said I could kill a god." Kensy pulls his gun from its holster. "And I did." His grin is rotten and smug. "How do you think we got to this island, Black Wolf? Do you think Ithika offered it up?"

Ren takes a step back, eyes wide. Her fingers twitch at her side, shoulders drawn in defense. But he can't take his eyes off Kensy. He can't show a moment of weakness.

Ithika has long been dead, Ko told them.

"Of course not," Kensy continues. "I orchestrated this moment. I slaughtered Ithika and took to her waters. I offered up this island in the name of the queen so that I could kill this god, too." Kensy's boot kicks at Sa-cha's statue. "The god of all gods."

Sa-cha's shrine.

"That's not possible," Basuin grits through his teeth, body rigid. "Ithika—"

"Do you know how many gods like you I've had to kill?" Kensy interrupts, eyes wild and teeth mean. "Hosts I've had to massacre to get what I want?"

Hosts. Gods without a body. Gods like him—Gods like Ren.

"Do you think you're the first?" Kensy straightens and stands at a lazy attention and it sends a shattering of ice through Basuin's veins. "Do you think you'll be the last?"

"Ithika has been dead," Ren finally speaks. There's no emotion in her voice at all. Purely blank. Iced over. "You killed her last host."

The waters Ren died in—Ithika's first death. And then, the death of Ithika's host, who protected her waters—Kensy killed them so he could reach the Winter River. Well, here they are now. They've walked right into another trap, just like Valkesta.

Gods damn him. He did it again.

"I did," Kensy says. "And you know what?"

With the butt of his gun, Kensy breaks Sa-cha's idol clean in half.

Something inside Basuin shatters. A piercing ache, burrowing deep into his guts. He reaches, and his hand doesn't belong to him anymore. The shrine crumbles into the water, hissing with steam. It curdles his innards. The wolf-man lets out some half-whine, half-snarl sound and it vibrates through Basuin's ribcage.

Beside him, Ren doubles over, clutching her chest and heaving, gasping for air. The pain infects her too. Her eyes blown wide, struggling to breathe.

"No," she whispers. A bright ray of light beams from the broken shrine and into the sky to the godrealm.

Sa-cha is dead. No shrine. No host. The loss of it is heavy, dragging Basuin toward the ground. Ren falls to her knees. Sa-cha, who arose from the Winter River, died here. And from the godrealm, he has no power. No one protects the River now.

No one but Basuin and Ren.

"I'll kill all the gods," Kensy spits. "I won't stop with Grimmalia and Xalkhir. I'll go straight to the godrealm and kill them, too. I'll begin anew, everything new, at my hand." He smiles. "Glory to the gods."

Basuin draws his sword from his back, gritting his teeth. "I won't let that happen." Not if it means putting the world in Kensy's hand—and not if it means Ren's death. A godless, evil world. A world, empty, without Ren. "If you thought me weak, you were wrong."

"You're nothing but a dead man," Kensy snarls. "I'm going to rip that god right out of you and watch you die thrice over."

Then, Kensy points his loaded rifle at Ren. "And you're next."

Bass rushes him without another thought. Not Ren. In the same moment, Kensy's drawn the sword at his hip and their blades clash in a crack of steel that rings out across the clearing. Bass pushes and Kensy relents, their swords singing against one another as Bass grapples to get the upper hand. He yanks the dagger from his hip—it's gone, laid at Yaelic's side while he slept. Instead, he reaches for the dagger he knows Kensy wears and slashes—Kensy blocks it with a pistol he whipped from another holster. But Basuin is backed by magic. There's a wolf inside him raging and ready to take control.

With a grunt, Bass shoulders Kensy off him, red magic rising from his skin. The force of it sends Kensy staggering back, panting, still wearing that feral grin. He looks like he's having fun. Like they're in the training arena still, having a friendly spar, wagered and counted in mugs of ale after the sun set and the old commanders all went to bed.

Behind him, there's movement. He hears the shuffle in the grass—Ren's footsteps, all lithe and airy. Before he can turn, Kensy reacts first. With a flick of his wrist, a gun is back in his hand—no, not a gun. It's the hand cannon that set Yaelic's den aflame.

It clicks, spewing flames. Kensy hurls it toward them, across the space between Basuin and Ren, and as soon as it hits the forest floor everything ignites. A wall of fire spurts up and starts seizing ground. Ren jumps out of the way, but it creates a dangerous barrier around Kensy and Bass.

Good. He's glad for it. She may burn for it, but at least the flames won't kill her. Kensy will.

Anger and fear are turning into something fearsome inside of him. If Ren is wounded in any way, then only the gods will be able to help every man and animal in this forest. Only gods will save the rest of them from Basuin's wrath. He'll have nothing left.

"You're weak," Kensy shouts over the crackle of fire. Basuin lunges, sword hilt wrapped in both hands. Kensy unsheathes his blade and redirects Basuin's with a fluid movement that reminds him—this isn't just a man. This is a god killer.

"What will power matter when you're at the top?" Basuin grunts and kicks at Kensy's knees. Kensy falters but rolls to the left and outside Bass' vision. Smoke fills the clearing, making it harder for Bass to see. "Not everything you destroy can be rebuilt."

The thought of it—the image of his scarred hands beside small, graceful Ren's as they weave Gyeosi's ashes into thread to stitch the village he destroyed back together—prickles his skin for one singular moment and that moment is enough to throw him off. Kensy strikes with his pommel and Bass can't dodge.

A shock of pain rams his shoulder blade. Bass stumbles and lands on his knees but Kensy grabs his armor and drags him in close. The gun's barrel presses into Bass' side.

"I built you," Kensy snarls in his face. "You think I'll let you win?"

Basuin remembers the stricken, incredulous look that

darkened Kensy's face after they stormed a Grimmalian church—a battle which Basuin asked him, not as a soldier, but as a human, to reconsider.

What of gods? Kensy asked, staring at his hand, covered in blood drawn from the priest who fought for his life in the name of Ke'the, the god of harvest. *Do they bleed?*

Basuin said, *Does it matter?*

And Kensy's hand shook as blood dripped from his wrist. *No*, he said. *All that matters is who stands at the end of it all.*

Now, Kensy's face leaves no room for doubt. Bass braces his blade against Kensy, struggling. "Then why didn't you kill me when you had the chance?"

Kensy shoves the gun into Bass' side so hard it makes him groan.

"You've always been stupid, but you're a loser, too." Kensy barks a laugh. "You're the one that led me here. Only that heathen god inside you knew where Sa-cha was, and you took me right to him."

The pain is sharp, but the knowledge of his mistakes is sharper. He's the reason Kensy found the River. He's the reason Sa-cha is dead.

But even before that, even before all this, Basuin is the reason Kensy's cruelty has been allowed this long. Because Basuin always bowed his head to Kensy.

"You're a disgrace," Kensy says, "but you're a damn fine soldier. I made sure of it."

He enabled Kensy's cruelty, year after grueling year. Battle after battle. Kensy wrote every war story and Basuin performed it, the last one left alive to tell it.

Kensy lodges a boot against Bass' stomach and kicks him away. Bass rolls across the field before finding purchase and getting back up on his feet. Nothing aches more than those words. Kensy throwing everything back in his face. All his mistakes. All his failures.

"Why?" His sword hangs at his side. His grip is limp. But he tightens his fingers and readjusts, ready again. "I don't get it. What did the gods do to you? This isn't about winning—it's more."

Kensy stares down at him, glare hot. "You've gone soft. The Basuin I knew first cared for nothing but blood."

"The Basuin you knew was angry," he says. "The Black Wolf was angry. The disgraced Captain Basuin was angry."

He's always been filled to the brim with it—an anger and a rage that can't be pacified. Can't be soothed. His mother used to try, but what exists in him can't be killed. There are parts of him that have stayed the same since he was a boy—his anger is but one of them.

"I'm still angry," he admits, breathing hard. "But all anger stems from fear." Ren told him that. He was angry when he met her first. When he thought her to be the one who kept him trapped here, in this forest, the forest that she loves so much.

But in truth, he was afraid of himself; afraid of the war his hands know, the blood he's picked from beneath his nails. And he was afraid to know Ren because of it, and afraid that she might know him, too.

So now, he asks, "What are you so afraid of, Kensy?"

Kensy's ice-blue eyes go wide and stricken for a split second. Then, he narrows his gaze into something cutting, sharp, as he stares Bass down.

"Gods fear nothing," Kensy says. "No one."

"That isn't true," Bass shoots back. "I fear much, Commander. So, I'll ask you again. What are you afraid of?"

Another memory from long ago colors Basuin's mind. Something that raises the hackles on the back of his neck now. From before Basuin was promoted to Captain, when they culled the rebellion in a Grimmalian village that was led by teenaged boys. Kensy's hand gripped Basuin's shoulder, hard.

If you don't fight, Kensy said, *then everything will be taken from you. That's why we fight, Bass. We fight so we don't lose anything.*

Fire roars behind him, a reminder that Ren is still here. A reminder that his race toward the River, toward Kensy, means his life is tied to Ren's. If Kensy kills him here, Ren dies too. He swore he wouldn't let that happen.

"What will you lose?" Basuin asks him. "If you don't become a god and you go back to Ha'riste, what will they take from you?" A lick of sympathy coats the back of his mouth. They were friends, once. Weren't they?

Everything is quiet. In this pocket of peace, protected from the outside world, the forest is so silent. He can almost hear himself breathe, it's so quiet out here. Breathe in, breathe out, chest panting to keep his lungs filled.

Then, Kensy pulls out a cocked pistol and shoots him.

There is no pain—he flinches but there is no pain—and then a body falls into him, and when he opens his eyes, it's Ren, and Ren is collapsing in his arms, and he smells blood, and Ren is bleeding, and her shirt is bloodied, and his knees hit the ground and Ren is so heavy in his arms and—

"Well, that's one." Kensy cocks his pistol again. "Now, two."

In an instant, the field explodes in a shattering of blue magic too bright to comprehend and Ren lunges out of Basuin's arms on all fours, a wild animal. Her limbs stretch into long legs and her spine crooks and then breaks, hunching and shifting. Her body grows into something imposing, larger than any animal he's seen before, glowing with the blue of her magic as antlers sprout from her temples.

In her place stands a deer, fur white and glowing cyan, tall enough that her antlers scrape the trees. Inside of its trunk, Ren's human body sits on her knees, palms pressed to the belly of the deer. Basuin reaches a hand out for her.

Before Kensy can shoot again, Ren charges him, impaling him on the end of an antler. Blood drips down the bone from Kensy's disemboweled stomach.

The monstrous, beautiful deer that is Ren's spirit turns and looks at him, viscera decorating her crown like jewels. Back arched, hooves dug into the earth, head dipping low with the weight of Kensy's body. Her eyes are blank, white, wide, glowing. Her human body is outlined in the blue that belongs to her, sitting on her haunches, staring at him.

Inside, she presses herself up from its belly and stands, a vision, a bright flash of light filling the clearing. When it fades, Ren's hair whips against her cheeks, human again, but still coronated with blue-boned antlers. Kensy hangs from her laurels.

Then, she slams her hands upon the ground. Ren sprouts a tree made of blue magic out of nothing at all. This time, without his help. Basuin watches every cycle—seedling to sprout to root to tree as it grows and thickens and branches unfurl and leaves plume from it. Ren rams her antler into the tree, slamming Kensy into the trunk and pinning him there. And as her body slowly shrinks, magic waning away, her human hand reaches and snaps the antler from her hair. Blood stains her god mark.

"The gods did not choose wrong," she speaks, her voice echoing with tones that don't sound like her at all, overlapping voices carried from her mouth. "They abandoned you."

And then, light bleeding from her body, Ren sinks. Basuin dives to catch her, skidding into the creek as he holds her in his arms. Red blooms from the shot in her chest, leaking blood from an exit wound in her back that he presses a hand against to staunch the flow.

The fear is so suffocating that when he opens his mouth, no words come out at all.

"Not so unfamiliar, is it?" Ren says, but it's breathy and strained.

"Stop," he whispers. "No."

Ren reaches up, hand on his cheek. It's sticky with blood—Kensy's, or hers? He's going to vomit. He's going to lose it. Bass' hand covers hers in desperation. The water beneath Ren turns red as it streams through the field.

"I've loved many things," Ren says, "but why do you feel like the first?" She smiles, but it's weak and trembling. "I love you, Basuin. Of Ankor, of the Wolf God—all of it. I love you, Basuin."

The tears break with shuddering breaths and swimming vision. He hurries to wipe his eyes because he can't do this right now. He has to save her. He has to heal her. He has to look at her face and commit it to his frail, lying, terrified memory so he won't forget her.

"Don't say that." Basuin presses his hand to her chest and pumps red magic into her wound. Stitch it up, mend it, damn it. Damn him. "Don't say it like that. We'll rebuild." His magic feels like it's pouring into nothing, going nowhere. It's just being leached away. "Say it then, once we've rebuilt our home."

"I've never killed anyone before," she says. She sounds tired, like she's beginning to drift away in the quietness of it all. Basuin chokes on a sob and pours everything he can into his hands to heal her, but his magic keeps filtering through her. Ren reaches up and clutches his hand instead, grip feeble. "I hope I did it right."

He makes a noise, half laughter and half shock. "Everything you do is right. Everything—please, Ren." He can't bring himself to do anything more but beg. "Please."

Basuin covers her with his body, cradling her tight. He cries into her neck. The magic he possesses won't stitch it back together, won't close the wound she's losing life from. He's losing her. Stitch the wound, stitch it up. Mend her, heal her, save her, anything.

But Ren stills in his embrace, and when Basuin pulls away to look, her eyes have closed. Her chest doesn't rise again.

And just like that, he's lost everything. Kensy won.

CHAPTER THIRTY-FOUR

THE DARKNESS OF his mind has never been this dark before. It's pitch and stuck, limbs moving so mechanical and slow that it's painful. Burning. Every part of him feels heavy, packed ice and snow atop him, weighing him down on the battlefield. The winds of Valkesta howl. They howl so loudly that the echo could shatter metal and bone alike.

He covers his mouth with his hand. Rust on his tongue. Bile in his throat.

Ren is dead. Ren is *dead*.

Basuin takes her face in both his hands, gentle. Still gentle. Maybe he can wake her.

"Please," he whispers, again and again. "Please, Ren," he begs. With shaky fingers, he fumbles with his mother's godstone, squeezing it in his hand so hard it aches. "I've never—"

He's never asked for anything like this before. He's never begged for something so bad.

Basuin begged when his mother died—to go home and bury her. He begged Tehali to kill him when they returned to Ha'riste with fewer bodies than they left with. He tried not to beg when Kensy said they were going on this godsforsaken crusade to claim this uninhabited island. Uninhabited because Ithika and her host protected it—until Kensy slew her, again.

But he hasn't begged like this.

"Please!" he shouts again, looking up to the sky, looking around the field, looking at the broken statue. "Please," he cries, watching the way the stream soaks Sa-cha's shrine in red the shade of Ren's blood. "Take me. Take mine, my life."

Barely twenty feet away, Kensy's body hangs from Ren's antler. His blood runs thick and dark, his hand still twitching. Basuin should've killed him first. He should've done what he does best. He's a murderer. He failed at the one thing he's good at.

The roar of the waterfall grows into screams in his ears. He can't move. Ren has chained him here—he'll stay until he's washed away with her in tow.

"It was supposed to be me." He chokes on his own tongue. "It was supposed to be my life."

Fuck Valkesta. Fuck it all. He shouldn't have died there. He's glad he didn't die there, in those mountains, under that ice. Because he's here. And this is where he should've died. This is where he was meant to.

"Say something," he begs. Not to Ren. Basuin hits his chest with his fist. "Say something!" he screams at the wolf-man.

Fuck's sake. Basuin cries. Fat, hot tears. He claws at his face, nails in his eyes, wanting to tear his flesh raw.

"You've never been silent before," he snarls. "You've always had something to say. So fucking say something." He bows his head, dropping his forehead against Ren's, frantically working to wipe away the tears that fall upon her perfect, cooling skin.

It should've been him. Why'd she take the shot? His sobs are the only sound in this place—this sacred place, defiled with blood and dead gods.

Come to the River, someone says. He nearly screams again out of pure rage.

"I'm here!" He turns his face upward. "I came all the way here and there's nothing." The River is nothing but a dream.

Ren lies in its water and she lies there dead. Eyes closed. Limbs heavy.

The ghost of hands fall to his back and over his shoulders. *Come to the River, my son.*

Basuin whirls, but no one is behind him. "Ma?" He knocks his fist over his heart again. No wolf-man is home.

But something sparkles in the water, a glint of light. Not a reflection. Something real. It skips down the stream, bounding off the broken idol and toward the waterfall. When it slips inside, the water parts as if making way for a body.

Come to the River, his mother says again.

Basuin gathers Ren in his arms—she's so heavy, blood smeared across her skin and water dripping from her clothes—and drags himself toward the falls. He tucks Ren's face into his shoulder as he wades through the curtain of water, shielding her from the spray. Everything here is dark, except for the glow of the light jumping through the cave. It draws him forward, further into the falls, until his eyes adjust to the blackness of the cave.

Here, a true river runs through the earth. The stream of it is cool on the crags, peaceful and unending. When he takes a step forward, the movement creates a blue glow from the water. Another step and the surface ripples in the same hue as the barrier that hid this place from them.

This is what he was looking for. The Winter River.

Place her in the water, his mother says again. With no hesitation, Basuin does as she instructs, moving further into the River and letting Ren's body sink into the water. He cradles her head with one hand, his arm still wrapped around her waist.

"I love you," he finally says, too late. It's too late. "I want peace—I want to find peace with you, whatever that means. I'll learn to let go. I'll learn to forgive myself. We can find peace, together." A trembling thumb runs over her bottom lip. "Please, Ren."

His heart is tearing into two. Someone's claws are sunk into him and ripping him apart. Breaking him. He'll never see her smile again. Never see her twilight eyes, gorgeous eyes, anxious eyes. He'll never hear her laugh. Never again will he borrow anything from Ren—not the floral smell of her or the feeling of her hand in his. Not her lips against his or how they move when she talks.

It's unbearable. He's lost his home again. It's dead and his hands have left imprints in blood behind.

"I'll do anything," he bargains. "Just please, Ma. Let me wake up. Let this be a nightmare. I'll do anything, I swear."

The gods won't speak to him anymore. Good. Because if they could, he would be offering everything he has. His eyes, his mouth, his hands, his bones. Anything to bring her back. Anything.

There's something buzzing in the water. Something fizzing against his skin. When he opens his eyes, Ren's body is aglow with blue magic. Not hers, but from the River. He pulls away, heart beating rapidly, afraid to disturb her. Then, the image before his eyes shifts and changes as a spirit emerges from Ren's body—a deer.

No; half deer, half woman.

She stands before him, naked, tattoos running blue along her pale skin in long swathes and winding around her limbs. A deer's head replaces hers, eyes glowing cyan, with long antlers the same color as Ren's stretching out like a flower in bloom. White hair falls in long rivulets around her shoulders, covering her breasts and ending below her waist.

The deer-girl tilts her head to the side, assessing him. When she blinks, her hand falls just above his chest, then pulls back as if he's burned her. She makes no sound at all. Basuin stills himself, takes shallow breaths, but his heart races.

"You..." Her voice sounds like Ren's did before, linked with other voices until a buzzing harmony is reached. It echoes in the cave, bouncing off the water. "You are lucky somebody loves you," the deer-girl says, as if confused. As if she doesn't believe it to be true. It sounds so familiar, but deadly all the same.

"I am," he says, voice smaller than it ever has been.

"And…" She tilts her head to the other side now, hair falling over her antlers, a jingling of bells coming from nowhere. "And you loved her, did you not?"

"I did," he answers. "I do."

The deer-girl stares at him, like she can see inside of him. "Then so be it."

Her hands reach for him, arms encircling his shoulders to pull him into a tight embrace. As their bodies clash, her tattoos shed from her skin and jump to his, wrapping around him like vines, squeezing and constricting him until they've cut into his flesh and his bone to entangle in his organs. She reaches for his sternum, his heart-bone, plunging herself inside of him.

As the deer-girl slithers into his skin, his head burns and screams, agonized by the prayers and cries and songs of thousands of others ringing out in the hellscape of his mind. Blinding white. Her fingers dig up the roots of his eyes and rip them out, then replace them with her palms.

An anger, unlike anything he's felt before, consumes him. Sweeps him away in a blaze burning so bright and hot he feels like he's suffocating beneath it. Desert dry, no air that isn't burning with the heat of Elka's sun to gulp down. The Forest God fits herself into every single corner of his body as if she looks to become him—not just to possess him.

It's heavy. This anger, so sudden and unbidden, is oppressive. It's so hot it burns him from the inside out and then creeps back inside him again. There's no way to shake it. No water to drink down and cool him. Valkesta is a gift compared to this molten, sticky, suffocating fury. Basuin falls to his knees on the bank of the River, choking and coughing and pounding his fist on the ground.

Was this the anger that possessed Ren? The anger she felt at every moment since godhood, the anger that consumed her, but didn't control her the way it would control him?

And despite it, Ren chose peace. Over war, over killing, over everything, Ren chose peace. He was the naive one all along. Not her.

She's dead. Sa-cha help him, Ren is *dead*. He can't bring her back. He's lost again. The Forest God's anger wraps him up, blankets him from the grief, turns his heartache into a hunger for war. It's changing him, he can feel it. Basuin's body, broken with anguish, is pieced back together by the Forest God, sinewed and stitched up with fury.

His back hunches and cracks. Fur grows on his skin. His mouth turns to maw and his teeth into fangs and his nails into claws and Basuin, rage like a brand igniting his skin, throws his head back and howls across the forest.

"Yaelic!" he growls at the top of his lungs. "Qia!"

He calls them to duty. They are his charges. Ren no longer lives, and she is no longer the Forest God, and now the Forest God has possessed him.

The bubble around the River breaks, shatters into nothing but a shimmer of magic, and beyond it—beyond the daylight that's frozen in time, the night still black on the other side—waits Haaman with Yaelic and Qia in tow.

Behind them, all the faces and the spirits of the forest who are left. They've answered his call, or perhaps this is all the distance they could cross in time. Maybe they were stopped here by the barrier. He doesn't care.

There's no time for words, and even if there were, he's being eaten by the burning ire that's healed all the breaks in his bones, suffused through him.

"Qia," he barks. "Ren is in the river. Tend to her. Call on Hou-tou." Then, he turns to Yaelic, too boyish and too little and too young to be in a war. "Stay with her and protect her."

"I want to come with you," Yaelic starts, but a snarl from Basuin shuts him up.

"You will stay," he bites. "Haaman!"

The sparrow looks at him warily. Like they don't know if they should bow or puff out their chest.

"Watch over them." Basuin waves a hand over at the spirits lining the trees. "Get them somewhere safe."

"Where are you going?" Haaman asks, but Bass has already turned his back.

Kensy still hangs from the tree Ren grew from her magic, her antler stabbed in his gut. The blood is shiny, still trickling down and feeding its roots. Thick vines, grown from the tree, have begun to coil around him. It'll feed on his matter, feast on his decay.

Bass braces his foot on the tree trunk and, magic running through him, rips Ren's antler from the tree. The roots wrapped around Kensy tighten, but those calculating blue eyes have gone dark. Basuin wasn't sure he'd ever see the day Kensy died.

If only Basuin had killed him. He wishes it. If only he could've saved Ren from killing; if only he could've *saved her*.

But, more than that, Basuin was meant to kill Kensy. For as much as Kensy made Basuin, Basuin made Kensy, too.

Kensy trained him like a dog, and every time Basuin rolled over and did as he was told, it grew the cruelty that Kensy was capable of. An obedient dog makes for an arrogant master.

But that arrogance brought him here. How far Commander Kensy has fallen, to die in the forest he lay claim over. Struck out to colonize. Basuin licks his lips—there's blood on his mouth.

"I'm going to the bastion," he says. "Back to Shaelstorm."

He's going to where everything began. Where he first set foot on this island.

With one last howl, stood up on his two legs, Basuin's heart thunders and his body bends and breaks and grows until he falls onto his hands and knees—on all fours on the forest floor. He can see above the canopy. He can see the whole forest stretched out before him. Basuin growls, all wolf and no man, and then he lunges and breaks for the trees. He leaps through the forest, large and unending. But he is larger, and he sees everything. The southern coast where Shaelstorm is built.

How will you end it? the deer-girl asks.

The same way it started. With fire, and with blood.

CHAPTER THIRTY-FIVE

THERE ARE NO tears left to be shed. The sting of his eyes is the sting of fire, of heat, of anger, of fury and of rage. It boils through every part of his body. Every limb, every bone, every nail, every hair. Covers him and burns through him like the itch of the poison ivy he got into as a boy, before he knew it could sting as much as it did.

I'm fine, he tried to tell his mother when she came close with a balm that smelled of grass and something astringent.

Even if you are fine, she said, pulling one of his reddened hands toward her, *that doesn't mean you should let your hurt continue to hurt. We make remedies so we can soothe the pain and heal the sick. Doesn't the itch drive you mad?*

Yes, he admitted to her, and then he let her smooth the pasty balm on his rash. The relief of it made him cry, and his mother laughed.

My Basuin, she cooed. *A son who feels such emotions, so fully. You are full.*

Of what? he asked her.

Everything. Joy, and sorrow, and sometimes anger. But it is better to be full than empty.

Are there people who are like that, Ma?

Yes, she told him, pulling him close and kissing his hair. *People like that are the ones who let their pain linger instead of soothing it away. They like the hurt, because it makes them feel less empty.*

He understands it now—Kensy, and Isaniel, and him. All the same, hands sunk into different vices. What would his mother think if she saw him now? Would she cry for him, or would she give him that proud smile, the soft one with knowing eyes, now that he's become a god?

His whole body feels like he's lit aflame, standing atop a funeral pyre. There are two gods inside of him, eating at what's left of him. Blood pounds between his ears as he runs through the forest, growling and snarling until foam bubbles on his maw, southbound.

In true god form, Basuin phases through the trees as if they are nothing to him. They shake and sway in terror of him, bowing their heads as he goes crashing through the woods. He feels free. He feels what Kensy craved so violently, so brutally. Enough to kill for—enough that it killed him in its stead. A power no one else can rip from you. A strength that only comes from godhood.

But Kensy was wrong. Basuin has lost so much, even as a god.

A bright blue-white light sparks to life beside him, and when his eyes shift to look, it's the deer-girl. She prances through the forest beside him on the air, one long stride met with a skip, then starting over. Then, she bounds even further than his legs reach, taking flight to zip in front of him.

Basuin runs, and the deer-girl turns to look at him. She tilts her head in that same way again as the trees rush by them.

What did you think of her?

He huffs a laugh. It makes him sound like the wolf-man.

Whip-smart, he tells the deer-girl. *Full of grace. So much grace and diplomacy—I've never met anyone like her. And beautiful. She was so beautiful it hurt at times.*

Beautiful enough to kill for? the deer-girl asks.

Something from deep below, the wolf-man or his own soul,

reaches up and squeezes his heart until it simply turns to blood.

Beautiful enough that I shouldn't have—but I love her too much not to kill them anyway.

Basuin closes his eyes. And when he opens them again, he sees Ren. The deer-girl moves with the same grace, the same arm's-length dance, that Ren always did. Twirling away from him, slipping out of sight, playing right on the edge of his vision. It's her, really. How much of Ren was the Forest God and how much of the Forest God is Ren?

How much of him is the Wolf God—and how much of him is Ren, now?

There are no camps left. Basuin destroyed them all, remains left behind and decaying. But the further south he gets, the more damage he sees. He skids through the center of the island, the Crying Trees almost entirely decimated. Ko's home. The only thing left—too hard to kill, maybe—is the elder tree, which was supposed to sever Basuin's tie with the Wolf God. A beacon of this forest and its proof it won't die willingly. He cries, howling into the night. All his fault. All his fault that they've burned down this forest, cut these trees down where they stand like enemies on a battlefield.

Godless, soulless. His fault. Treason.

Basuin's pace quickens, gunning for Shaelstorm. They'll pay for the damage they've done. No more sabotage. No broken weapons and barren fields and shriveled grains. No more nightmares. Basuin won't stop at driving them out of his forest. He'll squash them like bugs, hunt them down like prey, paint the forest with their blood and leave it as a warning.

There, in the distance, he can see smoke rising. With the forest cleared, there's almost a straight shot to the bastion. It makes him snarl, ferocious, bleeding from his gums from gnashing his canines together.

The first soldiers who see him run. Basuin grins.

Are you prepared to end this war? the deer-girl asks him, eyes blank and glowing white.

I should have ended it much sooner, he answers. *But I loved her.*

Captain Basuin, the Black Wolf, she says it like she's scolding him. *Always decisive, isn't that what you told them?*

With one last long, painful howl, Basuin lunges. First, for the farms that Ren kept barren and lifeless. With one long swipe of a paw, claws stretched out, he destroys one of the fields and takes the barns with it.

Screams and shouts begin to stream from Shaelstorm. He barks a laugh as he tears through another farm, and another, and another. On the exterior walls they've built to keep the forest out, he snatches a flaming torch and the force of his jaws splinters it in his mouth.

From the watchtowers, the soldiers begin to fight back. With war cries, they let loose arrows of steel at him. He doesn't even feel them, as if the arrows run straight through his fur and out.

Basuin leaps over the wall and crashes into the bastion, maw full of fire. Some men are running and some are standing and fighting. Swords drawn, spears in hand, others loading their rifles. He skids through all of them, nails on cobbles, swiping out at the soldiers with giant paws and clawing through them like they're made of paper. Bits and pieces.

Then, he crashes, head and body, into the grain sheds. The Wolf God spits fire as he bashes through the wooden sheds, the bags of food they've stored inside going up in an instant. The scent of fire and ash spreads through Shaelstorm.

A gun fires, echoing through the night. A prick of pain runs through his back leg as something wraps around him, tight. He turns, looking behind him at the soldiers who've raised their guns to him.

On his hind leg, where a bullet was drawn, thick roots covered in dirt and moss twine together and solidify into a forest-made armor. Another soldier shoots—into his stomach. But roots grow out of his body, from his ribcage, to ribbon through him and create the same living armor as before.

The Wolf God laughs, voice dark and growling and not all his. "You are foolish to think you can kill a god you've wronged."

Another gunshot, into his haunches. Another plate of living forest armor to cover his body. Rage and fury and grief mix in his gut until it bubbles up into his throat and he snarls at them, lunging.

His teeth sink into the first body he finds. He tears that man in two. Then, he skewers two more soldiers on his canines, crunching down on their bones and drooling them back out from his maw in a mix of blood and entrails. The air tastes of something sweet and smoky. There isn't enough fire. Not enough of it.

Magic collects on the surface of his body, unable to contain itself within him. His black fur glows red, ominous and dangerous, and when he rears back and opens his jaws again, flames burst from his mouth. The Wolf God breathes in embers, spits fire onto the bastion, and everything goes up. This place burns. Shaelstorm is swallowed up by the very thing they've destroyed his forest with.

This isn't cruelty. It's punishment. The same thing that brought him here.

He can't tell what they shout and scream and cry at him while they shoot their guns. More and more root-armor pads his body with every bullet they attempt to lodge into his skin. He sweeps them up in his paws and plays with them, teases his prey right before he slams his snout into them and breaks their little bodies. Kills them.

"Please!" someone shouts above the rest. His head snaps to them, sunk low to the ground and ready to pounce. A man drops to his knees, bows his head to the ground, crying.

"Have mercy, please! Gods, have mercy, we are weak. We are wrong. We are only human!" he prays, sobbing with his face pressed into the dirt.

Other men toss their weapons in futility and do the same, dropping to the ground and bowing, begging for mercy.

"You would ask for mercy after what you've done?" he growls at them, teeth dripping with blood. "Insolent men. You beg for forgiveness even in the wreckage of what *you've* destroyed!"

The Wolf God howls, neck stretched up to the missing moon.

"Gods, have mercy," another begs. "Gods, be good."

He slams into another building, destroying one of the large barracks, shredding through wood and setting it aflame with a snuff from his snout. And then he lunges for another. The mess hall, he remembers. He thrashes it and breathes fire into the building's bones until it catches like a match head.

He turns for the next barracks, but a woman stands before him. Small compared to him. She's shed her armor already and bows her head at him, hands upturned and palms stretched out to him in surrender and prayer.

"From the Winter River, there arose a god," she recites, eyes closed. "And that god was Sa-cha, and he was good."

Basuin recoils, jerking his head away.

"Our good Sa-cha cried until the River ran, and his tears birthed more gods, and they birthed man."

Man is weak and man is small, his mother would recite from memory, her hands moving across his own as they sat up late at night in her bed. *But Sa-cha's River has love for all.*

A man, and another man, shuffle toward the woman. Each places their palms out to him in worship, soot-streaked faces and fingers covered in blood. They look weary, not scared. They have already lost.

"Be us weak and be us small, we turn to Sa-cha, for he is ever and he is all. Our gods give the gift of light and night, birth and death, mistake and mercy," they pray to him. To the Wolf God.

"And if we are good," a voice pants, breathless, over

everyone else's. Tehali is waiting behind him, blood streaked across her face. "The Winter River opens its gates and grants forgiveness to those who are worthy," she finishes, closing the prayer. Her hand is dripping blood.

Cold, freezing guilt replaces the burning heat of anger. Shaelstorm is ruined. Dead bodies litter the ground. The bastion is half destroyed, lit aflame, and continuing to burn to pitch. These soldiers aren't the ones standing in their own wreckage. It's him.

Kensy really did make him. Desperate enough to become violent out of fear. Out of love. Out of losing something.

Ren—if Ren saw this, she'd be ashamed. He can hear her voice perfectly in his head, a blessing and a curse. Her voice is an echo on the roar of the flames around him.

The way her lips form his name and the way she told him that she didn't want to go to war with an army she couldn't fight. Her voice is clear, and stubborn, and still gentle somehow. The way she told him that she loved him. That he was the first.

She'd be disgusted if she saw him like this. Horrified at the beast he's become. A monster, just like Kensy. Basuin kills everyone he loves. It's a curse to love Basuin, but worse a curse to be loved by him.

Ren wanted peace. She didn't want things to end in blood.

But he's glad he did it anyway, because it's ended. No matter how horrified she'd be.

An animalistic cry tears out of his jaws and Basuin leaps across the bastion and toward the watchtower. His claws scrabble for purchase, turning into fingers once again as his tree-bark armor chips away and his body wanes into something not quite human again. Still godly, still rife with scars and blood and red magic, but human as he climbs over the guardrail to fall onto the platform. His body aches.

Part of him believes it was a mistake. Part of him thinks it's righteous. A means to an end. He told the deer-girl he would end it in fire and blood and he did, but Ren wanted peace. Ren is dead and she wanted peace and he should've honored that. But he couldn't. The anger inside him, half human, half god, or maybe all him still—it consumed him.

Ren is dead. He can't bring her back. They deserved to die for that.

No, they didn't. It was Kensy who brought this war, Kensy who shipped them over the sea and to this island, Kensy who commanded they destroy the forest. It was Kensy who killed Ren.

They were just soldiers, like Basuin.

He stands now, grunting as he pulls himself up just to sag on his feet. To see his destruction. To face what he's done. Basuin grips the railing of the watchtower—he's been here before. Overlooking the forest before. Questioning his duty, questioning himself.

And now, he overlooks Shaelstorm as it sinks into the fiery pits he's made, all to avenge a woman who never wanted it.

Far out, people are rushing to row their boats out toward the sea. In the long distance, one ship sits on the water. Good. Good riddance. They should have left so long ago. Should've fled before they destroyed half of this forest and killed its god.

Basuin rests his head on the railing.

Rushing footsteps find the stairs up into the watchtower. He doesn't bother to look at the intruder. He sets his chin on the guardrail and stares into the black sea before him. Lit lamps dot the water as the soldiers row toward safety.

"Are you done killing?" Tehali asks. She's out of breath.

He doesn't respond.

"Are you Basuin of Ankor?" she asks, too. "Or are you Basuin, the Black Wolf?"

"All and none," he answers. "I don't know anymore."

After a moment, Tehali moves to rest against the railings beside him. She smells of ash and gunpowder. It makes him gag, makes him slap a hand over his mouth. She smells of death—of the death he razed.

"Are you going home?"

After a long moment, Basuin gives her a curt nod. "I will, after this. We'll replant the forest. Rebuild." The word tastes like metal pressed to his tongue, branding it into his flesh. He wanted to do it with Ren. With Ren.

Tehali looks at him, dark eyes wide. "You're staying here?"

"It's my home."

She drags a bloodied hand over her face, thinking. They take that moment, standing in front of the burning bastion, together. It's been a long time since they've been together like this. The last time, they were in this very watchtower. And this time, he understands much more than he did then.

"I want to shed my armor," he says, swallowing hard. "I want peace now."

Tehali gestures out at Shaelstorm. "This isn't peace, Captain."

"I know." He hangs his head. It hurts worse to hear it aloud, to hear yet again that his hands brought war instead of cultivating peace. Ren would've found a way. "She didn't want this." If they had more time, she would've found a path to peace.

For better or for worse, Tehali doesn't ask who he speaks of. Basuin's eyes burn something rotten, not with smoke, but with another wave of tears wanting release. He already misses her.

He wants Ren beside him, even with disgust. Even with shame. Even if she hated him after all of this, he wants Ren here.

"You should go home," he says finally. "Go back to Jankri. Visit with your family again."

"My father would send me away," Tehali says with a bark of a laugh. "After this shitshow?" She shakes her head and the chime of gold rings in her ears is so familiar it aches. "My mama would be happy, though."

"Then you should."

Tehali's mouth makes something of a smile, pained but heavy with the duty of a soldier. She's still a soldier, through and through. Less than he was before, but more than he is now.

"I'm sorry," he says. "I didn't mean for any of this."

She shrugs. "We do as we're told, Bass. It's how we scrape by. But you—" Tehali takes a deep breath and sighs. "You've never had anything but war to love."

"War is easy." He tightens his grip on the railing. "War doesn't die."

"And look at what it's killed," she says.

He swallows.

"You should go home," Tehali tells him. "If this is your home, then you should go back to it. Stay here. Be happy, Captain." She beats her fist on the railing in a soft rhythm. "I'd like to go home, too."

"Then go," he says.

"Will you let me?" Tehali stares into him with a gaze that burrows deep down inside of him. "Will you grace me with your mercy, Wolf God?"

Basuin flinches. More than ever, he doesn't know who—or what—he is. He closes his eyes. The image of Ren, soft and a little sharp and so forgiving, paints across the back of his mind. Worst of all, if she could see all this, she would be sad. For him, for the burden of war he carries. At least it wasn't her. He would do it thousands of times over, as long as she wouldn't have to bear this sin.

"I've done enough harm. To you, and to this forest." To Ren. He's done enough. Basuin waves his hand out at the bastion. "Good night, Tali. Be well."

He doesn't turn to watch her leave. It isn't fair of him, but Tehali is the only friend he's ever had. The only person who's truly cared for him as if they were family. And it hurts too badly to say goodbye to her.

But Tehali reaches and grabs Basuin's hand, giving it a firm squeeze.

"Good night, Bass," she says. Then, her steps start back down the ladder and fade down the stairs as Tehali descends.

If he's ever to move on, ever to rebuild this place, ever to go back home again, he needs to let go. The blinding, howling winds of Valkesta. The death of his squad. The death of his mother. The death of Ren.

Forgiveness is so hard. The thing in his breast aches. He clutches at it, wishing he could wrench it out and destroy it the way he's destroyed everything else. But all he can do is live with it.

Once, Basuin wanted to throw himself off this watchtower and find the death he felt was all he had left. Now, he jumps from the watchtower and lands in the center of Shaelstorm, right atop Kensy's office with a slam. It draws shouts and shrieks from the remaining soldiers still scrambling to get out of Shaelstorm alive.

When he stands to full height, he's different. His skin has gone black, red lines of magic running up and down his bones like tattoos. Like the wolf-man. He can feel it, see his black snout in his watery vision. He's become the very thing he tried to escape from.

"I will give you a choice," he shouts above the bray of the destruction. His voice sounds like a growl, archaic and consuming. Some soldiers flee, but others stay to look up at him. "You are free to stay and fight and die."

Freedom. He used to pray that someone would give him a choice. But now, he makes his own. It's his choice, war or peace.

"Or you can leave and never return." His voice reaches across Shaelstorm. "Send word to Xalkhir of us—of powerful gods, of what destruction we can bring. Tell them that we're here, and that we live, and to never set foot in our forest ever again."

Basuin holds out a hand and gathers magic on his god mark. Then, something materializes, the Wolf God's black staff of red crystals, glimmering in the light of the flames. It pulses with his anger, his fury, his scalding wrath. It's made of him. He points it at the crowding soldiers.

"Choose what you will," he tells them. "Be free of this place."

The soldiers scatter and scurry off, grabbing what they can. Grabbing the bodies of their friends, dragging them to the docks and the beach. They'll save who they can. They'll bury who they can recover. The rest will burn with Shaelstorm and their ash will turn to fodder for the new forest Basuin will grow.

His new duty still belongs to Ren. He'll rebuild their island, heal the scars and burns and bruises he left here.

The deer-girl appears in a blink, sitting on the end of his staff with her tilted head and her white hair tangled in her antlers.

Is it over? she asks him.

Almost. Basuin reaches out his hand to her, and when she slips her fingers into his, it's a ghost of a touch. Nothing real. But he pulls her from his staff and she takes flight, disappearing in a blink. Almost over.

Basuin raises his staff high above his head and stakes it straight through the roof of Kensy's bunk and into the ground. Fire bursts forth from it, setting the building aflame. A crack runs through the stone-bricked streets of Shaelstorm, running through the earth in lines of lightning. A fissure in the earth. A split in bones.

The Wolf God fractures Yesua, the earth quaking beneath his feet. In a thunder, the island snaps at the breach, ground collapsing and sinking into the ocean which once belonged to Ithika. The ocean he sailed here on. Hungry waves devour the war that was wrought, gobble up anyone who is left. The Shaelstorm bastion finally falls at his hand.

Basuin shuts his eyes tight, his scar aching. No longer will this land belong to anyone but the gods and the spirits who roam here. No longer will death and destruction place its flag here. Let them know—let them know that the Wolf God protects this land again. Let them know that he kills in the name of peace, and peace only. But that he kills.

"Now, it's over," he says, standing at the precipice. It ended with fire and with blood, just like he said it would.

It's time to come home. Ren's voice is sweet in his ear. Basuin closes his eyes, breathing in. *Come home, Basuin.*

CHAPTER THIRTY-SIX

FOUR FEET ON the ground, Basuin slinks back through the forest. He's weary and worn, guilty and ashamed. Grieving. He has to go back. She's waiting for him, but he'd kill again if it meant he wouldn't have to drag himself back to see her dead. It aches, even from this far away.

The land aches, too. Where the legion has sawed trees down and burned brush to make room for their construction, it hurts as he walks along it. Most of the spirits are gone from here, dead or having fled already. He doesn't blame them. He blames himself for letting the army get this far.

He blames himself for Ren's death. She shouldn't have taken the shot meant for him.

Beside him in a twinkle of light, the deer-girl appears. Her white skin is nearly translucent in the thin light of twilight as it struggles to dawn. But they walk together, side by side. It's comforting in a way. He's not alone, even as he walks the shameful path back to Ren.

Do not be so sad, the deer-girl tells him. *Without war, there is no peace. With everything, there is balance. Humans always struggle with balancing their scales*.

Basuin looks up at the sky. The shadowed lavender above their heads doesn't feel like homecoming. It feels like the break in a nightmare he can see, but he can't reach. It's too far.

She told me that, too, he says.

Yes, she did. The deer-girl nods.

It aches. He almost wishes the wolf-man were still here to shred his insides. It always liked to eat at him when Ren was hurt. He's surprised the wolf-man didn't show up to kill him in light of Ren's last breath. But he's become it. The wolf-man has become him. Finally.

Ren is dead and he marches toward her. To come home and to lay her to rest. It's agonizing.

Basuin closes his eyes as the burn of tears begins. The deer-girl walks alongside him as they weave between what's left of the forest. He can feel the eyes of spirits who have yet to leave on him, can feel the weight of their stares.

His heart is heavy in his chest, weighing him down until his belly almost scrapes the forest floor. His bones ache with every step. Basuin misses his mother. He misses her terribly.

If she were here, he'd lay his head in his ma's lap and let her stroke his hair and soothe away the pain. He'd cry to her, tell her that the girl he loves is dead. The home that he found in her is gone now, laid to rest in her stopped heart.

Will you continue to love her? the deer-girl asks. *Even in death?*

Of course, he answers. *I'll love her even once I end up in the Blacksalt Sea.*

His paws are bloodied and raw by the time they return to the flowered field where the Winter River lies waiting. Before he enters, the deer-girl disappears in a mist of something warm, and then it's only him. He passes through the barrier, shifting until he's on two feet once more, where day is never-ending and water still flows. It's bright here, too bright, and he winces from the light.

Spirits have gathered in this sacred place, many of whom he recognizes and many he doesn't. They bow to the broken statue of Sa-cha sitting in front of the waterfall, its pieces littering the stream. The blood has already washed away.

Basuin picks up a large shard of the idol, turning it around in his hand. Sa-cha, in all his glory and godhood. Because this is his domain, the first, and this was his shrine, his hiding place, and Kensy destroyed it. Glory to the gods.

With a gentle hand, he places it back down in the creek, then presses his hand to the statue in promises to fix it later. He'll put it back together. It won't resurrect Sa-cha, but maybe it will give him a home to come back to. Another reparation to pay.

When he ducks through the waterfall, everyone is there waiting. Not for him, but for Ren, he's sure. They all look so broken—and he feels it. He feels shattered, in pieces, like Sa-cha's shrine. When Yaelic sees him, he scrambles to bow to Basuin. Qia, face streaked with tears and eyes reddened with grief, does the same. Nobody needs to bow to him, especially children. Especially those who grieve their friend.

As he passes them by, he places a soft hand on their heads. He takes Qia's chin and raises it, but can't bring himself to smile.

Haaman sits further inside the cave, resting against one of the walls with their head thrown back. Staring up at the stalactites in a numbness. They look as though they haven't moved at all.

And Hou-tou, blue eyes milky and long, dark hair spread across the cave, sits by Ren. Her hands are still hovering over the wound in Ren's chest, and when she upturns her face to look at him as he approaches, her cheeks are stained with tears.

"Wolf God," she calls him, pressing herself up off the ground to make room for him. "I tried—I'm sorry."

Ren's body lies in the River, floating and still, but glowing blue. When he kneels beside her, the ripples fluoresce with his movements.

"Don't apologize," he says. "There was nothing you could do." Ren's death colors his hands, not anyone else's. But her killer is dead. And he's here, and her family and friends surround her, and this is all anyone can do for her now.

The ache and the exhaustion finally sets in and Basuin collapses beside her in the River. One of his hands finds her cheek, soft and cold, and he closes his eyes.

"I went against you," he admits, as if she were still here. Still housed in this dead body. "I chose war. I went down to Shaelstorm and I killed them—many of them. Burned the bastion down. I wanted them to hurt." He breathes out, looking over her pallid face. "I was angry and I wanted to kill them, and I did. But—"

Basuin slips his hand into Ren's, jaw tight and trembling.

"How did you do it?" he asks her. "With all that anger, you still chose peace. I felt it and I ran straight to the legion. Brought war to them the way they brought it here—we brought it here." That blame still lies on him as much as it does anyone else. "How were you strong enough to keep choosing peace over war?"

He brings her hand up and kisses her knuckles. "But I did, at the end of it all. I chose peace, after everything. They're gone now. We can regrow the forest, rebuild Gyeosi. I'll do it. I'll keep choosing peace."

Tears break, and Basuin leans over her to press his lips to her forehead. "Are you proud of me?" he asks, a tremble to his voice. A sob in the back of his throat. "I'm sorry, truly. For not seeing it before. I love you, Ren."

And now that it's over, now that he's ended the war and there's only peace left to be found, Basuin lays his head on Ren's chest and cries. Like he first came into this world, like he's been reborn again, like the god inside of him is renewed, Basuin cries in the sanctity of Ren. Her heart beats beneath his ear.

No.

Her heart is beating. Basuin looks up, and where he thinks Sa-cha to be, at the mouth of the River, there stands his mother. She looks the same as she always did—threads of silver running through her dark hair, a soft face full of laugh lines and wizened dimples. Age spots litter her face and her hands, but she's still as beautiful as she always was.

"Ma," he calls, voice thin. But she only smiles, not saying a word. Then, she reaches into his chest. With one hand, she pulls something dark and pulsating from him. It aches like a wound. In another, she takes something white and shimmering. It burns as it leaves the cavity of his chest.

Two spirits, two gods inside him, both in the palms of her hands the way her godstone used to fit in her fingers. His mother's lips curl, worn in that knowing look she always had.

And before his eyes, both the wolf-man and the deer-girl come to life. Out of spirits, they morph into bodies, beautiful god-things he's seen before, when they chose to deify him. A man with the head of a wolf, a girl with the head of a deer.

The wolf-man holds out his arms and the deer-girl rushes forward, jumping into his embrace. Their twinkling laughs fill the cave, loud over the stream of the Winter River as the wolf-man twirls the deer-girl around. Around and around until they form one body, one soul—black and white and white and black.

Lovers. Like Ko said: *Always together, until they weren't anymore*. How the wolf-man thumped its tail when Ren touched him, how it howled for her, how it pressed Basuin toward her. They were lovers, the Wolf God and the Forest God. It sinks deep into him somewhere with an ache, watching them reunite with laughter. Tangled in one another, embracing the other until they are so close they make only one body. Basuin closes his eyes. The wolf-man wanted to protect his lover.

It wasn't the gods who bound them—it was love. The Wolf God chose to be the guardian of the Forest God. Like Basuin chose, in the end, to be Ren's protector. It was choice.

But then, they separate again in a shower of light that

glitters across the cave walls. The wolf-man, standing tall beside the deer-girl, looks at him.

"Thank you, Basuin of Ankor," he says.

In turn, all Basuin can do is bow his head, tears falling down the planes of his face. There's an emptiness inside of him, an eviction he didn't realize he would feel this deeply. The empty space where his heart used to belong, ripped out.

"Basuin," the wolf-man calls again, and he looks up. The wolf-man's eyes glow red, and beside him, the deer-girl's eyes are glowing blue. "Would you continue protecting this forest?"

"Of course," he answers. "I told her—we'll rebuild. The army left scars, I know. I've left my own share. But I'll work to heal it. We'll grow again." He bites his tongue to hold back a sob from his chest. "I want to do that, for her. For those who I hurt and those who lost their lives."

In the corner of the cave, Haaman cries into their hands.

After Valkesta, he wanted so badly to die. And when he came here, deified to be a god who was only meant to protect the forest and its god, he wanted nothing more than to die again. But now, he has a job to do. A duty he chooses to take on, not one he's commanded to. Ren is dead, but he needs to keep the memory of her alive. He has to. The hurt will linger and he will live on, even without her by his side.

And in the time it will take to rebuild, Basuin will learn forgiveness. He'll do as Ren told him and he'll learn to forgive himself—even for the death of her. Not today, not tomorrow, and not soon. But one day.

Basuin looks down at her, the softness of her sleeping face. "This is our home. I want to protect what belonged to her. So I'll stay. I'll protect the forest."

The wolf-man laughs that huff of a laugh it always did, then sweeps the deer-girl into his arms. They spin around, happily, until they form into one soul. Together again, they shoot like a star across the sky straight into Basuin's chest, and he staggers back. It feels familiar again, hot and bright but familiar. He's full again, the gods nestled in the space in his ribcage.

But Basuin falls to his knees and sobs, clutching his chest. The Wolf God and the Forest God are inside him, both of them. There's no one left to deify Ren. No one to bring her back. She's gone—she's really gone. Basuin sinks, on all fours, coughing out a sob.

Ren's dead, and he's left behind.

But over the roaring in his ears and the rush of water, Yaelic gasps. "Captain," Yaelic calls. "The River."

It's enough to make Basuin look up, vision blurry with hot tears. The cave is awash in blue, so brightly blue. Walls painted in all shades and facets of sapphires. Magic floods the River, fluorescent, but then it trickles right back to Ren's body. She's absorbed it, encased in it, like a cocoon webbed around her. Breathing in and out as if the magic has become a lifeform.

White lines, tattoos and leylines and scars like a god mark, thread through her body and drip down her limbs. It starts at the crown of her hair and draws down her arms, her stomach, and down her legs to wrap around her ankles. A split in a chrysalis.

Then, Ren's eyes open. She takes a breath and consumes the magic on her skin, alighting her in something only described as godly.

He's stunned. But not stunned enough. Basuin rushes to cradle her, pulling her body against his in a crushing grip. He cries into her wet hair, tucks his face into her neck to feel for her pulse. It beats, and it beats, and Ren wraps her arms around him.

"Basuin," she whispers, clutching him. "It's all right. I'm here."

He sobs in her arms like a child would, purely and freely as the grief breaks from him. There's magic on her skin and he can feel it. Taste it. A buzzing in the air like static that he still isn't sure is real.

"How?" Bass pulls back enough to look at her, to run his hands over her face and smooth her hair out of her eyes. He needs to know how she lives, needs to understand before she's ripped from him again. "How are you here? The Forest God—"

"*You* are the Forest God," she says, placing her hand on his chest. "You reunited them." It makes her smile. "They were eternal lovers. Separated in death, when their shrines were destroyed. And you reunited them." She repeats it with pride.

Basuin almost laughs. He could shake her. Cry again, because this isn't real. "Ren, how are you alive?" he pleads. If this is a trick, if this will only last a second, it'll devastate him. He's already so broken. It won't take much.

But Ren smiles that beautiful smile, infused with the sun. "I house a new god," she tells him. "Sa-cha has chosen me. When Kensy broke his shrine, Sa-cha had no home left, not without a host. But he chose me." Ren takes his godstone into her hand where it still hangs around her neck.

Then, a hand on his shoulder, Ren surges forward and kisses him, desperately, until they're both breathless. She wipes away the tears that continue to fall from his eyes.

"I remember it now," she says. "How I died before. When Ithika was killed, my family and I were on a boat. It sank, but the Forest God found me. It was lonely." Ren presses her hand to his heart again. "It didn't have its other half, its guardian—the Wolf God. So it saved me."

Ren takes his hand too, god-marked and all, and presses it to her own heart. He feels it fluttering under his palm, racing in response to his touch. He watches her breathe, listens to her heartbeat, and even still his eyes burn with tears when she looks up at him, alive.

"It saved me so I could house it until it found the Wolf God again," she says, staring at him so fondly.

Basuin laughs, resting his forehead against hers. And he laughs, and he laughs. And then, he laughs again until Ren wipes those tears away, too.

"Then I am glad," he tells her, nose bumping hers. "I'm glad that I died to meet you. That I was deified to protect you."

He breathes in, the scent of her still the same. White lilies and grass and upturned soil. She's the same. His Ren, more woman than god, with her twilight eyes.

"I am glad, because I can love you," he says. "I love you, Ren." And he means it. He means it in the deepest sense, in the forgiving sense, in the sense of gratitude for all the mistakes he's made and the losses he's grieved and the pain that clung to him with every step he took here. To Ren.

"Then rebuild with me." She grins against his mouth. "This is our home."

"Our home," he agrees. No longer a soldier, and not quite a man who lived on the outskirts of a village in Ankor. He'll build a new one, here in the forest, with Ren. A place of peace he'll carve out for himself with two scarred hands—of wars, and of gods.

CHAPTER THIRTY-SEVEN
EPILOGUE

Basuin bounds into the ocean, cool water splashing against his legs as he turns back to smile at Ren. "C'mon," he says, reaching out a hand to her. "I've got you." Beyond the rolling waves, he can hear Yaelic chasing Qia back toward Gyeosi after he shooed them off to go play with Haaman.

Ren shifts from foot to foot on the pebbled sand, eyes glancing between him and the water. "I trust you," she says.

"It doesn't seem like it."

"I trust you!" she repeats herself, louder. "I'm just..."

A breeze blows through the shore, whipping through her hair as much as it musses his. The sun is hot on his bare shoulders, a quick contrast to the cold waters climbing up his legs. Ren is beautiful, even with that look of apprehension she wears. It mars her lips, turns them downward in a frown. He considers kissing it away.

"You don't need to fear anything," he tells her. "I'm right here. And I'll always protect you."

That brings a smile back to her face and a little light to her eyes. Ren slowly moves toward the water and he strides forward to take her hand. She grips it tight, like a lifeline, teeth biting into her lip in fear.

"Be still," he says. "Just wait."

Then, the water rushes up the shore and rolls over their feet. Ren flinches at first, but it draws a laugh from her as the foam bubbles against her skin.

"It's cold!" she cries, nose scrunched in the way he loves so dearly.

But Ren lets Basuin guide her further into the water, one tiny step at a time, until the water meets her knees. Then, a little further, not far out enough for the waves to crash into her but he blocks her with his body anyway.

"You did it." Basuin smiles down at her, all fondness and all heart racing because even after all this time, his heart goes off like a wild horse when he's near her.

"I'm scared," she admits, squeezing his hands to keep her balance. "The waves might drag me away."

"Not with me." Basuin wraps an arm around her and kisses the top of her head. "I've got you, Ren."

Basuin looks out beyond the water, into the horizon where he came from by ship. There's nothing out there anymore. And no one will come either—he'll make sure of it. But there's a certain tug on his heart he feels when he looks out there, where it all began and where it all ended.

"Thank you," he says, to no one in particular but Ithika. "Be well."

ACKNOWLEDGMENTS

To MY EDITOR, Amy Borsuk, who saw the darkness in this book and embraced it—thank you. You shaped this book into the best version of itself. Thank you to Jess & Natalie, as well as the entire team at Solaris, for all your hard work to make this book happen.

Thank you to my absolute kickass agent, Allegra Martschenko at Bookends, who took on a book that was less than perfect and helped bring my vision and heart to life. Thank you for guiding me and being kind the entire way, even when I overthink literally everything.

Thank you, before anyone else, to my first readers, Cara and Olivia. When I believed this book wasn't good enough, you saw the merit and beauty in it and pushed me further than I would've gone alone. Thank you for being by my side through the trenches. I would not be here without you thinking Kensy was hot and calling Bass "wolf zaddy."

To Team Harrow, who have been with me the whole way. Matt, Sandra, Caroline, Jackson—you've been the best crit group ever. Thanks for celebrating every secret I've sent your way. I'm so glad we met and bonded over the political state of witches.

I'm endlessly grateful for Sonora Reyes, who guided me through publishing when I had no clue what I was doing. I couldn't have done this whole shebang without your advice.

For Chezza, who was the best mentee I could have ever asked for—you taught me much more about friendship than I taught you about writing. You have an eternal, and very large, place in my heart.

The biggest thank you to my circle, and to the BIPOC Book Babes—Bita, for trying to Pygmalion me so I could get through publishing; Simren, for being my crash out buddy; Claire & Rukman for being angels. Thank you to my writing friends, Steph, Viraj, Skaz, & Kaja, for supporting me from across the world even when I'm being dramatic.

Much love and many kisses and so much gratitude for my fave group chat—Cat, for actually making me write; Tiffany, for being good at everything; Risa & Jess, for supporting my crash outs and inspiring me to be better. We are exactly where we need to be.

Thank you to the Moth Lair & all its iterations. Couldn't have written this book without watching you all lose every Counter-Strike game. For playing Monster Hunter: World with me and inspiring this entire book. Thank you to my dads, who don't know what the heck I'm doing half the time but have supported me through anything and everything. Yes, we're still meeting for BG3 tonight.

For my very best friends in the whole world, Kyndall, Cas, & Cara. You will never understand the depths of my gratitude. You have been my strength, my guidance, my absolute most stubborn of supporters. I hope in the next life, you'll be there, too. I love you, I love you, and I love you.

To Pat Murphy, who wrote *The Wild Girls*, which inspired me to do the whole "writing books" thing. To all the Asian & Korean-American authors who paved the way for me, and who inspired me to embrace my identity. To all the poets who gave me my first love for language.

The biggest thank you to all my readers. Without you, this book would simply be a bunch of words. It's your vision and heart that brings this to life. This book was written as a love letter, and I hope you've found what you're looking for in it.

Thank you to the past version of myself, who didn't think she would ever write again. Thank you for trusting in me, and trying again, and refusing to let go of the passion that became too hungry to contain.

And lastly, to my mother. Everything I have has been a gift from you. Thank you.

FIND US ONLINE!

www.rebellionpublishing.com

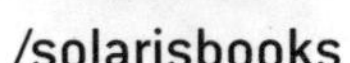

/solarisbooks

/solarisbks

/solarisbooks

/solarisbooks.
bsky.social

SIGN UP TO OUR NEWSLETTER!

rebellionpublishing.com/newsletter

YOUR REVIEWS MATTER!

Enjoy this book? Got something to say?

Leave a review on Amazon, GoodReads or with your favourite bookseller and let the world know!